The Enemy's Wife

DEBORAH SWIFT

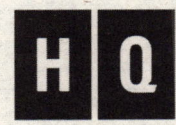

ONE PLACE. MANY STORIES

HQ
An imprint of HarperCollins*Publishers* Ltd
1 London Bridge Street
London SE1 9GF

www.harpercollins.co.uk

HarperCollins*Publishers*
Macken House, 39/40 Mayor Street Upper,
Dublin 1 D01 C9W8
This edition 2026

1

First published in Great Britain by HQ,
an imprint of HarperCollins*Publishers* Ltd 2026

Copyright © Deborah Swift 2026

Deborah Swift asserts the moral right to be identified as the author of this work.
A catalogue record for this book is available from the British Library.

PB ISBN: 9780008739737
TPB ISBN: 9780008823634

This novel is entirely a work of fiction. The names, characters and incidents portrayed in it are the work of the author's imagination. Any resemblance to actual persons, living or dead, events or localities is entirely coincidental.

All rights reserved. No part of this publication may be reproduced, stored in a retrieval system, or transmitted, in any form or by any means, electronic, mechanical, photocopying, recording or otherwise, without the prior written permission of the publishers.

Without limiting the exclusive rights of any author, contributor or the publisher of this publication, any unauthorized use of this publication to train generative artificial intelligence (AI) technologies is expressly prohibited. HarperCollins also exercise their rights under Article
4(3) of the Digital Single Market Directive 2019/790 and expressly reserve this publication from the text and data mining exception.

Printed and bound in the UK using 100% Renewable
Electricity by CPI Group (UK) Ltd

Praise for Deborah Swift

'A thrilling, immersive and beautifully written historical novel that will resonate long after the last page is turned. Highly recommended'
Marius Gabriel

'Taut, compelling and beautifully written – I loved it!'
Daisy Wood

'This impeccably researched wartime thriller had me gripped from the opening pages – I loved it'
Eliza Graham

'A fast-paced, exciting read … kept me reading late on several nights. Will appeal to all lovers of both romance and wartime novels'
Kathleen McGurl

'Had me gripped from beginning to end … Swift portrays the last desperate months of the war in Holland so vividly I found it hard to put *Operation Tulip* down'
Eva Glyn

'A nail-biting read from start to finish. Edge-of-your-seat action and a desperate romance make this a must for WW2 fiction fans'
Tessa Harris

'With real history in the raw, heart-pounding drama, bone-chilling cruelty, plot twists, and the sheer power of true love, this is a terrific finale to an unforgettable series'
Yorkshire Post

'I loved it. The book is fast-paced and page-turning, and at times has the quality of a thriller'
Ann Bennett

'A fascinating and original read'
Catherine Hokin

DEBORAH SWIFT is a *USA TODAY* bestselling author of historical fiction, a genre she loves. She lives in a small village on the edge of the English Lake District, an area made famous by the Romantic Poets such as Wordsworth and Coleridge.

In the past, Deborah used to work as a set and costume designer for theatre and TV, so enjoys the research aspect of creating historical fiction, something she was familiar with as a scenographer. More details of her research and writing process can be found on her website www.deborahswift.com

Deborah likes to write about extraordinary characters set against the background of real historical events.

Also by Deborah Swift

The Secret Agent Series:
The Silk Code
The Shadow Network
Operation Tulip

Survivors of War Series:
Last Train to Freedom

The plum blossoms at the corner of the wall
Blossom all alone in the chilly snowfall;
You can't mistake them for snow mass from afar,
For a subtle fragrance keeps coming forth.
                                        Wang Anshi, 1021–1086

The plum blossom, known as the *meihua*
is a common flower in traditional Chinese literature.
A symbol for resilience and perseverance in the face of adversity, plum blossom blooms even amidst the harshest winter snows.

Chapter 1

Shanghai, December 1941

Zofia unhooked the grey coat hanging from a nail on the rafters. It was a little too big, but what could she expect from a shared coat? She was lucky her young friend Hilly had returned it, because sometimes she forgot, and Zofia had to go without and shiver all the way to work. She buttoned it, and took her shoes outside to the doorstep to polish them. She ignored the holes and the fact she'd no shoe polish, and rubbed in a sliver of soap saved from the luxurious bathroom of her American employer, Theodore Carter.

Of course, Mr Carter had no idea what Zofia's living conditions were like here in what was called the 'Restricted Sector for Stateless Refugees', and nor would Zofia ever tell him. She did her best as his children's after-school teacher to be neutral, almost faceless. Clean, tidy and respectable. Though Mr Carter must surely have noticed she wore the same two plain dresses for work every day, no matter the weather, and had no stockings on her skinny white legs.

Zofia ignored the hopeful Chinese and Jewish children who

gathered to watch as she hunkered on the wooden steps outside the cramped Chinese house which fronted the alleyway of their *lilong*, or neighbourhood. The children always hoped she'd have a treat for them; scraps gleaned from her employer's pantry. But today was a day when she'd nothing to give.

'Scoot!' she said, flapping them away. They didn't move.

She sighed, hunching her shoulders against the December damp. If she looked up, she'd feel guilty about the fact these children had bare feet while she still had shoes. A final rub of her black lace-ups to get a bit more shine, and she was ready. The dust in the streets of Hongkew blew everywhere; the area north of Soochow Creek had been obliterated by Japanese bombs and was cratered with dirt and potholes.

She shivered and hoped Hilly wasn't cold without a coat. Hilly, always in a hurry, had left Zofia's that morning on a tram, and so now they had only the one coat between them. Second-hand, like everything else they owned. Hildegard, who Zofia called Hilly, was thirteen, but seemed to be half child, half adult. She certainly ate as much as an adult whenever food was about. During the day Hilly was kept busy taking coppers at the news kiosk on Avenue Joffre. Madam Wang, the elderly widow who owned it, had taken Hilly under her wing, and paid her in loose change and bottles of the ubiquitous Coca-Cola. She'd not be back for a while, not until dark.

Zofia brushed herself down and set off at a brisk walk. Slung over her shoulder was her bag with the exercises she'd prepared for her American charges, the Carter children, who unlike the neighbourhood children, would have their soft pink feet encased in white socks and shiny leather shoes.

She bounced along the crowded pavements, sidestepping the beggars, and with her bag firmly clamped to her hip. Jewish refugees had rebuilt these rubble-strewn streets, setting up cafés in the Viennese way, and selling black bread, strudel, and sauerkraut. Or at least, impersonations of them with Chinese ingredients.

Like the rest of the residents in her street, Zofia hadn't chosen Shanghai. Jewish refugees were no longer welcome in Japan, but nobody else wanted Jewish refugees either. Poland, Lithuania, Russia, Japan and now China. Five countries in less than two years and now all Zofia longed for was to settle down and be still. To fit in somewhere, to look at the same four walls, and have a place to call home. She yearned to plant seeds in a pot on her own windowsill and know that in the summer she'd see them bloom. But already she could feel the Japanese army closing like a noose around the International Settlement, and she knew that would mean the inevitable – moving again.

Be grateful to be alive.

She weaved her way through the crowds. Not an inch of bare pavement anywhere, and traffic crawling along in a cacophony of yells and hooting horns. She jumped out of the road as a bicycle teetered by, the rider swamped by what looked like a small haystack. Then she had to leap off the pavement as two women lurched past her, poles on their shoulders, wild finches strung on them as if the poor creatures had somehow keeled over on their perches.

A dog barked and tried to nip her calf but Zofia dodged its snarling teeth. Poor mutt would be hungry, like all of them. The crowd didn't thin until she reached the north end of the Bund and the Garden Bridge over Soochow Creek, the border to the International Settlement. There, two Japanese guards examined everyone's papers. She stopped and pulled the coat collar more tightly around her neck as she waited in line. Every time she crossed this iron bridge and looked into a guard's face, she was reminded of how much she missed her husband Haru and wondered when she might get news of where he had been posted.

Almost as soon as he'd gone to war, the Japanese had rounded her up, along with every other Jewish refugee, and by the end of August she'd been sent here to Japanese-occupied Shanghai. No matter how often she'd protested that she was wife of a Japanese businessman. She was still reeling from the shock; the realisation that she meant nothing, and even though she was married to a man fighting for Japan, she was still an alien in their eyes.

It made it hard not to resent them all. And now here she was, in a land struggling under Japanese occupation.

Her turn. She was at the front of the queue for the International Settlement. The Japanese guard waved her briskly through the checkpoint and she thanked him in Japanese, something few Western people did. Haru had taught her the language. Avid to learn and be able to speak to her husband in Japanese, she'd been a diligent student.

Now though, Haru was gone, and the days grew greyer with every passing week. Zofia comforted herself with the fact that she was on her way to the Carters' house and at least she would be fed. With luck she'd be able to put a few treats in her bag for Hilly. She walked straight up the road before heading for the bicycle hire shop.

The owner, Kung Liew, knew she'd be coming at that time in the afternoon and had the old contraption ready for her. She called it 'the Banana' because at some point in its life it had been painted garish yellow with gloss paint, and the cross bar had been bent downwards to accommodate lady riders. She slipped Kung the coin, and he grinned and waved her off as she stood down on the pedals to wobble away, heading from the Soochow River and into the French Concessionary area where most of the well-off Westerners lived. *Taipans* they called them, the men like Mr Carter – foreign businessmen who controlled all the global trade in Shanghai. They had built their huge, white-painted houses well away from the pollution of the factories, the laundries, and the stinking waterfront.

Another mile of pedalling against the bitter wind and she was turning left onto Avenue Joffre. A sleek Packard car glided by in a rumble of rubber tyres and a choke of exhaust fumes as she turned into Mr Carter's road. The uniformed chauffeur passed as close as a whisker, but the couple in the back, felt-hatted and smoking cigarettes, didn't turn to look at her. At the Carters' gated entrance, where the name 'Fairhaven' was carved into the gatepost, she dismounted and pushed the Banana through a gap in the hedge to get to the main drive. At least she was warmer now, though out of breath from pedalling on bad tyres.

Zofia left the Banana propped up against a drainpipe, near the servants' quarters that flanked the manicured lawns. This wing boasted the kitchen, (complete with gas, instead of the smoky coal stoves everyone else used) and the living quarters of their nine Chinese servants.

She took a deep breath, preparing herself for the feeling of being a servant. In Shanghai all Westerners had staff – as many as possible. It was an obligation, because that's what enabled many of the thousands of destitute Chinese to earn a few coppers a week.

As she sprang up the front steps, Zofia thought ruefully that Evelina Carter probably considered her to be the tenth servant, though because Zofia had the appearance of a white European, Evelina would never be so ill-mannered as to say it to her face.

Still, she expected a certain deference and it always galled Zofia that she must somehow shrink into that role.

Chapter 2

The Carters' house was a rambling stone villa with red roofs, built in the 1930s in the colonial style. A wide veranda ran all the way around it, with a carved wooden balustrade. Curved bays of art deco windows winked in the pale December light. Most of the Americans' homes were called after their inhabitants – Proctor House, Lovell House, Hutton House, and so on. But the Carters had gone for a more English-sounding name, as if they were deep in some romantic English idyll, and not here in Shanghai at all.

Zofia went in through the flyscreen and the glass-windowed door, where Chen, the so-called 'number one boy', greeted her. He served as general factotum, ran the rest of the staff and answered the door. She never tipped him, because no doubt he collected *cumshaw* – the sweetener from the shophouses for giving them his household's business, and she was sure he creamed off a portion of the wages of the other servants too.

Bo, the scrap that was Chen's assistant, a boy of about seven, took Zofia's coat as if she were a visiting royal. When the coat came back to her later it would be sponged and pressed, though nothing was ever said about this. If anything was in the pockets, it would be gone. She didn't mind, because she knew for Bo it was survival, and not greed.

She went straight up the staircase and turned left into a dining room the Carters had renamed 'the schoolroom'. They'd extended the house and now their own dining room was a palatial space with a table that could seat thirty.

Evelina Carter was already seated at the table with the children and their exercise books, and stood up immediately, glad to see her arrive.

'I gave Mai Ling the evening off,' Evelina said. 'Was the traffic bad?'

'Not more than usual. Sorry I'm a bit late – a queue at the checkpoint.'

Evelina was dressed in a powder-blue afternoon dress of shantung silk with a matching jacket. Her blonde hair was immaculately set into waves. There was always something slightly stiff about Evelina, and her clothes were the same, tailored to perfection, all rigid darts and seams. She looked afraid to move in case she should crease. But often her eyes were liquid and far away, as if she was never quite all there.

She tapped the shiny-topped table with her pearly fingernails, a vague expression on her face. 'Can you stay longer today? We're going out. The American Club. Just drinks. Should be back by nine.'

'That's fine,' Zofia said. She would be paid extra, and every little helped.

'Oh good!' Nine-year-old Jimmy said, eyes bright with excitement, 'We'll be able to play that game again.'

'What game?' Something approaching a frown appeared on Evelina's face.

'It's the one where we've made a board, Mommy,' Daisy said. 'We showed you.'

Daisy was in a hurry to open the cupboard to get it out, but Evelina was already gliding out of the room. 'Not now, sweetie, later. Mommy's busy right now. And fix your braids.'

And just like that she was gone, lost in the vast bowels of

the building. Zofia could hear stairs creak and high heels on floorboards echoing through the house even as she pulled out the home-made board game.

'Let's see to your hair,' Zofia said.

Daisy, dressed in immaculate school uniform of skirt and blazer, was fiddling with one of her plaits that had come undone. Zofia replaited it and tied the ribbon tight. Daisy was a stubborn but studious child, unlike her more mercurial brother.

Daisy wriggled, trying to unfold the cardboard layout of the game. It was designed to teach the children the Japanese names for shops as they navigated their counters around the board.

Here, the bakery, there, the shoe shop, and on the corner there, the bank.

Evelina didn't know that the *kanji* were as unfamiliar to Zofia herself as they were to the children; she assumed that if Zofia could speak Japanese, she could also write it. Although Zofiia had been in Shanghai for six months, the Chinese banners on the streets of Shanghai were hard enough. So Zofia was learning as much as they were, and hoping when Haru came back from the war she'd be able to surprise him by being able to speak and write more fluently. He'd come to find her when it was all over, wouldn't he?

The thought gave her a momentary pain, but she thrust it to the back of her mind to concentrate on her work. She'd drawn out little squares and just last week they'd started filling them in with things they could buy with their counters, their fake money.

'I hope I land on the bread shop,' Daisy said throwing the dice. 'I want to buy a bagel.'

'They don't have bagels in Japan, stupid,' said Jimmy.

'They do! Don't they, Zofia?'

'They don't have bagels, but they do have pancakes, with sweet red bean paste,' Zofia said. 'They're called *dorayaki*. Shall we have those instead?'

'Yes, yes! Give me the crayons.'

She got them both colouring in pancakes with red wax fillings whilst she looked up in the Japanese dictionary how to write the kanji. Jim was getting more awkward because he was coming up for ten years old and inclined to be bored. She watched him poring over the paper, his blond flyaway hair sticking up from the crown of his head. He coughed and put a hand over his mouth.

'You okay?' she asked him.

He didn't answer but sighed and pushed his drawing towards her. 'This is kid's stuff,' he said.

Like all the British and American boys in the settlement he was obsessed by war, and she worried he'd get himself into trouble. Since the Japanese had invaded China, the American quarter clung to its uneasy peace, though many Americans had already gone back, leaving businesses struggling to carry on. There was a strong sense of decline, as though one world was ending and a new one was about to begin.

'Finish it and then we'll have a game of Battleship. Can you remember the word for it?'

'*Senkan*,' he said, 'Easy.'

'Well done.'

Japanese battleships were in the harbour and the Western enclave was surrounded by Japanese troops who had taken over the rest of China and now wanted to snag Shanghai, the so-called Pearl of the Orient. All of this Zofia recognized, and dreaded, as she watched her blond American charges colour in their drawings, oblivious to the tightening of the net around them. For Zofia, the signs were all too visible; she'd seen the same scenario played out in Poland and in Lithuania before she'd arrived in Shanghai. Her ruminations were interrupted by a slam of the door, and both children looked up.

Theodore Carter's footsteps thudded up the stairs.

'Dad!' shouted Jimmy, charging out into the hall to grab him by the waist. Daisy followed, with Zofia waiting politely in the doorway. Theodore Carter was a stringy-limbed man with the neutral good looks of a clean-cut diplomat. She liked him; he always paid on time without fuss. But today his face had a ravaged expression, his eyes restless. He clung to his son a moment before asking Daisy, 'Where's Mommy?'

'Theo?' Evelina appeared across the landing, a mascara brush in her hand. 'I thought we were meeting at the American Club.'

'I know. Something's come up. You need to pack.'

'Why? What's going on?'

'The Japs tried to assassinate Prescott of the *China Weekly Press*. A journalist for Christ's sake. He was attacked with a grenade.'

'Is he all right?'

'He survived, but he's leaving. And it's time for you to get out with the children. I've booked you a passage to Manila.'

'You've done what? When?'

'This evening. Eight forty-five. You need to hurry.'

'Now? Don't be crazy. I've got to organise the children's Christmas party for the Club.' A shake of the head as if to deny what she'd heard.

'There's not going to be a party.'

'Mommy?' Daisy was getting upset.

'Not now darling. What about you?' Evelina seemed unable to move, as if frozen in place.

'I can't come. The Chamber of Trade need me. We're still lobbying the government back home, telling them the transfer of American assets and equipment is a national emergency. Since our ships stopped calling here, we can't get anything in and out of port.'

'I won't go, not without you. The children need their father.'

'Let's go in your room while your daddy's talking,' Zofia said, shepherding the children away.

Theo's voice was audible outside the door. 'It's for them I'm doing this. I'll leave when I've secured the business. If the Japs take over our shipping accounts, we'll be left with nothing. They're looting everything in the Chinese quarter. Not content with bombing it to smithereens, they've taken every lightbulb, every doorknob; they'd take the wallpaper if they could scrape it off—'

'Don't be ridiculous.'

'No, it's you, you have to face it, our time here is up and I just need to salvage what I can, or how will we ever pay school fees, buy us a house, for God's sake? Twenty years of damn work down the pan.'

Zofia could hear the desperation in his voice, but she didn't like the way he referred to the Japanese, as if they truly were the enemy. She hovered in the doorway, unsure what to do, and knowing with a sick sense of dread that this meant the only real source of her income would soon be gone.

Mr Carter seemed to suddenly realise she was there.

'Zofia, can you run to fetch Mai Ling and help her pack the children's things? One suitcase each, their passports. Warm clothes?'

Zofia nodded, told the children to find their favourite toys, and shot away down the servant stairs, her thoughts in a panic. She knocked on the door of the room Mai Ling shared with Suzi, the female number two cook. Mai Ling was sleepy-eyed and grumpy because it was her evening off. The room was dark, and as cramped as a broom cupboard. Zofia explained they were to pack for the children and Mrs Carter.

Mai Ling gazed at her in shock. 'Where they go?'

'Manila. By boat.'

'Mr Carter-Boss?'

'He's staying.'

She looked visibly relieved, but like Zofia, she must be worried about her job, about what would happen if there were no Americans to serve anymore. They'd both seen it enough times – Chinese thrown out on the streets after having served years in these luxurious houses.

They clattered back upstairs, and into the children's rooms. Jimmy and Daisy were full of questions they couldn't answer.

Evelina and Theo were still arguing outside the door. 'Can't it wait?' Evelina said. 'I can't possibly leave today, I have my appointment at the hairdresser tomorrow morning and I was meeting Gloria for *mah-jongg* then lunch at the—'

'You don't understand. It's not safe, there's no army here to defend us. The government are doing nothing. Nothing, I tell you!'

'I can't leave Shanghai! What about my medicine, for my nerves?'

'You'll have to manage without.'

'I can't, I just can't.' The sound of hysterical weeping.

Zofia tried to close her ears as she folded Jimmy's school shorts and jumper and rolled his grey socks into balls to squash them in the corner of his case. She turned to him. 'That's right, put the Meccano in here.'

Across the room, Mai Ling was doing the same for Daisy, smoothing out winter dresses and little white lacy vests. She was listening first, packing second. 'Manila. Where is that?' Mai Ling asked.

The question was never answered as they both cocked their ears to Evelina's protests.

'But we've been okay so far, haven't we?' whined Evelina in the hall. 'They wouldn't dare attack us here.'

'They already have. They raided Hongkew – supposedly searching for Chinese guerrillas. The ones that have been sabotaging Japanese garrisons. They killed the suspects, but foreigners were caught in the crossfire. It was savage. Two Englishmen are dead.'

Daisy and Jimmy began to tussle over who was to take ownership of a toy car, but Zofia was too busy listening to stop them.

'Dead?' Now Evelina sounded less certain. 'And you didn't tell me?'

'Honey, the Japs are getting bolder. I didn't want to worry you. I'm afraid it's only a matter of time.'

'But I don't want to go to Manila.'

'It was all I could book. You can go to a hotel. Any safe place. Anywhere's better than here. Beggars can't be choosers.' Zofia heard him go into the bedroom and the noise of closet doors opening and closing. 'Take this. Your best fur coat. And this.'

Then the noise of more crying. Evelina trying to persuade him the only way she knew that worked.

'Listen, darling, the Consulate told us Shanghai's indefensible. They withdrew all our troops. The British have done the same. Once the Japs get aggressive, we can't do a thing. We're in a bubble here, and it's about to burst.'

Mai Ling's eyes met Zofia's in silent anguish. Ten thousand British and Americans still worked in Shanghai as well as the wealthy White Russians who had fled the Bolshevik Revolution. These foreigners were the only people who would give either of them a decent wage, and now they would be leaving, exactly like Mrs Carter.

And when they'd gone, what then?

In less than half an hour, the bewildered children were packed into the back of the Carters' chauffeur-driven car, and Evelina, in a mink coat and hat, had given her husband a dry kiss on the mouth. Zofia stood to watch them go in the bitter cold and remembered her own leaving from Kaunas. It made her want to cry, but as usual the tears sat in a hard knot in her belly, unshed. Crying never achieved anything, she thought. Just wasted water.

She watched the two fair heads, one each side of Evelina, as the car drove away, her fists balled tight. She would miss Daisy and Jimmy, and no one had thought to let her hug them goodbye. With a feeling like she'd swallowed stones, she went to fetch her coat then untied her bicycle from the drainpipe and pushed it around to the front.

To her surprise, Theodore Carter was waiting there for her.

'I suppose you won't need me now,' she said dully.

'No.' He stood in the path of the bicycle. 'I'd like you to stay on.'

She frowned. There was no one for her to teach, now the children were going to the Philippines.

He answered her unspoken question. 'You can teach me.'

She clung to the cold metal of the bicycle frame. 'I can't ... I don't know enough.'

He shrugged. 'You speak Japanese. You know more than I do, don't you?'

She weighed it up, aware that to teach Mr Carter would cast doubt on her relationship with him. It would make her seem like another of the cheap Chinese concubines that nearly every Shanghailander had tucked away in a hotel somewhere.

'I'm married,' she said.

'I didn't mean ... Look, I need to know a little Japanese if I'm to stay here. As much as you can teach me. Enough to understand what they're saying when they come for my shipping business, which I'm sure they will. Enough for me to be able to secure it somehow so they can't get their dirty hands on it.'

She glared at him. 'The Japanese are the cleanest people I've ever met.'

He capitulated immediately. 'I'm sorry. I wasn't thinking.' At least he had the guts to apologise. 'Look, this crisis is getting worse and the government is supposed to be having talks with the Japanese to smooth things over but—'

'I can't. It wouldn't look right. What about the other staff here? Won't they help you?'

'I don't know. I hope they'll all stay on. Though my wife's gone, I'll still need Mai Ling to pack her other clothes and shoes and the rest of her things, so I can ship them back to America for her. And I'll need Chen to do the same for me. And obviously I'll need meals, so Suzi can stay, and my chauffeur. And the gardeners and maintenance man ... well, I guess I'll need them all.' He looked at her with a rueful smile. 'I guess I've gotten used to them.'

'I'll think about it,' she said.

He stood aside to let her pass. 'I'm serious.'

She saw from his face that he was, but she jammed a foot on the pedal and set off.

'Same hours, same pay,' he called after her as she cycled away.

As she pedalled she ruminated on it. She could see why Theo Carter didn't want to give up his business. Many Americans were in shipping like Carter & Co. You didn't need to be a genius to see why American shipping companies had made money in the port of Shanghai. The Chinese were hungry for US goods like cars and refrigerators, and the Americans loved the Chinese silk and porcelain that came back on the return journey.

She knew it wasn't a good idea to work for a lone man, but she needed the money. Her Saturday job running parcels of laundry around the International Settlement would soon stop too if there were no Western women to demand clean clothes. She returned the bicycle to Kung Liew, and began the walk home, barely seeing the refugee Chinese now crowding the pavements, mulling over Theo Carter's offer and what Haru would think if she were to take it up.

Such evil luck that Haru's conscription dates had fallen during a war.

He had waited as long as he could, pacing their small apartment, unwilling to volunteer, but in July the call had come, nevertheless. All Japanese men had to take a spell in the army before they were twenty-six, so when Haru's papers came he was not surprised.

For the next week, the dark shadow of worry never left his eyes. 'I'm sorry,' he'd said, pressing his forehead to hers as they lay sleepless on their futon in the summer heat.

'It's not your fault. What will be, will be,' she replied to smooth the parting for him, because she couldn't bear for him to see how much it hurt.

'Perhaps it will be the making of me,' he'd said.

But the army? It was the last place on earth she could picture her mild, bookish husband.

Now the memory of him leaving – the overcrowded station, the hiss of steam, and his too-polite goodbye that felt as if both of them might break, was a tearing pain that still closed up her throat. It seemed so unjust, and those few months with him in Kobe, her few months of stillness, of mutual trust, seemed to be a mirage, a wrinkle in time.

Her thoughts were interrupted when a man carrying a sack on his back bumped into her as he passed.

Now there was Hilly. She had to be practical. With no other work, what would they do? Somehow they'd have to eat.

Chapter 3

Back in the dark streets of the ghetto, Zofia was just hanging the coat back on the hook in the rafters when Hilly arrived, out of breath from running.

'You get paid?' Hilly asked. She spoke in English because she'd learned it in school and it was what all the *farangs* spoke in Shanghai.

'No. Not today. It slipped my mind to ask.'

Hilly's blue eyes widened. 'You forgot? How could you forget? My stomach's rumbling thinking of those noodles!'

Zofia and Hilly had an agreement – twice a week they'd have a proper meal; once when Hilly was paid and once when Zofia was paid, though Hilly's pay from the kiosk was only a few coppers – mere pocket money.

'Sorry. I had some bad news. Mrs Carter and the children have left. Gone on the boat to Manila.'

Hilly didn't react but sat down at the rickety table by the window, less interested in the Carters than in her stomach. 'What shall we do for food then? Let's empty our pockets, see what we've got. We can go down to Ward Road and get something.'

Zofia obliged, feeling in her purse for the last few coins. 'Only a few *jiao*,' she said, laying them out on the table.

Hilly raked through them and added her few coins to the pile. 'It's enough for two dumplings anyway. I need something hot. My feet hurt. I think my chilblains have frozen.'

'You can have the coat then. It's still warm.'

'*Hao!*' Hilly said. Like Zofia, not only did she speak English, but she'd picked up the Chinese for 'good' along with many other useful phrases.

Hilly grabbed the coat from the hook and Zofia layered herself with another cardigan and a padded Chinese jacket left behind by someone else. Hilly always managed to turn heads no matter what she wore. Partly it was her blonde hair, and partly the waif-like face made fragile by perfect bone structure and a winning smile.

On Zofia, their winter coat looked baggy and too big, whereas on Hilly it always made her look like she needed looking after. Which she did, because her blonde hair and good looks brought trouble in their wake, and Hilly could never see it coming.

They weaved their way down the crowded alley, under the quilts hanging up to air, and past roughly painted German and Polish signs for '*Wascherei*' – the laundry, or '*delikatesy*' – the delicatessen. Zofia hooked Hilly's arm in hers as she steered her down Ward Road towards the green area they called Wayside Park. Hilly was always staring about, as if looking for something lost. It drove Zofia crazy, but she had learned it was part of Hilly, and she'd have to put up with it.

At their favourite street vendor's stall in Liao Wang Market they stopped to buy dumplings from the gap-toothed Chinese man they simply called Feng. He smiled at them, eyes creasing as he handed them a hot tin pan with two of the steaming savoury dumplings. Neither of them could wait to get to the park to eat them, so they tossed them from hand to hand until they were cool enough to eat and then bit into them, the juice of the hot vegetables running down their chins.

A sudden noise made Zofia almost choke.

At first she didn't recognize the sound, but then she saw people running down the street towards them from the tall buildings of the British Cigarette Company near the border to the International Settlement. Smoke and the smell of gunpowder.

Another blast. The unmistakeable sound of machine-gun fire. Zofia dragged a bemused Hilly off the road as Feng leapt to trundle his handcart away on its iron wheels, his legs in their short trousers scuttling through the muck and debris.

Zofia stood back hurriedly as a group of gesticulating Chinese men came running past, in their midst a man on a stretcher, blood dripping from wounds in his arms and chest.

'Oh!' Hilly had seen it and was mesmerized with shock, standing in the road so no one could pass.

'Get out of the way!' Zofia pulled Hilly off the road. Hilly buried her head against her shoulder to hide her eyes.

In the wake of the stretchers came a stream of Western cars, the British flag prominent at the front. They hooted and pipped their horns to move people out of the way. As one of them passed she glimpsed an Englishman holding his arm, his face white as a mask. Blood was seeping through his suit.

'Doesn't look good,' a man next to her said in English. 'Let's get out of here.'

Zofia agreed and she pulled Hilly away and down the road to the White Horse Café.

Hilly was rigid with shock. 'Is it Nazis?'

Zofia passed her a handkerchief and held her hand. 'No. Just trouble with the border. It's over now.'

The café was empty, people streaming away from the site of the blast.

She caught up with Karel and Jan, two young Dutch refugees, hurrying away.

'I knew there'd be trouble,' Karel said. His beaky nose was red from cold. 'Now the British Army's gone, there's no one to stop them. If people try, the Japs just claim they're looters and gun them down. You mark my words, there'll be a Japanese takeover of this whole damn place any day now.'

'I know. I feel it too.' She suppressed a shiver. 'But keep your voice down. You'll upset Hilly.'

'No, he won't,' Hilly said, clinging to her arm. 'I heard that. Stop treating me like a baby.' Then a moment later, 'Do you think they'll shoot people?'

'Not if we concede quietly.' Jan, a short youth in spectacles, paused to catch his breath. 'They don't want any damage to the Bund or any of the infrastructure. They just want American dollars and access to their champagne lifestyle.'

'One look at the river tells you all you need to know,' said Karel.

Zofia knew what he meant. She'd passed the harbour yesterday and looked out at the grey hulks of the ships. HMS *Peterel* and the United States gunboat *Wake* were the lone remnants of the British and American presence, whereas the Japanese fleet had increased, and the shadow of the massive warship *Izumo* loomed over the Allied vessels.

'Did you hear about the man from the *China Daily News*?' Jan said as they jostled through the crowd towards Hongkew.

'Uh-huh. It's always the newspaper men who are first to be targeted,' Zofia said. 'It's about control of the propaganda. So if I were you, I'd pack just in case. Get your things together, because if they come, it will be without warning, and then there's never time.'

'Know what I'm scared of? There are Nazi sympathisers all over Shanghai,' Karel said, as he and Jan peeled off down a side street. 'If the Japanese take over, and there's no international protection, they'll let the Nazis have free rein, because they're allies.'

Nazi sympathisers. This was a thought Zofia hadn't considered.

It made up her mind about Mr Carter. If she kept working for him perhaps it might give her a measure of protection against any Jew-hunting Nazi. But what about Hilly? She wouldn't last two minutes against the Nazis.

'Come on, let's get home,' she called as Hilly fell behind.

She was always chivvying her, though she tried not to. She remembered how Hilly had latched on to her on the boat to China. She looked so lost, all on her own.

It started at passport control. Hilly had mislaid her passport and begun to weep. People were staring at this girl who was sobbing like her heart would break, so Zofia, feeling sorry for her, had taken charge. It had taken a few panicked moments to find the passport where it had fallen through a hole in Hilly's pocket and into the lining of her coat.

'Here it is,' she said.

'You look after it for me,' Hilly insisted.

Hilly's trust in her warmed her heart, and after that, Hilly treated Zofia like an older sister. At the immigration control all that seemed to matter was that they had the 'J' stamped on their passports. Zofia looked at Hilly's to find out she was thirteen – she'd thought her much younger. Hildegard Hoffmann, daughter of Franz and Zara Hoffmann.

'Where are your parents?' Zofia asked. 'Are you travelling all on your own?'

'The Nazis took them,' she said. 'They took Mother away. She wouldn't do favours for the Nazis like I did, so they took her.' She took a ragged breath and pressed a hand to her mouth to staunch another sob.

This bald statement filled Zofia with horror. She didn't dare ask what favours, or what had happened to her father, but instead hugged her tight and gave Hilly her only handkerchief.

There seemed to be no other adult with this girl, and Zofia knew what it was like to be lonely and afraid. From then on, they had become inseparable, which was both comforting, and frightening.

Chapter 4

Theo heard the crack of distant gunfire from his villa. It was unnervingly quiet in the house without Evelina and the children, though he had to admit, it was also a relief. He'd time and space to think, to work out what to do. It was pretty obvious the Japanese were going to invade the settlement; they'd been stringing it out for weeks. So what the hell were they waiting for?

He went to the drinks cabinet, poured a whisky, and helped himself to ice from the tray in the refrigerator. As he came back, he saw his silver cups for last year's American polo season, and a panic began in his chest. It was all over. The end was coming, like the fall of Rome, and there was crap all he could do about it.

On the lacquered sideboard Evelina and the children smiled at him from the photograph in its silver frame. Had he done the right thing? He couldn't have borne it, her witnessing the collapse of his business. And he was sure it would send her looking for opium again, now in ever shorter supply. Evelina coming down from that stuff was a sight he'd carefully kept from everyone else. He shuddered. Much as he loved Shanghai, the dragon breath of the poppy had all but ruined his marriage, and he'd have to get out of here himself soon; he didn't trust Evelina with the children. But not until he'd secured Carter & Co.

Theo didn't call for Chen or any of the other servants, because he wanted time to think. He spread out the *China Daily News* and the *Shanghai Evening Post* on the dining table and leaned over them, looking for clues as to what might happen next, but then closed them in frustration. Just the usual society gossip. Photographs of the steeplechase race winners, reports of charity dances at the Cathay Hotel. No reports of Japanese incursions, though any fool could see they were happening all over Shanghai.

He sat back and picked up his tumbler with its chinking ice and knocked back the shot of whisky in one gulp. The press were burying their heads in the sand. He got it – their hands were tied. To say anything would be to invite reprisals. Nearly all his friends had gone, deserted the sinking ship, but Theo wasn't the giving up type; he hadn't worked all these years to have it looted by someone who had no idea what it was worth – what it had cost him in grit and sleepless nights.

So that night he didn't undress and barely slept. He got out his passport and all the certificates of financial holdings he owned, the deeds to the offices by the port, the deeds to this house. He'd die before giving them up.

When he had it all together in his briefcase, he stared out of the windows across his lawns. There was a hole there where he'd dug out a Christmas tree last week. This relic of home had been lovingly watered and kept in the shade every year they'd been here. Now it was wilting in the hall, still undecorated.

What a bloody Christmas.

He poured another shot of whisky, knowing he shouldn't. He'd do what it took to save his business. Perhaps if he was polite to the Japs and showed he could be useful to them, they'd let him retain shares in Carter & Co.

He was relying on the children's tutor to teach him enough Japanese so he could negotiate. She was always so self-possessed, that one. It made him nervous even to give her orders. And besides, he'd no language skills to speak of, except basic Chinese, and he feared she might laugh at his incompetence.

It caught Theo by surprise the next day when Zofia Kimura actually turned up. He'd been to his offices and collected all his personal things – his desk photographs of Evelina and the children. A few other keepsakes like the fountain pen left to him by his father, and his college certificates. He'd withdrawn dollars a week ago from the Shanghai Bank, as much as he dared, and hidden them in various places, some in his socks, some in his luggage, some in the house. He didn't know what was coming, but American dollars always seemed to smooth the way.

When the bell buzzed, he heard Chen go to the door and Zofia's voice in the hall as Bo took her coat.

He went to the landing. 'Come up,' he said. He watched her as she hurried up the stairs, light on her feet, her arms clutching a scuffed canvas bag heavy with books, a bag she seemed to take everywhere with her. He smiled and wondered if he'd be given exercise books like the children.

'Right on time,' he said. 'I wasn't sure you'd come.'

'I always keep my appointments.'

Ouch. She waited for him to show her through to the dining room where the children usually did their homework.

Instead he led her to his own study at the back of the house. The other room reminded him too painfully of Jimmy and Daisy. He sat down at his desk before realizing he looked like he was about to interview her for a job, so he jumped to pull another chair next to the end of the desk and, self-conscious, cleared a space for her books. She had a Japanese textbook, some lined exercise books and, strangely, a copy of what looked like *The Tales of Beatrix Potter*, but in Japanese.

Theo picked it up and thumbed through it. 'Gee, I'm really going back to class, aren't I?'

'*Otogi Shosetsu Itazurana Kousagi*,' she said. 'A Fairy Tale of Mischievous Little Rabbits.'

'Will that really be any use with the invading Japanese?'

'We have to start somewhere,' she said stiffly. He liked her slight accent, her very definite consonants. When she was in the room it made him wake up. She tapped the book where he'd left it on the table; 'And you'll be able to share it with your children when all this is over.' Her serious eyes looked into his. He wasn't sure if she was for real, but grasping that she was, he shrugged and picked up the book again.

She was a patient teacher, considering he could only sit still for about fifteen minutes before he had to go and light another cigarette.

'You want to learn?' she asked. 'Or smoke?'

Seeing her disapproving look, he stubbed it out. Somehow, she'd got the upper hand.

After they'd been going about half an hour with her repeating the Japanese from the book and showing him the illustrations, and him parroting it back, he suddenly slumped and said, 'It's useless isn't it. It was a crazy idea to think I could talk to them. I'm going to lose everything, aren't I?'

She leaned back in her chair. 'Maybe. We don't know. But even if you lose it all, life still goes on afterwards. I can tell you that much, that even with nothing, life goes on.'

Now he was hooked. 'It happened to you?'

'I fled the Nazis and Lithuania with one rucksack. As long as your family are safe, that's all you can ask for.'

'When was this?'

'End of last year.'

'Did you come to Shanghai on your own?'

'Long story. My brother Jacek set off with me from Lithuania, but he got arrested by the Russians on the way. I think he's in Siberia. In a gulag.'

The one word sent a shiver down his spine. 'God, I'm sorry.'

Her eyes slid away and she pressed her lips together. This was obviously something she didn't want to talk about.

She turned back and her tone sharpened. 'You need the Japanese numbers, Mr Carter. *Ich, ni, san, shi* …' She started to recite them and draw the characters on the lined page in front of her.

He stared at it. Even after living among Chinese kanji for so long, he still knew few words of Cantonese, and Japanese looked just as baffling, but he persevered, reciting the numbers and drawing out the kanji in rows on the paper.

After a while, he paused, pencil in hand. 'Don't you want to leave? The Japs don't follow the Geneva Convention, you know.' She looked up with interest, so he continued. 'They signed it in 1929 but never ratified it. We heard they did awful things in Burma.'

'Like most men in war.' She frowned as if he'd said something to offend her. 'Where would I go? I've no money for a passage to America, and Nazi-occupied Europe would be a death sentence for a Jew like me.'

He sat back and ran a hand through his thick light-brown hair. 'I can't help. I've dollars but there are no more boats. The government have given up on those of us that are left.'

'Then I'll have to sit it out. One thing I learned though. The things you own, they're not important. They can take those away, and you'll still be you.'

Still be you. Her words fell into a deep well inside him. But who was he? He had a shaky feeling he didn't know. He looked at her where she sat in her too-thin print dress and darned cardigan, nothing like his wife in her couture clothes, and yet she seemed far more self-contained than Evelina ever did, and her eyes were bright and alert, not like Evelina's vague, evasive gaze.

She interrupted his thoughts. 'You'll need the words for banking terms. Here, I looked them up in my Japanese dictionary. Investment. Property. Loan. Payment.' She reeled off a list of terms. Consulting the dictionary, flipping through its flimsy pages, she scribbled the kanji and then the phonetics onto the paper for him to copy.

'This is better,' he said. 'I can imagine asking for an investment but I can't imagine asking the Japanese invaders if they're after the cabbages in Mr McGregor's garden.'

She smiled, and it lit up her face. 'Might work,' she said. 'It seems unlikely they'll listen to you anyway. Perhaps instead of arresting us, they'll want to put us in a pie!'

It tickled his sense of humour and he let out a guffaw. 'God, it's a good job we can laugh, isn't it?'

They spent another hour working on the business terms before she stood to put everything away.

'You know, I enjoyed that,' he said. 'I like learning new things. Though I have to say, learning the lingo would be more fun if it wasn't for the fix we're in. Can you come tomorrow?'

A nod. 'I expect you miss them,' she said, pointing to the photo on his desk.

'It hasn't sunk in yet that they've gone.' He sat back. 'See, I'd forgotten how noisy they are – the clatter and bustle of them. Jimmy running in every two darn minutes saying something's 'not fair'. Daisy demanding to be picked up and swung around. Their Christmas gifts are still in my closet, but I haven't had time to wrap or send them.'

Zofia was packing up her books as he talked. 'They'll understand. They know you love them, don't they?'

Did they? He hadn't ever questioned it. 'I guess.'

'Till tomorrow then, Mr Carter,' she said.

He stood up and spread his arms. 'Look, can't we drop the formality? Can't you call me Theo?'

'Only if you've read the whole of *Peter Rabbit* by tomorrow, and then we'll have a test.' She lay an English transcript of the Japanese text on the table. 'If you pass, you can call me Zofia. Otherwise, it will be Miss Kimura.' Her mouth twitched with a smile, because in all the months she'd been coming, he'd always called her Zofia.

He saw her out, and strangely, the house seemed even emptier than before.

Chapter 5

Zofia didn't cycle straight back home but pushed her bike round to the servants' entrance and knocked there. Mai Ling answered it with a guarded expression. She was obviously unaware Zofia had even been in the house that day.

She let her in with a wordless gesture. Zofia knew this was because she was 'white' and not Chinese, and Mai felt obliged to. The invisible pecking order demanded it. Mai led her through to the kitchen where a pot of Chinese tea stood on the table, and Chen the butler and two other Chinese men turned to gawp at her. Their eyes were not welcoming. A pistol and a few empty cartridges were on the table. Zofia recognized the gun from her time in Poland – a German 22-caliber Mauser with a long barrel, a military-type weapon.

It was quickly pulled out of sight.

'What you want?' Mai asked her.

Zofia took in the hostile atmosphere. 'I just wanted to know if you were leaving. Mr Carter says he's staying, but he seems to think it's only a matter of days before the Japanese army takes over. I was going to ask if you knew anywhere safe to go.' She was thinking of Hilly. 'Hongkew is getting dangerous; they blew up the cigarette factory.'

Mai Ling glanced at the men who were watching the conversation like snakes.

'We're going nowhere,' she said. 'If they come; we'll fight.'

'No need to worry, little lady,' said Chen. 'The Japanese won't dare hurt anyone in the International Settlement. They don't want war with the Americans.'

She suddenly understood. The Chinese were using this house as a place to meet and plan their resistance. They must all be men working for French or American families.

'So you don't know where to go?' Zofia asked.

Nobody answered, they simply watched her squirm.

'I'll see you out,' Chen said, standing. All at once he seemed unlike the friendly servant she knew; someone more threatening had taken his place.

He ushered her to the door then stood watching in the light of the doorway as she mounted the bicycle. A glance back showed him still staring as she pedalled away. It made her aware all at once that the Carter household was two separate worlds – the upstairs world where Theo lived and the world downstairs where something else entirely was at play.

That evening, in their shared lodgings, a draughty room roughly partitioned from the one next door, Zofia and Hilly were unpicking second-hand wool jumpers to reknit them. Zofia was concentrating so it was a while before she noticed the necklace glinting over Hilly's faded dress.

'Where did you get that?' Zofia tried to touch it, but Hilly put a protective hand over it. 'It's mine.'

'I know, but where did you get it? It looks like it might be valuable.'

Now she moved her hand away so Zofia could see. 'Someone gave it to me.'

'Madam Wang?'

'No!' Hilly scoffed. 'She's too poor. He's called Goro. He's nice. He comes to the kiosk every day and he told me he liked my hair.'

A Japanese name. Zofia stared. She suddenly saw what should have been glaringly obvious. Hilly's dress was too tight over the chest. Hilly was growing up, becoming a young woman. 'Is he a soldier?'

'Uh-huh. Very smart. His uniform's always so clean.'

Oh no. 'And when did he give you this?' Zofia pointed to the necklace.

'When we shut for lunch. He waited for me so we could sit together in the park. He smiled at me, and then sat next to me on the bench when I was eating my noodles.'

'Wasn't Madam Wang with you?'

A shake of the head. 'She had to go to get more change from her friend in the market.'

'And did he do anything, this soldier?'

'What do you mean?'

'Did he touch you or anything?'

Hilly looked at her knees, so her hair swung over her face in a blonde curtain.

'Hilly?'

'Madam Wang wasn't pleased about the necklace. I think she wanted it for herself, but I wouldn't let her touch it.'

She'd evaded the question and it made Zofia's spine prickle. 'Will you let me have a look?'

'It's pretty.' Hilly unclasped it reluctantly and handed it over.

Heavy, so real gold, made maybe fifty years ago, in a design of curlicues with a central red stone. Ruby? Or paste? The hallmark seemed to be British with a lion and a few other marks. Zofia suspected it had once belonged to someone in the British concession, someone like Evelina who'd left in a hurry.

Hilly was holding out her hand impatiently so Zofia passed it back. 'Does this man know where we live?'

'He's called Goro,' she insisted. 'You said not to tell anyone, so I haven't. I said I'd meet him in the park again tonight. Not here. That was right, wasn't it?'

Zofia took a deep breath. 'It's better if you don't, or at least not on your own.'

'But he'll be waiting for me. At sunset, he said. He might give me something else. I'd like a bracelet.'

How could she explain? From this she saw all too clearly Hilly was still a child, but Zofia wasn't family. She'd no real right to dictate what Hilly should or shouldn't do. 'I'll come with you.'

'No. I don't want you to come. He didn't want to see you, did he?'

'It's dangerous after dark. And I'm not sure we can trust a Japanese soldier.'

'Why? You're married to Haru, and he's a Japanese man. A lovely man. You said so.'

Zofia sighed. 'It was different then. That was before there was a war. Now everyone in Shanghai is the enemy of the Japanese.'

Hilly frowned. 'Well, I'm not his enemy. We're friends. He likes me.' A tinge of red in her cheeks.

'I don't think you should—'

'I'm going and you can't stop me. You're always trying to stop me doing things.'

This was completely unjust. She'd never stopped Hilly from doing anything, except if it spelled danger. 'Look, you can keep the necklace, but I don't want you to meet this man, not until I know more about him.'

'But he said he'd take me for a meal at Wing On's.'

Wing On's was a vast department store with a well-known restaurant and even Zofia had never been inside it. Would this soldier really take her there? Little Hilly in her shabby frock? But she could see the temptation, and knew Hilly was more motivated by food than anything else.

Zofia had a brainwave. 'I'll tell you what, I'll take you. Let's go there now. You're hungry, aren't you? Put the necklace on, and we'll go right away.'

Hilly's eyes brightened. 'Really? To Wing On's? Hadn't we better wait for—'

'Yes. Right now. Here, let me help you put it on.' She fastened the clasp behind and while Hilly was busy touching its cold weight at her throat, Zofia, desperate to distract her, fetched the coat. 'Here, it will be cold out.'

'But what about Goro? He'll be waiting.'

'Maybe he'll find us there.' She helped Hilly into the sleeves with a guilty feeling she was manipulating and diverting her, but couldn't think what else to do. She took her arm and led her out onto the street, steering her through the narrow alleys heading for Nanjing Road.

They hurried through the gloom, with Zofia fearing to slow down lest Hilly should dig in her heels about the soldier, Goro.

Wing On's was the biggest most luxurious department store in the whole of Shanghai – five storeys of opulence and wealth with curved iron balustrades on the balconies, and a flagpole with a dragon flag flying from its mast like a giant ship. Its annexe was a modern building, the highest in Shanghai at seventeen floors.

The window displays to the street were still showing Chinese goods but Japanese soldiers manned the doors. Zofia hurried Hilly forward, following on the heels of two businessmen. She hoped the Japanese would think they were with the men in front. There was no doubt Hilly's blonde hair and gold necklace helped this illusion.

They took a lift to the fourth floor and alighted into the baroque splendour of the restaurant. Hilly gazed around at the white-clothed tables, the triangular art deco lamps on the pillars, her mouth open.

The man at the menu stand found them a table for two, and thank goodness it was in an unobtrusive place, for the restaurant soon filled with well-dressed night-time customers. They looked at the menu and Zofia found herself worrying if she'd actually have enough to pay the bill.

'How about the mushroom and scallion noodles?' she asked, steering Hilly to the cheaper options. Fortunately, the items were listed in English as well as Shanghainese.

Hilly would not be persuaded and spent so long looking and deciding on salted beef with rice, that the waiter had to return three times before they were ready. Zofia surreptitiously counted her coins. Without dessert, there'd be enough.

When the menus were finally removed and Zofia had asked the wine waiter for 'just water, please', she was able to exhale with relief. After they'd chatted a little about how the building had been repaired after the bombing, Hilly pointed to a couple by the door. 'He looks too old for her,' she said.

'Sssh! They'll hear you.' It was true. He was an old grey-haired businessman, and she was a vivacious black-haired Eurasian with a flower tucked behind her ear. Zofia glanced around hoping to divert Hilly's attention. Her gaze was caught by a group on a table to the left of them. Mr Carter, dining with a couple of other men in suits. He smiled and lifted a hand in a wave, just as Zofia tried to pretend she hadn't seen him.

Hastily she smiled back, her face flushing.

'Who's that?' Hilly's sharp eyes missed nothing.

'Mr Carter. The one whose children I teach.'

'He looks like a film star.'

'Of a B-movie you mean.' But Hilly was right; he was attractive, and Zofia was already far too aware of it. Being near him made her snappy and awkward.

Hilly laughed. 'Aren't you going to go and talk to him?'

Thank goodness the food arrived and Hilly's attention was taken up with the plate in front of her. 'Eat slowly,' Zofia reminded her. 'Enjoy the surroundings. We might not be able to come back again.'

'We will,' she said, her mouth full of beef. 'Goro will bring me.'

Zofia mentally gritted her teeth. But the food was good, hot and plentiful, and she couldn't be cross for long. As she ate, she noticed Theo kept glancing over at them.

When she'd finished her meal, and Hilly had scraped the last juices from the plate with her spoon, the waiter reappeared and put down the dessert menus. 'No, thank you,' Zofia said firmly.

'But I want dessert,' Hilly said, putting her palm on the menus so the man had to leave them there. He shrugged and said, 'I'll leave it with you, ladies.'

'We can't afford dessert,' Zofia whispered. 'I haven't enough money.'

'You said you'd bring me out for dinner. Dinner means I get dessert too, right? They've got sundaes. With cream.' Her voice was rising.

Please, don't let her make a scene. Not in front of Theo Carter.

'I'm sorry, sweetheart, but we haven't got the money.'

'They'll give me it if I ask nicely and give them something in return. They always do.'

'We haven't got anything to give them. Look.' She took all the coins and notes from her pocket and placed them on the table.

Just at that moment the waiter returned with his notepad and pen. Zofia felt like sinking through the floor.

'We haven't enough money for a whole dessert,' Hilly said to him without any apology. 'Can you do half one?' She batted her eyelashes at him. 'A small pineapple sundae with lots of cream?'

The waiter's eyes skidded around looking for help, but he soon realized he was on his own. 'Very sorry, miss, but we're not allowed. I'll bring you the bill.'

'I'll give you a kiss if you'll bring me a sundae.'

Zofia's eyes widened in horror, but Hilly was looking up at the Chinese man, her eyes beseeching.

'We'll have the bill please,' Zofia insisted.

'But you promised!' Now it was a loud voice everyone could hear. People looked up to stare.

The waiter grabbed the menu from under Hilly's hand and sped away.

'He would have said yes,' Hilly protested. 'I know he would! Why are you so mean?' Her hand swiped across the table and a spoon clattered to the floor.

Mortified, Zofia bent over to pick it up. When she sat up again Theo was at their table. 'Are you in some kind of trouble? Can I help?'

'No, I—'

'We were going to have dessert,' Hilly said, eyes full of tears. 'But Zofia said no. She says we can't pay.'

Theo looked at her, blinked, and then a realization came over his face. 'Then let me help,' he said. 'I'll ask him to bring the dessert menu again—'

'He's bringing us the bill,' Zofia said stiffly, embarrassment making her shrink inside to the size of a bean. 'And we couldn't possibly—'

'A loan. A loan against your teaching, okay?' He was insistent. 'So this young lady can have her dessert.'

Hilly was beaming now. 'A pineapple sundae with cream. Can you ask him for that? A big portion.'

Theo waved a hand at the waiter who came scurrying over. 'One pineapple sundae with a big portion of cream – that's right isn't it? And for you?'

Zofia shook her head. 'No I don't want anything, I—'

'Then I'll order for both of us. And two of the *hudiesu* please.' He'd ordered the expensive butterfly crackers – puff pastry sandwiched with sweet cream. He grinned at her. 'I love them. And I'll need my energy if I'm to tackle Mr McGregor's garden before tomorrow.'

Zofia put the backs of her hands to her cheeks to cool them as Theo went off for a word with his friends on the other table.

'Who's Mr McGregor?' asked Hilly.

'Just a friend of Mr Carter's,' she said, still feeling like she'd been peeled raw.

A few minutes later Theo was back with an extra chair. She noticed he was carrying his briefcase with him, even dining out in the evening. 'I hope you don't mind.' He sat down, squashing himself in next to the wall, and tucking the briefcase under his chair. 'If my colleagues are right,' he gestured to the table he'd just left, 'it seems we might not have much time left to enjoy ourselves, so we should make the most of it.'

'Are you rich?' Hilly asked.

'Hilly!' Zofia said sharply.

But Mr Carter smiled. 'A proper Rockefeller. But probably not for much longer.' He turned to Zofia. 'Since Evelina's gone, I thought I might as well come out to eat. No point in moping at home. And my friends from the American Club are spooked about the war. I thought it might be an idea to pool our knowledge.'

'And?'

He shrugged. 'Too much rumour. Nobody really knows. Ah. Here come the desserts.'

And they did look splendid. Hilly gasped at the mound of ice cream over chunks of pineapple, and the wafers shaped like fans.

Zofia tried to eat her dessert gracefully, but it was one of those pastries that simply wouldn't behave and they were all soon giggling as she and Theo tried to tackle the escaping cream.

When they'd finished Mr Carter summoned the waiter and took charge of the bill, waving away all Zofia's protestations. 'I have an account here,' he said. He signed a docket the waiter brought. 'And if the Japanese take over, serve them right, they'll get my bill.'

He was treating them like the enemy, and it filled Zofia with unease because she knew that if Haru were here, he would be offended. On the way home Hilly had forgotten all about Goro, thank goodness. 'Mr Carter likes you,' she said. 'He has nice teeth.'

Zofia let the comment go by. 'Come on, let's get home.'

'Can we go again next week?'

But by next week the world would be changed, and it would be the last time they would ever eat at Wing On's.

Chapter 6

'Additional Training.' That was what they called it.

As if they needed any, having been beaten with bamboo flails from the very beginning, and told that to disobey would mean not only ignominy, but torture and death.

Haru Kimura had spoken back only once and now he had a livid scar across his cheek from the sharp cut of bamboo, and the whole unit had been beaten blue because of his insubordination. Terrified to object, but terrified to obey, he understood all too soon what life was to be like in the cold brutal family of the Japanese Imperial Army.

The unit of new recruits, all soft faces and innocent eyes, had been in China less than a week when they were brought to a village square – a rough, sandy clearing surrounded by decrepit wooden buildings – and handed bayonets for target practice. Even before the instructions from the NCO were given, Haru registered the silence. That was before he saw the pit on one side of the square and the mound of bodies. On the other side of the square stood posts made from trees.

His knees began to quake.

No. What kind of practice was this? He started to say silent prayers.

The posts were smeared red, and tied to them were six squirming Chinese men – men who looked like poor farmers, their chests and stomachs bared. Men they'd been told were *chancorro* – bugs, lice, less than human. Haru saw their flesh was white in comparison to their sun-baked, weathered arms.

Refusing was not an option. The captain asked for a volunteer and the man beside him, almost wetting himself to get it over, ran with his bayonet, uttering a fearsome yell. A squint, and Haru saw one of the Chinese sag to his knees over a carpet of blood.

'It's war,' he told himself. 'They would kill us too.' Wouldn't they?

The order came. Haru closed his eyes. A fraction of a second before his legs started to run. He'd have to do it. Get it over with, that was all he could do.

Eyes squeezed shut, he felt the slip of the rifle in his hands, his feet thumping on the dusty ground. At the last moment he opened his eyes, surprised to see another human being there, but it was too late to stop, his bayonet sank easily into the man's chest. As he withdrew it, he felt his own amazement, that to take a life was so easy, like piercing a mango.

The man's eyes were open, looking at him. Accusing him. Then he slid down leaving Haru with a view of a bloodstained post.

From behind, he heard the cheers of the rest of the men as if he'd done something heroic. 'Another victory for the Emperor of the Rising Sun!'

The words swilled in his head like soup.

Chapter 7

After dining at Wing On's, Theo went home, but unable to sleep, he caught a rickshaw to his office that same night. He left his car at home, safe in the garage of his house, but carried his most valuable documents – his passport and bank books – with him. His offices were close to the American Consulate, on the Bund, the long stretch of Western-style shoreline where all of Shanghai did its business.

The weather was sharp and his coolie was in a padded jacket and quilted hat, despite his exertions. He would have liked longer to talk with Zofia, but she was with that other girl. On the journey through the city, Theo wondered about her. The blonde girl was much younger than Zofia, he realized. Maybe eleven or twelve? She'd behaved exactly like Daisy. Zofia seemed to be looking after her and his heart went out to her. It would be no easy task. The girl had a knowing look about her that was disconcerting.

The rickshaw man stopped before Carter & Co and waited for him to get out and hand over his fare and the tip. Theo was jumpy; the rumours of a Japanese takeover hung over him like the weight of a tropical cloud before a downpour. He glanced up at the company building, a three-floor edifice of colonial splendour, and his heart swelled with pride and a tang of bitterness it might soon be lost.

He crossed the marble-floored lobby and nodded to Chan Yeung at night reception, before taking the lift up to the second floor. There, in his personal office, he switched on the desk lamp and took out a ledger. Still in his overcoat and muffler because it was too cold to go without, he got out his pen and ink bottle. Painstakingly, he copied down a summary sheet naming all the business assets, the ships, the routes they travelled, the firms with whom he did trade. His ships brought butter from New Zealand and beef from Australia, and the routes from San Francisco and Honolulu brought in fruit and returned with bolts of cotton. A complex web, in which when one thing failed, everything else was put in jeopardy.

Shanghai was a paradise in comparison with where he was brought up. As a kid he'd been raised in the Dust Bowl, where hardly anything grew, and he'd watched his father try to literally scrape a farmer's wage out of the dirt. But drought had destroyed the fragile green shoots his father had laboured over for so long, his thin arms straining to yank a crop from the soil, and his ma had wept from hunger when there was no more wheat for gruel.

He wasn't going to let his kids have that kind of hardscrabble life. His staff knew him to be stubborn as a mule. He'd built his business stone by stone, never letting anyone say no. Until now. He loosened his tie under his scarf, trying to dispel the panic in his guts. He was losing control, and he needed to know what he was worth and how much of it he could hide.

All night he stayed there, and all the following day, frantically going through the files and invoices trying to get his affairs in order. He couldn't trust anyone else to do it. By midnight on the Sunday evening, he was too tired to go home and dozed in the chair in his office until a horn somewhere out on the river made him look up. His eyes were gritty and he still hadn't finished the accounting. The telephone shrilled, making him startle.

Chan Yeung, at reception. 'A message came, sir. Head office in Washington telephoned. Not good news. The Japanese have bombed Hawaii. America is at war with Japan.'

'What?'

'War, sir. They dropped bombs on the American fleet.'

'When was this? Why didn't they call me on my direct line?'

'I don't know, sir. Head office sounded panicked. They bombed Pearl Harbor. But because of the time difference we've only just got the news. New York says there's nothing you can do except secure your assets as best you can. Get cash and get ready, because if America's at war, you can expect a visit from the Japanese at any time.'

Theo didn't take the lift but ran down the stairs two at a time. In the main office on the first floor, some of his Chinese employees had heard the news too via the radio and had arrived early, their faces as worried as his own.

'Sir, is it true?' 'Sir!' A cacophony of demands.

He brushed them aside, and seeing he wasn't going to answer, they moved silently away so that he could look out to the street below. Though it was early, not yet dawn, the jetties were crowded with the usual silhouettes of sampans and junks, bobbing on the swell. Beggars clustered on the boardwalks in huddled heaps; dark figures wrapped like mummies against the cold. Theo glanced to the grey bulk of the HMS *Peterel*, and his belly tightened.

'What's that, sir?' One of his secretaries pointed.

It was still dark, but he made out a launch flying the red sun as it powered over to the British gunboat from the Japanese warship *Izumo* and disgorged a group of dark-clad Japanese. He fixed his eyes on it, wondering what they were doing, but it appeared they were turned away because no white flag or Japanese flag went up and instead the launch returned to the *Izumo*.

He was about to walk away from the window when an almighty boom shuddered the whole building.

'Christ almighty!' The words were out of his mouth before he could think.

Smoke engulfed the *Peterel*. On the street, beggars leapt up to scatter like ants.

A few moments later and machine-gun fire blitzed through the air with staccato efficiency and a few Japanese fell, but this was instantly rebuffed by huge shells aimed at the British ship. The explosions threw up white flashes and great spouts of water.

Theo blanched. There was actually a battle going on right here.

Another blast. The windows shuddered. 'Whoa!' Behind him the rest of his workers crushed up to the glass to see what was going on.

The *Peterel* was struck and began to list heavily to one side, gushing flames and smoke. Small black figures rushed hither and thither on deck trying to escape the firepower of the Japanese guns and the burning deck. Several men plunged into the sea.

Theo leapt away from the window. 'Don't just stand there gawping,' he shouted. 'That's the British ship! We've got to help them!'

At the door, he paused, holding it open. But nobody followed him. It was then he saw all too clearly where people's loyalties lay. They'd all turned away, as if they had seen nothing.

Sickened, he hurtled down the stairs alone, running, dodging all the Chinese beggars running in the other direction, away from the shore. The streets cleared like they did before monsoon rain. The stink of oil and gunpowder filled his nostrils. Theo ran hell for leather along the water's edge, as wounded men splashed through the murky swell towards dry land. The water was a foul concoction littered with debris and rotting funeral flowers from the beggars who could not afford to bury their dead, and instead cast the bodies into the belly of the river each night.

As he reached the shore, the surface oil slick caught fire and Japanese snipers tried to pick off the men as they flailed and staggered towards land. Theo shouted in rapid Chinese to Lee, the sampan man who often took him across the river. Lee, a balding man with a face like old leather, and trousers tied up with string, grabbed an oar as Theo fumbled aboard.

'Row!' shouted Theo.

Together Theo and Lee tried to drag a man out of the river but the pepper of machine-gun fire forced them to crouch and duck. A whine of bullets zipped and splashed past and frothed the surface.

The boat turned slightly. A man's head, white in the remaining moonlight, bobbed above his thrashing arms.

'Here!' Theo shouted. He plunged his arms into the freezing water to help the man climb aboard as the sampan swayed and rocked.

'Thanks,' the man gasped, rolling himself into the boat.

Lee rowed them towards the shore, head low as bullets streaked past. Over the wooden edge of the boat Theo fixed his gaze on the concrete jetty. Beneath it, a few exhausted, wounded men had crawled up onto the mud. In the confusion, further down the shore men were being picked up and taken away in Japanese launches.

Just shy of the mudflats Lee stashed his oars and refused to row on.

'What's the matter?' Theo yelled, conscious of the man crumpled in a wet heap at his feet.

'Give me your watch,' Lee said.

Theo frowned and held out his arm. 'This?'

'Yes. I take. Or no row. Okay?'

Theo felt he'd no choice, but it brought home to him that even now in this madness, Lee had only ever thought of him as a rich foreigner to be fleeced if possible.

He took the watch off and dangled it before him by the strap. Lee swiped and pocketed it in one deft movement.

Theo and the injured sailor clambered out onto the scummy shore, sinking up to their knees as Lee rowed off without a word. One of the men dumped by another sampan died before his eyes, bleeding out from his chest into the black oily mud. The man he'd rescued and hauled into the shadow of the steps had a wound to the arm and was white with shock and terror.

'Lie still,' Theo said as he dragged him out of view of the Japanese snipers. 'Pretend to be dead.'

The man curled himself into a small ball under the concrete walkway. Theo himself took cover huddling next to the steps in the overhang of the jetty.

By now a pale sun was illuminating the carnage on the water. Theo's trousers and arms were soaked with icy water. All at once everyone's attention was diverted by the rumble of heavy engines as, at the north end of the Bund, Japanese tanks rolled over the British-built Garden Bridge. They were followed by the dirty green trucks flying the flag of the Rising Sun.

The diversion was what they needed to get off the beach.

'Quick,' Theo said to the wounded man. He stripped off his overcoat and blue woollen scarf and thrust them into his arms. 'Walk with me, buddy. Just stroll, like we're two businessmen having a conversation.'

In the end he had to help the sailor into the coat as one arm was bleeding and the man was shaking all over with cold. Theo tied the scarf around his neck and buttoned up the coat like dressing a toddler. The man's eyes were blank with shock, but he did as Theo asked, stumbling after him up the steps and walking on unsteady legs. Theo suspected he was bleeding into his brand-new overcoat.

'Act like a businessman,' he whispered. 'We're having a business conversation, right?'

He marched him as quickly as he dared towards his offices, passing the trucks as they growled down the main highway scattering people in their wake. Grimly, they marched on, each step feeling like a mile. In through Carter & Co's big double doors to the lobby, his hand on the stranger's arm, where this time he ignored Chan Yeung's stare and took the lift.

In the whirr of the ascending lift, the rescued man leaned against the walls, grey with pain, taking deep ragged breaths before following Theo as he walked purposefully to his private office. Theo opened the door, then gestured the man inside.

Fortunately, his staff were all on the lower floor watching the street. 'I thought I knew my staff,' he said to the man slumped in his office chair. 'But not one of them was prepared to come with me. You all right?'

'Just a bit faint.'

Brits and their stiff upper lip. 'Well don't bleed to death before we can get you to a medic, all right?'

'All right.'

'We'll have to wait until it calms down a bit. Think you can last?'

'I shouldn't be here. I need to be with the rest of my crew.'

'No, you don't. You'd be dead or arrested. Sit tight here, we'll figure out what to do. What's your name?'

A long pause. 'Charlie … Charlie Hargreaves.'

Theo strode to the window and returned his attention to the street. 'They're coming down the Bund.'

The Japanese troops in their white helmets were everywhere, rifles and fixed bayonets glinting in the weak morning light. He watched several parties of these troops approaching, accompanied by what looked like Japanese officials in suits with the Japanese flag on their armbands.

With dawning realization, Theo saw they were going systematically into each building on the waterfront. He watched as they emerged from the American Consulate. 'Shit. They're coming in,' he said. 'There's nowhere to hide. I'll stall them. We'll have to brazen it out.'

The party of officials came out of the neighbouring hotel and disappeared from the pavement, and all too soon there was a commotion in the outer offices. 'Sit tight and stay *shtum*,' he said to Charlie.

He went out into the outer office to find a party of armed Japanese crowded there.

Shouts of protests as his Chinese workers who'd returned to their desks were led away at gunpoint.

'Is this really necessary?' he said, trying to intervene.

'You are Mr Theodore Carter?' A scrawny Japanese man in a pristine civilian suit approached him, with a clipboard in his hand.

'Can I help you, gentlemen?'

An older Japanese man in a thick camel-coloured overcoat, his grey hair oiled to his scalp, rattled off a few words and the skinny interpreter leapt in to translate. 'These premises are now under the control of Lieutenant-General Shigeru Sawada, commander of the 13th Army.'

'I understand,' Theo said.

More words. The interpreter bowing to his boss, and then; 'All transactions must be approved by Sawada. One of his employees will be coming tomorrow to assist you in the transition.'

'I'm sorry, but my existing staff are invaluable. They know how the business runs. Will I not be allowed to keep them on? They have families to support.'

The interpreter frowned and translated, though what he relayed seemed very short. The Japanese official shook his head in an impatient way. Theo wished he'd been able to have more time to learn Japanese, though he also realized no amount of Japanese would soften these men, who had probably had the same conversation a dozen times. What was more, they knew his name, so this raid had been carefully planned.

'I repeat, these premises are now under the control of Lieutenant-General Sawada.'

Theo felt fear tighten around his ribs. He was getting nowhere. It was really happening. His offices had been cleared of all his Chinese and Eurasian staff.

'You will hand us your spare keys,' the interpreter said.

Meanwhile, two soldiers strode past him into his office.

Theo's stomach clenched. God knows what kind of penalty he'd get for harbouring an escaped Brit.

Heart sinking, he followed them in. Charlie's face, lean as a wolf, was tense, but he ignored Theo and looked up at the visitors. He didn't attempt to come out to greet them and had the good sense to stay behind the desk. He'd dried his hair and his face somehow, so his hair looked as if it was slicked back with brilliantine. The interpreter asked him for his papers.

'Sorry, old chap, but I left them at home.' Charlie didn't stand up, and Theo knew exactly why. Under the scarf and overcoat, his trousers and shoes were covered in black mud.

'This is my logistics man, Mr Hargreaves,' Theo said, feeling a cold sweat beading on his brow. 'My assistant. I'm sure he will supply you with his papers when you return tomorrow. We weren't expecting you today.'

The interpreter rattled off what he said and the camel-coated official nodded impatiently, looked at his watch and spoke rapidly for a few more minutes. His body language said he was anxious to tick these premises off on the clipboard, the one held by the fawning official next to him.

'Make sure you have all your papers tomorrow,' the interpreter said. 'My assistant will come back to inform you what to do next. The keys, Mr Carter.'

Theo walked around to the desk drawer and withdrew one of his spare sets of keys. He held them out and counted them off. 'The front door, the stationery cupboard door, the keys to the three private offices on this floor. The key to the main office. Oh, and the key to the cellar storeroom.'

'The safe?'

Theo dug into his pocket. Good thing he'd emptied the safe yesterday.

The camel coat man didn't appear to take any notice, just watched as the sets of keys were tied and tagged with a brown label and a scrawl of Japanese kanji. The man with the clipboard scribbled something on the list.

'Business will continue as usual,' the interpreter said, as if it were an order. 'You will work as normal.' Theo felt like saying, *How can I, with no staff?* But he merely nodded.

From the corner of his eye he caught sight of Charlie, still seated behind his desk, a slight tic twitching in his cheek, his face pale as ivory.

Mr Camel Coat tossed the keys in his palm like toys, then turned on his heel and the whole entourage hurried away back down the stairs.

As soon as they'd gone, Charlie slumped over the desk, head in his hands.

'You okay?' Theo asked.

'I thought I might have a heart attack. Sorry, but there's mud all over your carpet. And my arm throbs like crazy.'

'Give them a few minutes and then I'll try to get a rickshaw to take us both home. There's a woman nearby, a Russian nurse. Speaks good English and she'll help sort out your arm.'

'You don't need to do this.'

'I know I don't, but I want to. We're allies aren't we? The Yanks and the Brits? And what's the alternative? Give yourself up? You'd be dead inside a day. Besides, we'll be safer there in a civilian area, not the business district.'

Chapter 8

Zofia woke to shouting and gunfire and was out of bed in an instant, gathering together all her belongings.

'Hilly!' she yelled. 'Get dressed!'

Hilly too was on the move, hastily thrusting her clothes into a bag, but they were too late; Japanese soldiers were already in the house, rousing everyone from their beds and pushing them out onto the street. Those tenants with Chinese clothing were immediately arrested and taken away in armoured trucks. Those who looked European were frisked for their papers.

Zofia held her passport open, and helped Hilly find hers amongst her mess of belongings. Hilly was still in a nightdress with a coat on top, the necklace around her neck. 'Take that off, you might get mugged,' Zofia yelled. 'And find your shoes!'

Hilly stumbled into them, but there was no time to take off the necklace.

'Out, out!' the Japanese soldiers said, prodding with their bayonets. They shoved everyone onto the street, like sweeping a tide of cockroaches out of a slum. Zofia was prepared, her bag already packed, but Hilly was still trying to find her woollen hat as they were ordered out. Behind her she heard explosions and saw one building engulfed in flames. Chinese people emerged coughing from the textile mill at that end of the street and were swiftly rounded up. They had no choice but to follow the billowing crowd, like flotsam on the tide.

'Where are we going?' Hilly kept asking as Zofia was dragged along, Hilly's arm hooked desperately around hers.

'We'll try Mr Carter's. It's all I can think of.'

Everyone had the same idea, to head for the International Settlement, but the barrier was a wall of sandbags and barbed wire and guarded by Japanese. They found themselves wedged in a crush of beggars and refugees. Hilly was on tiptoe peering over their heads.

'I can see Goro!'

'What?' Zofia couldn't see anything, but Hilly was dragging her towards the barrier. Zofia's arm was almost wrenched out of its socket but she daren't let go.

No one could go through without showing papers and all the Chinese servants were being turned away, even when they sobbed that their children and relatives were left inside. Word soon spread and a ragged queue of Westerners began to form. From the fevered talk in the queue, Zofia discovered there'd been a raid on Hawaii, and Japan was now at war with the US. At war!

Hilly was dragging her forward but she pulled her back. 'No,' she shouted over the din. 'We have to queue!'

They waited, with Hilly still desperate to go to speak to Goro. Zofia followed her gaze and saw it was fixed on one of the men near the entrance. He was a young man with a thin moustache and a very upright bearing. His mouth was turned down in a frown. He swiped a sobbing Chinese woman across the face with his bayonet when she came too close, and the queue fell back in horror.

Hilly faltered.

When it got to their turn Hilly held out her passport and smiled shyly at him. 'Look, I'm wearing it,' she said, pointing to her necklace.

He didn't react, merely snatched her Austrian passport and glanced at it. 'Move along now,' he said in broken English. 'Next.'

'Goro?' Zofia saw the confusion in her face. 'It's me, Hilly.'

'Move along.' They seemed to be the only English words he knew.

'I'm sorry I didn't come to—' Hilly's words were cut off as he stabbed the bayonet in her direction so the tip just touched her chest.

Hilly recoiled. 'It's me,' she said again, eyes wide with shock.

He withdrew the bayonet and in one whip-like movement slapped her hard across the face. 'Whore.' The English word was unmistakeable.

Hilly staggered and almost fell forward. Zofia could do nothing. Nobody said anything.

Zofia held her breath as her own pass was examined by his companion, a heavier man with a face like iron.

For a moment she thought she'd be turned away. Desperately she explained in Japanese that she was a teacher tutoring American children to speak their language.

He grunted and waved her on. She almost collapsed in relief. 'Thank you,' she said in Japanese, almost ashamed she knew their tongue. These men were nothing like Haru, these men were thugs.

Hilly was waiting, one cheek red as fire. It made Zofia so angry she could barely speak. She wrapped an arm around Hilly's shoulder. 'It's all right.'

'I didn't go to the park, so he hates me now.'

'Forget him. Keep your head down, and don't stare at anybody,' she said.

'It's your fault. You should have let me go with him to Wing On's.'

'He called you a foul name. He didn't deserve you.'

'Are we really going to Mr Carter's?'

'Yes.' Though she hated to beg. He was her employer, not

a friend. Perhaps they would be able to stay a while until the Japanese army had done whatever it was going to do.

Hilly was quiet, and she saw her touch her cheek where it burned red.

The two of them set off walking, for the Chinese bicycle hire place had all its shutters down. Nor were there signs of life at the cobbler's, or at the man who sold umbrellas. All the small businesses were closed. Word had spread in the space of hours.

The Carters' house looked just the same, and knowing Theo would be out at work, she went to the servants' entrance. Nobody there. Not even Chen or Mai Ling. She peered through the windows but the place was deserted. Cups and bowls littered the table as if a meal had been left in a hurry.

At the front, she knocked again but Chen didn't answer the door. Instead, to her surprise, Mr Carter shouted, 'Who is it?'

'Zofia.' she said. 'And my friend, Hilly.'

The door opened a crack and Theo's face peered out. He had dark circles under his eyes, his jaws were shadowed with stubble and his hair hung over his forehead as if he hadn't had time to brush it.

He opened it wider to let her in. 'Are you all right?'

She shepherded Hilly inside. 'The Japanese have taken over our lodgings and kicked us out. Did you know they—'

'Yes, I got the news. If you come in, you have to promise not to tell anyone what you've seen in here.' He put a hand on her arm. His gaze was intense, and it made her shiver.

She shot Hilly the expression that meant 'do as I say'.

Hilly drew a finger across her throat and said, 'We swear.'

'Then come in both of you. We're in the sitting room.'

He let them in, then relocked the door. Zofia followed as he bounded up the stairs ahead of them.

She'd never been in his sitting room before but was unsurprised to see a blend of East and West with bamboo tables and pictures of dahlias embroidered in silk. Sitting on the sofa with his feet up was a wiry young man with sharp features and curious brown eyes. His arm was strapped to his chest with a sling made from a tea-towel.

'This is Charlie,' Theo said. 'He was injured this morning in the fight on the Bund.'

'Zofia.' She gave him a nod. A British sailor. His trousers gave him away, and the fact there was a bloodstained navy uniform jacket, with its distinctive brass buttons, slung on the back of the chair.

'This is Hilly,' she said. 'We share lodgings in Hongkew.'

'We used to. They took over our street,' Hilly said. 'Can we stay here?'

'You Jewish?' Charlie swung his legs down and was leaning forward in his seat.

'Yes, from Poland,' Zofia said.

'And Austria,' Hilly said proudly.

'It's okay, Charlie,' Theo said. 'Zofia taught my kids Japanese. And it could be useful. Seems we might need a lot more things translating now.'

'I've been thinking,' Charlie said, 'I need to get some way of contacting the boys back home. Don't suppose you've got a radio?'

'Not a transmitter,' Theo said. 'Only a receiver. For the BBC World Service. To get the news. I tried earlier but could only get interference.'

'Bastards have probably jammed it.'

Zofia frowned at the bad language in front of Hilly. But then realized she'd certainly heard worse.

Charlie leaned forward. 'I need to know more about Pearl Harbor. Whether the US are coming into the war against the Nazis.'

'Nobody knows,' Theo said. 'It's chaos. The Japs are obviously expecting us to carry on under them, but how can we, with no Chinese staff? I called Mitchell from the city waterworks and Bathurst from the bank. They've been told the same. All Chinese sewerage workers have to stop doing their work, and the bank's assets have been frozen.'

'They'll replace the staff with Japs, I suppose,' Charlie said.

'I don't see how. Japan's a tiny country whereas China's enormous.'

'But not as ruthless and organized as the Japanese,' Charlie replied.

'Are we going to have some breakfast?' Hilly whispered to Zofia.

'Ssh. We'll find some soon.' Zofia took her into the children's room where on the dressing table there were crayons and a colouring book belonging to Daisy and Jimmy. There was still a pair of Daisy's patent-leather party shoes Mai Ling had discarded from her case. Their absence stung. 'Draw me something cheerful,' Zofia said, passing Hilly the colouring book.

'With this?' Hilly curled her lip in disgust. 'I'm not a baby. Just show me where the kitchen is.'

'We're guests. We have to be polite. Five minutes, then we'll find it, I promise.'

By the time Zofia came back into the sitting room, Theo was talking, but he stopped and lowered his voice.

'Is she all right? It's hard for a kid.'

'It's been a shock. She's at an awkward age. She just … she needs looking after. She only half understands the war, what it's all about.'

'Where are her parents?' Charlie said.

'Don't ask. She should be in school. But we can't afford the International School. She's got no family to pay. And I can't leave her just wandering the streets on her own.'

'Well don't let her blab,' Charlie said. 'If she blabs that I'm here, I'm done for.'

'She won't,' Zofia said. But a creeping tension grew in her stomach.

'I've got to go,' Theo said. 'I'm meeting Mitchell at Bathurst's.

We can't meet at the Shanghai Club anymore; it's been taken over. We're not sure how to trade or whether it will all be subject to new laws. Just thinking of it gives me a headache.'

'Where are your house staff?' Zofia asked. 'I need to fix us something to eat. Nobody was in the servants' wing.'

'Hell knows.' Theo ran a hand through his hair. 'I woke up this morning and they'd all vamooshed. Maybe they knew this was coming.'

'Do you think they'll come back?' Zofia asked.

He shrugged. 'Don't know. But when I'm out, don't open the door to anyone, there've been looters at the empty houses now people have left. And anyway, the Japs could come looking for Charlie.'

'Don't worry about me. I'll be out of here as soon as I figure out a plan,' said Charlie.

'Let it all die down first.' Theo turned to Zofia. 'Sure you can stay, but you have to know there's a risk.'

'Everywhere's a risk,' Zofia flashed back, suddenly defensive because she knew there was nowhere else. 'Out there, in here. It makes no difference.'

'I meant if the Japs find Charlie here, you could be labelled enemy sympathizers. Because technically now, the Americans and the Brits are their enemies. And they're not above torturing people to find out what they want. Even kids. Promise not to open the door. I don't want anything to happen.'

'It won't. You go to your meeting. We'll keep the door locked.'

While Theo was out, Zofia found some sesame rolls in the kitchen and some soybean milk. Eating felt like normality. Like they actually lived somewhere. Hilly ate quickly, as if it might be suddenly taken away. Though her face had lost the redness of the slap, her eyes were flicking place to place like a wild animal in a trap.

After they'd eaten, Charlie prowled the place looking for anything useful. 'Hey, can you ladies sew?' he asked.

Hilly rolled her eyes. 'We don't bother usually.' In Shanghai it was cheaper to get it done by a tailor.

'Can you fix these?' He'd picked out a pair of trousers from Theo's wardrobe, along with a shirt and tie, and a sweater. 'They're too long for me; can you turn them up? I can get away with the rest of the things.'

'Won't he mind?' Hilly said. 'It's not allowed. Taking things without asking.'

'Look at my trousers, they're filthy. Better to look like I'm a toff than a British sailor, don't you think? And besides, I can't do it – there's my arm …' He waggled it in the sling.

Hilly stood and walked up close to him. 'Does your arm hurt? What happened to it?'

'A bullet tore through it,' Charlie said, with a hint of a swagger. 'But nah, it's only a flesh wound. A friend of Theo's came this morning to stitch it. A Russian nurse, Olga. But she had to go to the hospital to see if there were any other injuries. Shame, she was a looker.'

'What's a looker?' Hilly asked.

'Never mind,' Zofia said. 'Hilly'll fix your trousers. She likes sewing, don't you, Hilly?'

Hilly looked dubious, but Zofia went on the hunt and after a bit of searching in the *amah*'s room below, found a box with needles and thread. It felt strange to be wandering about the house with nobody to stop them, but then again, the world had gone to war overnight.

Back in the sitting room, she handed the box to Hilly, who held the trousers up against Charlie to get them the right length. 'You're not as tall as Theo,' she said.

'Tall for a sailor. Tallest in my squad. Used to call me String Bean. It was a joke. Cause I'm only five foot five.'

'String Bean!' Hilly giggled.

Zofia helped her to pin the hems, then Hilly started sewing. Painfully slowly, but with complete concentration.

Zofia couldn't be still though; the house was cold, and as there were no servants to light the fire, she started to lay kindling in the grate with newspaper from a basket next to the fireplace.

Her mind was distracted, wondering whether Haru was somehow involved in this theatre of war. Her heart ached for him.

Haru wouldn't even know where she was. She'd written from Shanghai to his training camp, but had no reply, and the silence made her want to scream. She stood up from the grate, and went to the window to gaze out through the mosquito screens to the dark beyond. Was he fighting against the Americans and the British now? She baulked at the idea that the Japanese, and by extension, Haru, were on the side of the Nazis. And whenever anyone called them 'the Japs' or 'the Nips' as if they were all bad guys, it made her uncomfortable.

A noise from below of a door slamming made them all start.

'What the hell?' Charlie was out of his seat in a moment.

Voices from the servants' quarters.

'Is it Theo?' Charlie asked.

She shook her head. They were speaking Chinese. 'Get out of sight,' Zofia said. 'I'll go and see who it is. It's probably only Chen and the servants come back.'

'Who's Chen?' Hilly asked.

'Servant. Number one boy.' Zofia went to the top of the stairs and called down. 'Chen, is that you?' Silence. 'Mai Ling?'

Nobody answered so warily she went down the stairs. Shouting came from the kitchen, raised voices she couldn't make out.

She opened the door and the scene that met her eyes made her step back.

At least ten Chinese people were in the kitchen. They seemed equally shocked to see her standing there. Chen she recognized, and Mai Ling and Suzi the cook. But the rest were strangers. Chinese men. But what shocked her the most was the pile of weapons on the table. Rifles, and what looked like machine guns, mortar bombs and grenades.

Chen came towards her with his hands outstretched.

'Missy, what you do here?'

But he'd barely time to speak when another Chinese man elbowed his way past him. He was squat but powerfully built, dressed in an expensively cut suit and burgundy silk tie. His expression was one which made Zofia step back. 'Where's Carter?' He spoke in well-educated English.

'He's not here,' she replied, trying to keep calm. 'He's gone to a meeting.'

'Is that right? Well, we're having a meeting ourselves, right here. You want some work?' It was not what she was expecting. His English was better than hers and when he spoke a tooth flashed gold.

'I already have work,' she said. 'With Mr Carter.'

He laughed. 'Mr Carter won't be here long.' He came closer. 'The tables have turned. Tell him this from me; the days of being his servants are over. We are fighting for our country. The rules are different now. Now you Westerners will serve us.' He poked a finger towards Zofia's chest. 'Tell him that.'

Zofia didn't flinch despite the shudder inside. 'You're trespassing. If Mr Carter—'

'You dare talk to us about trespass?' He laughed, a harsh mirthless sound. 'Now you listen to me, Miss Smarty-pants; if I were you, I'd go back upstairs before we shut your mouth in a more permanent way.' He mimed a gun with his two fingers and a few of his companions sniggered.

She drew herself up but said nothing. No point in antagonizing him further, and besides, she didn't want him to see her shaking knees. She retreated upstairs with as much dignity as she could.

'Who is it?' Hilly asked. 'Is it Theo?'

'The servants, and a lot of other men. But they're armed – rifles and grenades.'

Charlie emerged from the box room where he'd been hiding. 'What gives?'

'The Chinese servants have taken over the kitchen. They were deliberately intimidating. They're saying the rules have changed and they're not going to be servants anymore.'

'Will they come up here?'

'I don't know. One of them was pretty aggressive and threatened to shut me up. The rest all seemed to kowtow to him like he was the man in charge.'

'Bad guys,' Hilly said, as if it was a given.

'Armed is not a good sign. I lost my gun in the water,' Charlie said. 'And I couldn't fire it now anyway, with this arm.'

'What shall we do?' Zofia asked.

'Dunno. Wait for Theo to return, I suppose. They're his servants. He knows them. Maybe he can reason with them.'

They spent an uneasy few hours hearing noises and voices in Chinese from below, but Zofia didn't want to go down again and it was obvious Charlie was in no fit state to take them on.

At the slam of a car door, they all froze.

The sound of the key in the front door was a relief. It must be Theo.

As he walked into the room, he threw off his hat and slumped into a chair. 'It's grim,' he said. 'Our accounts are frozen and we can only make limited withdrawals. All travel permits out of the country have been revoked, and we have to show our papers as we move between the different concessions – travelling between all the sectors will be hell now, and there'll be lots more queueing. Barricades are up everywhere. Barbed wire. Spiked palisades.'

'Palisades,' echoed Hilly, repeating the new English word.

'Are all sectors the same?' asked Zofia.

'All except for here in the French. They're more lax with the French Concession because the Germans are their allies under the Nazi-controlled Vichy government, and there are so many of them here. One of the Germans at my meeting was wearing the Nazi armband with the swastika. Since the takeover, they're keen to advertise themselves as being on the Japs' side.'

Noises from below of footsteps coming up. 'Shit. They've heard your car,' Zofia said. 'There are Chinese downstairs, more people than just the servants, I think they're—'

'What do you mean? Isn't Chen down there?'

'Uh-huh. But it was another man who looked to be in charge …' Her words died and fell to a whisper. The man she'd talked to earlier was striding into the sitting room, a bunch of others massed behind him.

'Ah, Mr Carter.' The Chinese man's words were polite, but he had a revolver pointing at Theo's chest.

'Zha Wei. I should have guessed. What's all this?' Theo's tone was polite but cool.

'We are taking over this house for the National Communists. You'll have to find somewhere else to stay. After all, you owe me some hospitality for feeding Evelina's habit.'

Theo took a step back, frowning. 'Now just wait a minute, I've always paid my dues, right on the button. Isn't there someplace else you could go?'

'The Japs have taken over the nightclubs and casinos. Closed them until further notice. Same with all Chinese premises unless they've been given special dispensation.'

'And yours? The Blue Lilac?'

'Exempt for now. I'm sweet-talking them and it's still open, but for how long? They're putting pressure on me.'

'Isn't there anything you can do to stop them?'

'Yes. Organize. That's what we are doing. And your house is where we'll do it.'

Theo kept his unruffled air, though Zofia could see a vein throb at the side of his neck. He turned to his servant. 'Chen. You know me. I'll do what I can, but I'm not moving out of my house. I have guests, as you can see.'

Chen looked away as if there was suddenly something fascinating out of the window. His mouth was pressed together in a sharp line.

'See?' Zha Wei laughed. 'He's not answering your orders anymore. I'll give you half an hour.'

Now Theo looked rattled. 'But it's getting dark! We can agree something, surely? The downstairs servants' quarters can accommodate you all.'

Zha Wei stepped forward with a thrust of the revolver. 'Like I said to the lady, we're nobody's servants now. Not yours, not anybody's. So get packed and get out.'

Charlie got awkwardly to his feet. 'Hey, there's no need to be so—'

'All right, sailor boy, you want to be handed over?' Zha Wei gestured at the uniform jacket on the back of the chair. He swivelled to point the gun at him. 'We know who you are. You're the missing crewman from the *Peterel*. But we'll turn a blind eye so long as you get out of here. We don't want any whiteys spying on us.'

'Have we to leave now?' Hilly's expression was one of disbelief. 'Again?'

Zofia knew how this would end. She grabbed Hilly by the arm. She couldn't leave her here. It was always the same, leaving Hilly would be like leaving a kitten in a lion's cage. 'Let's get your things,' she whispered in a kind, sing-song voice. 'Put your coat on.'

'I can wear it, can I? You don't want it?'

'No, it's cold out, so button it up, and fetch your hat.'

Hilly scooted away but Theo seemed unable to take it in. She saw that the ridiculous idea that everything in the world belonged to him was still there.

'Warm clothes,' Zofia urged him in a whisper. 'Good shoes. Practical things. Your personal papers, dollars, anything gold. Any way of getting money. Medication if you take it.' She pushed him towards the bedroom. 'Go with him, Charlie,' she ordered. 'Make sure he packs as much as he can. Two bags. Things for you too.'

Charlie was at his heels like a terrier, and she heard their low voices talking in frantic whispers.

Meanwhile Zha Wei had found a cigar box on top of the piano and was taking out a cigar. One of his men lit it for him whilst he kept the gun pointed in their direction. The smoke was pungent and thick. Zha Wei had a lazy air about him, but his eyes were sharp as stones. The other men were prowling, looking in all the rooms as if they'd never seen anything like it.

A tense silence as Zha Wei looked Zofia up and down, as if he was assessing her worth in currency. She felt her face redden but maintained an icy stare.

One of the men came back with a pink and diamanté evening dress of Evelina's. He hung it up next to his emaciated frame. 'My wife would like this,' he said.

'Then take it,' Zha said. 'Be no use to his woman now. She's gone, hasn't she? Mai Ling can have the rest, she's worked hard enough for it.'

'Oh, that's pretty,' said Hilly, 'is it silk?' She stepped out from the bedroom to try to feel the material before Zofia could stop her.

The young man whipped it away, shouting at her in Chinese.

Hilly shrank, afraid, while he bundled up the pink silk as if it was laundry. Hilly had her coat buttoned up wrong and it made Zofia's heart constrict. She took her by the arm and pulled her back until they were standing against the wall.

Mai Ling wouldn't meet her eyes, but Zofia watched her go into the bedroom and come out clad in a black Persian lamb fur coat. Several sizes too big, it swamped her tiny frame, but she stuck out her chin and looked at Zofia with defiance.

Zofia gripped Hilly's arm tight, willing her to keep quiet.

Theo emerged from the landing with two suitcases, dropped them by the door and went into his study. A moment later he came out with a folder of papers which he hastily shoved into his briefcase. Charlie picked up one of the cases with his good arm.

All this time the Chinese men watched like birds of prey. Theo and Charlie did not look at the men, but she felt their resentment like a knot in the chest, the compressed anger that they couldn't fight, that they were unarmed and vulnerable.

'Car keys,' Zha Wei said.

'What?'

Zofia saw by Theo's face that until this moment Theo had actually thought they'd let him keep his car. Let him drive somewhere.

Bitterly, Theo took the keys from his pocket and threw them on the ground at Zha Wei's feet.

'Out,' Zha Wei said. 'All of you. Before I lose my temper.'

Hilly bowed her head and moved stiffly towards the stairs like a doll. Zofia grasped her by the arm and propelled her towards the front door. 'Whatever happens, stick with me,' she whispered.

A few moments later all four of them were standing outside the house, looking back at the lights in the windows.

'What now?' asked Charlie. 'Is there anywhere we can go? We sure as hell can't ask the Japanese for help.'

'Olga and the Russians?' Theo asked. 'We have to hope she's in, because sometimes she works nights.'

By now it was dark, and in the distance the occasional burst of gunfire echoed amid flashes of light. The roads of the French Concession were quiet, with hardly any cars, and no rickshaws.

'It's eerie,' Theo said. 'Like the heart's been hollowed from the city.'

'I don't like walking.' Hilly was reluctant. 'Aren't there any coolies?'

It took about a half hour before they arrived outside Olga's house, a *lilong* at the edge of the French Concession – one she used to share with two other Russian women, both of whom had left in recent months. The house had no lights showing.

'Shall we wait until morning?' Theo asked. 'She might be sleeping.'

Zofia gave him a push on the shoulder. 'It's no good being polite now. You've just lost your house to a gang of Chinese rebels and you're in a war zone. Just knock on the door.'

'If it had been my house back there, I'd have stood my ground and fought for it,' Charlie said.

'Oh yes, two unarmed men, a woman and a kid,' Theo said, rounding on him. 'Fat lot of use that'd be.'

'I'm not a kid,' protested Hilly.

'Americans always roll over,' Charlie said. 'They won't take on Hitler and they didn't fight when the Japanese Navy started this whole thing. They just handed over the *Wake*. They didn't fight like we did on the *Peterel*.'

'Because it was pointless. There were too few men on board,' Theo snapped. 'And the Japs are trained to fight to the death. *Never surrender*, that's their motto. It's insane. They'd rather die than give up, no matter the odds. And as for the British, they were outclassed! But oh no, they had to make a stupid show of defence. For what? So men like you could get killed and act like heroes?'

'Bet the Americans did the same in Pearl Harbor. Just gave up.'

'Pearl Harbor was an unprovoked attack,' Theo said hotly.

'Shut it, Charlie,' Zofia said, disturbed by this talk, and unaccountably guilty on account of Haru. 'Without Theo you'd have been in a Japanese jail by now.'

Charlie looked sheepish. 'Sorry. My arm throbs like the devil.'

A light flashed on in the hallway, and a woman's voice called out, 'Who is it?'

'Theo Carter again.'

The door opened and Olga's cat-like eyes assessed the four of them, coming to rest first on the suitcases and then on Charlie's arm still in the sling she'd given him earlier. 'What's all the noise?'

'Sorry to barge in on you,' Theo said. 'We need your help.'

She gave a wag of the head to invite them in. Her house was cramped but as neat as Olga herself. Three Russian icons of bearded saints glinted gold in the hall. In the living room a radio was tuned to a foreign station, all crackle and interference.

Olga gestured to it. 'Can't pick up anything Russian anymore.

They must have jammed the frequencies with a local Jap station.' Like everyone else in the settlement she spoke accented English; it was how Shanghailanders got along. She offered them coffee and they accepted.

While the kettle boiled, she shouted, 'Let me guess. The Japs have taken over your house.'

'Wrong,' called Theo. 'The Chinese. Zha Wei and his men.'

Now she came back into the room, eyes wide. 'The nightclub owner?'

'They were armed,' Zofia said. 'Like they're planning a rebellion.'

'He's a gangster. Drug-running, prostitution, you name it. The churches tried to get him shut down, but it was no use. Rumour is they're Triads. Him and his two sons. They can't shut down his club, the Blue Lilac. Too many big men in Shanghai go there.'

'He's at Theo's,' Hilly said. 'We had to leave. That's three places I've been thrown out of in two days.'

'What are you going to do?' Olga asked Theo.

He shrugged. 'I don't know. I'm hoping they'll get arrested once the Japanese get wind of where they're based, and I'll be able to get my property back.'

There was a silence but Zofia, like everyone else, said nothing. Better to let him hope.

'I suppose you want to stay here,' Olga said. Her tone was one of resignation.

'We'd be very grateful,' Charlie said, giving her a big smile.

She sighed. 'I have only two spare beds. And they're in one room. You'll have to make do.'

'The ladies can have the beds,' Theo said. 'We'll take the couch and the floor.'

Hilly nudged Zofia. 'Ladies!' she whispered with a big grin.

They drank coffee while Olga re-dressed Charlie's arm and offered him a sedative to help him sleep. Charlie basked in her attention and pretended to be brave. 'I don't need it,' he said, pushing the bottle of tablets away. 'It's just a scratch. Hardly hurts at all.'

Olga showed Zofia and Hilly to the spare room. Again it had pictures of saints on the wall and a statue of the Virgin Mary on the lace mat on the dressing table.

'Want my advice? Get some sleep,' Olga said. 'We'll all need our wits about us tomorrow when we see how things fall out.'

They thanked her as she went, though Zofia didn't like her abrasive manner. She hadn't exactly been welcoming.

'I wish everyone would leave us alone,' Hilly said. 'Why do we keep having to move? Can I go to the kiosk tomorrow?'

'No,' Zofia said. 'Not for a while.'

'Why?'

'It's because there's a war … oh, never mind. It's too complicated to explain.'

'It's not. I get it – the Japs are fighting to take over. Stop treating me like I don't know anything.'

Zofia took off her shoes and put them neatly under her bed. She didn't know what would happen now. It was hard to guess because of all the other nations involved in this settlement. The French, the Dutch, the English, the Americans – Japan traded with them all. Surely they'd want to retain some sort of cordial relationship?

Hilly rolled over onto her back. 'It's nice here, better than Hongkew.'

She was right. It was civilized. Everything clean and tidy and scrubbed.

'Charlie's got the hots for Olga,' said Hilly with a giggle. 'He kept looking at her, all moony.'

'It's just because she's a nurse and fixed his arm. You're imagining it. Nobody with any sense would start a romance at a time like this.'

She turned over so her back was towards Hilly. She remembered being Hilly's age and her own young dreams of romance and how they had been shattered by war. How her body had changed and become something men stared at. Now it was happening to Hilly, and she worried in case Hilly did something to put herself at risk.

Talk of love had made her think of Haru. Where was he now? She'd heard nothing. She couldn't believe he was out there somewhere with those instructions, to fight to the death. The words Charlie said, *never surrender*, echoed in her head. And now she wasn't sure whose side she was on.

She reached for her purse to find the only photograph of Haru that she had. A wedding photo of them both standing stiffly without smiles, the Japanese way. She smoothed her thumb tenderly over his face. His eyes were blank in this image, yet she remembered the soft light in them as he looked down at her to make his vows.

So many conflicting loyalties, and none of them of any use in the situation she was in now.

The only thing she knew was that she had to keep Hilly out of trouble, because to a soldier, whichever side they were on, Hilly's mix of innocence and naivety, combined with a worldliness beyond her years, would be hard to resist.

Chapter 9

The next morning Zofia awoke to find Theo had already been out to buy the only newspaper available, the *Shanghai Times*, which was much shorter than usual. It had been purged of any reference to Christmas celebrations, and now bristled with Japanese propaganda.

Theo spread it on the table as everyone clustered around.

'Instructions and demands from our new overlords. We've to register at Hamilton House opposite the Metropole Hotel,' Theo said. 'Then they'll give us some sort of pass.'

'All of us?' Hilly asked.

'Wait a minute—' He was reading as he spoke. 'It says here just British, Americans and Indians – you know, the Sikhs who direct the traffic.'

'They've got to be kidding,' Charlie said. 'No way am I going there; not unless I want to lose my head.'

'Then it's just you, Theo.' Zofia said. 'Are there no Chinese or English newspapers?'

'Not that I could find. The Japs have a stranglehold on it all. They're well organized. I saw what they're calling a "news dissemination truck".'

'What the heck's that?'

'A truck with loudspeakers, telling us to go about our business as usual. As if. But they were chucking out leaflets of anti-US propaganda. Here.' He fished a crumpled flyer from his pocket and handed it to her.

An ugly cartoon of Churchill and Roosevelt clinging to each other, their faces a caricature of dismay. 'Yikes.' Zofia put it on the table so the others could see.

'I'm off to the Chamber Offices in the American Club,' Theo said. 'See if I can do anything about Zha Wei.'

'Wish I could come with you.' Charlie looked considerably brighter today.

'Yes, what about Charlie?' Olga asked. 'He's got no papers, and if they find out he's a British sailor, he'll have no chance.'

Hilly raised her eyebrows at Zofia as if to say, 'I told you so'.

'I've a contact in the Jewish ghetto,' Zofia said. 'If I can find him. He used to forge papers for Jews; people who'd lost their identity cards getting out of Europe. He made what they call Nansen passports. Hey, Charlie, how do you feel about being temporarily Russian and Jewish?'

'Russian? You joking? I can't speak a word of it.'

'And neither can the Japanese,' said Zofia. 'It will be a lot less suspicious than being English or American.'

Charlie screwed up his face. 'If you can find this forger man, then why not?'

'You could be the brother of one of my flatmates,' Olga said. 'They left, but there's no reason the Japanese will know. Here are their names.' She got out some paper and wrote them down. 'Viktoria Khorkina and Yana Produnova. And you' – she gestured to Charlie before writing down the name – 'you are the brother of Viktoria, Maksim Khorkin.'

'Oh gawd,' Charlie said. 'I really don't think it's a good idea to have a name I can barely pronounce—'

'It'll mean you can go out,' Olga said. 'We'll get you a pair of glasses and make you look like a Russian intellectual.'

'I am an intellectual,' Charlie said, miffed. 'Just a British one.'

'Am I the only one all of a sudden who's got to register?' asked Theo.

'You're the only one who's not a refugee like the rest of us,' said Zofia.

Theo bent his head over the newspaper. He sighed. 'I suppose I'd better go and do it. It feels so strange that just last week I was planning Christmas with my wife and children, and now I'm homeless and need some sort of pass to even go into my own office.'

'War's like that,' said Zofia bitterly. 'It just tramples over everything like a great threshing machine.'

The next day Hilly wanted to go back to work at the kiosk as usual, so Zofia made a few enquiries and discovered that Madam Wang seemed to have escaped the Chinese cull, probably because she was providing a service – the Japanese soldiers needed their cigarettes and snacks, and somewhere to sell their propaganda newspapers.

Today she'd go to the forger Isaac Finkelstein, to get Charlie's papers.

Though Olga had let them stay, there was a coolness to her Zofia didn't like. But there was nowhere else to go, so she reckoned she'd best keep on the right side of her. And Hilly was right, Olga seemed to have taken a shine to Charlie.

After dropping off Hilly, Zofia headed down Avenue Joffre, an area known as 'Little Moscow' because of the number of Russian shops. It was already thronged with Chinese women who screeched and fought with their nails, stockpiling rice and flour and any other goods they could grab. After a half hour of grappling, Zofia managed two small bags of rice and beans and some bottled vegetables.

The change was only a few *jiao*. She counted the coppers before slipping their cold weight into her purse. So few. The little money she had left – all her wages from tutoring at the Carters' – was dwindling fast. As she walked away, her bag weighing on her shoulder, she wondered how Theo's family were, Evelina and the children. Whether they'd heard what was happening here in Shanghai and if they'd got safely to Manila. And she couldn't push away the thought of Haru and wondering where he was. Malaya, Singapore or Hong Kong. Names she read in the newspapers. She couldn't imagine him patrolling like the soldiers here. He'd probably be in an office somewhere, his fingers wrapped around a pen.

In Hongkew, Zofia hurried around the corner to where Isaac had his business, a single-room apartment on the top floor of a crumbling block of mansions. Her knock was answered warily by his wife, Sarah.

Isaac, dressed in a worn old cardigan, was poring over a document being inked by one of his two sons, friends of her Dutch pals, Jan and Karel. They looked up at her as she entered, and their dark eyes stayed fixed on her the whole time.

When he heard what she wanted, Isaac was impatient. 'No no no. Too busy. Look at this.' He pointed to a pile of papers. 'Business has exploded. Everyone wants new papers.'

'I can pay. It's urgent.'

'They all say that.'

'I'm trying to help a friend, that's why. He's a Brit.'

'Don't tell me. Not the one they are all looking for? That sailor from the *Peterel*?'

'Bob Dering, father,' chipped in the eldest Finkelstein boy. 'He's called Bob Dering.'

Zofia masked her shock. 'No. This man is Charlie Hargreaves. What's this about a sailor?'

'The escaped man from the boat they sank. One of the sailors is unaccounted for, a petty officer. He escaped into Shanghai and they're offering a hundred US dollars as a reward. The Japanese think they're losing face the whole time he's on the run. They want to catch him and make a big song and dance about it.'

Bob Dering. It had to be Charlie. He'd given them a false name. With a sinking feeling, she realized Charlie might not be fully trustworthy. 'My man isn't him,' Zofia said firmly, 'This man has no papers.'

'Then where did he come from?'

She trotted out the explanation she'd planned. 'He used to work for Carter & Co, but his house in Hongkew got bombed and now he's no papers.'

The Finkelsteins exchanged glances, which made Zofia squirm and her face flush.

Mr Finkelstein sighed but agreed to do the work. She'd to deliver his photograph and then collect the new papers the following week.

Hilly had already forgotten Charlie, or Bob, or whoever he was, was supposed to have a different name and Zofia had to remind her again she must start to call him Maksim.

'Why?' she asked, swinging her legs back and forth over the edge of her bed. 'It's stupid. Is it because of the Japanese?'

'They're on the same side as the Nazis now.'

Hilly thought a moment. 'But we have to learn to live with the Japanese. We can't go on just fighting them all the time. And some of them are nice. Just normal like us.'

'True enough.' Then she frowned. 'Who said that? Madam Wang?'

'No, my friend. He comes to the kiosk every day. That's what he says. That we should try to live in peace.'

'Is he Chinese? Or what?'

'He's nice. Today he bought a pack of rice balls, a newspaper, and twenty cigarettes.'

'Hilly. He's not another Japanese man, is he? Which friend is this?' Zofia sat forward, suddenly on high alert. Hilly had made many friends at the kiosk because she was always so cheerful.

Mostly these were old Chinese grandfathers who came daily for their tobacco.

'He's not a soldier. He's much older, and very polite.'

From that she assumed he was Japanese. Zofia reeled at this news. 'But I told you to stay away from the Japanese! He might be like that other one, Goro.'

'Keep your hair on. I know what I'm doing. He's like that kind man you talked about on the boat, the Japanese man in Kaunas who gave you the visas to get away from the Nazis. Not like Goro.'

'Goro was nice at the beginning. Until he hit you, remember?'

'He's not like Goro. I told you. You don't know him! You're always trying to interfere. You make it so I can't breathe. "Don't go here, don't go there!" You make my life a misery.'

'I'm just trying to protect you—'

'You're not my mother. It's none of your business what I do! I look forward to Eiko-san coming. I always give him a bit extra if he buys our sweet crackers. He likes me too, I can tell.'

That's what I'm afraid of. 'You'll make other friends. Try to make friends with Westerners or Chinese boys.'

'The Chinese boys are horrible. Poor and ugly.'

'That's not true.'

'It is so. Madam Wang doesn't treat the Japanese the way she treats everyone else. It's embarrassing. She was cross at Eiko-san. She was rude when he asked to see me. I hope he comes back.'

Let's hope he never does. 'Forget it, let's just sleep.' Zofia lay down and pretended to sleep, but in fact her mind was churning. Hilly was attracting another Japanese man's attention, and if he decided he wanted her, there would be nothing anyone could do to stop him. At the same time, she hated the hypocrisy of her own argument, and the deep discomfort of being married to the 'enemy'.

She sent up a silent prayer of thanks for the sharp eyes of Madam Wang; it must have taken courage for an old Chinese woman like her to stand up to the Japanese.

Chapter 10

Zofia spent the morning trying to cram Japanese kanji into Theo's head.

'I'm sorry,' he said. 'I'm not with it today. It's not you. You're a good teacher. But I just can't concentrate. Too much on my mind.'

'It's okay. We'll try again tomorrow,' she said. She enjoyed his company and she felt for him, sensed his distress and worry.

He put a hand on her shoulder as he left and she felt the burn through her blouse and the flip of her stomach. *Calm down, don't be a fool.*

As a kind of penance, a punishment for her disloyalty to her husband, Zofia gritted her teeth and spent the day laundering the men's shirts. All the laundries were closed because most of the Chinese had been cleared out of the settlements, but Olga's house had water piped in, so washing was not too hard. Olga was out delivering Charlie's messages to contacts in the fire service who might help him get word to the British.

Charlie was restless and spent a lot of time pacing when he wasn't reading the paper again cover to cover. He smoked too much and was never still. It made Zofia tired just to look at him.

When she went to collect Hilly that evening she saw there

were no trams, no squeak of them on the rails and no rumble of wheels from rickshaws and carts. The streets were full of dispossessed Chinese who had come on foot from the burnt-out, ruined villages further down river, carrying their salvaged bundles, and cowering from the Japanese soldiers who were on every corner.

As she passed a lamp post she saw it had a poster taped to it and a single glance brought her up short. It was Charlie's face, a bad photograph of him in naval uniform. It was in English, Dutch and Chinese as well as kanji. 'Bob Dering.' *No use you pretending to be Maksim now*, she thought.

When Zofia arrived at the crossroads, she was confused, thinking she'd got lost somehow. She expected to see the kiosk, festooned with its good luck red envelopes, lottery tickets, packets of salted corn and stacks of cigarettes, and Madam Wang greeting her with a big toothy grin.

She looked from left to right in a panic.

The kiosk had gone. As if it had never existed.

This was the right place. But there was no sign of Madam Wang. No thick-waisted woman in a worn apron, no sign of her greedy parrot, Pipi, just a dirty patch where she used to stand, and where she lit her small charcoal stove so her feet didn't freeze.

Zofia turned around on the spot searching for any trace of it. Right here was where people queued. She looked down at the pavement.

And then the fact of it hit her and she started calling, 'Hilly!'

She ran down the nearest street still calling Hilly's name, but no one answered.

'What happened to the kiosk?' She grabbed a man by the sleeve but he shook her off. She hared back to the junction of the road. 'Hilly!' Her voice sounded high and desperate.

She ran into the nearest shop, a German ironmonger's.

'The kiosk?' she said, breathless. 'What happened to it? Have you seen a girl, a blonde girl in a grey coat?'

'The Japs knocked it down and took it away,' the hard-eyed man behind the counter told her.

'What about the girl? Did you see a girl?'

A shake of the head. 'I didn't see anything. Just one minute it was there. Then it was gone. Good thing too, it left so much litter.'

'What about Madam Wang?'

'That old ragbag? Don't know. Never saw her go.'

Zofia's heart constricted. She shot back outside, scanning every street for that blonde head. 'Hilly!'

Glancing side to side, she rushed down towards the harbour but then retraced her steps. Where else to look? She made another fruitless search down the other road, asking in every shop. No one had seen a thirteen-year-old girl. Had she run away? She shouldn't have shouted at her last night.

With rising panic Zofia returned to the spot where the kiosk had been.

Movement caught her eye. A gangly figure, running towards her, grey coat flapping.

Thank God.

Hilly saw Zofia and stopped, waiting, her head down. She had that hang-dog look that meant she'd done something Zofia would disapprove of.

Zofia walked up to her, suppressing her anger. 'What happened? Where the hell have you been? Where's Madam Wang?'

A shrug.

'What were you doing? You know I always come for you at four.'

'It's not my fault. The soldiers came.'

'And what happened to Madam Wang?'

'They took everything off the shelves. The cigarettes, the tobacco, everything. They shoved me out, but Eiko-san was there and he told me they'd come to take Madam Wang away.'

'What?'

'He said he'd look after me … and it's best to be nice. Like with the Nazis. I didn't want them to take me away with Madam Wang. Eiko-san pulled me away and wanted to sit behind a tree, but he hadn't brought a blanket for us to sit on. The ground was wet and dirty. He tried to get me to lie down but I thumped him hard and jumped up and ran away. He was shouting and yelling after me but I didn't stop and when I got back, the kiosk was gone. I looked everywhere. I kept on screaming for Madam Wang. A woman came to stop me yelling.'

'What did she do?'

'I was crying by then and … and another Chinese woman came and I asked her about Pipi and the woman said they hit Madam Wang with sticks, and let Pipi out of the cage and tried to hit him too, but he was flapping and squawking and he … he … flew away.'

Zofia tried to unravel what had gone on, but Hilly refused to answer any more questions.

Later Zofia told Olga what had happened.

Olga was unsympathetic. 'She's a liability that girl. I worry every minute she'll say something to some Jap. I mean, about Charlie staying here, and then we'd all be sunk.'

'It's not her fault. She's young and men think they can take advantage.'

'I know. That's the problem. You'll have to keep more of an eye on her. She can't go out on her own. It's just too risky.'

Zofia glared at her bullish expression. 'What should I do then? Tell me that? Lock her up? Or stick her out on the streets to fend for herself?'

Charlie appeared. 'What's going on?'

'The Japanese bulldozed the kiosk,' Zofia said. 'So there's no longer a safe place for Hilly to go in the daytime.'

'And the little fool's been fraternizing with the Japs,' Olga said.

'It's not her fault. She had no choice. You know she hadn't.'

'Whoa, ladies.'

Charlie stepped between them, but Olga wouldn't lay off. 'You should have been watching her.'

'I can't watch her every minute. You have to help me.'

'Help you? Why? We didn't ask for this. She's not our responsibility.' Olga stuck out her chin. 'We don't have to do anything.'

'Now hang on just a minute.' Charlie held up a hand. 'Is it true? Is she sleeping around?'

'No! She was hit on by some creep. She didn't do anything.'

'What did she tell him?'

'Nothing. She was scared. She ran away.'

Charlie rolled his eyes. 'Christ, what a mess. We have to be more careful. Keep Hilly busy indoors, where we know where she is.'

'Like a prisoner?' Zofia stood her ground.

'And what the hell do you think I am?'

There were a few moments where no one spoke.

Then finally Charlie sighed. 'So how about she helps me. Does a few jobs for us. You too.'

Zofia was wary. 'Who's "us"?'

'The Resistance,' Charlie said. 'Then you'll be on the right side, for a start.'

She was indignant. 'There is no right side.'

Charlie pushed his face towards hers. 'Theo says you're married to a Jap. That's why you speak Japanese.' His expression was accusing.

'But Haru's not like these men! He's a charity worker for the Jewish Association in Japan. He got conscripted, that's all.'

'Are you on their side?'

'No … I mean, I don't know.'

Olga threw up her hands and let out a frustrated breath. She took Charlie by the shoulder and whispered, 'You'd be crazy to trust them. They'll ruin everything.'

Zofia caught the words and it was enough to make her bridle. She turned to Charlie. 'What Resistance are you talking about?'

'Chinese Guerrilla fighters,' Charlie said, 'Communists. They're picking off the Japs one by one.'

She gave a laugh, but it was to mask her horror. 'We can't do that.'

'You don't do anything,' snapped Charlie. 'You and Hilly and Theo just use Olga's house like a hotel and give nothing back.'

It was an unfair accusation and it rocked her. 'Who fished you out of the burning sea? Who went to order your fake papers? Look, I'm doing the best I can. Things keep changing. We didn't ask for this war.'

'None of us did,' snapped Olga. 'The hospital's full of bomb and burn victims.'

Zofia stood her ground. 'So what exactly are you doing that's so great, Mr Resistance Man?'

'I've gone in with Zha Wei.'

Dumbstruck, she couldn't take it in.

'He approached me yesterday. Actually I didn't have much choice.'

'How did he know where to find you?'

Charlie glanced at Olga. Zofia saw the look and stiffened. So Olga was in on this too. Zha Wei would keep quiet about where Charlie was, if the rebels could use him. It was blackmail.

'Does Theo know?'

Charlie stuck out his chin in defiance. 'No. None of his business.'

'Of course it is! That bastard stole his house.'

'They needed a base.'

'If we're all in this together, why can't Theo go back there?'

Charlie's expression was sheepish. The question went unanswered. 'Zha Wei says the old government under Chiang Kai-shek is hopeless against the Japs. Too much infighting between rival warlords. And Chiang's afraid to confront Wang, the Japs' puppet, who does sod all, just lords it over the country from Nanking. But the communists are fighting back. They have the support of every Chinese peasant who's sick of being shat on.'

'So what are you going to do then, with this mob?'

'Stuff like drawing up the maps of Jap activity from the BBC and making a note of where their checkpoints are. General reconnaissance. Zha Wei's got Chinese runners all over Shanghai spying, telling him where the next Jap patrol will be and how we can target and take out the Japs involved. For every patrol that goes out we want only half to come back. Japan's a tiny country. China's a huge one. Japan will run out of men long before China does.'

The words took her breath away. 'It sounds like you'll enjoy it.'

'It's the only thing I can do – I'm too recognizable to risk getting caught. And I want to be of use. What's wrong with that? It's what I joined up for. It's better than just sitting here doing nothing.'

'But I can't see how I'd fit in to that? If you think I'd kill anyone … it's ridiculous. And what about Hilly?'

'You could transcribe news from the BBC. Any outside news about Japan. No matter how small. We've a contact too in the US – sends us classified stuff. News not tainted with Jap propaganda. We copy it all and distribute it to the network. Hilly can help you – if she can write, she can copy. And you could be useful. You'd be a good courier, you can speak Japanese. That's if you're really on our side.'

Zofia turned away from his belligerent scrutiny. What choice did she have? He was right; transcribing was something they could do. Even Hilly. But she didn't want to admit it yet; the argument still seethed in her chest. And she didn't want to be sending men like Haru to their deaths.

She turned back to face him. 'I'll do it, but on one condition – we don't have to kill anyone, and you keep Hilly busy and out of trouble.'

Olga tried to take Charlie to one side again. 'Think! She's married to one of them. I don't think we should—'

Charlie took hold of Olga by the shoulder. 'We need Zofia,

especially since those 'wanted' notices. I can't go out, can I? And if that means some babysitting, then we just have to do it.'

'Hilly's getting us a reputation and I already have trouble convincing people I'm not one of *those* Russians.' She meant the women who worked as prostitutes or paid escorts.

Charlie took hold of Olga around the waist. 'She's just growing up, doesn't know what's what yet. Surely you remember those years? It's not her fault.'

'What can I tell Father Rostnikov when I go to confession? That I live with a girl who consorts with the Japanese?'

'You don't have to tell him anything. Just like you don't tell him about me. All right?'

Olga pulled away from him. 'You don't understand. You don't understand anything. We're already sitting on a powder keg just having you here. And now you tell me you're going to risk the whole network for some half-wit of a girl?'

'Calm down. It'll be okay, you're getting overwrought.'

Olga gave him a look of pure loathing and marched out of the room.

The door slammed so hard behind her that Zofia winced. 'She cares about you, that's all. She doesn't want you to get caught.'

'I know.'

'Then go after her, try to make it up. Otherwise they've already won, haven't they?'

Chapter 11

One month later

Theo had got his official pass from the occupying Japanese, but he'd had to surrender his passport. This small act of taking away his ability to travel hit him hard. How was he to get back to his children? He chewed over it, even as he wrote them long, scrawled letters assuring them he'd see them soon.

Foreigners in essential services were told to remain at their jobs. Theo was to show a Japanese 'assistant' the running of Carter & Co. Nokomo spoke little English and, irritatingly, followed Theo around like a small dog. It gave Theo the same sort of wariness – that Nokomo might turn and bite at any moment.

Brits and Americans were forbidden from entering places of entertainment such as cinemas, dance halls, nightclubs and the Shanghai Racecourse. His group of friends was fracturing, some giving in to the occupiers, some arrested, some already fled. It was hard to find out what was really happening in Shanghai because the Japanese had clamped down hard on leisure, outlawing anywhere people could meet to exchange news.

Theo fretted over the loss of his house. What was going on

in the place? It was still legally his, by rights. It rankled that he could do nothing. A cowboy would have got together a posse or a militia and gone to sort them out. But this was 1942 and those things were just not possible here in China.

One night, too restless to be indoors, he walked warily around the British and American areas, to see if his was the only house used by the Chinese. It shook him how many houses lay empty, the weeds growing through the paving on the drives, and whole streets of villas had Japanese requisition notices pinned on the gates. He guessed these would be occupied by Japanese families, connected, he presumed, to the military.

His walks became a habit, but it was a few weeks before he realized what he was really doing was reconnaissance. Observing the lie of the land and working out how best to function in this changed environment. He made maps of all the checkpoints in secret in his office when he got a few moments away from his 'minder'. He wasn't sure why he was doing this, but he needed to keep moving, and besides, it was the only protest he could make.

Today, striding home along the Bund, an army truck drove by, blaring out another announcement. It took him a moment to realize what the words were. An order to surrender all radios, cameras, binoculars and telescopes.

When he got back to Olga's, he found they'd been searched twice by the Japanese guard.

'What the heck did you do when they came?' Theo asked Charlie.

'Olga saw them coming, so I dodged out and hid in the privy next door. I was shitting myself I'd be discovered. She was a genius, she kept the radio safe, stashed in a pillowcase under her bedding.'

'Good thing they were looking for radios not people.'

'Too flaming close for comfort,' he said. 'What's it like near the harbour?'

'Unrecognizable,' Theo said. 'Four times as many beggars

– people who've suddenly lost their jobs, or their house, or both. The bay crowded with sampans, but with nothing to sell. Children crying. Germans walking the streets openly wearing swastika armbands. Japs everywhere demanding your papers at every intersection.'

'Sounds grim.'

'And I'm one of the lucky ones. My business is limping along, scrutinized every minute by my Japanese friend, who sticks to me like a louse and demands a long-winded explanation for everything I do.'

'At least we kept the radio. We'll still be able to get news out to the Resistance. It seems Zha Wei's been busy.'

Theo hid his repugnance. Charlie should be grateful to him, shouldn't he? Yet here he was, colluding with the biggest shark in Shanghai waters.

'By the way, one of his men brought you your mail.' Charlie pointed to the sideboard.

'Oh, how very good of him.' He couldn't hold back the sarcasm. Theo looked it over. Bills. 'Does the bastard expect me to pay these?'

Charlie shrugged. 'I've contacts in the Shanghai fire service. One of them came to see me. Says Zha Wei's a big noise, and they're planning on destroying the Japanese supply train.'

Theo didn't respond. He didn't want to know what Zha Wei was doing. He had only one goal, to keep his head down and save his business. He was single-minded about it in the way he'd been when building it. It was inconceivable he would fail.

One of the letters had caught his eye. Evelina.

He slit it open with a finger.

Dear Theo, just to let you know we have arrived. It is warmer here than in Shanghai and I have no summer clothes, so please send my luggage as soon as you can. We are staying in a suite in the Manila Hotel, recommended to us by a doctor

I met on the boat. You'll need to wire us some money as the room is fifteen dollars even for long stay. Fortunately the restaurant is top notch. Jimmy and Daisy have been enrolled at the local international school as a temporary measure, though the discipline is terrible and there's no proper uniform. I hope they will make new friends there of a good type, but they keep asking when Daddy will come. Jimmy still has a cough, so he can't start yet, and I've had to employ an amah to mind him. She is costing me twenty cents an hour. Daylight robbery!

Let me know your plans, darling,
Evelina x

Chapter 12

Haru pinched his nose against the stench of rotting vegetation as he and the rest of the men rattled south through the countryside by train. The vast interior of the country had been flooded by the Chinese to stop the Japanese advance. The water had engulfed Henan, and Jiangsu, changing the course of the Yellow River, shifting it hundreds of miles to the south. Four thousand villages underwater, hundreds of thousands dead, and millions of peasants searching for somewhere to go. Talk about China shooting itself in the foot.

The railway line ran through this desolate land of stinking slurry, and still after all this time, the floating bodies of their Chinese enemies were a common, nauseating sight.

Haru thought of Japan, of its peaceful cherry-blossom-lined gardens, of its Zen temples and *onsens*. He dreamed of those bathhouses, of the scouring of hot springs, of clean sweet-smelling skin, of jasmine soap and clean cotton *yukatas*. He thought of Zofia too, waiting for him in Kobe, of how they would start a family together once this war was over. If it was ever over. Impossible to imagine his shaking hands on her naked body. He gripped his fists as the train swayed, until the nails cut into his palms.

He'd had no concept of the vastness of China until coming here.

'How much longer?' his companion Yoshio asked.

'Another hour.'

'Do you know why we're being deployed in Jinan?'

Haru shrugged. He'd learned never to question orders. 'No, but I heard Chinese raiders keep trying to take the city back. We're to be its defence.'

When he got off the troop train at Jinan he saw a city in ruins. The railway station was intact, but almost two-thirds of the place was uninhabitable from earlier Japanese bombing. He wasn't surprised; every city was indistinguishable from the next – each one a grey pile of rubble and dust, with shuttered streets where you had to step carefully, and you didn't dare look too closely at the piles of rags on the ground, in case they were people.

Their barracks had been newly constructed but looked as if they had been there forever, so ingrained were they with grime blown off the streets.

Haru's superior officer approached him after only one night in these desolate bunks. Haru shrank back but then found his backbone and stood straight. He'd been kicked until he bled by that same man.

'Our commanding officer gave his life for the Emperor last night,' he announced. 'I am taking command in his place. You are therefore promoted to be my deputy.'

It hit Haru in the guts like a grenade. A shock wave that rippled up his spine. Best not to ask questions. He saluted as was expected, but knew this change in position would mean he'd have to inflict terror on his fellow men. Seasoned recruits were expected to beat new ones harshly, NCOs had to beat privates senseless, and officers were expected to beat NCOs unconscious.

His commanding officer wasn't done yet. 'You will get your ration of amphetamines, too, a perk of the promotion.'

'Thank you, sir.' It was well known the officers got meth. Haru wondered if it helped, or whether it made everything brighter and more vivid. That he couldn't bear.

'Dismissed.'

Haru crumpled as soon as he'd gone. As it was, his body was already divorced from his mind. His former self was closed like a scroll in a cabinet, whilst his body was here in this hell on earth.

At night he would occasionally let his old self loose, to write to his mother.

> Last night I went out to a field of Chinese milk vetch and lay down, thinking about home. It smelled like you, Mother. It was the only beautiful thing I have seen in weeks. The delicacy of flowers reminds me of you.

He dared not write to Zofia. That part of him, the part that was in love, would be spoiled if it had to witness the killing machine he'd become. And now he'd have to hurt his own men. He pressed his uniform sleeve hard to his eyes and tried not to weep.

Haru's days at the checkpoints to the city went slowly, his spine stiff with tension, fearing a Chinese dagger in the ribs every time darkness fell. One day, his friend Yoshio did not return from his patrol.

Broken by losing his only friend, and brimming with rage, Haru found the next Chinese person and disembowelled him alive as a lesson to the others.

Chapter 13

Theo went through the days in a kind of numb acceptance, but inside he seethed. At his office over the next few weeks he made hundreds of telephone calls, but stopped most of them when he heard another click on the line.

Every ship he tried to book passage on had been appropriated by the occupying forces. He bought the Japanese newspaper every day, hoping to find a way out. All propaganda of course, so he had to read between the lines.

One morning, when he bought the paper, he was astonished to see a half-page splash in English and Chinese – a reward offered for the capture of Bob Dering, a radio operative from HMS *Peterel* who was on the run. He stared at it, feeling like a fool.

It was Charlie. He'd given them a false name. The reward for his capture was a hundred dollars, a sum most Chinese wouldn't be able to ignore, and it put them all in instant danger of being rumbled. The penalty would be death, both for him and those hiding him. And worse, Charlie was hobnobbing with Chinese Triads like Zha Wei. Theo read it again with growing unease. Harbouring Charlie would be a threat to the women too – to Zofia, Olga and Hilly.

When he got home, he beckoned to Zofia, who was ironing one of her few dresses, and placed the paper flat on the table. 'Look at this.'

'I know,' she said. 'The Finkelsteins told me about the reward. I realized then that Dering must be Charlie. And I saw a notice, pinned to a lamp post.'

'So what do we do?'

'Nothing. If he wants to be Charlie, let him be Charlie. It's only a few more days, then he'll get Russian papers and we'll have to call him Maksim. Olga's getting his photograph developed. There was a long hold-up because we hadn't been able to source any developing fluid for the photograph.'

'It feels odd he didn't trust us enough to give us his name.'

'I thought that. But then I wondered what I'd do if I were him. After all, when you brought him to Olga's he didn't know if he could trust us. And still now, he doesn't know if one of us will hand him in and claim the money.'

A rustle behind him alerted him to Charlie's appearance. 'Evening,' he said. 'Any news?'

Theo and Zofia looked at each other and moved away from the paper. 'Read it for yourself,' she said.

They watched him read.

'It's all right, Charlie,' Zofia said. 'No one here is going to say anything.'

'You don't know what it's like, feeling like I should have died like the rest. That I'm worth less than they are – that because I'm not dead I'm somehow a traitor.'

'No one thinks that.'

'They do. They think I should give myself up. Do the honourable thing.'

'It's not dishonourable to want to survive,' Theo said.

'I'm trying to get someone from Blighty to get me out, but so far, it's no go. Can't even get a contact. Shanghai's sealed off. The only thing I can do against the Japs is help the Chinese.'

'Is there no one else but Zha Wei? I don't trust him,' Theo said.
'He's got the most contacts. And the power to use them.'

The next day Theo was at the barricade onto the Bund as usual, his pass in hand. Being shut out of a city he'd helped to build did nothing to improve his mood.

As he got close to the barrier be saw a Chinese bean curd seller hawk and spit on the pavement, a common enough occurrence in Shanghai. But immediately, a Japanese soldier came and beat the man savagely with a truncheon, smashing the poor man's head until he fell to the floor unconscious, bleeding from the ears.

Theo turned away, nauseous.

Nobody dared do anything in case the same treatment was meted out to them. Theo felt bad walking away. This inability to act combined with having no home to call his own made him feel less of a man. All through the day, the image came back to him. He should have done something. The feeling wouldn't go away.

He wrote to Evelina to tell her he'd try to get cash transferred at the bank, but it didn't seem likely he could do much, the situation being what it was. He told her to write to him at the office, not at home. He didn't dare tell her their house had been taken over by Triads.

That night, when he got back to Olga's, he saw Zofia and Hilly sitting hunched over the radio, scribbling down every word, and Olga filling envelopes with anti-Jap propaganda. They were all working for the Resistance. It made him feel guilty.

Maybe he should get over his antagonism towards Zha Wei. Everyone was making hard decisions, and he didn't like being the odd one out amongst his friends. He opened his briefcase and drew out a sheaf of papers he'd hidden inside a file of accounts.

'Here,' he said to Charlie. 'These might be useful.' He held out all his hand-drawn maps.

Charlie took a look at them. He was thinner now, and his arm was out of the sling, just wrapped in a grubby bandage. 'So you decided to join us,' he said. 'About bloody time.'

Theo ignored the jibe. 'You forget. I've a wife and kids to support. My main priority is to secure Carter & Co. Ten years ago it was worth peanuts. Now it's worth a million. I built that business from nothing, and nothing on this earth will make me give it up.'

Zofia turned to stare at him, and he felt somehow exposed, as if she'd understood a part of him he didn't want anyone to see.

Chapter 14

Six months later, July 1942

The city limped on, now humid in the summer heat, and beset by beggars pouring in from burned-out villages. The shop shelves were empty; stocks were used up, and shortages had kicked in through lack of imports and exports. Everyone was hungry, tired and tense.

The first intimation that Theo wouldn't be allowed to stay in Shanghai was when Japanese officials took over the municipal services, removing them from British, American or Dutch control. Next came the humiliation of the armband with 'A' for American that he was forced to wear.

He was tall, so like most Westerners he stood out, and if he didn't wear the damn armband he was invariably stopped and forced to put it on. The Brits had one with 'B' and the Dutch one with 'N' for Netherlands. Only the stateless Russians, Germans and French escaped this indignity – and it was clear that these labels were designed to show the Japanese who was an ally, and who was not.

Nokomo continued to follow him round like a bad shadow. Japanese officials manned the front desk now, replacing his loyal Chinese receptionist, and they stared at him each day as if he didn't belong.

Today he needed to speak to the bank urgently and had left several messages. He had to find cash to repay the loan on Carter & Co's warehouses. He feared that if shipping couldn't continue, then the bank would foreclose on the loan and it would be the ideal time for the Japanese to take the company over.

Theo's Chinese secretary had also been removed, so he made himself a strong black coffee and inhaled its bitter scent. He could hear the replacement Japanese office workers clacking away on their abacuses and typewriters – that daily rattle that used to be soothing was now an irritation. He shut the door on them all with a bang. It made him depressed to see his business slowly ebbing away.

The telephone shrilled and the receptionist said, 'Call for you' – words the man had only just learned in English.

He leapt to the phone but it was not the bank, but his contact in Egypt. 'Your ship didn't arrive to pick up the oranges. They'll rot if they're left here any longer.'

'I'm sorry. The situation's bad here, as you know. We no longer have control over our own shipping timetables and—' Theo paused. A series of clicks on the line again. This undoubtedly meant his calls were being monitored. 'I'm afraid there's nothing I can do,' he said. 'The transport will be with you as soon as the Japanese release it from its holding slot. They are searching every American vessel for spies or ammunition.'

More angry protests from the other end. He let the man rant a bit before pressing the cradle and pretending they'd been cut off. He stared at the phone a few moments, before thumping his hand down on the desk.

He could do nothing, he realized. He wondered if his father had felt that way when the rains didn't come.

The weather grew even more sultry and suffocating. The whirr of the fans in his office did little to help, and the sea of Japanese clerks with their blank looks did nothing to ease his comfort. A letter came, summoning him to a meeting of the shareholders of Carter & Co, and the Japanese administration. But as soon as the delegation came through the door he knew something was off. These were not his shareholders. They were all Japs.

Two men in suits, accompanied by four fully armed privates in uniform. They didn't sit down at the boardroom table, but indicated that he should. As if he was a schoolboy in detention.

Sweat broke out on his brow to see this cordon of unsmiling men. His hackles raised as Nokomo joined them, a smug smile on his face. He had a file of papers under his arm. Theo wiped his palms on his trousers.

The papers to transfer the business to the Japanese were already prepared. A quick glance showed they had been translated into English and the words 'transfer of all assets' stood out starkly on the page.

'Sign,' Nokomo said. 'Here.'

At first he refused. But Nokomo spoke smoothly. 'Matthewson, he not sign. Most unfortunate. Dead now, and Japanese state has his hotel anyway.'

'You bastard,' he said. 'I hope you rot in hell.'

'Sign.'

There was no choice. His pen ran out of ink as he signed the papers, and he thought bitterly that even the pen knew this was wrong.

Nokomo snapped at him in Japanese as if it was his fault, brought him another fountain pen and pushed it into his hand. It felt unreal to be surrounded by a cordon of armed soldiers, just so he could put pen to paper.

He scratched his signature in an angry scrawl, recapped their pen and thrust it into Nokomo's hand. 'I hope someone shits on you, the way you shat on me.'

Sitting in this familiar boardroom, under his own portrait, at the polished table where he'd brokered so much trade, he felt the exact moment of transfer like an amputation.

He'd lost his house, and now this was the end of his business. He was sleeping on the floor of a Russian refugee, and today his assistant had ceased to be his employee and had taken control of Carter & Co without even a memo. Zofia's joke that the Japanese might put them all in a pie came to mind, and he smiled grimly at the thought. It was a physical pain to realize everything he'd worked for for years was just to be handed over in an afternoon.

He stumbled from the room, blind to everything, hoping the blur was rage and not tears. The Japanese doorman stopped him at the door and asked for his keys.

'Take them!' he shouted. He ripped off his jacket and threw it on the ground. 'You want the shirt off my back too?'

The doorman picked up the jacket and fished the keys from the pocket. 'You need pass,' he said in his pidgin English. 'No need trouble.'

The man was right. He'd need the pass and the blasted armband. Reluctantly he took his jacket out of the man's hand. To do this felt like he was letting Carter & Co down. But he slung the jacket over his arm and walked out of the swing doors, wondering if it was for the last time.

Ten years of effort and all gone in the swipe of a pen.

Down the steps, and out onto the Bund where the familiar view of sampans and junks pierced him to the core.

Zofia knew something was the matter as soon as Theo came into the house.

'That's it,' he said, throwing his jacket onto the dining table. 'They've got Carter & Co. No amount of learning Japanese would have stopped them.'

'Did they give you any kind of payment?'

'None. I suppose they'll repatriate me. Meanwhile, I have to wear the blasted armband and pretend I'm still a man who has something to do with his life.'

He sat down on the sofa and put his head in his hands. The back of his shirt was transparent with sweat.

Zofia went to sit next to him, hurting for him. 'Do you want to walk?' she asked.

'Walk where? We can't go anywhere in this damn city.'

'We can. Let's just get out of the house.'

'What about Hilly?'

'I'll go and tell her we won't be long. She's still excited about the whole idea of being a rebel against the Japanese. To be honest, the fact she's so interested is a godsend.'

She hurried through to the box room where Hilly was copying a newspaper article. 'Have you seen this?' Hilly said, excited, stabbing down a finger on the paper. 'The Americans have won! The Japs hoped to defeat them and take Midway. It's good news because it'll stop them launching any more attacks on Pearl Harbor. I'm just copying it now.'

Zofia was happy to see Hilly smile. She was growing up fast. Had become older in just a few months. 'I'm going out with Theo for half an hour or so,' she said. 'We just need to get some air.'

'Okay.' Hilly wasn't even listening, she was back to poring over the article she was reading from a smuggled English newspaper.

Zofia left her and went back to Theo. He'd changed his shirt and put on his jacket again, despite the fact it was so humid. Thundery clouds were massing over the distant rooftops.

Theo walked fast down the road and away from the city. She hurried after him. 'Wait up,' she called. 'I can't walk that fast.'

'Sorry,' he said. He stopped and waited until she was beside him. 'I guess my body just wants to run away from it all. I can't believe I'll never go back there.'

'What will happen to it?'

He shrugged. 'I don't know. I feel worse about this than I did when Evelina left.'

She raised her eyebrows.

'I know, I'm a terrible person.'

'You're not. You care really. You've just had a shock, that's all. You'll survive it. You're standing here, aren't you? And there are still people who need you.'

'No one will need me now I'm not the head of Carter & Co anymore.'

She slowly shook her head. *You can't see for looking, can you?*

A crack of thunder and the first spots of rain. He didn't pick her up on it. 'How will I tell Evelina? It will be the end between us. She'll be expecting me to pay for her hotel ... everything. All she ever wanted was the lifestyle. To send our kids to the best schools. Not for them, not for their benefit, but because then she could say, "Ooh, my children go to such and such a place." And if I can't support her needs, she'll take the kids away, I know she will.'

The rain was coming harder now. 'Plum rain season', they called it. They'd have to find shelter or be soaked.

'Come on.' She ducked her head and ran for the shelter of a gingko tree that shadowed the pavement. He joined her next to the trunk as the rain spattered down. 'You're worried about Jimmy and Daisy?'

'I remember being their age and it was ...'

'What?'

'Hard. What we would have given back then for a drop of this rain. Where we lived in the States we had not a drop of rain for four years. And because of it, no crops. The dust was savage. It got in your lungs and in your eyes. Grit was in everything.'

'Jeepers.'

'Have you ever had people throw bricks at you because your pants are tied up with twine and your hair's full of dirt? I vowed I'd never be poor again. And neither would my children. I wanted to leave them a legacy. Now it looks like I'll have nothing to leave them but regrets. And rain.'

'Nah. You're young. When the war's over everyone'll be crying out for men like you, men who can rebuild it all.'

Rain poured through the branches of the tree canopy, and the splash of it drummed loud on the pavement. The wet made her dress stick to her back and legs.

He looked down at her, droplets beading his hair. 'You're always so positive. What makes you so certain everything will turn out good for folks?'

'Don't. You make me sound like some kind of Pollyanna. I just don't see the point in doom-mongering. It's the way I get by. Just do the next thing and don't look back.'

He was looking at her very intently. The tension between them had been building for months, like a solid wall. A spark flashed between them, like a flash on water.

It was so powerful it made her step towards him.

'Theo … I—'

'Don't say anything,' he said, holding up a hand to ward her off. 'I know. But I can't deal with it right now. We'd better walk.'

He set off into the slash of rain, his head down, and with that peculiar intent stride that he always had. She let him go, reluctant to go into the downpour but also embarrassed he'd rejected her and she'd made such a fool of herself.

Chapter 15

Over the next couple of months the weather grew more bearable. September arrived – cooler with fewer tropical storms. Zofia still felt awkward around Theo, knowing she was just too aware of him, though she tried not to let it show. The attraction ate away at her; she was helpless to stop it even though she was consumed by gnawing guilt about Haru. Being so close to Theo, day in, day out, didn't make it any easier. When he wasn't meeting fellow businessmen to try to sort out his dwindling finances, he was working beside her, transcribing broadcasts. Although Olga had curtained off an alcove in the living room for Theo to have some privacy, Zofia was always intensely aware of him whenever he was behind that curtain.

Charlie was able to go out now with his Russian papers, and a new moustache, as long as he shadowed his face with a hat and kept Olga by his side, and they all had to remember to call him Maksim in public. Olga was protective of him because she and Charlie had become like a married couple. He'd even moved into her room, though he made out he still slept on the floor.

Hypocrite, thought Zofia, the thought tinged with envy.

Olga was resigned to them all being there; she couldn't throw

Theo out, because of the debt Charlie felt he owed him. And Theo insisted she and Hilly stay with him, under male protection, because Hilly was so young.

It wasn't exactly cosy, but it was the only way they all felt safe.

For Hilly, being a revolutionary was a continued source of excitement and interest, but Theo still refused to talk to Zha Wei, and who could blame him? Zha Wei retained an iron grip on Theo's house. Every now and then, a batch of mail would arrive from the house, the bills and warning letters Theo routinely ignored.

Once, Theo walked back to the Bund to look at the outside of Carter & Co and came back to tell her they'd hacked off the stone logo from above the door, and the Japanese flag was flying on the roof. Tears had sprung to his eyes when he told her, but he took out a handkerchief, coughed as if he had a cold, and tried to hide them.

She'd embraced him then, and he'd held her so tight it almost hurt. The feeling between them had grown into a palpable thing with its own moods. Every day they watched each other, like wild animals, circling. Whenever Charlie had any ideas, she would glance to Theo to see if he approved, only to find him looking at her in the same way for her reaction.

There was something as strong as steel binding them together. Zofia wished it would stop; the feeling of it was driving her to distraction. Today she staved it off by handing him his mail.

'This came for you. I hope it's not what I think it is.'

She passed him the typewritten brown envelope. It had the official chrysanthemum stamp of the Japanese and kanji in red ink. She remembered Lithuania, when that seal had been a symbol of safety. Now it was a symbol of all that was wrong in Shanghai.

He slit it open and pulled out the paper.

'What does it say?'

He swallowed. 'It's my date. Four days from now. I'll be interned at Woosung Camp with the other Americans.'

'That soon?'

'Looks like it.' He gripped the door jamb as if it would support him. 'I suppose at least I'll have a chance of being repatriated.'

A drowning sensation, though her voice came out bright and brittle. 'I heard they were doing this. Interning all the Brits and Americans. Olga told me the British are even offering a reward for Charlie's capture. His own people? Can you believe it? The Brits heard they were to be put in camps and are blaming Charlie. They think the Japanese are punishing them because he's still at large, and he should surrender. They just don't realize the camps are happening to everyone, Dutch, Americans, the lot.'

'Charlie won't give in though, will he?' Theo said. 'If he did, it would be torture and beheading. That's what the Japs do to their enemies. I wouldn't like to be in his shoes.'

'He's safe for now. He's got Russian papers.' She didn't mention Charlie was also under Zha Wei's protection because she knew that name would not go down well with Theo.

'He'll find it harder now all his contacts have gone though,' Theo said. 'They took his British friends in the fire service and the police. They're in Bridge House for interrogation.'

She watched him re-reading the letter. 'We'll all miss you when you've gone.'

'I don't have a choice.'

'I know.'

There was a moment when they just looked at each other. It was the end, Zofia thought. The end of whatever she thought was between them.

'I hope the government will get me out soon.'

'And get you home to America.'

'Yes.' He took a step forward and she was sure he was going to embrace her again, but then he turned away. 'You know what I hate? The fact we built it. Shanghai was nothing before we came.

We built it all, us Westerners. And now they just come and take it. It leaves a bitter taste in the mouth.'

'You should make the most of your freedom,' Zofia said, rallying herself to be cheerful. 'What do you want to do with your last four days?'

He seemed taken aback. 'I hadn't thought of it like that. You make me sound like a condemned man.'

'You are. Four days of freedom left before you'll be shut away for heaven knows how long. How will you spend them?'

'I don't know. Sort out the essentials. I expect they'll search us and take our valuables, but I could make sure what I'm taking is clean and practical.'

'No, not those things! I meant what sort of fun? Do you want to see a film, go to a bar, find a cabaret? There'll be little enough luxury once you're in there. Don't you want to hit the town?'

'I'm not much of a one for all that, and I don't suppose the Japanese would let us in anywhere. But I suppose it would be a good idea to eat well before I go. Spend my money before they confiscate it all.' He came closer and looked into her eyes. His were brown and had an expression of longing that made her heart leap. 'Hey, you're right. Want to join me for dinner one night?'

'Tonight,' she said, failing to keep the emotion from her voice. 'Let's not waste any time.'

'Then let's push the boat out and go to the St Petersburg. It's the best.' St Pete's was an elegant restaurant owned by a former White Russian cavalry officer, and popular with the Japanese.

Zofia's smile seemed to rise up from her shoes. 'Then we'll get the others together and go out on the razzle. And anyway, it could be us tomorrow. They may decide to intern the Russians and Jews too.'

'You know what?' he said, 'Making the last four days fun has made me feel like a kid on an outing.'

He was right. It had taken away the sting of the order.

And when he went into his alcove to begin sorting out his possessions, she could even hear him whistling.

Zofia dressed in her most tidy dress and brushed her hair until it shone. She resolutely pushed away thoughts of Haru. It was only one night, she told herself. Hilly had grown again and now her best dress was too tight, and it showed off her figure in a way that was provocative. Not that Hilly noticed. She never noticed her own appearance, only that of other people, observing them with the sort of curiosity you might give to animals in a zoo. Hilly suffered from bouts of sorrow Zofia could do little to prevent. Once, Zofia caught her staring at the raindrops on the window, her cheeks wet with tears.

'What is it?' she asked, thinking something had happened.

'The sky looks so sad,' she said. 'I never realized the sky is as sad as I am.'

'It's just rain,' Zofia said. 'And it's just a shower. What's making you sad?'

'The war, I guess. The sky can see everything. It sees what we are doing – all the bad things – and it can't stop crying. Crying for Madam Wang, and all the other women.'

Zofia sighed and hugged her.

'Why are the Japanese so cruel?' she asked.

'It's because to them we are all just enemies stopping them getting what they want.'

'We're going to stop them though,' she said decisively. 'The CCP and us.'

Now Zofia looked at Hilly. What would happen to them both when Theo was gone? Without Theo to sweet-talk Olga, life would be harder. Would Olga let them stay? It seemed inconceivable Theo would be locked away in only four days' time.

'You look different,' Hilly said to her. 'You've got lipstick on. Can I have some?'

Zofia didn't think this a good idea, but she couldn't really refuse.

She watched Hilly apply the greasy red stick to her lips. 'Blot it now,' she said, handing Hilly her handkerchief.

Hilly pressed it to her lips and fortunately it didn't smudge, just left a scarlet residue on the white cotton. Even with a cardigan over her frock Hilly would turn heads, and when they went into the living room Charlie openly stared before dropping his gaze.

Charlie had one of Theo's hats pulled down over his face and a pair of tortoiseshell glasses Olga had found somewhere. He was wringing his hands with nerves at going to a restaurant, but had agreed to risk this one night in the city to toast Theo and bid him farewell.

'Let's go,' he said. 'Olga?' He called her and she arrived all neat and sophisticated in her belted jacket and little felt hat. She gave Hilly a look of disgust and it made Zofia want to slap her.

'Will it be like Wing On's?' Hilly asked.

Charlie frowned. 'You've been to Wing On's?'

'Zofia and Theo took me.'

'Zofia and Theo,' Olga mocked, and nudged Charlie.

'He just happened to be there,' Zofia said huffily.

'Talk of the devil,' Charlie said. 'Here's the old charmer now.'

Theo emerged from the alcove in his only suit, and Zofia's heart tightened. She grabbed his arm and they all headed out, determined to spend the last of his money. Zofia tried to be lively and cheerful, knowing this was all a front for the fear inside. After the initial crackdown, some places of luxury entertainment remained open – the ones the Japanese wanted to frequent, where no Chinese dared to go, and she suspected soon there would only be Russians and Germans left on the streets of Shanghai, and of course the Japanese.

The Chinese were already treated as an underclass. There had always been professional beggars in Shanghai, the ones with deliberate injuries, the weeping women with emaciated children, the old women unable to stand on their disfigured bound feet.

She winced, knowing they were about to go and have more food in one night than these people would have in a week.

Theo looked down to her and exchanged a glance, and she knew he was thinking the same. How quickly fortunes can change. Today, for these last days, he was a rich American, tomorrow he'd be a penniless internee.

St Pete's was crowded with Russians and Germans. Their little group filed in past the tables, which were pristine with their white cloths and the obligatory metal ash trays and water jugs. Like most Russian restaurants, St Pete's had a cabaret floor in the centre for the entertainment of the Japanese and their allies, which tonight was to be an Armenian gypsy singer. Surprisingly there seemed to be no Japanese on the door, though there were a few seated at tables nearer the centre of the action.

Still wary of being spotted, despite his Russian papers, Charlie ignored the waiter and led them to a corner table away from the bright lights of the chandeliers, where he could have his back to the Japanese.

On a few of the other tables Americans with the 'A' armbands had obviously had the same idea and were already knocking back Russian vodka from trays of tiny glasses.

Hilly's eyes roamed the restaurant, wide and curious.

'Don't stare,' Zofia warned, but too late, the Japanese men at the table near the dance floor were already looking at her with appraising eyes. A bit of lipstick made her immediately a woman.

Zofia pulled out a chair for her. 'Sit down,' she hissed, taking off her coat.

They let Olga lead the conversation loudly in Russian. After a few moments in which they were watched with steely attention, the Japanese group soon assumed the rest of them, apart from Theo, were Russian and lost interest.

Charlie was sweating though, and she could see he looked uncomfortable. 'Was this really a good idea?' he whispered.

'Relax,' Olga said. 'If anyone approaches, let me or Zofia do the talking.'

A waiter brought them menus and they ordered beef stroganoff and wine. When the wine arrived, red and vinegary, they toasted each other with a clink of glasses. *Za zdorovye!* called Olga. 'Health and happiness.'

'To the future,' said Theo clinking his glass first with Charlie's and then with the rest.

Hilly tackled her food with gusto, but Zofia could hardly eat. Theo would soon be locked up in a camp. The thought was inconceivable.

Theo too was barely eating.

'You must eat,' she said. 'Build your strength. You don't know what it will be like in there.'

After that he made more of an effort and she was glad to see he'd forced the meat and rice down. She tried to give him what was left on her plate, but he pushed it away.

'I'll have it,' Hilly said.

After they had eaten, Charlie said he and Olga were going to go home. Charlie was still twitchy being out in so obvious a way.

'Can I stay here?' Hilly asked.

Olga nodded, but Charlie nudged her and said, 'Nah, she can come with us.' He turned to Hilly. 'We'll have a game of cards. I'll teach you how to play poker. You'll be a right card sharp when we've finished with you, okay?'

So it was settled. Zofia realized Charlie was doing it on purpose so she and Theo would have time to be alone together. The thought made her face hot and her heart beat faster, though she was conflicted; she hoped she could trust Charlie, and Olga would be kind to Hilly.

'I'd like to take a walk past my old house,' Theo said. 'I know it's a stupid idea, but just for old times' sake. I had some happy times there.'

'Okay,' she said. 'I've not been to that part of the French

Concession since we left. Will there be more checkpoints?'

'I don't know. I guess we'll find out.' They walked side by side, Zofia conscious of him the whole time, of his long loping stride and serious expression.

As they rounded a corner they came slap bang into a barbed wire barricade, surrounded by sandbags. At the sound of their footsteps, two Japanese soldiers leapt out and put up their rifles.

Theo stopped dead. Zofia was suddenly aware of Theo's red armband with the big 'A' on it.

'This way,' Theo said, hurriedly steering her away.

'So much barbed wire,' Zofia said.

'The Chinese have assassinated too many Japanese soldiers at their posts, so they've stepped up security. We have to be careful.'

She glanced and saw the sentry box had been reinforced with steel plates.

'I know a short cut,' Theo said, grasping her arm. 'Round the backs of the houses.'

She was aware of the heat of his hand through her sleeve, and the warm wind blowing about her bare legs.

'I worry about you.' He stopped on the sidewalk, frowning. 'What are you going to do?'

'Do? There is nothing to be done. There is nowhere I can go. When I left Lithuania I'd hoped to go to America. But things haven't worked out. And besides, there's Hilly. I can't go without her.'

'And you took that on?'

'It just sort of happened. On the boat to Shanghai. Hilly had travelled from Vienna via Italy, and I'd come all the way from Lithuania, and there was something in common there. We met on the last leg. I never found out why she was alone, a young girl like her. She's cagey about her past. But I was on my own and so was she ...' She shrugged. He stopped to listen. His silence and attention encouraged her to carry on talking. 'She's only thirteen, so any fool could see she wouldn't be safe on her own. I thought when we got to Shanghai someone would help us. I didn't know what it would be like. So much poverty, so much misery. Dead beggars on the street. And I couldn't just leave her, could I?'

'Many would have,' he said. His eyes held a light she couldn't ignore. It set off an answering tension in her stomach, like something stretched to breaking point.

He reached an arm around her neck to draw her towards him.

By instinct, her arms closed around his waist, and she felt the thud of his heart against her chest as his hand tilted her face towards his. 'Zofia,' he whispered. And then his lips closed on hers, soft and warm.

The kiss lasted a long few seconds. It was as if her mind had dropped into silence, only their touch was real. Her palms felt the dampness of his shirt, her cheek the scrape of his stubble. The noise of a car engine backfiring brought her back to the present with a gasp.

Thoughts rushed in. Immediately she backed away. 'No, Theo. We mustn't. You're married and so am I. And what would be the point? You're about to leave. It would make far too many complications.'

The spell was broken. His shoulders sagged and he shook his head, let his arm drop. 'Sorry. I know. It's just … I wanted to do that for so long.' A pause. 'I'll take you back if you like.'

'No, it's all right.'

'You sure? You don't have to—'

'No, I'll come with you.' She was confused, her heart still beating too fast, her mind stuck between Haru and this man who was just about to leave her life. She forced herself to think of practicalities. 'Let's see if Zha Wei and his men are still there.'

'If there are lights on, we won't go near though. Too dangerous. I just want one last look at it.'

'Okay,' she said. But she followed him, her body still feeling his kiss, as he skirted past a blacked-out house with an empty garden, its pond dry, and the lawns unkempt and straggling.

Theo's house was in darkness. The lamps by the front door were out and a broken window gaped where his study used to be. A requisition note in Japanese was pinned to the gate.

She pointed. 'Looks like Zha Wei's had to move on. The Japanese army have driven him out.'

'About darn time.'

It was silent, and looked deserted. She followed Theo up the front steps as he tried the door. It opened at his push and he put a hand out to the light switches, but they didn't come on.

They walked down the hall, in the dull gleam of the moonlight from outside, their feet crunching on broken glass. The place was empty. Completely empty. No furniture remained. Everything that could have been stripped had been removed. Brown telephone wires dangled from the wall with no telephone attached.

She followed him in silence as he walked from room to room. When he got to the master bedroom he opened a closet. It was empty too. 'Will you look at that? They took their Christmas presents.' He was choked. 'Her puppet pony ... and Jimmy's Airfix plane.'

Without a word he turned and walked past her and down the stairs, moving fast, as if holding his breath.

She hurried after him until he stopped on the driveway, head in his hands. She put a hand on his shoulder, but he turned, eyes full of anger. 'Bastards, they couldn't just leave it, could they? Had to ruin it all ... turn it all to shit.' He was incoherent, but she knew the feeling because it had been like that in Lithuania.

'Oh, Theo,' she said. She wrapped her arms around him, and they stood for a long time in the dark, as if she was just holding him together.

Finally, he freed himself from her grip and said, 'Now I believe it's over. That my Shanghai is gone, and all that's left is an empty shell. The communist Chinese are as bad as the Japanese; they have no respect for land or property.'

She swallowed back her reply that the Chinese had an equal

right to be angry; it was their city as much as Theo's. But she felt the weight of his distress and sorrow. It took twenty more minutes for them to avoid the patrols on their way back to Olga's house. In the distance the sound of a machine gun punctuated the night.

As they walked, Zofia cursed herself. She felt the loss of their intimacy – she'd ruined something she'd longed for. It had been so brief, their connection, so intense. But now she missed it like the rush of a tide that had already retreated.

Theo tossed on the sofa at Olga's, disturbed by images of his house, and by the memory of Zofia's face. He was too angry with himself to settle. He should never have propositioned her. It was crass. But he was aware that time was short and he didn't know if he would see her again, and somehow that one thing seemed to matter more than all the rest. She held a fascination for him that meant he couldn't get her out of his head.

He toyed with the idea of trying to get out of Shanghai, but it seemed impossible. There were no boats. Every road was guarded by the Japanese. Chinese guerrillas were everywhere in the suburbs, looking for anything they could steal. At about three in the morning, he finally fell into an exhausted sleep.

The house was woken by the sound of rapid hammering on the door.

Theo's first thought was they'd come for Charlie. He scrambled up, throwing off his blanket at the first sound. 'Quick! Get Charlie out!' he yelled.

He was halfway through putting on his suit jacket with its armband when Olga burst into the living room. 'Who is it?' she asked, throwing on a robe.

Her question was answered before he could utter a word. 'Kempeitai. Open up.'

Everyone was up and running into the corridor wild-eyed. Charlie emerged, still in his pyjamas and looking panicked, from

Olga's room. 'There's no way out,' he said, putting on his fake glasses. 'The back window's jammed solid. I'll have to bluff it.'

Olga rushed to the door. The military police, now Japanese to a man, strode in.

Dark blue serge uniforms and American style caps, yet beneath them the faces were cold and motionless.

The man in charge demanded papers and, hair still tousled from sleep, Charlie dug out his Russian permit from under the newspaper on the table.

'You too.' The man stabbed a pointed finger at Zofia and Olga, who were in their nightwear, thin arms folded around their chests for protection. They hurried back to their room and the next time they emerged Zofia had Hilly in tow, her eyes bewildered, her coat over her nightdress.

'What's happening?' Theo heard Hilly whisper, and Zofia said 'hush' and smiled stiffly at the Japanese policemen. Olga held out her papers and they glanced over them.

'Russian too?' one of the men asked Charlie.

'Yes,' Zofia replied firmly in Japanese. 'Russian.'

Theo saw they had no interest in the women at all, but only in him and Charlie.

'Mister Carter.' The Japanese accent made his name sound unfamiliar and the officer had to repeat it before Theo understood they meant him. So this was no random round-up – they'd actually come for him. That must be why they gave Charlie's papers only a cursory glance.

His armband showed plainly he was American, Theo thought, but still he had to hand over his pass.

'Mister Carter, you come,' said the Kempeitai man in charge, gesturing at him. 'Internment.'

'Already?' Zofia said to the men. 'But it wasn't supposed to be today.'

'Yes. Today.'

Theo held up his hands. 'I'll pack, okay?' He mimed filling a bag and made to go behind the curtain but was stopped by the sharp thrust of a gun to the belly.

Zofia said something angry to them in Japanese, and Theo saw them start, surprised at how well she could speak the language. The officer in charge shot a reply back to her and she replied in a heated manner, gesticulating.

A little discussion ensued until she turned to Theo, her eyes distraught. 'They'll let you have one bag! Make every last thing in it count.'

Theo was so clumsy with shock, that he almost tripped as he went to get his case from the alcove. But he threw in a jumper, his sturdiest shoes, shaving soap and brush, clean socks, as Zofia's bright, clear voice continued to interrogate them with questions. But he heard no reply. He grabbed a coat from the back of the sofa, to find it was the one still stained on the inside from Charlie's blood.

When he pushed aside the curtain, Zofia was stepping distractedly from foot to foot. 'They won't tell me why it has to be now,' she said, her eyes full of distress, 'when you were not supposed to go until Tuesday.'

'Can you ask them where I'm being taken? Is it Woosung, like they said?'

She asked them and received a terse reply. She turned to him. 'They say to the Haiphong Road.'

Theo felt himself stiffen. It was not what he'd been told before.

'Come now,' the Japanese policeman said in English.

Charlie and Olga were quiet, he noticed, standing back in the shadows of the bedroom door, but Hilly's eyes were round, and she clung to Zofia's arm.

Theo placed a hand on Zofia's shoulder. 'Thank you for trying to help.' His throat was tight, his eyes dry as tinder. 'Thank you for ... everything. Keep well,' he said, not knowing what else to say. The eyes of the Kempeitai were watching and it made him stiff. 'You mean so much to me ... I'll try to write.'

She reached out and gave him a hurried peck on the cheek. It made his heart leap, and he saw her eyes were shiny with tears.

'Good thing we dined out last night, wasn't it?' she said.

'We'll dine again at the St Petersburg, I promise.' He didn't know what he was saying; his mouth was forming words he shouldn't say.

Zofia looked him dead in the eye. 'I'll hold you to that.'

The Kempeitai officers led him at gunpoint to a truck which was already full of confused but silent Brits and Americans, judging by their clothes and luggage. The stars were bright dots in an ink-black sky. Nobody spoke and the truck rumbled out towards the suburbs.

Stay alert, Theo told himself, trying not to think of Zofia, or what might happen next. *Every landmark. Note where they take you.* He forced himself to map the route as they went.

After a twenty-minute ride they were unloaded at the Haiphong Road camp. He should have guessed they'd use this place – it was the former barracks of the US Marines, and like everywhere else, it was now under Japanese control.

The barracks were spartan, like most military accommodation, but made draughty by bomb damage, and unsanitary because the Japanese army had brought in three hundred internees overnight. One of the men, another American, was so badly beaten he had to be dragged from the truck, and he was pushed roughly through the door to the billet. His legs gave way and he collapsed onto the dirt floor until Theo and a few others rushed forward to help him. Both arms seemed to be broken, and his knees concertinaed oddly the wrong way.

'Bridge House,' said an older British man who had the military bearing of an army officer. 'They all come back like this, or worse.'

Theo stared at the crumpled man's injuries and wondered if they were survivable. They immediately called for a doctor, and a man who looked far too young to be any kind of doctor came running. They watched him do his best to bind and splint the man's legs with shaking hands, using only another man's walking stick and a few spare shirts to tie it together.

'It could be any one of us,' said the man Theo was mentally calling 'the captain' because of his upright posture. 'And we have sod all to tell the Japs that they don't already know. But knowing nothing doesn't help – it's just another excuse for them to beat the crap out of us.'

'Why have we been brought here? I was told I was going to Woosung?'

'Because they think we know something. Look at us,' said the captain. 'We're all men who could have some sort of intelligence or information they need.'

He was right. Apart from those who had come from battle or been shot down, all were prominent business traders such as himself, ex-officers of the Shanghai Municipal Police, or retired old codgers from the US Navy. Like a collection of elite men from a New York social club.

'They'll want to know what we know,' the captain said. 'That's why he ended up like that.' He pointed to the injured man.

'Is there any chance of escape?'

'No. They make us sign a docket to say we won't try under pain of death. Of course they force you to sign it. No one gets out of here except with a Jap on either arm.'

Chapter 16

The way Theo had been taken, with no warning, prompted an earthquake of memories for Zofia. It reminded her of Russia; of her brother Jacek being taken by the NKVD on the train out of Moscow. That grief still pulled, deep in her gut. The human heart was a mystery. Last year she'd been under Haru's spell, like Alice, in a kind of Wonderland where nothing had seemed real because their time together was so brief. They'd had no time to build anything solid. Her old life was like a page in a book, an old story that had no bearing on today.

And now she hardly dared think about her strange connection to Theo, and what it meant – if it meant anything at all.

But she wasn't the only one who was jumpy. Charlie was short-tempered, and Olga had become obsessed with locking doors and windows and watching Hilly as if she might suddenly turn around and bite. Hilly was quieter. She didn't like going out and kept asking if the Japanese soldiers would come back and take her away too.

It was a relief in a way that Charlie gave them deliveries to do, mostly in the French Concession where more Chinese guerrillas hid out in abandoned houses. Zha Wei had got his way after all, and now she was in effect working for him but only because having somewhere to live was paramount. She did her deliveries dutifully, and in the sweltering summer heat she and Hilly copied out transcripts from the BBC and other Allied reports for distribution.

Zofia never minded listening to the broadcasts. She was avid for news from the rest of the world, but trying to speculate where Haru had been posted, and whether she would ever get a letter from him, was like rubbing salt into a wound.

Hilly was on watch by the front window while they listened in, to warn them if anyone was coming. Since Theo had been taken, they'd scraped the paint from the back windows and unjammed them to make a back exit route.

Fretting about Theo and how he was doing made Zofia restless. She decided to go and see if she could collect his mail. She didn't interrogate herself too much on exactly why she was so interested in his affairs, or what was driving her. Instead, she told herself she'd try to get an address so she could send a message to Evelina and the children that Theo had been interned.

She left Hilly on watch as usual with Charlie and Olga.

'Will you be long?' Hilly asked, her forehead furrowed with worry.

'Just an hour or so. Don't worry, Hils. I'll be back soon and I'll go by the market, see if I can find fruit or something nice to eat.'

It took a good hour to reach Carter & Co. The multiple checkpoints were a constant irritant. Zofia trained herself to look calm as she passed through each one and headed for the Bund. Bodies lay in the street and the place stank of decay and misery, its former prosperity all gone.

This was it. She took a moment to compose herself before pushing through the imposing swing doors, grateful to be in the cool, and marvelling that this whole building had once been owned by Theo Carter. The Japanese man on reception was an older man in wire-rimmed glasses, not a soldier, and he had the manner of a clerk.

She bowed low and spoke to him politely in Japanese.

He blinked, surprised to find a Westerner speaking Japanese and asked her where she'd learned it. 'My husband is Japanese,' she said. 'He's in the army.'

'Where is he fighting?'

'I don't know. His mail doesn't come to me in Shanghai. But I've come to collect the mail of my employer Mr Carter who is about to be interned before repatriation.' She struggled with the Japanese words for 'repatriation', apologized profusely, bowed low again and let him help her.

'Has mail come for Mr Carter, I wonder?' she said, eyes lowered. 'He would like to deal with it before he goes.' The white lie. She sweated, hoping this man wouldn't know Theo had already gone.

The man smiled and drew out a wad of mail tied with a rubber band. He handed it over and she saw it had all been opened. 'It's been processed,' he said, 'and anything of importance will have been dealt with. But you can take it if you wish. We have no further use for it. The boy was going to take it to the trash.'

'Honoured sir; that is most kind. Mr Carter will be pleased. Thank you so much.' She bowed once more for good measure, then thanked him again profusely before he could change his mind.

Afterwards, she wondered at their encounter. He'd seemed polite and pleasant, just like the Japanese people she'd met in Kobe. It made her ask questions about what she was doing. Why was she doing this for Theo, an American, against the wishes of the Japanese? As Haru's wife, she should surely feel loyalty to Japan, not to the Americans.

The thoughts were uncomfortable. As soon as she was outside the office, she hurried home, the letters stuffed down the front of her dress. If her bag was searched, she didn't want to lose them to some over-zealous soldier.

'You're back!' Hilly had left her lookout post at the window and was busy copying again.

Anxious not to be interrupted, Zofia took the mail into their bedroom, sat on the bed, and sifted through it. It gave her an odd feeling of excitement to see his name *Mr Theodore Carter Esq* on the envelopes. She felt guilty even touching his personal mail, but she intended to reply to his wife or children, didn't she?

She fingered her way through the typed bills, then stopped. This one was personal. Tidy upright writing, a letter mail on a single sheet. A hotel in Manila. That must be their address. She flipped it over to read the signature. Evelina. When she flipped it back, she couldn't help her eyes skimming the first few lines.

She let it fall to her lap. Oh no. It couldn't be true.

She picked it up to read each word again.

I don't know why you've cut off the phone. Over the last weeks I've tried every possible way to get you and still no reply. I've been dreading saying these words to you but it's been like shouting into a void. And now it's too late. Jimmy is dead. There, I've said it. He went down with the whooping cough on the boat. It made his chest weak.

He was just settling in school then a few weeks ago he caught pneumonia. I was out of my mind with worry and though I got all the best specialists, no doctor could do anything to help. Where the hell were you? I couldn't do anything. He just coughed and coughed and called out for you. It's so hot and humid here. Air too thick to breathe. He died three nights ago. I can hardly bear to write the words.

This letter was written at the end of June. It was more than two months old.

Theo wouldn't know anything of this.

She felt a piece of her heart heave in her chest as she remembered Jimmy, never still, whizzing from place to place, impatient with his lessons, and always chock-full of energy.

And Daisy? How would she manage without her brother? It didn't bear thinking about.

She put the page down as if it was hot. She shouldn't have read it. Her mother always used to say bad things come to those who snoop.

Her mind kept replaying that sentence. *Jimmy's dead.*

It didn't seem real. And now she knew something she should never have known. It sat in her heart like a lead weight, but she couldn't unsee those words. What should she do? Ignore it? Get a message to Theo? Or better to leave well alone? Bad news like this could break a man.

She remembered Theo's eyes when he was taken away, as if he wanted to say something, but the words were left adrift, unspoken.

He wanted such great things for his children; he was always talking about it, building a better life for them. If she were him, she'd want to know. He deserved to know. She should try to get the letter to him. She closed her blurry eyes and then reopened them to refocus on Evelina's address at the top of the page before taking paper and pen and composing a carefully worded note.

She'd made a mess of it, but now she should do the right thing. Evelina would no doubt wonder how Zofia got her address, but it was too complicated to explain. And the most important thing was for Evelina to know why Theo hadn't got the news or replied. Zofia aimed for a professional tone. She didn't want Evelina to know she'd read Theo's personal mail.

7 September 1942
Dear Mrs Carter,
I am writing to let you know that Mr Carter has been interned in the Haiphong Camp for International Prisoners in Shanghai. I thought you should know as I do not know when he will be sent back to the USA or when they will

> *release him. Carter & Co is fully under the control of the Japanese.*
>
> *I'm sorry this is bad news. I'm sure he will write to you when he can.*
>
> *Best wishes*
> *Zofia Kimurai (Tutor)*

Yes, better not to mention she knew anything about Jimmy, at least for now.

'What are you doing?' Hilly was at the door.

She started. 'Writing to Mrs Carter to tell her where Theo is.'

Hilly didn't seem interested. 'Can we go out? I'm bored.'

'Has Charlie got anything for us to deliver yet?'

'Don't know. I'll ask him.' And her head disappeared from around the door. Zofia didn't wait for her to come back, but sealed the envelope to Evelina Carter and addressed it. Perhaps it would get past the censor. She hoped so. She was pretty sure all outgoing and ingoing mail would be scrutinized, especially if it had a foreign address, like a hotel in Manila.

When she went into the sitting room, Charlie looked up. 'You okay? You look a bit washed out.'

She rallied herself. 'No. I'm all right. Are these to go today?' He had a row of packages lined up on the side table near the radio.

'Yes,' he said. 'They're all addressed.'

'I did it all,' Hilly said. 'Stuffed the envelopes, copied the addresses out and everything.'

'Well done,' Zofia said, her mind still in shock.

'And you're in luck,' Charlie said. 'I've managed to get you a bicycle. Help you get around to the drop points.'

Zofia brought her thoughts back to the room and tried to summon enthusiasm. 'Really?'

'It's an old one, but heavy duty. It's chained up by the front door.'

Hilly raced downstairs, with Zofia behind.

The bicycle was a black-painted delivery boy's bicycle, one that looked even less roadworthy than the Banana.

'How come you get a bike, and I don't?' Hilly said, staring at it with envy.

'They're hard to come by, and I'm used to riding a cycle.'

'I used to have one too,' she said. 'I'd nearly grown out of it. Before the Gestapo came and everything changed. It was a red one.'

'What happened when the Gestapo came?'

A shrug. 'Mother wouldn't let me go out on it anymore. Not after they arrested my father. They didn't like him because we're Jehovah's Witnesses. They came in the morning before he went to work. A man in a raincoat, and two Gestapo officers. They had guns and made him go with them.' She stared at the bicycle as if she couldn't really see it. 'Father hugged me so tight it hurt. Then he asked them, "Shall I bring a toothbrush?" and when the Nazi in the raincoat said yes, my mother began to cry.'

Zofia moved closer to Hilly in the dark hallway. She'd never heard this story. 'Where did they take him?'

'Mother said she was sure he'd come back soon, but though we waited and waited, he never did. They didn't like it that he wouldn't make the Nazi salute. And Mother was afraid they'd come for us too and take us somewhere called Ravensbrück. I asked her if there were ravens there. There were no ravens there, she said. No birds at all.'

'Where is it, this Ravensbrück?'

'In Germany. She was worried if we were sent there then …'

'What?' She tried to probe gently.

'I don't know. That it would be very bad and we might get separated.'

There was a pause while Hilly twined her fingers in her skirt.

Zofia sat on the step and gestured for Hilly to sit next to her. 'So why did you come to Shanghai?'

'Mother decided we had to leave as soon as Father came home

again. She was so sure he'd come back. She sold our best dresser and all the cutlery to get boat tickets to Shanghai. Vienna then Genoa then Shanghai. That was her plan. She had the map and kept on unfolding it to look at it. But one day after school, after she got the tickets, the Gestapo came again.

'One of them wanted to touch me and lift my skirts. Mother stood in front of me to stop them. She was screaming, telling them to do it to her instead, but they dragged her away, and left one man behind. A big fat man in black boots. He took off his cap and pointed a gun at me, so I had to let him do it. The pushing thing. When the man finished, he said he'd come back. I thought he meant just then, so I was too scared to look out of the window.

'When night came, I pulled the curtain back, but I couldn't see Mother. So I didn't go anywhere, but I hid in a cupboard in case the Nazis came back. No one came back. Not Mother, or Father or anyone.'

Zofia had moved to put a hand on hers, but Hilly pulled it away. Her eyes were glazed with tears and she could hardly get the words out. 'I heard noises in the house but I was too scared to move, I just hung on to my knees, kept counting to ten. I was suffocating in there. But when the cupboard opened it was my neighbour, Mrs Stieg.'

'Mrs Stieg?'

'Mmhmm. She swore when she saw me. She'd got an armful of Mother's clothes, her flowered dressing gown, and her best blouse. I told her, don't take them, because Mother was definitely coming back, she had to because we were going to get the boat. Mrs Stieg asked, what boat? And I told her Mother had tickets for Shanghai and she'd be back soon. She made me show her our tickets, all on one document, Mother, Father and me. They were with our passports. Mrs Stieg got very excited, her face went red and her eyes all shiny. She looked at the tickets and she said, "We'll go together. Your parents have gone ahead. They'll meet you in Shanghai." I wanted so much for it to be true, I didn't think properly. I was so scared, and I trusted her. I believed her, that Mother and Father were in Shanghai waiting for me. So the Stiegs took our tickets and passes and we went. Her and her fat husband took the tickets and brought me here.'

'So where are they now, these people? I didn't see them on the boat.'

'I don't know. But as soon as we were on board, they took my money and then they pretended they didn't know me. They would walk off if they saw me coming. It was confusing. I looked for my mother on the ship, but she wasn't there. She'll never be here, will she? It was a lie, and I should have known, but I didn't understand then. I thought grown-ups knew everything.'

Zofia took all this in. 'Who were these people again, the ones who took your tickets?'

'Mr and Mrs Stieg.'

'And they got off at Shanghai?'

'I think so. I didn't see them again. They didn't want me, only the tickets. And I felt such a fool, and I kept thinking about Mother and Father and how I'd let them down. I was glad you came. The Stiegs didn't want to know me anymore, and I didn't know what to do.'

Zofia mentally cursed them. If she ever set eyes on them here, then they'd have some questions to answer and no mistake. She didn't know whether to agree with Hilly that her parents had probably never left Germany. It just seemed too cruel.

'I was so stupid. How will they find me, now I'm here?' Hilly asked, a fat tear sliding down her cheek.

Zofia hugged her, feeling her shoulders heave. She had had to grow up too fast. She remembered the confusing feeling of being thirteen years old, and that was without a war to upend everything.

'You'll be together one day. They'd be proud of you if they could see all the work you're doing for the CCP.'

'D'you think so?'

A hug was the only answer she could give.

Chapter 17

Zofia had found out through the underground grapevine that American businessmen like Theo had definitely been taken to Haiphong Camp, so after much soul-searching, she'd decided to try to get Evelina's letter to him.

She couldn't get hold of binoculars as they were banned, but she hoped to get close enough to get a view of the camp by bicycle. She'd told no one she was going, grateful that Charlie and Olga were occupying Hilly with copying and printing on a machine supplied by the CCP. She hoped Olga wouldn't find Hilly's constant need to chatter irritating.

She pedalled hard, her leg muscles aching, even though she was strong and fit. She was wearing a navy Chinese jacket to blend in, and kept her head swathed with a cloth, like a peasant woman on an errand. When the houses ran out, the bomb damage made the landscape a wasteland of shattered warehouses and broken shacks.

She slowed, watching for the Haiphong barracks. Well before she got to the perimeter fence, she scraped to a halt and squatted in a bomb crater, the bicycle beside her. She could see the camp easily from this distance, and even from here she could make out the posts with barbed wire and electrified fencing. A single fence. That was good.

A wooden shelter was by the main gate. Two Japanese guards were standing just outside it, shuffling from side to side as if bored, but they launched into conversation with two more uniformed soldiers who returned from patrol.

As one turned to look towards her, she ducked down out of sight. A large water tower loomed above the camp, but no tower for guards. The fence ran close to what she guessed were new bunkhouse billets at the back of the compound. She could see their roofs from here. Some of the brick-built buildings in the compound had been bomb-damaged, and rust-coloured rubble strewed the road nearby.

She hunkered down, prepared to wait. She took careful note of the soldiers' patrol times on her watch – noting it took a full quarter hour for the patrol to go right around the perimeter and return. She cursed her layers of clothes – under the frogged jacket she was wearing a dark blue jersey and black slacks – and they were itching furiously in this afternoon heat and humidity. The guards seemed to spend more time hiding from the sun in their wooden shelter than out of it. Both smoked long bamboo pipes not cigarettes, and these seemed to need a lot of care and attention.

She watched for a couple of hours in her hiding place under the burning sun. No one came near, except a Chinese man who appeared at dusk with a bundle of sticks on his sweat-soaked back, and he turned away across the field, giving the camp a wide berth.

As soon as the patrol had set off for the fourth time, she was confident she had the gist of their routine. By now the sun was low in the sky and smoke was wreathing around the sentry hut. No other guards were in sight.

Zofia stretched her cramped legs, stiff from waiting in this hole for nightfall.

When night came it was black with no moon, and a sky peppered with stars. The silhouette of the wire fence was eerie, until electric lights on stanchions suddenly blinked into life-like eyes.

Zofia tensed, an involuntary shudder running up her back.

Between the stanchions were deep pools of dark. There was no sign of the patrol so she had to wait until it reappeared and set off again before she could risk going nearer. She hoped the bright lights might make a dark figure harder to see.

In her bicycle basket she had newspapers, Evelina's letter about Jimmy's death, and a handwritten note addressed to Theodore Carter explaining. They were all tied together with raffia onto a stone she hoped would be heavy enough to lob over the fence. She prayed she would be able to throw it over, if she was quick. It would show Theo he hadn't been forgotten – that he still mattered. She prayed someone kind would pick it up and get the message to him. It was what she hoped someone would do for Jacek, locked away in the gulag, although she knew this idea was a forlorn hope.

As soon as the Japanese patrol set off around the camp perimeter again and the other two men had gone back inside their hut, she launched herself forward on the bike, pedalling after the guards and hoping they would keep walking onwards and wouldn't decide to turn back.

The chain gave a squeak so she slowed, mentally crossing her fingers and hoping only she could hear it. Around the back of the fence, close to the roofs of the barracks, she dismounted. Everything was hot and dusty, including the parcel she was about to throw. She closed her nose to the strong smell of the latrines.

God help her if it landed in there. And she had to hope no soldiers were patrolling inside the fence.

Her first attempt to throw wasn't high enough and it landed on her side of the barbed wire. She scrabbled after it, listening in case the Japanese had heard the thud. She knew she would have to throw much higher and much further to clear the wire and the fence. She plucked up the parcel and took a step back.

She raised her arm and threw with all her might. On the other side of the fence she heard a yelp. 'What the …?' Then a whisper, in English. 'Who's there?'

'A friend,' she whispered back. 'Can you deliver to Theodore Carter? He's an American.'

'Okay. Will do.' The anonymous person spoke back in hurried whispers.

A glance at her watch made her start. That time already. She made a grab for her bicycle. The patrol would be nearly back to the gate, and they'd catch her on their second round if she didn't get away quick.

She scrambled onto the saddle and pedalled back the way she'd come – towards the hazy lights of the city, wavering in the heat. Just as she was about to come out of the lee of the fence, she heard the door of the guard house open and had to jam her heels into the dirt as one of the guards, complete with rifle on his shoulder, emerged into the slash of light.

Quickly, she dragged the bike into the shadows, away from the perimeter. The noise she made had alerted the guard because he raised his rifle and crept forward looking towards the city.

Sipping in small breaths of air, she stayed motionless, fearing to make another sound. If he turned and looked her way, she'd be done for.

'What are you doing?' A call in Japanese from the guard house and the other guard, shorter and heavier, emerged.

'Thought I heard something.'

'Just birds. Or rats.'

The guard laughed, his attention on his friend. It meant they didn't see her in the shadows. But the delay meant that to her horror, she could see the patrol coming back around the edge of the camp towards the gate.

She'd no idea how she would get away if they started the circuit again.

But then, just as the patrol were about to set off again, a pair of headlights flashed up the road, accompanied by the distinctive rumble of a truck. From her position, crouched in the shade of the fence, Zofia saw all four Japanese soldiers stroll out to meet it, the noise forgotten.

Another load of internees. The truck stopped and in the dark more people were unloaded, their faces white in the glare of the lights by the gate. Mostly men, she noticed, all Westerners, with downcast eyes. They stumbled as if tired. The gates were creaked open and just for a moment all the guards were focused on shepherding the men inside the camp.

Seizing the moment, she took a deep breath and legs pumping, shot away down the road, fearing a bullet in her back at any moment. But after a few frantic minutes of pedalling, she risked a look over her shoulder and saw the pinpoint lights of the camp in the distance.

She pulled over to try to catch her breath. She was gasping with the effort and with the terror of how close she'd come to being caught. But also with elation. She'd done it.

But could she do it again? That was the question. In the letter she'd promised Theo she'd be there again in two weeks' time to take a reply and try to get it to Evelina. But that was before she knew just how exhausting it was to stay out of sight, and how scared she'd been of being caught. The reality of doing it was so much harder than she'd imagined.

Inside the camp, Theo was trying to sleep. There was little else to do, and he hadn't slept at all for the first few days. The air was humid, and clouds of mosquitos were feasting on his ankles. The hardness of the wooden bunk, and the fact there were so many other men, all snoring or moaning, made it hard to drop off.

He wondered if they would all be repatriated and when. He wondered how Evelina and the children were doing, whether they were still in Manila. He worried about Charlie and whether he would get caught. And he felt guilty about Zofia, how he'd tried to kiss her and she'd refused. And yet still he couldn't get her out of his mind. She must have quite a brain to know all those languages, and yet she was wasted with no proper work and looking after Hilly all the time. But he couldn't imagine Zofia ever getting out of Shanghai with Hilly in tow, and the thought of her trapped in that war zone disturbed him.

He was just musing on this when he heard his name being called. At first, he thought he must be dreaming. He sat up, surprised.

'Theodore Carter?'

'Here!' he called.

A small wiry man with a big nose was waving something at him. The man looked over his shoulder warily, before approaching.

'Special delivery!' his visitor said, grinning. 'It just came over the fence. Nearly brained me! A woman brought it. Quick, take it and get it out of sight.'

Theo frowned and stood up to take the parcel.

'Hit me right on the bonce, it did.' The man rubbed his head ruefully. 'Must have a good aim, your girl.' His accent pinned him as a Scot, and he showed no sign of going away. 'Name's Mac. MacIlhinney, but they call me Mac.'

'Theo,' he said.

'I know, your name's all over the sodding parcel. You gonna open it?' He moved round to shield Theo from view. 'Open it under your blanket, I would. Keep it oota sight.'

Theo felt obliged to open it in front of him. He undid it carefully, keeping the raffia because there was no paper or string in the camp, and he knew better than to discard anything useful.

He drew it out from under the blanket so Mac could see.

'A bloody newspaper! Lucky devil!'

The *Shanghai Post*, but it was the note that interested him. His heart was already beating too fast.

He turned away so he could read it. It was frustratingly dark, so he had to squint and hold the paper right up to his eyes. He saw the 'Z' signature and wanted to whoop, but the writing was hard to read in this dim light. He stared at the paper until his eyes accustomed himself to the pleasantly rounded writing and he could make out the words.

Dear Theo

I thought you might want news from outside about your business, and a way of keeping in touch. I went to your office and asked for your mail. It had all been opened. But they gave me it, all neatly wrapped in a rubber band. Seemed to be mostly empty envelopes. I've kept any correspondence safe for you for when you return. But there was one I thought you should have. It's inside the newspaper.

I'm beyond sorry to bring you such bad news.

I'll be outside the fence again same time in exactly a fortnight. If you actually get this, wait by the fence and I'll try to throw over more news. You can throw over letters you want posting, or any request, and I'll see if I can do anything. If I don't come, it's because they have changed the patrol.

Z

Theo read it again. Zofia had been outside the fence? 'Has she gone? The woman?'

'If she's got any sense,' said Mac.

What bad news? Surely being in here was bad enough. Zofia said it was in the newspaper.

He opened it up, expecting to see a headline, but instead a blue folded letter dropped out. From Evelina. He recognized the spindly handwriting. The paper was flimsy, an international mail where the letter was simply folded and the address written on the outside.

His first thought was that now he'd lost Carter & Co, Evelina had left him. He wouldn't put it past her.

Again he struggled in the dark, but he made out the writing because he was familiar with the way Evelina formed her words.

No. He couldn't take it in.

Not Jimmy. He couldn't be gone. He'd been fine. Was never ill.

'Good news?'

He started, suddenly realizing Mac was still there. 'A letter from my wife. About the children.' His mouth formed the words, though they felt like they didn't belong to him.

'Hope you don't mind me asking, but can I have a look at the newspaper?'

'Here.' He handed it over in a daze. 'Yes, take it.' How could he not have known? If he'd known he would have swum there, anything to save his boy.

'Aw, thanks pal. I've been here three weeks and I'm that bored I could murder someone just for the entertainment.'

'Better not try it on me,' Theo said, his mind still not able to process what he'd just read. He kept looking at the letter expecting it to say something different.

Mac was still talking. 'Wouldn't dare. You look like you can handle yourself.' He waved the newspaper. 'News type's small,' Mac said. 'Better wait until daylight and find somewhere out of sight to read it. I'll have it back to you pronto when I'm done.'

'Yes, yes. Okay.' He just wanted Mac to go away.

'It's good of you to let me have it. I owe you.' Mac tucked the paper down into his shirt – a regulation issue of dark blue corduroy along with baggy pants, the outfit prisoners who had no other clothing were issued. Then he gave a wave, just as a Japanese guard stuck his head around the door.

Theo grabbed the blanket and hastily threw it over himself and the letters and feigned sleep.

Footsteps prowled past but then receded.

Theo remained motionless until the guard had gone away. Then he stood up, unable to be still. He couldn't accept it. Wouldn't accept it. He paced, his throat tight, wanting to hit something. He should have gone with Evelina, and then this might never have happened; he should never have trusted her.

He'd been blithely carrying on, trying to salvage his business when all the time Jimmy needed him.

His business. How stupid. How could he have thought it even mattered?

Maybe Jimmy would have lived, if he'd been there? He could have done something, got the doctors to do something. And now he was stuck here in this bloody camp. He kicked out at the wooden pallet over and over.

'Stop that bleeding racket!' Another man raised his fists at him.

'Wanna fight?' said Theo, eyes blazing.

'No. Just shut the hell up.'

Theo felt the prick of tears. He crushed both letters into a ball in his fist and strode over to the latrine. There, he tore them into shreds and cast them down into the dark depths. He'd never got the letters. His son was still alive. He was out there in the sun in Manila, playing football and demanding ice cream.

Theo struggled through the days under the weight of grief and disbelief. Some days he pretended to himself he'd never had the letter. Others he crumpled in misery and frustration. He just wanted to get out of there as soon as he could. He paced the boundary fence looking for any weakness in the wire. On one occasion he was beaten across the head by one of the guards who thought he was too close to the fence. He could do nothing in here. He was excluded from his own life.

'Do people ever get out of here?' he asked Mac.

'Nah. Only way out is Bridge House. The Japs keep sending people there and they either just disappear, or they come back worse than they went. Torture. Terrifies me I'll be next. I'd rather die on the wire trying to get out of here than die in there with what they do to you. Fingernails torn out, half dead.'

'We need an escape plan,' Theo said.

'You mean dig our way out?'

'Are you up for it if we do?'

'Dunno. Maybe. Could be useful to have someone like your missus on the outside as well.'

'She's not my ...' Theo broke off. It would be too difficult to explain about Zofia. He was wracked with guilt about her. And he feared if he tried to explain anything about Evelina to Mac he might cry.

Even now he was amazed Zofia had risked being arrested to get this letter from Evelina to him. For days he'd cursed her, raged at her as the bringer of bad news, his emotions churning, his pain too near the surface for reason. Today he was able to be grateful, but there was also something else there, excitement that Zofia had thought of him and was prepared to do something so kind. He couldn't imagine Evelina braving barbed wire for him, even with such desperate, awful news.

But then he felt guilty for thinking of Zofia; it seemed disrespectful to his wife and son.

How short Jimmy's life had been. And yet here was his father, living half a life for God knows how long, shut up in here. And what about Daisy? What if something happened to her?

'We have to get out,' he said to Mac, 'or I'll go insane.'

Chapter 18

Zofia hoped the message had got to Theo and was counting the days until she could go back. She didn't want to risk it too often, and even now she worried the letter might have fallen into Japanese hands and a patrol would be waiting to arrest her. But she knew Theo would want some sort of message to get to Evelina.

In the meantime, under the pretext of delivering laundry, she'd fallen into Charlie's routine, running messages to Zha Wei's contacts. Dangerous work because some Chinese were collaborators with the Japanese, under the dubious orders of Wang Jingwei, long-term enemy of Chiang Kai-shek, who ruled China in exactly the same way that Nazi collaborator Pétain ruled Nazi-occupied Vichy France.

The messages Zofia had to deliver for Zha Wei were packaged in the bundles of sheets and shirts. The Japanese soldiers at the checkpoints never seemed to notice it was always the same two bundles, they were used to Zofia coming and going on the same route every day. She bowed and greeted them with some subservience in Japanese.

Hilly had finally understood she was under a kind of house arrest, and it almost broke Zofia's heart.

'I wish I had a bicycle,' she said wistfully to Zofia. 'You're always going out and you never give me a go.'

'It's too dangerous, with the Japanese out there.'

'It's not too dangerous for you though. You go out every day. Can't I come too?'

This sort of conversation went on for a few days, until the day Charlie was out at a meeting with Zha Wei. Olga was at the hospital, so Zofia saw no harm in taking Hilly with her. They'd walk instead of going by bicycle today. The air was damp and warm, and the sky steamy with low-hanging mist.

The coolies with their rickshaws and passenger wheelbarrows were doing a brisker trade now the situation was more settled. The Japanese had taken rigid control, and some sort of order had returned, though it was laced with resentment from both the Chinese and Western populations.

Their first delivery was a bunch of correspondence to one of Zha Wei's houses – he'd a few now, dotted around the International Settlement, the homes of interned diplomats. They rarely saw anyone because the drop boxes were always in the grounds – under a tree or in the mailbox. Hilly enjoyed peeling back the laundry to find the slim packages and then leaving them in the drop boxes. 'Like a proper secret agent,' she said.

It wasn't until they got back that Zofia noticed a bloodstain on the back of Hilly's skirt.

When she pointed it out, Hilly was shocked. 'I must have sat on something.'

'Do you have stomach ache?'

'A bit.'

She explained it might be her own blood.

'What's happened to me?' Hilly said in a panic. 'Get it off!'

'Nothing to be worried about. Just what every woman has every month, that's all.'

'Every month!' She looked horrified.

She made Hilly change her clothes and found some spare

rags for her to put in her underwear. It took her a long while to explain. Hilly was unwilling to believe she was going to have this happen again.

And in truth, it seemed a hard extra thing to deal with in the midst of this war.

Maybe Olga and Charlie were right, and they must keep her indoors. Hilly had become a woman and in occupied Shanghai all women watched their backs.

Chapter 19

Bridge House, September 1942

Theo counted the days until he could make contact with Zofia. He was anxious about Daisy. He'd written a long letter to Evelina, begging for more news. He concealed it under the inner lining of his shoe. Though he'd asked the Japanese camp commander if he could write to his wife, permission was denied.

Mac had become a firm friend, though there was hardly anything of him; his ribs showed even through his shirt and his bony face was gaunt and hollow. He was always watching out, eyes darting here and there to warn anyone when a Jap was coming. He had scars across his back where one of them had beaten him up, so it made him jumpy whenever one was near.

He let Theo talk incessantly of escape. Mac was twitchy, always wary of trouble, but it made him a good lookout. They made a note of the times of the patrols, and of which soldiers were possibly open to a bribe.

Sadly, the wooden fence and electric wire were insurmountable, and there were too many guards to risk climbing it. Digging was impossible as they had no suitable tools, and it would be too visible to anyone passing.

'Can we get your wife to get us something for digging?'

Theo still hadn't told Mac that Zofia was not his wife. 'Can't imagine her being able to chuck a spade over.' His mouth twitched with the first inkling of amusement at the idea of Zofia lobbing over something so big.

'I know. We couldn't use it anyway. We'd be too much in view. When's she coming again?'

'Day after tomorrow, I hope, because I need to send a letter.'

Mac didn't know about Jimmy either. Theo couldn't bring himself to even talk of it, because he thought his carefully built protective shell might collapse and leave him a blubbering mess.

'What's her name?'

'Zofia.' Saying it, when she wasn't really his wife, filled him with misgivings.

'Have you asked her for cigarettes?'

'No. But I've asked her to send as many newspapers as she thinks she can throw over.'

'Get her to bring cigs next time. We can trade 'em.'

'All right. You can come with me to wait, show me exactly where the stone came over.'

'Yer'll need a hard hat then.' Mac grinned.

Theo smiled back. He'd realized that life was going on regardless, no matter what he felt inside. He wasn't sure why he was trusting Mac, but he didn't doubt him at all. Intelligent, and good with his hands, Mac was a working-class Scot who'd been an engineer on the docks. He was in a different hut from the one Theo was billeted in, but they'd often chat in the evenings to while away the time, and they had managed to get a pack of cards so they could play poker. Mac always won. Theo's mind was never on it. He made stupid mistakes, ones Mac seemed to think deliberate, and designed to let him win.

Another day passed. Theo worried about how Daisy was,

whether she missed her brother. Whether Evelina was giving her enough affection – or if Evelina had reverted to her opium habit which made her ...-centred and distant. When he heard sparrows chitter... outside the camp, he ached for his children ...past.

Since ...f the news about Jimmy it had been the longest two ...re of his life, but now there was only one more day to ...he might hear more from Zofia. He prayed for good ...ther that night, and that she would come.

He settled down to sleep hoping it would make the time go quicker.

Okiru! Okiru! Theo flinched as rough fingers bit into his arm. The nose of a rifle was at his throat.

He was instantly awake as he was hauled to his feet by two Kempeitai officers, men the Westerners had nicknamed the 'gendarmerie' before discovering that, unlike the French, these men had an appetite for unspeakable brutality.

The man in the bunk above watched Theo be dragged out without a word, but he shook his head and mimed the sign of the cross at him as he was pulled away. There was no time to collect any belongings or to tell anyone where he was going. They simply bullied him, bleary and disorientated, to a car waiting beyond the gate.

Theo found himself shivering. He'd had no time to put on his shoes, and he caught sight of himself in the car window, unshaven, haggard, his hair over-long now and straggling. He didn't look like Theodore Carter anymore. He didn't know where he was going and he was acutely aware Zofia would be taking risks to get a message to him in a matter of hours.

Not now! A sense of injustice threatened to overwhelm him.

The car rolled over the potholes of the road, jerking and swerving. Finally, the surface levelled out, and he saw they were coming back into Shanghai. As they came down the Haiphong

Road and into the Bund, the certainty of where they were t... him sank in. The infamous Bridge House, an eight-storey art deco building that now housed the Japanese Gestapo, the Kempeitai secret police.

He was forced to get out right in front o... no illusions that this prison was a place of to... Theo was under Would he have the strength to survive it? Now Jin and death. he was tempted to just let them do what they wante... was gone a deep breath. The sun was just coming up in a pink ha... the rows of boats on the harbour and gulls wheeled and so... over them with their haunting cries. It caught him like a hook, how it could lift his spirits. Even now there was still this beauty in the world.

One of the officers informed him in broken English that he was there for interview. But he was treated like a criminal, told to empty his pockets, and they took his watch and his pen and anything else that hadn't already been taken. They even cut the buttons off his shirt. The messages to Zofia and Evelina were still in his shoes back in the camp. He hoped Mac would find them, rather than the Japs.

He smelled his cell before he got to it. The whole corridor stank of human misery. He was shoved into a cage that was already full of people. He'd expected to be a lone captive, and this was a shock, because already there was no room to move. About fifteen people were crushed together or crouching there, and he was astonished to see there was a woman in there too, huddled against the barred wall. He turned back to look at the door to this cage which was constructed of wooden bars each about six inches thick, spaced about two inches apart. A small square aperture, presumably for food, was cut into it, not big enough for even a head to get through.

It was immediately obvious some of the prisoners had been there weeks if not months, because the first thing that struck him was they looked like old men, hunched and bowed with matted whether she missed her brother. Whether Evelina was giving her enough affection – or if Evelina had reverted to her opium habit which made her self-centred and distant. When he heard sparrows chittering outside the camp, he ached for his children and the summers past.

Since he got the news about Jimmy it had been the longest two weeks of his life, but now there was only one more day to go before he might hear more from Zofia. He prayed for good weather that night, and that she would come.

He settled down to sleep hoping it would make the time go quicker.

'*Okiru! Okiru!*' Theo flinched as rough fingers bit into his arm. The nose of a rifle was at his throat.

He was instantly awake as he was hauled to his feet by two Kempeitai officers, men the Westerners had nicknamed the 'gendarmerie' before discovering that, unlike the French, these men had an appetite for unspeakable brutality.

The man in the bunk above watched Theo be dragged out without a word, but he shook his head and mimed the sign of the cross at him as he was pulled away. There was no time to collect any belongings or to tell anyone where he was going. They simply bullied him, bleary and disorientated, to a car waiting beyond the gate.

Theo found himself shivering. He'd had no time to put on his shoes, and he caught sight of himself in the car window, unshaven, haggard, his hair over-long now and straggling. He didn't look like Theodore Carter anymore. He didn't know where he was going and he was acutely aware Zofia would be taking risks to get a message to him in a matter of hours.

Not now! A sense of injustice threatened to overwhelm him.

The car rolled over the potholes of the road, jerking and swerving. Finally, the surface levelled out, and he saw they were coming back into Shanghai. As they came down the Haiphong

Road and into the Bund, the certainty of where they were taking him sank in. The infamous Bridge House, an eight-storey art deco building that now housed the Japanese Gestapo, the Kempeitai secret police.

He was forced to get out right in front of it. Theo was under no illusions that this prison was a place of torture and death. Would he have the strength to survive it? Now Jimmy was gone he was tempted to just let them do what they wanted. He took a deep breath. The sun was just coming up in a pink haze over the rows of boats on the harbour and gulls wheeled and soared over them with their haunting cries. It caught him like a hook, how it could lift his spirits. Even now there was still this beauty in the world.

One of the officers informed him in broken English that he was there for interview. But he was treated like a criminal, told to empty his pockets, and they took his watch and his pen and anything else that hadn't already been taken. They even cut the buttons off his shirt. The messages to Zofia and Evelina were still in his shoes back in the camp. He hoped Mac would find them, rather than the Japs.

He smelled his cell before he got to it. The whole corridor stank of human misery. He was shoved into a cage that was already full of people. He'd expected to be a lone captive, and this was a shock, because already there was no room to move. About fifteen people were crushed together or crouching there, and he was astonished to see there was a woman in there too, huddled against the barred wall. He turned back to look at the door to this cage which was constructed of wooden bars each about six inches thick, spaced about two inches apart. A small square aperture, presumably for food, was cut into it, not big enough for even a head to get through.

It was immediately obvious some of the prisoners had been there weeks if not months, because the first thing that struck him was they looked like old men, hunched and bowed with matted hair and beards. Stinking of sweat and excrement, they were the poorest specimens of humanity Theo had ever seen.

He pressed himself into the crowd, almost gagging. After he'd been in there about an hour, two stone-faced guards came round and immediately everyone dropped to their knees to face the door. Theo had no choice but to do the same.

'Head count,' whispered the man next to him. 'Don't look at them.'

Theo dropped his gaze but one of the other prisoners, a Chinese man in a bloodstained shirt, his face black and blue with bruises, stayed defiantly standing.

'Oh no, not again,' whispered the man next to Theo.

The guard barked out a command, which a second officer interpreted as 'kneel for the Emperor'.

Still the Chinese man stood. The guard pulled back his fist and smashed it with all his strength into his face.

The Chinese man reeled and went down, falling on top of another man, but scrabbled back to his feet, his mouth gushing blood.

The command to kneel was repeated, but the Chinese man was immovable. So the blow was repeated and again the man struggled to his feet, staggering as if drunk.

The third time the blow knocked him out cold. The other prisoners shuffled aside so he could rest on the filthy ground. The guard rubbed his fist, satisfied, and told his friend to count.

Theo's knees were hurting from crouching in this unfamiliar way, but the count was repeated three times – he was sure just to make them endure it – until after what seemed an interminable time, the door slammed shut and they could all creak back to upright. All except the Chinese man, who remained flaccid on the floor.

There was nothing they could do for him. They had no clean water, no painkillers, nothing. Such inhumane treatment was totally beyond Theo's understanding and left him in a state of terror which was only mirrored by the rest of the men, and the woman, in the cell.

Time lost its meaning as there was no daylight, only electric bulbs, where they were kept, and those only on when the guards did their rounds.

Sleep was impossible unless you clung to the bars to keep yourself upright. There was no room to lie out or stretch his legs. Twice the guards appeared to take someone away and everyone winced at the thuds and shrieks and moans, before the man was brought back, mutilated and barely alive.

The other prisoners stared blank-eyed like animals in a slaughterhouse pen, but Theo tried to close his ears to the whimpering of the woman by the wall, and the groaning of the Chinese prisoner, whose face had swelled up like a balloon. A few of the men arranged for them to shuffle around the small space, all going clockwise, just to move their legs to relieve the pain of so much standing.

Theo quaked, wondering if he'd be able to take it, and whether the fear alone would kill him. He'd no information they could possibly want. He wracked his brains trying to decide if there was anything he could tell them – anything at all that might stop the inevitable torture.

Chapter 20

Cloud obscured the moon and Zofia's knees trembled as she waited again in the bomb crater outside Haiphong Camp. As soon as the patrol was well out of earshot, she set off in the same direction as before, around the perimeter fence. The bicycle juddered over the rough ground as she bounced her way to the dark space between the concrete stanchions and the perimeter lights.

She had transcripts of news from the BBC ready for Theo, facts about what the Americans were doing in the war. Olga's radio was a lifeline to them all, to hear what was really going on outside the limited Japanese propaganda. The papers were still full of the aftermath of Pearl Harbor, and of how the Americans were now at war with the Axis powers.

Zofia had parcelled up the handwritten news from the radio with some Shanghai newspapers and some dried fruit, bought on the black market at incredible expense, and she'd packaged this with a stone for weight.

Nervously she dismounted, close to the glint of the fence, hoping Theo would have got the last message and be on the other side waiting for her. There was no time to lose so she stepped back and, taking a deep breath, threw the parcel up over the fence. She heard a thud and then voices as it landed. She turned the bike quickly around and sat astride it, ready to pedal for her life.

'Hey!' A hissing voice from inside the fence. 'Is that Zofia?'

'Yes. Who's that?'

'Mac. Theo's friend. I've got bad news. He's not here. Been taken to Bridge House. They came for him in the night.'

She went closer and put her face close to the fence. 'You mean arrested?' A whisper.

'Heck knows. They just take people. We dinna know why. Interrogation. Look, I canna stay to talk. Come next week and I'll tell you if he's back.'

'Thank you. Thanks for telling me.'

'He'd want you to know. He was always talking about his wife.'

'I'm not his wife.'

'You're Zofia aren't you? He was always talking about you.' A pause. 'He had letters he wanted you to send. He was going to meet you himself before … well, before they took him. He kept them in his shoes. I'll send them over.'

'What?' But she'd no time to ponder it because a black shape came hurtling over the wire, swiftly followed by another. Then rushed words. 'Shit. Have to go. Bring us a paper with a crossword, can you? And cigarettes.'

Then she heard men's voices and Japanese commands that sounded like 'Away! Out of there'.

She searched the stony ground on her hands and knees. Shoes. His shoes. Why wasn't he wearing them? Would there actually be messages inside? She gathered them both and shoved them into her bicycle panniers, and set off to pedal home, her mind in turmoil. Theo was in Bridge House. The thought of it made her feel sick. He'd been taken without his shoes. She wasn't watching where she was going and the cycle careened into a pothole. It bounced and then the pedals started to spin.

Damn. The chain had come off.

Zofia leapt off and tried to feel for its slippery oiliness in the dark. She found the sprocket but couldn't get the chain to bed into it. The more she tugged at it, the more slippery grew her hands and the metal links, and the more impossible it seemed.

Her mind whirred through the possibilities, her mouth dry. She'd have to push it.

She took hold of the handlebars and hauled it forwards, its chain dragging and the pedal hitting her ankle, making her wince in pain. It was taking too long, but she couldn't move the beast any faster.

She'd have to dump it and run.

Fumbling to retrieve the shoes she knotted the shoelaces together so she could hold them in one hand. She was reliant on the darkness beyond the camp lights. She peeked around the edge of the fence to see if the guards were there.

One of them was out front, his long bamboo pipe in his hand. The thin stream of smoke rose into the air as if from a miniature chimney. When he turned to go back into the guard hut, she let go of the bike, heard it crunch to the ground, and ran.

Her feet barely touched the ground.

'*Yame!*' A sharp yell.

They'd seen her. She sprinted, legs pumping. A shot rang out behind her, but she didn't stop running into the thick dark. Another shot followed but it was well off the mark, hitting the road just as she dived into the ditch.

Her breath rasped in her throat, her lungs heaving fit to burst. She kept her head down, listening. Nothing. After a few moments she dared to raise her head, to see the guards standing over the bicycle.

They dragged it to the side of the gates and dumped it there, more interested in it than in her. She watched them mess with the chain before one of them climbed on the bike and the other pushed it until his friend could wobble down the road. A whoop and a cheer before the first guard got off and turned to drag it back to the compound.

They'd know someone had been there and she hoped it didn't mean the people inside would be punished. She didn't dare come out onto the open road in case they spotted movement and shot at her again. Instead, she kept moving alongside the road in the ditch where the refuse collected. Few cars passed because the Japanese had requisitioned them all, but at one point a Japanese army truck passed her, heading for the camp, and she had to crouch out of view.

The skulking and brief interludes of walking meant it was three hours before she got back to Olga's. When she let herself into the house the place was quiet. Hilly was asleep, motionless, her breath regular, in the bed next to hers.

She put the shoes on the bed and felt around the insides.

There was a slight gap between the insole and the leather base, and she wriggled a finger under it. She could definitely feel paper. It took a moment to prise up the insoles of both shoes enough to draw out the contents. There were three letters. Only one was addressed to her.

Feeling a little light-headed, she took the letters to the bathroom and slid the bolt across. There was no toilet, just a sink and an old, enamelled bathtub set into a panelled wood surround. She lit the old gaslight and sat on the edge of the tub to read. She set the other letters, addressed to Evelina and Daisy, to one side.

Dear Zofia

Here are the letters to Evelina and to Daisy. I thought Daisy should have her own letter at a time like this. She will be lost without her big brother. I feel terrible, stuck here, unable to get home. Please see if you can find envelopes and get the letters sent care of the post office to the Manila Hotel. I will repay you once I get out of here. We will need your help but don't take any risks on our account. I am grateful beyond words that you were brave enough to bring me the news, for I would not have liked to go on imagining Jimmy alive when he was already gone. It can't have been easy to do. You are a true friend.

Yours
Theo

Zofia looked at the other two letters. It was oh-so tempting to read them, but she squashed the desire. Instead, she carefully hid them back in the shoes.

Why had he gone without his shoes?

Too much adrenaline was whooshing through her. She thought of Theo taken barefoot to Bridge House, a place spoken of with horror by the Chinese. But then she also thought of how the man behind the fence, Mac, said Theo had spoken of her. Often.

The fact Theo's friend thought her to be his wife – well, she didn't know what to make of that. On the one had it was flattering, but on the other hand the feeling of longing was drowned out by the feeling of guilt, both for Evelina and for Haru.

Theo and Evelina had just lost a child, for heaven's sake.

Yet she couldn't help remembering Theo's serious face when he was going to kiss her. The touch of his lips.

Stop thinking of it.

But her mind kept churning. How could she go back there now? Number one, she no longer had a bicycle. Number two, they'd be looking out for someone now, could even have extra patrols. It would be foolish to return. Yet the thought of not knowing if Theo was alive or dead – well that was something she couldn't bear. She'd been waiting over a year to find out about her brother Jacek, and that long wait of not knowing still twisted like a wire around her heart. She was not sure if she could bear another lost soul.

She took the shoes back to the bedroom and she was about to put them under her mattress when Hilly sat up in bed.

'You've been out,' she said. 'I woke up and you weren't there. Where did you go?'

'Just out for a walk.'

'Not a walk. I went to find you and your bicycle was gone.' Hilly was sometimes surprisingly sharp.

'I needed some air.' Zofia shrugged, pushing the shoes out of sight.

'What's that? Did you go dancing?'

'No, of course not.'

'Why've you put those shoes under there?'

'Because a refugee left them on the street.'

'Ha! Those aren't a refugee's shoes. They're Theo's. The ones he was wearing when he went away. With the little fancy holes all cut in them.'

'Not much gets past you, does it?'

And then a pause before she looked up. 'Is he dead?' It was almost a whisper.

'No!' Zofia was vehement, and she rushed to hug Hilly tight. 'Of course not.'

Hilly squirmed away. 'Then where is he? Have you seen him?'

'Just in a camp.' She thought quickly. 'I'm to get them mended for him. A friend from the camp gave me them. But it's a secret. A present. So we won't tell anyone, will we?'

She frowned. 'There are a lot of secrets. Zha Wei told me I was to keep his secret.'

Zofia stiffened. 'When? Has he been here?'

'When you were out.' Hilly shuffled back on the bed.

'What secret? What's he done now?'

'Nothing.' Then under Zofia's scrutiny, she tilted her head and said, 'Just a kiss. And before you ask, no I didn't like it. But I couldn't refuse, could I?'

Zofia tried to stay calm. 'You must never do anything you don't want to do.'

'He's Charlie's friend and I don't know where we'd go if they threw us out.'

'But Hils, Charlie would be horrified if he thought Zha Wei was taking advantage of you like that.'

She stood up, indignant. 'Charlie saw! He went to get some papers and when he came back, he saw him through the open door, trying to kiss me, and afterwards I told him I didn't like it and he … he told me not to tell Olga or it would cause trouble.'

'What?'

'He told me to keep it a secret too. Like everyone has to please Zha Wei and nobody can say anything against him.'

Shit. It was worse than she imagined. 'If anyone asks you to keep a secret again, you must tell me.'

Hilly looked doubtful. 'But what about Theo? You asked me to—'

'That's different. We're friends, okay? Sisters.'

'Then if we're sisters, can I come with you next time? I'm scared. I don't like being here all on my own.'

'There won't be a next time because I haven't got my bike anymore.'

Hilly came back to sit on the edge of Zofia's bed. She picked at the edge of the blanket, pulling off fluff. 'Why not? Where is it?'

'It was stolen. By the Japanese.' This wasn't the truth, but it was the best she could offer.

Hilly sighed. 'I miss Madam Wang. I miss how it was before the Japanese came. Do you think she's forgotten me?'

'No. She liked you – she told me you were good with the customers.'

'She might be in a camp like Theo.'

Zofia sighed. 'Get some sleep.' But at the same time, she herself couldn't sleep. She'd too many worries. And now Hilly and Zha Wei to add to them.

But more than that, the message from Theo replayed over and over behind her eyes. The neat slope of his writing – *you are a true friend*. She wondered if he would ever be released from Bridge House. Some people who went in there were never heard from again.

When Hilly was sleeping, Zofia took Charlie to task over Zha Wei. Olga was working nights at the hospital, so Charlie was still up, poring over messages and transcripts.

'Hilly says Zha Wei forced her to kiss him and you told her not to tell.'

'She's making it up.'

'You know damn well she's not. She told me you saw. You told her not to tell because Olga would get mad.'

Charlie glanced around guiltily as if Olga might appear at any moment. 'I don't know what the fuss is. It was only a little peck. She was making eyes at him.'

'Don't be crazy. You know she smiles at everyone, because she's too terrified to do anything else.'

'She was fraternizing with the Japs, that's what Olga said.'

'Oh Olga this, Olga that! She's so obsessed with being a good Catholic. Yet she's in your bed every night, the hypocrite.'

'You can't talk, you and Theo—'

'Never had a chance!' she shouted over him. 'We never had a chance. And do you know why Hilly's like she is? Because she was raped by a Nazi soldier when they took away her mother, that's why. So if I find out anyone, and I mean anyone, has interfered with that girl, they'll have me to deal with, and I'm not above reporting the pair of you if I think he'll do anything to her. I'm not the one on the run, Charlie Hargreaves, or whoever the hell you are, remember that.'

'Shut up.' Charlie's face was red and his mouth pressed together, but he finally capitulated. 'All right. I'll tell him she's out of bounds.'

'You'd better.'

Charlie gave her a glowering look, turned his back and began to fiddle with the radio.

It was then she turned to see Hilly staring at her, stricken, from the doorway.

Chapter 21

After two nights of hell in the cage at Bridge House, Theo was finally summoned for his first interview in the Kempeitai offices on the fourth floor. As he was taken, all the other prisoners looked at the ground. They were so cowed, no one would even wish him luck.

The interrogation room was three times the size of his cell, and well appointed in the Western style. Theo noticed the teak sideboard and the glow of parchment shaded lamps; he supposed it was his mind searching for something else to think about other than torture.

'Be brave for Jimmy,' he thought.

The interrogator, Lieutenant Yamamoto, was a thin-faced man, a good foot shorter than Theo, but he sat down in a leisurely way as Theo was brought in.

'Aha, Mr Carter,' he said, puffing out smoke. 'We need to ask you a few questions.' His English was passable, or at least understandable, although the accent was thick. 'It is about business.'

Theo raised his eyebrows but waited. He knew better than to assume anything. He remained aloof and impassive and stuck his trembling hands in his pockets.

'The rice shipments from India to Shanghai don't come. We have trouble now from the Chinese, from beggars, thieves cutting rice bags, stealing food from our shop counters. We deport them when we can catch them. But our stores are low. So, you will help us.'

'How can I help?' He'd try to be pleasant, even though he was sure some worse treatment would be coming.

The Kempeitai officer directly behind him lit a cigarette. Theo startled at the strike of the match behind him, the hiss of the flame and the officer's sharp indraw of breath.

'Your account with Bombay. We need a signature. The India office will not send supplies without a signature.'

Theo's eyes widened. So it was truly about business. These were deals he'd brokered before the invasion. Indian rice in return for Chinese silk. He remembered Abhishek from Bombay, who he called Abi – his polite, almost too rich English accent, his smiling expression when they last met.

There were papers on the desk in front of Yamamoto, a whole pile of them.

Theo knew he had to sign, there was no choice. And besides, it would make no difference to him if he wasn't to get out of here alive in the end.

He reached for the pen and started to read the document. Suddenly a piercing pain. The guard behind him had stubbed out his cigarette on the back of his hand.

'Sign quickly now, Mr Carter. We have no time to waste.'

Theo blinked the water from his eyes and resisted the urge to rub at the blister forming on his hand.

Behind him, he heard the strike of another match, and his stomach heaved. But he picked up the papers in a measured way and scanned each one, pretending not to be afraid.

Again, the hot stab of a burning cigarette to the back of his hand.

Now it was really smarting. There were several more to sign but he refused to be hurried.

By the end, he'd seven burns on his left hand, which had been holding the papers steady while he signed.

He pushed the last one towards Yamamoto.

'Get him on transport,' Yamamoto said to the man with the cigarettes.

Transport? Where?

They led him out into the night, his hand throbbing so much he daren't put it in his pocket or touch anything. A car was waiting and he was gestured into it. He was nauseous with pain and shock, and as the car drove off, he feared he might be going to his execution. The headlights of the car cut through the fog and showed they were headed out of Shanghai. At least it was away from the Bridge Hotel.

The driver was a man who could be Korean, not Japanese, because of his height. He glanced at Theo in the mirror in a way that made him think he was memorizing his face. The guard beside him stared fixedly out of the window with his hand on his gun. Theo too peered out as the car slowed. A crossroads. The car swerved left down a minor road.

Barbed wire. A watchtower.

Another camp, not the familiar Haiphong. Theo's spirits plummeted and he squeezed his one good hand into a fist.

A Japanese officer came out to meet him, and the driver wound down the window. 'Mistercarter,' he said, running the words together as if they were one word.

The officer nosed him out with the gun, shouting in frenzied Japanese. Theo had no idea what he was saying but didn't react, staring straight ahead as the car backed away and drove off. He refused to bow his head which was what was always expected. Insects bit his face and neck and he tried in vain to brush them away, before he was allowed indoors to a barracks which already housed about thirty other men.

In the back of his mind lingered the thought of Zofia, who would have risked her life to go to the Haiphong Camp tonight, and he wouldn't have showed. Maybe she'd think he'd forgotten her.

A big Australian man approached him.

'Read you the riot act, did he?' he asked.

'I didn't understand a word,' Theo said.

'Camp rules. No escaping, punishment of death. No breaking any camp rules. Punishment of death. No answering back—'

'I get it. Punishment of death.'

'Smart-arse.' The Australian grinned. 'Welcome to the Ritz. Otherwise known as Woosung Shithole. I mean Camp.'

Chapter 22

Zofia came out of the bedroom where Hilly was using the dressing table for her copying. She sat at the kitchen table and toyed with a pencil. She was unable to concentrate on the newspapers and documents she was supposed to be transcribing. Two days Theo had been in Bridge House and the corrosive thought of it made Zofia distracted and morose. Charlie was sitting by the sideboard and frowning, headphones on, his face pressed close to the radio.

'What's this? Two long faces?' Olga bustled in from outside. 'No Western bread, just rice cakes. You two been arguing again?'

'We never argue,' Charlie said, pulling off his headphones. 'Isn't that right?' He shot a barbed look to Zofia.

'If you say so,' she said.

Charlie pushed back his chair and his face turned serious. 'I just heard, not only have the Japs got deeper into the Northern territories, but they've taken the Philippines – set the Brits to slave labour. Hilly's copying the transcript now.'

'The Philippines?' Where Evelina and Daisy were. 'What about the wives? The children?'

Charlie shrugged. 'Dunno. Camps like here, I suppose.'

Oh no. Heaven help Theo if he ever found out. She sat down

on a chair opposite Charlie. 'I might as well tell you. Theo's been taken to Bridge House.'

Charlie started. 'When? Why the hell didn't you tell us?'

'I wasn't sure what to do.'

'When?'

'Two days ago.'

'How do you know?' Olga asked. The pair of them were hostile. It disconcerted her.

'I went to the camp.'

'What? To Haiphong?' Olga was astounded. 'And they let you in?'

'No. I talked to one of his friends through the fence. Went there at night, in the dark.'

'Are you crazy? You must be lovesick. Either that or you've lost your tiny mind.'

'Neither.' she raised her chin. 'His son died. It was months ago now. I thought he should know.' She explained about the letter from Evelina.

'My God, that's awful. Poor bastard,' Charlie said.

'And his wife and daughter, they evacuated to Manila. The Philippines. The place the Japanese have just taken over.'

This news moved Charlie not at all. He leaned forward, hands on his knees. 'What were you thinking? You should have told us about Theo as soon as it happened. He might blab. Might tell them where I'm hiding. It puts us all at risk.'

'He won't talk,' Zofia said.

'We can't be certain,' Olga insisted. 'They sometimes hold them for months, soften them up for interrogation. We'd better move on, find a safer space to hide.'

All of them were silent a moment. The thought of moving somewhere else was too hard to take in.

'Let's not be hasty,' Zofia said. 'Maybe Theo's out by now. Isn't there a way we can find out?'

'Maybe Zha Wei might have some ideas,' Charlie said.

Zofia sighed.

'Be snooty about him if you like, but he's our best contact. Information never comes for free in Shanghai. But Zha Wei's got a vested interest in keeping me out of Jap hands, after all. Without me, he'd lose his supply of information from the BBC.'

'You mean, without us,' Zofia said pointedly.

'I don't see the problem. Why don't you just go back to the camp?' asked Olga. 'After all, you did it before.'

Zofia shook her head. 'Too risky. The security will be tighter now … there's something else I need to tell you.' She hesitated. 'I'm sorry, but I had to leave the bike there.' She explained how she had to abandon it and run, and the Japanese had taken it. 'I can't get it back, and they'll be warned off now about messages from the outside.'

Charlie stood up, bristling. 'Will they be able to track it to us? You didn't leave anything in the basket did you?'

'Of course not.'

Olga threw up her hands. 'Bicycles are like gold dust – how could you be so stupid?'

'It was a clanky old thing. I told you; the chain fell off. It wasn't my fault.'

'It was stupid, to go to the camp,' Olga said.

Hilly came in from the room next door. 'What's all the shouting?'

'We're not shouting,' said Zofia and Charlie in unison.

'Zofia's lost her bicycle,' said Olga.

'Oh, that,' said Hilly. 'She told me.'

'Look, I'm sorry about the bike. But that's not important. We have to think about Theo. There has to be some way we can find out if he's still in Bridge House.'

'Bridge House?' Hilly said. 'Where's that?'

'Forget him. The only thing we know, is that we need to move on,' Charlie said. 'If he tells them I've got Russian papers under the name of Maksim … then we're toast. We must find somewhere else to go, the quicker the better. We'd better start packing.'

'No,' Hilly wailed. 'We don't have to move again?'

'It's for Charlie, to keep him safe.' Zofia said, trying to hug her and placate her.

Hilly pushed her away, hard. 'I heard what he said about me, that I was making eyes at Zha Wei. It's a lie. And I don't see why everything must revolve around Charlie. I need a life too!'

Zofia saw Olga fix Charlie with a look that clearly said 'say something'.

But Charlie was not courageous enough to throw Zofia out. He went up to Hilly. 'Now look, young lady, you should just be damn grateful you've got a roof over your head and you're not out on the street like the beggars.'

'Nobody takes any notice of what I want. It's just "do this", "do that, Hilly", and nobody even asks what I think about it all.' And she went out with a slam of the door.

Zofia sighed. She didn't want to move either, and more than that, she didn't want to live with these people. But it was the hand she'd been dealt and she'd do it to keep Hilly safe, even if Hilly couldn't understand that was why she was doing it.

Chapter 23

Woosung Camp

Theo grasped straight away that the camp was too far from Shanghai to get any message to the outside world. In here, he was one of a ragbag of people – US officers from the *Wake*, Australians, British and an assortment of other nationalities in this hut they called his 'section'. His bed was a bare splintery board on a raised platform. Four cotton blankets were thrown to each man, but these were too thin to be of any use to pad out their bunks. His clothes had been taken and he was put into camp uniform – trousers that were too short and a mildewed vest and jacket.

On the first night he was too tired and depressed to speak to anyone. He imagined Zofia waiting for him in vain, and it galled him he wouldn't be with his friend Mac. His hand festered and throbbed. He knew he'd escaped lightly. Others had smashed legs, dislocated shoulders or had endured the horrors of water torture. But he was beginning to realize he'd never see his son again, and none of the physical pain was as bad as the leaden grief inside his heart.

That night it rained, a thick downpour that battered the tin roof. Impossible to sleep, even if his hip bones hadn't dug into the bunk. A fetid wind from the Whangpoo river blew in through the broken windows.

When he woke, bleary-eyed, to roll call and shouts in Japanese, he staggered to his feet. The big Australian was just standing up too and gave him a grin.

It revived him enough to speak. 'Suppose it's too much to hope for breakfast,' Theo said.

The Aussie gave a rueful smile, 'Got it in one,' he said. He was large red-headed man with ruddy cheeks. 'Make sure you always sleep in your shoes. If you don't, someone'll have 'em. It's happened every camp I've been in.'

'No problem. I don't have any. I hadn't time to put them on before I got dragged to Bridge House.'

'Ah. They're always doing that. That's why the ones in here get pinched. Someone dies or leaves, they auction their shoes for cigarettes. Better start doing favours so you can trade for cigs.'

'Thanks for telling me. I'm Theo,' he said.

'Lennie. Used to work for the Telecom in Shanghai.'

'Shipping merchant,' said Theo.

Lennie made a face as if to say it wasn't a real job. But he stuck by Theo's side as they went out into the yard out front with the rest to be counted. 'I'll see if I can get you some sandals,' he said. 'Or you won't last long.'

He was right. The ground was stony and walking on it was painful. Theo hobbled his way into the line of men from his hut. Through spattered rain he was able to see the camp perimeter was surrounded by two electric fences and a ragged partial palisade. The sight made him sigh. There was a farm on one side by a couple of bare trees. A rough road ran by it and he could make out the badly tiled roofs of two shacks, presumably occupied by Chinese farm workers.

Theo felt bleakness descend. His third incarceration and it

looked just as soul-destroying – seven ramshackle old wooden barracks, each divided into sections, thirty men in each section.

The Japanese soldiers lined them up and kept them standing in the pelting downpour whilst they inspected their barracks. Afterwards Lennie and Theo were detailed to go to the mess hall – a draughty wooden building with large cauldrons set in brickwork over coal fires. About twenty other men were there to help prepare the food, which was rice and squid stew. At least it was warmer in there, though thick with steam and his clothes were still damp. The stew contained the ends of lotus root and *gai choy*, and it bubbled, greyish and greasy, more like dishwater than anything that could be a meal. The rice was full of stones and the congee overboiled to a sticky mush – and there was not enough of it. But at least they'd get to eat something. Theo's stomach was groaning with hunger.

Lennie was set onto making tea in a huge, blackened pot. It seemed the water wasn't safe to drink so 'tea' – boiled water with a few leaves chucked in, was to be their main liquid intake.

'The tea and the soup look the same,' Theo said.

'Too damn right,' Lennie agreed, shaking his big gingery head. 'There's not enough protein in that to keep a Jap alive, never mind a tall fella like me.'

'We'll have to try to grow something, or starve.'

'Got green fingers have you?'

'You've got to be joking.' He held out his hands – still peppered with blisters and burns from Bridge House.

'You've got fingernails though. Some bastards haven't.'

The four cotton blankets gave some sort of shelter, and many men wore them wrapped around their heads and shoulders in layers all the time, so it was like mingling with ghosts.

'Does anyone ever get out of here?' Theo asked.

Lennie laughed. 'In a box, yes. Otherwise, no. And to be truthful they don't even give you a box.'

'Well I intend to escape.'

Lennie rolled his eyes. 'Guess you'll be needing that box sooner then.'

All men were forced to sign a piece of paper to swear they wouldn't try to escape, on pain of death. Theo watched with amazement as one of the men, an old Brit, Major Griffiths, refused to sign.

He addressed the Japanese soldier with a haughty expression. 'I'll have you know it's my duty to try to escape and a matter of honour. None of the men here will sign,' he said.

Theo exchanged a glance with Lennie because he'd already signed.

The major gave a lecture about the Geneva Convention, but the Japanese were unmoved. Food would be withdrawn until everyone signed.

Mass groans, but nobody wanted to take on the ire of Major Griffiths. Theo, who found the old guy only marginally less intimidating than the Japanese, shook his head.

They were set to polishing shell cases in a long wooden hut on the opposite side of the camp. No talking allowed. He coughed through the day, his lungs protesting against the dust and fumes of rust and polish.

Fights broke out over lack of food, until Major Griffiths was ambushed by internees and reluctantly advised the men to sign the 'no escape' paper. Horror when they realized too late they had actually signed conscript papers for the Japanese Imperial Army. Complaining about being conscripted was useless. It did, of course, give the guards an excuse to beat them for insubordination whenever they felt like it.

Theo ruminated on the possibility of getting out and watched carefully when supplies came into the camp. Coolies arrived with carts of provisions each day, their chicken-bone bodies hauling the goods by sheer manpower, their worn-out straw sandals straining against the muddy, potholed roads. They rested the carts at the outside perimeter fence, by the electric wire. It was all strictly supervised by armed men.

Despite their regular appearance, Theo couldn't get close to any of the coolies, and he knew he would need help on the outside. His immediate thought was Zofia, and now he was in here, the CCP. Too late he realized he should have been more sympathetic to Zha Wei and his men. But Zofia was the only one who he'd had any contact with since being interned. Trouble was, how would she even know he was here?

He took a particular interest in the two shacks close to the perimeter fence. One near the gate – this he dismissed, and one to the south of the camp. Because the land there ran next to the road, the two sections of wire were closer together. There was a guard post on the corner though, so there was no easy way to get a message to the people in there, even if they were friendly.

He discussed it with Lennie. 'We need an excuse to be by that fence,' he said.

'Like what?'

'A football pitch, badminton net?'

'There's already sports in the yard. They'd just tell us to play there.'

'What about trying to do what you suggested – get a garden growing there.'

'The major's already starting one. But it's a scruffy affair, round the back of the kitchens.'

'Really? I never put him down as that kind of man.'

'Gives him something to organize, doesn't it?'

Theo went to have a look. The 'garden' was just being marked out in the dirt. The major had rounded up a few people to try to make a kind of allotment where they could grow vegetables. The other prisoners made fun of this scruffy patch of ground, but Major Griffiths was determined. He was intent on scrounging root ends or seeds and raising at least a few potatoes or greens to supplement the godawful gruel and soup. He had begun to lay it out with military precision and developed a round-the-clock watch in case anyone should interfere with it or steal his precious tubers.

There was only one problem with this garden. It was in the wrong place. It needed to be near the farmers' shacks.

Theo worried about Evelina and Daisy. He had this idea that if he could only get out of here and get home, then Jimmy would no longer be dead, and his life would go back to how it had been before. He knew rationally this was nonsense, but the urge to escape and go to his son, even though it was too late, was intense.

He recognized his body was getting weaker from lack of nourishment and activity, and so he took to a rigorous routine of push-ups and squats. To exert himself was excruciating, as his body lacked the fuel he needed; still, he knew he had to risk a break-out sooner rather than later. If he left it too long, he'd be too weak.

But he couldn't do it alone. He'd need to mobilize a few others to help him. The burly Australian, Lennie, was an obvious choice, but he needed someone else reliable. A team of three would be the best — as they would certainly need a lookout.

He told Lennie he was going to ask the major to move his plot, so the garden would give the team a chance for cover and to get messages to the outside world so someone could help them.

'Then what about asking him to join us?' said Lennie.

'Old Griffiths?' Theo made a face. 'I hadn't planned on asking him. Just seeing if he'd mind us starting up another garden. He'd probably try to stop us. Regulations and all that.'

'He's got authority. We need someone with that kind of mind. Someone who's not afraid and doesn't give a shit about anything except orders.'

'You sure? I don't want him bossing us about.'

A shrug. 'Maybe. But I'd bet your bottom dollar if he gave you his word, he'd stick to it through hell and high water.'

'All right. I'll ask him. But it's a risk. He might decide it's a danger to the other prisoners – that there might be repercussions. Then he might report us.'

'Can't think of anyone else with enough backbone. The rest are too unreliable.'

'Okay, matey. I'll see if I can find him.'

Major Griffiths was easy to find, in the 'garden' near the back of the kitchens.

'Hi,' said Theo approaching him with a smile.

Griffiths looked at him with cold blue eyes, his mouth a thin line under his greying moustache. 'What?'

'I'd like a few words, won't take long.'

'Something the matter?'

'No.' He beckoned him away from the other men who were scraping at the soil with their bare hands and trying to mark out areas with stones. 'It's like this. We wondered if you'd be interested in … well, Lennie and I thought …'

'Spit it out.'

'Getting out. An escape plan.'

'Hmm. Who's Lennie?'

Theo couldn't help but notice the spark of curiosity in those blue eyes.

'Big Australian, red beard.'

'Just three?'

'Yes. Too many would be hard to manage.'

Griffiths waited for more, eyes screwed up in concentration.

'And it would involve moving your garden.'

Now he looked Theo up and down with an assessing gaze. 'Why?'

'Can't tell you unless you swear your silence.'

'Then it's no go. You can see how much thought's gone into this already.' He gestured at the men shifting stones.

Theo couldn't, but he persevered. 'That's why we need you. We need a planner.'

Griffiths' eyes flickered, but his face was fixed like wood. 'I might be interested. But only if it's plotted meticulously. No half-baked rushing at it. A proper operation.'

Theo felt his shoulders relax. 'That's why we picked you. We knew you'd want it that way.' He held out his hand.

The major wiped the dirt off his hand with care and grasped Theo's. 'When shall we—?'

He bit off his words. A Japanese guard was approaching.

'Glad to have you and Lennie as volunteers in the garden,' said the major, slapping him on the back and nailing him with a meaningful look.

Oh shit. Now they were really going to have to dig with their bare hands.

Griffiths saw his expression and let out a bark of a laugh. 'Hard work never hurt anyone. I'll expect you both here after roll call.'

Now he was giving the orders. How had it turned from his plan into the major's?

The Japanese soldier approached. 'You.' He gestured at Theo to move off.

The major intervened, stepping between them, his upright bearing giving him a huge height advantage over the Japanese man. He spoke loudly and firmly. 'Carter has volunteered to help grow things in our garden. He will be here every afternoon.'

The soldier didn't understand or didn't like what was being said, or took offence at the man's manner, who knew? He struck the major a blow across the face with the truncheon he carried at his belt. Griffiths didn't move, though his head jerked to the side and the thud of wood on bone made Theo wince.

The skin of the major's cheek was broken, and his eyes watered. But the sight of his imperturbable expression sent the soldier into more of a rage and he carried on screaming at him for another few minutes. Still Griffiths didn't move. Finally, he gave the short man a look of disdain and turned away to carry on marking out his scrubby patch.

Theo was humbled by this. He went back to Lennie and said, 'You were right. He's a maniac. But he's our man.' He outlined what had happened.

'Told you. We can have the ideas, but he'll be the one who dots the i's and crosses the t's. And he'll never give up.'

Chapter 24

Major Griffiths, who Theo now familiarly called Griff, braved the guards to see if they could move the garden. He told them the light was better there and so was the soil. After a bit of argy-bargy they agreed, so long as they could have half the produce. Griff had no option but to agree as they would probably take it anyway, whatever he did.

The Japanese thought it a matter of great amusement that the major should want to dig all over again. On the first day, they watched him and laughed as if it were a big joke. But then they built a new guard post, right at the entrance to the garden, complete with a shelter against the rain. Each worker had to be checked in and out, as did any tools.

'It's going to be hard to do anything right under their noses,' Lennie complained.

Griff was pragmatic. 'We've nothing better to do, and even if it doesn't work, at least we'll have some fresh food.'

'Except we're going to get out of here before we eat a single bite,' Theo said. 'We need to focus on those shacks. Try to make contact however we can.'

They met every afternoon in the new garden. There was a four-foot distance between the first electrified fence and the 'garden', with a gravel path that ran right around the camp near the fence, so the soldiers could patrol there. In between digging out stones, pulling up tough fibrous weeds and trying to turn the claggy soil over with their bare hands, they watched the comings and goings from the southernmost shack, which seemed to be inhabited by an elderly bicycle-rickshaw man and his wife.

After a few weeks, they managed to make their first contact with the woman. A short, squat individual with a lined and weathered face, she'd been watching them scrabble in the dirt each time she hung out her threadbare clothes to dry. On that day, Theo, who had pidgin Chinese, wished her a good day, pointed to the ground and told her what they had planted.

'Good. You wait!' she mimed, wagging a finger at him.

She trotted into the house and after ten minutes or so, she came out with a piece of hollow bamboo with cloth tied at both ends. This container she placed close to the perimeter wire, walking along until she found a place with a gap beneath it where there was a depression in the ground. 'You grow,' she said. 'Pak choi. Understand?'

Theo looked hopelessly at the bamboo package. He bowed his thanks.

She seemed to understand he would need to devise a way to collect it, flapped a hand and walked away. Theo felt the first flutter of hope in a month. He immediately went to find Lennie. 'There's a package for us out by the wire,' he said, the words spilling out. 'The woman from the shack has given us some seeds in a bamboo tube. But we need a long stick or something to drag it in.'

'They'll shoot us if they catch us too close to the wire,' Lennie said. 'Best bet's in the dark after curfew, when the Japs can't see what we're doing. But I'll see if I can find something long enough.'

Theo grabbed his arm. 'Don't you see what this means? She might take a message. Find us help outside.'

'Now hold on, matey, she might, and she might not. She might report us to the Japs. We have to be careful.'

Of course Griff had to know too, and he planned the schedule. They used string to tie a broom to a hook fashioned out of a piece of metal cut from a milk tin. They'd been allowed to pierce milk tins to use as watering cans, and Griff had used the awl they'd been given to make holes close together so a part could be torn away. All tools were checked back in, but Griff kept the sharp metal hook in his sleeve until he got out of view.

In the black moonless night they sneaked out when the guard went for his smoke, and pushed this long hook contraption under the wire. Griff kept watch because they reckoned he'd be able to stall the Japs if they came. It was after curfew, and they would be severely punished if found outside.

Lennie, whose arms were the longest, had to lie on his stomach and push the thing through. Like some sort of fairground 'hook a duck' game, this wasn't nearly as easy as it looked. The precious bamboo container kept rolling away and once they thought they'd lost it.

A cough from too close behind. A Japanese guard on patrol.

Theo dragged the pole back as Lennie scrambled to his feet. Theo and Griff were quicker and dived for cover into the dark shadow of one of the barracks.

The Japanese patrol had spotted Lennie but he pretended to urinate against the side of the hut. They heard the soldier shout at him and Griff and Theo held each other's gazes as they waited, with bated breath. They heard a thud and a grunt of pain, sharp orders in Japanese, and then another groan and the scuffle of footsteps moving away. The patrol moved on.

They waited another ten minutes before daring to come out again, by which time there was no sign of Lennie. The only good thing was, they'd heard no shots.

'What do you think they'll do to him?' Theo whispered.

'The cooler, probably.' Griff said. 'What now? Carry on, or leave it?'

'We give it another go. It will have to be me because I'm tallest. You keep watch like before.'

After another frustrating time of juggling the hook to try and get the bamboo tube, Theo finally dragged it through.

He almost leapt up and down, so great was his excitement.

'Sssh!' Griff warned him. 'Get back inside where they can't see you. Open it in the light.'

They crept back towards the barracks and after waiting again for the guard to move away, let themselves in.

The next morning Theo was in the garden early waiting for Griff. Once he was through the sentry point, he had to wait until the coast was clear before they could see what was in the container.

'How's Lennie?' Griff asked.

'Not good. The bastard hit him in the kidneys with his rifle. He spent the night in agony. And this morning they came for him and put him in the cooler. Making an example of him to warn us all to stay in our billets at night.'

There was nothing else to say. The cooler meant solitary confinement in a small damp hut, half underground, with no light.

Theo pored over the bamboo tube as they knelt, backs bent, pretending to dig. He passed it to Griff, who carefully unwound the string, then peeled off the blue calico cloth. Nothing must go to waste. Griff drew out a small piece of paper and unfolded it to reveal the tiny black specks of seeds. On the paper there were some scribbled Chinese kanji. Both Theo and Griff recognized them as the Chinese for 'good fortune.'

'That was kind,' Griff said.

Theo grinned. 'But even better, it means she's literate and friendly. Are you thinking what I'm thinking …?'

'You bet. We'll have to think carefully about what to write. It might be our only chance to get a message out. And she could snitch on us and that could have repercussions for all the other prisoners too.'

'We have to risk it,' Theo said. 'Or who knows when we might get another chance.'

'But we should minimize the risk.'

Yes, that was Griff all over. Cautious, organized, and frustratingly pedantic.

They eventually settled on a short note. *Please will you take a message to our friend in Shanghai? We will send at night.* No signature, so they couldn't be identified.

They sealed the tube in the same way with the message inside. Next time the woman came out to hang her washing on the line, they were ready, with Griff keeping watch. Theo waved and pointed. They'd pushed the bamboo back through the fence with its message. He gestured with sign language she should open and read.

She seemed to understand but didn't pick up the message, scurrying behind the garments dangling on the line.

He saw why then – one of the guards was on outside patrol near the fence. Theo held his breath. Would he spot the package? To Theo it looked all too obvious, lying on the scrubby grass next to the track.

The woman stayed behind the flapping clothes and the guard glanced at her as he passed. She dipped her head in the kind of obeisance the Japanese liked. It was enough to distract the soldier from the bamboo parcel, and he walked on, but not without a quick look their way. Theo carried on scraping at the earth.

The man on patrol walked on, and several minutes later the woman darted over and picked up the parcel.

Theo hurried over to where Griff was working, with one eye on the sentry post. 'She's got it,' he said, elated.

'So now we wait. One of us must go every night and see if she leaves us another parcel.'

There was still no sign of Lennie, and they knew conditions in the cooler were hell. The tin roof made it freezing in winter. No bed, no blankets, no company, barely fed or watered. A sentry was on twenty-four-hour duty so they couldn't get near it to find out if he was okay.

For two nights they went out, afraid of being caught out of barracks, and ending up in the cooler like Lennie. No bamboo tube.

'She's got cold feet,' said Griff with a resigned sigh.

'Give her a few more days.' Theo was unwilling to give up hope.

The next day they saw them drag Lennie out. He'd been beaten and his face and arms were a mass of bruises. They didn't dare stare too hard, but could see he'd lost weight, and could hardly stand.

'Still want to risk going out tonight?' Griff asked.

A nod. Theo just wanted to be on the other side of that wire, no matter what it took.

'Not sure it's worth the risk to the others,' Griff said.

'Then I'll go alone.'

Griff sighed. 'All right, you've twisted my arm. Someone's got to watch your sorry arse.'

Theo smiled, and as soon as the soldiers left him alone, went to find Lennie.

He had two cracked ribs and a broken collarbone and could barely speak for pain.

'Sorry you had to carry the can,' Theo said.

'Haha. Bad joke. You get through? Any joy?'

Theo explained their contact seemed to have dried up.

'You've got to keep going. Or what's all this for?' He gestured to his bruised face.

The night was cold, and a swirling fog had wound its way into the camp. They could only see a few feet in front of them. Unsurprisingly it made everyone cough, including the guards, who turned up their overcoat collars against its creeping autumn chill and hurried on their rounds with their heads down.

'I think I can see something,' Griff said, peering through the gloom. 'I'll go keep watch.'

Theo squinted through the milky haze. He was right. There was something.

He had the technique a little better this time, and the long broom and hook worked well to drag the bamboo back in.

'Got it,' he whispered to Griff as they passed, and each melted away into the dark.

The next morning Griff accosted him even before their hot tea and congee. 'Well?'

'She'll do it.'

'Bingo!' His eyes fired up with glee. But then he immediately said, 'We can't waste this chance. We need proper watertight procedures.'

'And Lennie comes with us.'

'He won't be fit enough. He can hardly move.'

'We're all in it together. It's our fault he got hurt. I won't go without him.'

'He's a risk. We have to be prepared to lose men. That's war.'

'It might be your war, but it sure as hell ain't mine.'

Chapter 25

It was Hilly's birthday and Zofia was determined to make it some sort of occasion. Fourteen years old. Old enough to get a paid job, had there been no war. Hilly had been thrilled with a petticoat slip Zofia had made from peacock-coloured silk. She'd cut it from a disintegrating *changpao* found on a market stall.

'It's dreamy – like the sea and the sky!' Hilly hugged Zofia till she was breathless.

There were no gifts for Zofia on her birthday; it had passed unnoticed by anyone. The shophouses were impoverished. Japanese soldiers had collected Western metal goods for their war effort, so now their typewriter and alarm clock had to be hidden every day along with the radio. Shell or bullet factories had opened where textile factories used to be. Zofia had unpicked a man's pullover and knitted herself a cardigan. It was brown, not a very attractive colour, but at least it was warm.

Weeks had passed and they'd heard nothing more about Theo. Zofia prayed in the best way she knew how, a yearning plea made of the same longing she had for her lost brother.

Olga and Charlie were on edge and it made them short-tempered. Olga had been out every day scouting for a new place for Charlie to go, but it was hard to find anyone they dare trust, and so many houses had Japanese neighbours now, or Nazis nearby, or collaborators who would hand Charlie over. The women too would be in danger if anyone discovered they were in league with the CCP.

So when the knock came at the door, Zofia froze, before shoving all the documents she was transcribing under the rug at her feet.

'You expecting anyone?' Charlie asked.

Zofia shook her head, placed her chair over the rug and went to peer out from behind the bamboo blind. 'No Japanese soldiers.'

'Don't answer it,' said Olga. 'Charlie, get ready to go.'

'Shall I hide in the bedroom?' asked Hilly, her eyes wide with fear.

'There's no truck. No soldiers.' Zofia continued to look out and saw an elderly woman step back away from the door and look up. She seemed to be aware of them and that someone might be looking out. 'It's an old woman,' she said. 'Chinese.' She turned to Charlie. 'Is she one of yours?'

'It could be Madam Wang!' Hilly said.

'It's not her. Stay there.'

Charlie jumped up to the window and stared out. The woman was still waiting. She was dressed in a faded pink Chinese padded coat, a cloth bag slung across her shoulder and chest. Charlie shook his head. 'No. Don't know her. But it could be from the CCP. Go and see what she wants, but be careful.'

Hilly made to get up and come with her, but Zofia shook her head. 'Stay here until I know what it's about.' She hurried down the stairs and opened the door just a few inches.

'Zofia?' The name was mangled by the woman's toothless pronunciation. 'You Zofia?'

'That's me.'

'This is for you.' The woman thrust a scrap of brown paper into her hand.

Zofia was puzzled, but unfolded it and saw straight away it

was written in English. She scanned for a signature. Theo. Her breath seemed to stop in her lungs.

> *Zofia. Going to try an escape.*
> *We need:*
> *Chinese farmworkers' clothes for three men. 2 my size, one as big as you can.*
> *Cash, whatever you can get.*
> *Boots or shoes – most important. 2 pairs size 10, one size 12.*
> *Antiseptic cream.*
> *Thank our friend who brings this at risk to herself. We need a boat to take us onwards north up the Whangpoo. Can you arrange?*
> *You are our only hope. Will confirm date of attempt soon.*
> *Your trusting friend, Theo*

Zofia glanced back at the house where she could see the shadow of Charlie watching. 'Come,' she said leading the woman around the corner out of sight. She tapped the message. 'Where?' she asked. 'Where is he?'

'Woosung,' the woman replied, nodding and smiling, but added something unintelligible. It was not Shanghainese, but another dialect.

'Can I come?' Zofia asked, gesturing to go with her.

The woman flapped no, waving her hand to keep her away, but brought out another piece of paper and a pencil. She mimed writing.

Oh. She was waiting for a reply.

Zofia leaned the paper against the side of the house and wrote a brief note agreeing to help. Though how she could find such things, she'd no idea, but the adrenaline of seeing Theo's name had made her reckless. As she scribbled the reply she glanced over her shoulder, for she knew that agreeing to this, helping someone escape from a Japanese camp, would put them all at risk. A rill of fear made the hairs on her arms stand on end.

She folded the note and handed it to the woman. 'Thank you,' she said bowing and making the prayer sign with her hands.

The woman pulled another piece of paper from her cloth bag and pressed it into her hand. Zofia looked at it and saw it was a printed flyer for a pharmacy in the centre of town. The woman mimed more writing. 'You' – she pointed – 'go here. Good man. He fetch, he carry. Message with him good. I bring. You fetch from him. Not here. See?'

'Oh. You want me to collect from the pharmacy?'

A vigorous nod. 'Many come and go there. Safer. See?'

'This man' – she gestured at the brown paper note – 'you have seen him?'

Another nod.

'Is he well? Not hurt?'

'*Shi, shi!*' She grinned and mimed what seemed to be digging and planting.

Zofia frowned, trying to understand. But the woman put her hands together and bowed a farewell. Zofia followed her towards a waiting cycle-rickshaw until the woman made an angry shooing gesture and Zofia backed off. But not before she'd seen the elderly man between the shafts ready himself to go. This must be the husband mentioned in the note. He looked old and scrawny, and she immediately felt sorry for him.

Zofia watched the woman in the faded pink coat climb in and the wheels kick up dust as he began to pedal away, before she walked slowly back to the house, the note in her hand. Then she tucked it into her cardigan sleeve.

Something told her not to mention this to Charlie and Olga. She was wary of them, unsure whether to trust them with this information. Without Theo in the house, there seemed to be two distinct camps: Charlie and Olga, and Zofia and Hilly. Charlie seemed to tolerate Hilly only because Zofia could be useful in taking his messages. There were still notices out for his arrest, and Olga had insisted he should remain indoors, a fact that only made him irritable.

'What did she want?' Charlie asked as soon as Zofia came back. 'She gave you a note.'

'Just a list of prices,' Zofia said. 'She was wanting to sell us some rickshaw services, so I went to look at her husband's rickshaw. A rickety-looking tricycle thing and he looked old and slow. I told her we didn't need anything right now. It was sad. Just an old woman going door to door.'

Charlie frowned. 'She didn't mention me?'

'Of course not. Why would she?'

'There are spies everywhere looking to hand me in for that reward.'

'She was an old woman wanting a few fares. And the rickshaw trade's harder now most of the foreigners have gone.'

'I don't like it, people begging door to door.'

'She wasn't begging, just …' But Charlie had put his headphones back on again and had turned back to the radio. When he did that, to dismiss her as if she was of no concern, it made her want to slap him.

Hilly was biting her lip looking worried. She never liked it when people argued. It made her nervous.

'It's okay,' Zofia said, giving her a reassuring smile. 'Nothing to worry about.'

Hilly was always at her most bright when she was allowed to go out, often on the occasions when Olga was at work and Charlie plugged into a particularly juicy news item. It was painful to see her joy as Zofia scoured the second-hand markets looking for what Theo had asked for. She didn't tell Hilly what she was doing because she worried she might let something slip. It bothered her that this was exactly the way Charlie felt about Hilly.

Hilly wanted to haggle for the luxury items that had obviously been looted from some rich Westerner's wardrobe. The furs, of course, had gone first, because everyone needed warm clothing with winter on its way, but there were heaps of slippery satins and crêpe de Chine, all encrusted with diamanté, or embroidered with gold thread. Beautiful things hand-sewn by Chinese tailors, but non-Japanese were not allowed in the dance halls except on the arm of a soldier, and all the theatres had been shut down, so there was no one left to wear them.

'Look, Zofia, this is my size!' Hilly shouted. She was holding up yet another unsuitable garment, a narrow-waisted low-cut Western-style evening gown, made of silk and patterned with peonies.

'Where would you wear it? We need practical things. Let's look here.' Zofia hurried to the trestle table of indigo-dyed Chinese clothes and yanked out a frogged tunic and a pair of loose-fitting trousers.

Hilly frowned. 'Ugh. We can't wear those, they're dirty.'

'We can wash them and alter them.'

'I don't want to wear Chinese clothes. Unless it's a *cheongsam*.'

The thought of Hilly in a tight-fitting dress with side splits made Zofia shudder. 'Anyway, they're not for you,' she said.

'Then who?' Hilly insisted, as Zofia bargained for these bits of rag. After searching for the largest ones she could find, she bundled them under her arm.

'Why won't you tell me?' Hilly pressed at her shoulder.

'Three *yuan*,' shouted the scrawny stallholder, seeing his chance at a sale slipping away.

'Two,' shot back Zofia.

He gave a reluctant nod and the deal was done. That was the easy part; the hard part was always going to be the shoes. She had Theo's shoes already from his friend Mac and she'd gauged their size and spent a few days looking for big enough men's shoes on the stalls. No Chinese shoes in such big sizes were to be found, until she spotted a local man slopping along in a pair of large patent dress shoes. He'd stuffed them with paper to make them fit, but they still looked ridiculous on his skinny legs.

She stopped him and asked him where he got them and he led her to the seller, a wizened old man with a walleye and a cloth wrapped turban-style around his head, squatting before rows of men's shoes. The prices were scrawled in chalk on the pavement.

Zofia took her time choosing, looking inside the shoes for the Western sizing. All the remaining shoes were big sizes because Chinese feet were too small to wear them. She drove a hard bargain with the seller who eyed her beadily, and after examining the leather soles to make sure they were sturdy enough, she bought two pairs.

When they left, she saw the man pack up his things into a huge bag, and totter away down the road. Obviously their purchases were enough to sustain him for a day or two.

'They're for Theo, aren't they?' Hilly whispered. 'He had big feet like that.'

'Not a word to anyone,' she said to Hilly, forcing the heavy shoes into her bag.

'Why? You told me not to keep secrets.'

'This is different. You must swear not to tell. Not Charlie, not anyone.'

'D'you think they'd even believe me? They think I'm stupid. I'm not. I've spent weeks watching them and I can tell Charlie's just using Olga. She can't see it though. She thinks the sun shines out of his backside.'

'Hilly!'

'It's true. He doesn't give a fig for her, or us. He wants to be like his hero, Zha Wei. To be a big man, in control, to snap his fingers and have everyone at his beck and call.'

'Has he been near you, Zha Wei?'

'No. And if he did, I'd hit him. Or kick him in the groin.'

Zofia gave her a sharp look. 'Don't get in a fight with him. He's dangerous. Just avoid him, you hear me?'

Hilly didn't reply but Zofia felt the weight of it press on her mind.

She worried Hilly was getting bolder. Though it was a good thing in one way, it was a bad thing in another. It could lead her into trouble.

Zofia hurried through the deliveries so there was time to go to the pharmacy, and she waited her turn patiently in the queue of Chinese customers, inhaling the smell of camphor and a dry woody aroma she couldn't place.

Hilly hated the smell of the shop. 'It pongs,' she said. 'I'm not coming in.'

'Then don't move from there, okay?'

Hilly rolled her eyes.

'I'm serious.' Zofia left her outside, loitering by the street vendor next door. Poor man, he was captive to Hilly's scrutiny behind his stall. Her curious unblinking gaze was disconcerting to most Chinese people, who expected women to be more demure. This elderly man sold sweet chestnuts and bean curd strips, and Zofia reckoned Hilly would be safe there for a few minutes whilst she delivered a message for Theo and checked inside the shop for mail.

The pharmacy had the pharmacist's name, Hai Jun, written in *kanji* over the door. A small traditional wooden building, it was furnished with stools for people to wait, and two spittoons which Zofia avoided. Behind the counter, the shelves were stuffed with paper packets of leaf teas and tisanes. Rows of bottles below contained amber and green liquids, all floating with glutinous objects suspiciously like snakes or squid.

A set of about a hundred small drawers were labelled with their remedies in Chinese characters. She only recognized the kanji for a few – common cooking ingredients like root ginger – *Shen Jiang*, and lemongrass – *Xiang Mao*.

The pharmacy was busy but when her turn came a sturdy,

flat-faced man greeted her, elbows on the counter, his eyebrows raised in query.

'Anything for Zofia?' she asked. She kept her voice low.

'Ah.' He softened, and spoke to her in accented English. 'Ming Biyu told me you'd come. No mail today. Try again tomorrow, yes?'

She tried to hide her disappointment. 'From Woosung?'

He put a finger to his lips.

Heat rushed to her cheeks. But she'd noted the woman's given name, Biyu. In China the family name always came first.

'Take this.' His face was still expressionless, but he was handing her something. A liquorice stick. 'For your friend outside.'

She blinked, surprised. So he'd noticed Hilly. How strange. She thanked him and opened her bag to find her purse.

'No need to pay,' he said. 'Friends of Biyu. Come back tomorrow.'

She glanced out to check Hilly was still there.

'It's all right. The chestnut seller will watch her. He's my third uncle.'

Zofia found it odd how folk in Shanghai numbered their people – they had number one boys, and number two children, and now – a third uncle.

'Oh, that's kind.' She thanked him politely and went to find Hilly.

'You were an age,' Hilly said. It seemed she'd been unable to persuade the stallholder to part with a single sweet chestnut.

'Here,' Zofia said. 'Stop moaning.'

Hilly was mollified by the liquorice stick and was soon chewing away on it.

For several more days Zofia went to the pharmacy. Secretive smiles, whispers and sidelong glances were the currency there, as well as the pharmacy business. She overheard a woman ahead of her asking about having her fortune told, and she gathered that on some days an astrologer sat behind the red curtain to give advice and suggest strategies for living a long life. Mostly though, those coming out looked like hardened men, not like women wanting their fortunes told. These men eyed her curiously, as if she shouldn't be there, but she ignored them, keeping her chin up and her gaze calm.

She guessed she wasn't the only one using this place as a drop point. There'd always been communist factions in the city, and everyone had heard of the anti-communist massacres – the 'White Terror', where thousands were killed right here in Shanghai. One of the most famous quotes from Chiang Kai-shek was that he would 'rather mistakenly kill a thousand innocent people, than allow a single Communist to escape'.

This had forced the communists from the city and into the countryside, where the Kuomintang was less powerful. It was years ago, but for the ordinary people of Shanghai it was something hard to forget.

Each time they went, Zofia was able to pacify Hilly's impatience with a stick of liquorice. Hilly was not stupid; she'd guessed it was something to do with Theo, and she was aware not everyone in the pharmacy brought prescriptions or asked for remedies. The pharmacist, Jun, was a quiet man, but his eyes missed nothing. It was as though they looked through you, not at you. She kept hoping for another message from Theo, but so far, nothing.

During this time, the delivery of Charlie's messages for the Chinese rebels went on. They had to be careful to conceal everything in case they were stopped at a checkpoint and searched by the Japanese, so Zofia had made a body bag, a wide belt she secured around her waist under her clothes. If Olga was at work, Zofia always took Hilly. It was unhealthy for her to be cooped up with no exercise.

Charlie turned a blind eye and just said, 'Be careful.'

All went well until they were coming home one afternoon and went through the same checkpoint for the second time. There was barely a queue, and the Japanese soldier took his time looking at Hilly's papers. 'You are Austrian?'

Zofia had briefed Hilly to make sure she remembered to give the impression she was Hildegard the German sympathizer and loyal Nazi. Zofia held her breath and Hilly, terrified to have been stopped, stumbled a reply. The soldier seemed satisfied and shut her pass with a snap, before holding out a hand for Zofia's.

'Jewish?' he asked Zofia, seeing it on her passport.

She replied in Japanese, hoping to ingratiate and get by quickly.

'You pass here many days,' he said, smiling. His teeth were very white and even, his eyes intense.

'Yes,' she replied, 'with the laundry.'

'Where did you learn Japanese?'

'My husband. He comes from near Tokyo. He's in the army.' She hoped this would stop any further conversation, but it seemed to have the opposite effect.

'Where did you live with your husband?'

'In Kobe, in the Jewish settlement.' She held out her hand for her pass, but he moved it away and held on to it. Her heart sank.

'Ah. Jewish. So they sent you here.'

'Yes.' She glanced around to check what Hilly was doing. She was gazing around as if looking for someone. Her mother. The realisation came all at once. That hope had obviously never died.

She wanted to comfort her but the Japanese soldier was still talking.

'Where do you live now?' He was rifling through Zofia's papers. Shit. This interrogation didn't bode well.

He repeated the question.

'With some Russian friends.' Zofia tried to sound casual.

'On the Luosong Road,' Hilly said.

Zofia's heart sank. *Don't tell them anything.* 'I'm sorry but I have an appointment. Please, my pass. We must go. Very sorry.' She bowed and took hold of the edge of the pass, but he still clung on. A small battle went on between them for only a few seconds before he smiled and let go.

She called to Hilly, and stepped away, but the soldier stopped her by placing his rifle across her path.

'You like dancing?'

The answer couldn't be yes. She sought frantically for some way out. 'Sorry, my Japanese is not so good.'

He smiled, in a knowing way, and continued in English. 'Dancing – you like? We will go to the Argentina Ballroom tonight. Dance Western style, okay?'

'I can't, I think my husband won't like that I—'

'Your husband not know. You will come. I will buy you something nice. New shoes, new stockings.'

She would pretend to agree. 'Thank you. That would be lovely.'

'Meet me in the left lounge bar at nine o'clock.'

She nodded and bowed, and the rifle was lifted. 'My name is Kenzo. Nine o'clock. Don't forget.'

She grasped Hilly's arm and dragged her away. 'What were you thinking? You should never tell them where we live.'

'And you said we should never talk to Japanese soldiers, but you were talking to him.' Hilly's tone was full of accusation. 'You were being friendly, so I was just doing the same.'

'I had to. He'd got my papers and I needed them back.'

'But you agreed to go dancing with him.'

'I know, but I won't go. I just humoured him to get him off my back.'

'What will happen if you don't go? Will he come looking for you?'

Zofia had just had exactly the same thought, and the answer was one she didn't want to contemplate.

And it seemed ironic – after worrying all the time about Hilly's difficulties with men, that she hadn't given a single thought to how she might appear to the occupying Japanese. She could see now that using their language had bought favour with them just once too often.

Chapter 26

Haru's holdall was packed and he was glad to be moving on again. He'd made few friends or colleagues in his unit since promotion – his position as a Non-Commissioned Officer made the other soldiers shy away because of the necessary discipline he had to administer. Cowards, all.

Even though he hardly used the rifle and bayonet anymore, army discipline made him prepare his weapon. He dabbed more of the gun oil onto his cloth. He was glad to escape front-line fighting, because some days he could hardly see straight. Headaches blurred his vision and wouldn't leave him in peace. They came without warning, a throb as if his whole head was full of blood, compressing his skull. He suspected it was because of the tight muscles in his neck and shoulders. He couldn't relax; he kept thinking someone was behind him, ready to slit his throat, and the nightmares of the slippery bayonet, of men screaming, meant he hardly slept.

Any loud noise could make his stomach clench and squeeze his shoulders into rigid bands. He'd tried hard liquor but all that did was dehydrate him and make them worse. He looked down to see his hands were trembling, but he ignored it, ground his teeth and polished harder. When his bayonet was gleaming, he took the bottle of salt and ammonia to polish the brass on his uniform. The bad egg smell of it caught in his throat, and his head throbbed again, so he leaned out of the door of his office.

'Sakurai!' He summoned the private on sentry duty.

When he didn't arrive quickly enough, he hit him hard across the face and shouted at him. He didn't see why he should do the polishing himself. Sakurai set to it with his face red and tears dripping from the end of his nose.

Haru paced his room and stopped at the pile of books by his bedside. He'd hardly touched them since he came to China. He wouldn't need any of them. Commander Onozaka was moving him to Soochow near Shanghai, where he was to oversee two units who were guarding the canals. The canals were used by the Chinese Red Army insurgents to send explosives and weapons to those who were resisting Japanese occupation.

There was a book here in Russian. He looked at it almost without recognition. Had he read that? He couldn't remember it. Or even imagine reading anything that thick. He opened it and the small type shimmered before his eyes. He hadn't read anything except telegraphed orders for months.

Perhaps Zofia had given it to him. He thought of her, now he was a soldier, with a degree of resentment. She had it easy, in the orderly beauty of Kobe. He'd written to the Japanese Embassy to make sure she was treated with all courtesy, but he longed for her, and for home, in a way the Japanese army thought unmanly. She would be at home in Kobe, freshly bathed and sipping jasmine tea, away from the tang of blood.

The noise of polishing had stopped. He whipped around. 'What are you staring at?'

'Nothing, sir, sorry, sir.' Sakurai ducked his head and went back to work.

Haru turned the spine of the book in his hands. Dostoyevsky. Once, he'd been in love with Russia, with its snow-bound beauty, its deep green forests illustrated so beguilingly in his childhood books. But that was all childish fantasy. The Russians were communists, traitors allied with the CCP.

He couldn't imagine why he'd ever wanted to read that; he'd no use for the Russian language now. He'd leave it behind.

'Out! Get out!' He rounded on Sakurai and shooed him out. 'Get the bags ready for transport.'

It was cold in the early morning, so he put on his thick serge coat and his cap and checked his watch. The train would leave soon. His driver appeared and saluted him. It was a crisp salute and for once Haru let it pass without rebuke. He passed over his luggage and climbed into the back of the car. He saw Sakurai staring after him with a smile twitching his lips, but he didn't show any sign he'd seen him.

As they drove, Haru realized he was looking forward to his new post. Perhaps things would be better in Soochow. Onozaka had told him it was a beautiful place, known as the 'Venice of the Orient' by tourists, and even better, it was under full control of the Japanese. He hoped the gardens and waterways were as delightful as he said, though of course nothing could ever compare to Japan.

According to Onozaka, a few Chinese residents remained in Soochow under the control of the so-called Reorganized National Government, who in turn were under the thumb of Wang Jingwei. Wisely, Wang had surrendered himself to Japan, and recognized Hirohito's authority, so his government was effectively powerless. Wang hoped Tokyo might eventually negotiate a deal for peace with China, one that would allow the land of China to survive. Ha! That would never happen. The Emperor tolerated Wang only because he was useful, but he still had a creeping Anglo-American fondness for materialism that weakened their men.

The train journey in the cold compartment was long and even though he was accompanied by two bodyguards, Haru couldn't allow himself to doze. He gripped his fists, always too tense, like an over-wound watch. It gave him the jitters; the train track was exposed and they were a moving target for the Americans, who might bomb the line.

When he arrived at Soochow, his head aching like the devil, he was pleasantly surprised to see a large city with its canals and streets mostly intact, and orderly people going about their business. A Japanese private in pristine uniform, pistol at his belt, marched over to meet him, and ordered two riff-raff Chinese to take his luggage. They offered him a sedan chair, the only transport available down the narrow edge of the canal. He declined, but ordered the private to accompany him and his bodyguards as he walked. You couldn't be too careful; the Chinese were a devious race.

Haru followed the directions he'd been given. His house was the best in the row, the front edge jutting out on stilts above the water – well constructed, with a terracotta-tiled roof and a balcony overlooking the waterway. A tree by the stone steps to the upper floor was just sprinkled with pale pink petals – the *meihua*, or Chinese plum blossom that flowered in winter, a symbol of resilience and survival against adversity. He'd get that pulled up soon.

At the door a second Japanese soldier welcomed him with a sharp salute, said his name was Private Endo and that he'd been assigned to be his personal servant. Ah, this was more like it.

The bodyguards waited at the door and Haru walked through the gloom of the house to the windows and threw open the latticed shutters. Beneath him the canal flowed by, reflecting the pewter of the sky. A momentary pang that he'd no one to share it with, that the floorboards echoed to his boots.

After a few minutes, the private, his face taut with nerves, brought him tea, and handed him a message.

Haru read it quickly, annoyed he'd been so soon interrupted. It seemed the local Chinese police chief would like to see him that evening. Probably some sort of welcoming committee.

'Tell him to come here at nine,' Haru said. 'And bring me hot water to wash, and something to eat.'

The Chinese police chief, Pau Tsungjien, was a heavyweight man at least ten years older than Haru. Haru himself was skinny from lack of food in the army, and he regarded this fat oaf of a man with disdain.

Pau bowed to the bodyguards and greeted him in mangled Japanese.

'I speak Chinese,' Haru said dismissively. 'No need for you to massacre my native tongue.' He dismissed his servant too and shut the door.

This seemed to disconcert Pau, and he blinked and then cleared his throat. 'Your predecessor Kitaki-san was a nice man,' Pau said. 'We got along well, and I'd like to go along as before. It was a shame he—'

'Yes, yes.' Haru didn't want to be reminded of the manner of Kitaki's death, shot by a Chinese rebel. 'Why did you want to see me?' He didn't offer the chief a seat but left him standing awkwardly before him in the middle of the floor.

'Well, the unit you are to be heading … it's like this … they expect certain accommodations.'

'Accommodations?'

'To make their task easier.'

'Like what?'

Pau wrung his damp hands. 'In the police we have access to certain goods, trafficked goods you understand. And in return for a small fee, we supply the army with these. A kind of favour, you see, to your troops.'

'Are you saying you sell the army something?'

'It keeps many Chinese dockworkers happy and in work, sir, and—'

'I don't give a pin how many of you it keeps in work. What is it?'

'Paregoric.'

He'd never heard of it. 'And what is that?'

'A preparation of opium.'

Haru sat back on his chair, the breath gone from his lungs. Trust the Chinese to try to profit from them somehow. 'How many of my men do you sell to?'

'How many? No, you don't understand. They expect it as part of their ration.'

'And who administers it?'

A frown. 'Why, you do. The army. Or at least the commander of the unit.'

'But they already have amphetamines and tobacco in their issue. The field kitchen makes sure of it.'

'If you ask the men, I think you'll find they value this more. It helps them with the night terrors, with the thought of demons. Opium is like nothing else, like what you call a *baku*, a mythical creature that eats their nightmares.'

Nightmares. 'My men don't need this nonsense. They are fearless. There is no demon they fear.' As he said this he felt something shift inside him, like a roar waiting to escape. 'We will have none of it.'

'Then I'm afraid you will have mutiny,' Pao said. 'The suppliers have been packing these exact rations in the old dye factory for years. Of course, you need know nothing of it, so long as the bill is paid every month.'

Haru was tired. He didn't want a battle before he'd begun. Perhaps he'd wait to cut this peculiar ration until the men were more under his control. His predecessor must have been a weak man. Even more so to get himself killed. 'You have two months,' he conceded. 'And bring me a sample of exactly what goes into these rations. I want to see what is being peddled to my men, understand?'

'Of course. And welcome to Soochow.'

Chapter 27

Zofia spent many sleepless nights worrying about Theo and his escape plan. At night she mentally ticked off Theo's list and wondered how she would get everything to him.

The antiseptic cream Theo asked for was a problem. Was he or one of his friends hurt? Since the Japanese came, Western medicine had dried up. Everyone went to pharmacies like Jun's in wartime, for traditional remedies for strength and virility – tiger bones and shark's teeth. And since this brutal occupation, there was a bigger demand for Chinese herbal medicine for injuries or ill health.

She could only think of one person who might have access to real antiseptic – Olga. She'd tried to warm to Olga, but the truth was they didn't get along. She didn't know why, except she found Olga's manner abrupt and abrasive, and Olga had a knack of making her feel like a fool. She'd tried to be pleasant and make conversation with her, but Olga didn't do small talk. Olga would be sure to ask why she wanted antiseptic, and Zofia didn't want to tell her.

So one morning, she waited until Olga was out shopping and then went into her bedroom to search her things. Olga had a medical bag she took with her when she went to work, and Zofia hoped she'd find something in there.

Olga's room was oddly tidy as if nothing had ever been out of place. Not a speck of dust anywhere, and Charlie's clothes neatly hung on hangers on the back of the door. On one wall was a *Bogoroditsa*, a Russian icon of Mary and Jesus, and a red glass holder with a candle. Olga's rosary was there too, on the table under it, along with her tidily laid out brush, comb and mirror.

The icon's eyes seemed to follow her, making Zofia swallow hard. She assessed the room, homing in on Olga's nurse's bag. It was standing next to a chair on which her dark green nurse's uniform was laid out ready for her next shift. Feeling guilty, she stood the bag on the bed and searched through it. It was neatly ordered inside with everything in sealed paper packets. In a side pocket she found some tubes of ointment, and lifted one out to scrutinize the label. Was this antiseptic?

'What are you doing?'

She started and turned. 'I've stomach cramps. I was looking for some aspirin.'

'It's in the bathroom cupboard,' Olga said, arms folded across her chest, 'where it always is.'

'I couldn't see it. Time of the month.'

Olga curled her lip. 'I don't like you going into my bag. Everything in there is sterile. I don't want it messed with. Okay?'

'Sorry, Olga. I'll get some from the bathroom.'

Olga watched her silently as she went, a grim expression tightening her mouth.

Zofia felt terrible. What if all this was for nothing? What if the Japanese had intercepted Theo's messages and he couldn't risk a break-out? But then she thought of his face, his laugh, and the light in his eyes.

She imagined what it must feel like to have your freedom taken away. He was relying on her. She wouldn't let him down. When she got the next letter with the date of his escape, she'd be ready.

* * *

The next day, Zofia was out on a delivery and when she got back, two rickshaws were outside the house. 'What's going on?' she asked Charlie, who was on the pavement.

He glared at her. 'Olga only answered the door to a Japanese soldier. A Jap called Kenzo. Went all down the street looking for you. A Jew called Zofia Kimura.'

She swallowed. 'What did she say?'

'She told him a woman of that name had lived there once but had moved on. And no, she didn't know where. He wanted to come in the house, and Olga couldn't refuse, though she had to practically gag Hilly so she wouldn't give you away.'

'Shit. Where were you?'

'In next door's outside privy again. I couldn't risk having to talk to him. I've got no Russian or Japanese. Just too dangerous. He apparently asked about the men's things. Olga told her they belonged to her lodger's brother, Maksim. And all the time 'Maksim' was in the shithouse next door. So we're moving. Theo must have talked. The bastard. If they know about you, they must know about me.'

'No! It's not Theo. It was me. I mean … Calm down. No one knows you're here.' Zofia tried to explain about the Japanese man at the checkpoint and him wanting her to go dancing.

While she was explaining, Olga appeared. 'I should have known it would be you.' She curled her lip in disgust. 'You and Hilly haven't got the sense you were born with. If he asked you out, you should have kept the date.'

'Don't be stupid. What good would that have done?'

'Stopped him coming here! What do you think? Too late anyway,' she said. 'We're moving. To the Blue Lilac club.'

Zofia felt her heart plummet. 'No. We're not going there.'

'Well, you can't stay here,' Olga said. 'I'm renting it out, to someone from the hospital.'

'And you have to come with us,' Charlie said. 'Where we can keep an eye on you.'

The implication he didn't trust her struck her like a blow to the stomach. 'It's too far out of town,' Zofia said, hardly knowing what she was saying.

'Out of town's good,' Charlie said. 'They're searching for me in the settlement.'

'The Blue Lilac's a good place for Charlie,' Olga said. 'Plenty of other Russians there. Women who work the tables, bodyguards. Charlie will blend in. And anyway, Zha Wei doesn't like loose ends.' Olga's eyes were cold. 'You have to come with us.'

Zofia ignored the threat. 'Does Hilly know?'

'She's packing,' Charlie said. 'I suggest you do the same.'

He was loading a rickshaw with his few CCP essentials; a hand litho-printing kit, the forbidden typewriter, and a few clothes scrounged from Theo. Olga climbed into the rickshaw, belongings crowded at her feet.

Hilly came rushing from the house, her hair tousled and two big bags bobbing against her thighs. Zofia glanced to the other rickshaw where the coolie, old and bent with legs spindly as twigs, waited by the shafts.

She ignored him and instead took Charlie to one side. 'Charlie, do we have to? Theo didn't talk, and I don't trust Zha Wei; some of his men look like thugs.' Zofia whispered, so Hilly couldn't hear.

'They act that way so they don't get any nonsense,' Charlie said. 'But Zha's on our side. He's the man doing the most to try to sabotage the Japanese.'

'He's a gangster. You can't tell me he's turned good overnight. How can he be a communist when everything for him is about lining his own pockets? Last time I saw him he treated me like dirt and made threats to silence me.' She turned to see Hilly was talking to the coolie who was smiling at her, as if she was an old friend.

'So he's tough. You need tough guys in a war. Zha Wei's fighting the Japs. Just be grateful he's offered us a safe space to stay,' Charlie insisted.

Except it sure as hell isn't safe.

'Stop griping, woman.' Charlie shook his head impatiently. 'It's not like there's a choice. I need to be moving on, in case your precious American can't keep his mouth shut.'

'Don't talk of him like that. If it wasn't for him, you'd already be dead. He won't talk. I know him.'

'Huh. You can't know what someone would do under torture.'

He was right. But she had a sudden feeling she did know Theo. On some deep unspoken level.

'Cat got your tongue now?' Charlie planted his hands on his hips and stared her down.

Hilly was calling, anxious to be on the move.

Zofia hurried back into the house and grabbed the bundle of things she'd collected for Theo. Her own bag was already packed as usual, except for toothbrush and soap. She was always ready to run. It was a reflex from being in Poland with the Nazis. The spindly Chinese coolie nodded to her as she heaved her bags onto the seat and clambered up beside Hilly.

Zofia prodded the overstuffed bag on Hilly's lap. 'What's in there?'

'Olga was going to leave these behind, so I thought I'd have them. She'd ever so many stockings. And some blouses with pearl buttons.'

Zofia inhaled and then sighed the breath out. There was really no point in arguing. 'Come on then, shift over. Give me a bit of room.'

The other rickshaw was already bowling away on its huge wheels, and she could see Charlie and Olga's heads above and the soles of the coolie's feet below.

'All right, Suyin,' Hilly said. 'Chop-chop. Just follow the other one.'

'Do you know him?' Zofia asked her.

'He was one of the customers at Madam Wang's. He's a nice man. He has five grandchildren. He buys them lychee sweets.'

He was nippy, steering his way through the traffic, keeping up with Charlie and Olga. Zofia read the shop signs, and realized they were passing out of the International Settlement now and into Japanese-controlled China.

After fifteen minutes or so they were travelling along Bubbling Well Road and the houses were becoming poorer and more ill kept. Many were boarded up, with their signs broken or hanging off. 'Casino'. 'Gin House'.

Zha Wei's house was just outside the French Concession in what used to be called the Badlands. Not that it was really a house. It was a large sprawling warehouse with a casino attached and rooms upstairs. The warehouse part was boarded up with flaking hoardings plastered with garish posters, advertising blackjack, roulette and 'Beautiful Girls'. It was obviously some sort of gambling joint, like many on this road. Since the Japanese came, this road was the haunt of Japanese soldiers, and this in itself made Zofia's throat tight.

The 'Blue Lilac' sign had once been neon, but was now just broken black tubing.

When they got out, Zofia handed Suyin a few extra coins. He made a prayer gesture and Hilly bobbed a curtsey back at him which made him laugh.

It was a moment of sunshine and it was lovely to see two smiling faces.

Some young Chinese men, with tattoos on their hands and cigarettes stuck to their lips, came out to watch them unload, but didn't offer to help. They were flanked by two broad-shouldered men she assumed to be Russians. The way they silently watched them with predatory eyes made Zofia even more uncomfortable.

One of the men went inside through an unmarked side door, and a few moments later Zha Wei swaggered out.

He greeted Charlie like an old friend. And even kissed Olga's hand.

Zofia was wary. Zha Wei's allegiances seemed to shift to whatever best served his purposes. He was paid by the communists, and yet he was prepared to do business with the Japanese in his casino.

Charlie and Olga followed him towards a downstairs salon. A young Chinese boy gestured to the women to follow him as he grabbed Hilly's big bag to haul it upstairs. Zofia took her own and they passed through a ballroom with tables and chairs piled up as if it was no longer used, the bar at one end dusty, with unemptied ashtrays.

The boy led them up some back stairs, dumped the bag outside a door and then slunk away.

As they arrived two other women poked their head out of the door opposite. Both were Eurasian, their faces caked with white powder, their lips painted red. They giggled and then shut the door.

'Were they laughing at me?' Hilly asked.

'No. Take no notice.' Zofia already had her suspicions about the women, but there was nothing she could do.

Zofia turned the handle and pushed open the door.

It was a room at the back of the house, papered with dingy floral paper in the French style. Immediately she knew it had recently been used by someone else. There was only one bed, and it looked rumpled, the sheets thrown back, as though someone had just got out of it. Its slippery satin counterpane had slid to the floor.

Hilly immediately picked up on it. 'Someone's already living here.'

'They've gone. We just have to make the best of it.'

Hilly pointed to the counterpane. 'They only just left.'

'Just fold it up for now. Here, help me straighten out the bed.' She turned the sheets over and put them the other way around, and then tucked in the blankets. 'We have to share,' she said.

'I don't mind, Zof,' Hilly said. 'I like it when you're there. I didn't like waking up and finding you were gone.'

As they were sorting out their room and possessions, Zofia could hear men's voices below them. She tried to hear what they were saying but couldn't make out anything definite.

A few moments later Zha Wei pushed open their door. His

bulk filled the doorway. He looked them up and down. 'All right, ladies?'

'It'll do,' Zofia said.

Hilly had backed away.

'Don't be shy,' he said to Hilly. 'Come out where I can get a better look at you.'

Hilly cringed, her bravado evaporating instantly. Zha Wei strode in and grabbed her by the arm. He took hold of a strand of her hair and said, 'It's grown. Pretty.'

'Take your hands off her,' Zofia said.

'She likes me though, doesn't she?'

Hilly nodded dumbly before his smiling gaze, her vibrancy gone, like someone turned to stone.

'See?' He let her hair drop back to her shoulder. Then he turned to Zofia. 'If you're going to stay here then you'd better make yourself pleasant. The other girls here know how to do that. Maybe they can give you lessons.' He laughed, a throaty but unpleasant sound.

His whole persona was about intimidation and threat. Zofia had grasped that the minute she set eyes on him, and now he'd done nothing to dissuade her of the fact.

He sauntered away, leaving her seething.

'You okay?' she asked Hilly. 'If he asks you to do something you don't want to do, you tell me right away.'

'Do we have to stay here?'

'For now, yes. But you'll tell me if he does anything. Promise?'

'Stop fussing.' Hilly said, with a new attempt at boldness, now he'd gone. 'I can take care of myself.'

Later on, Olga came knocking at her door. At least she knocked rather than just barging in. She sniffed and made a face at their room. 'The men were talking and I thought you'd like to know. It's about Theo. Zha Wei says he's out of Bridge House and he's been transferred again to Woosung Internment Camp.'

Zofia tried to act as if this was news to her. 'Is he okay?'

'We still don't know if he talked. Zha Wei thinks he might have done a deal for information about Charlie.'

'He won't have talked. Where exactly is Woosung Camp?'

'About fourteen miles away – up river. One of Zha Wei's guys was the driver when they brought Theo out. He's a Korean, acting as a pro-Japanese runner. A man matching Theo's description was taken to the camp. And the Korean overheard them call him Mr Carter.'

'Then it's him,' Hilly said. 'When will they let him out?'

Olga shrugged. 'When the war ends, I suppose, if they don't repatriate him before. But Zha Wei keeps a hard eye on everyone going in and out of there. Charlie says it pays him to know who's been arrested and who hasn't. Zha Wei has business dealings with most of them. Supplies funds for their charity enterprises. Provided they give him a favour or two.'

Zofia made an expletive. 'Charity? Don't make me laugh. You mean gambling and corruption.'

Olga fixed her with hard eyes. 'You can afford to look down your nose at us, can you?'

'I'm not, it's just—'

'You're not living with it every day. A man with a death sentence on his head. Your man has fought no one and is safe inside a camp waiting to go home.'

Little do you know.

Olga didn't wait for a reply, and there was nothing Zofia could say in front of Hilly.

'Why does everyone have to argue all the time?' Hilly asked.

Zofia sighed. She'd learned something new though – Woosung Camp was a long way away. She would have to accept that the only way of getting any kind of message to Theo would be through the pharmacy and Jun.

The Blue Lilac was full of men coming and going at all hours. The rooms opposite Zofia's were obviously used for prostitution.

When the Japanese came, which was every night, they were all sharp with tension. Charlie kept a low profile, locked away with Olga. Olga was calm with these visitors, ready to field any questions about her 'Russian' husband. The Japanese soldiers were oblivious to everything behind the scenes because they were off duty and had called only for their dose of sexual satisfaction.

Zofia and Hilly shivered behind their locked door, desperate for the moment the men would leave and the thumping sounds from behind the doors would cease.

When she confronted Charlie about the dangers of being here, right under the Japanese soldiers' noses, he was tetchy. 'It's the safest place. They'd never think of looking for a British sailor here.' But he'd lost weight through worry, his face gaunt and lined, and though nobody said so, it was obvious Zha Wei ruled over them all like some kind of feudal overlord. He juggled all their lives like threads in his stubby hands.

They were working for him, when he deigned to appear. His men were always present in the house or the warehouse, where Chinese grain was stockpiled for backhander payments to the Japanese. At the same time, Zha Wei was in negotiations with the Chinese rebels fighting against the official government of Chiang Shek. This involved couriering messages between the houses in Zha's network, because all phones were tapped. Charlie was organizing this in return for their silence about his existence.

Zofia resented it, but there was little she could do. Any trouble with Zha Wei meant putting Charlie in danger. Charlie barely acknowledged this – the fact all three of the women, Olga, Zofia and Hilly were pawns in this game of keeping him safe.

Chapter 28

Woosung Camp was about twenty acres, and a second electrified fence ran around the perimeter, a short distance away from where the shack was. Griff made Theo walk the fence in sections to check the visibility of their escape route to any patrol.

The angles of the lights inside the perimeter fence meant this path was brightly illuminated but the actual fence was not.

'You have to choose a foggy night,' said Lennie, lying on his bunk.

'To hide your big butt,' Theo said. 'But it's good thinking, you can't even see the second fence when it's bad.'

'I'm not coming,' Lennie said.

'Yes, you are,' Theo said. 'This whole thing was your idea.'

Lennie gave a laugh and a cough. 'No it wasn't, mate, it was yours.' He'd tried to work in the garden that day, but it was obvious that even after weeks, he was still in pain and the fire had gone from his eyes.

'Well, whatever,' said Theo. 'We're a team. We don't leave our pals behind.'

'I dunno if I'm up to it.'

'You are. You will be. You're getting fitter every day.' He so much wanted it to be true. Griff was a great guy, but Lennie had a warmth about him Griff lacked.

Lennie gave a weak smile and looked away. In a sudden hollow flash of intuition Theo saw that Lennie's spirit had sunk to zero. His stomach dropped. Maybe Griff was right. But it was too late, he'd insisted Lennie should come, and now he couldn't back down.

At their next meeting they huddled together in Theo's billet, their thin grey blankets swathed around their heads. Being late October the weather had worsened, with thick wedges of bone-chilling fog blown in off the sea. The fact there was no heating inside any of their barracks meant the fog lingered.

Lennie's cough had got worse, but nobody mentioned it.

'We can't climb the fences so we'll have to tunnel underneath,' Theo said.

Griff nodded. 'But getting any kind of spade or shovel will be hard and we have to do it before frost season, or we won't be able to dig quickly enough with our bare hands.'

'Can we make something?' Lennie said. 'Find a bit of metal for a pick?'

'Where will we get anything strong enough?' Griff said. 'Tin will be too weak, and they won't even let me keep a rake or tools for the garden.'

'The kitchen? See if there's anything useful we can get from there.'

'There are no knives,' Lennie said. 'The vegetables come in already cut up by Chinese slave labour.'

'Well, keep an eye out for anything you can find.' Theo wasn't going to give up.

Over the past few weeks, they'd managed to get messages out via the bamboo tube, and Theo had asked Zofia to arrange a boat to take them up the river. Beyond that, they just didn't know. It was a big ask, he knew, and dangerous. He wouldn't blame her if she said no, or just ignored it.

He was determined to get out of China and back to where Evelina and his children were. Child. Oh Lord, Jimmy. He couldn't even bring himself to think of him.

But he shouldn't have doubted Zofia. The bamboo tube came back with her handwritten reply. It said simply: *Yes. All is ready. Tell me precisely where to meet you and on what day.*

Theo grinned, his shoulders light for the first time since he'd arrived, and read this brief note over and over, searing it into his mind. He hid it in his sleeve, and in the kitchen he dropped it from there into the fire and watched it shrivel. Any note like this spelled danger and must be destroyed.

She was their hope. They had to have someone on the outside who could help them blend in and then a way of getting away from Shanghai. He still hadn't got shoes, but had fashioned something to protect his feet with cardboard and twine. It wasn't ideal, but okay in the limited confines of the camp.

Conditions in Woosung worsened, not least because of the bad weather but because of one of the civilian staff – Ishihara, nicknamed the Beast from the East, or just the Beast. He'd been a taxi driver before the war, and because he'd learned English in the United States, he was given the role of interpreter. The 'interpretation' was often wrong, and he was renowned for his brutality.

The slightest thing would mean a beating or punishment. When a young internee, John Everley, who knew a little Japanese, challenged him about his translation, Everley was made to stand naked in the rain. Ishihara then hit him in the genitals until he was bent double. When he started coshing him on the head, Everley tried to run.

In his panic, he ran straight into the electrified fence.

Nobody would ever forget the sight of his convulsing body, or the hiss and crackle of that wire.

The guards left him hanging there for an hour and made everyone come out of their sections to see.

'You sure you want to carry on?' Griff asked Theo.

'Too damn right I do. Just to see the looks on those bastards' faces.'

They scrounged and planned, waiting for the right time. A time just after heavy rain.

The timing was crucial. They needed the fog and the dark, but also needed the ground to be soft, because they'd have to dig deep to clear the wire. No one wanted to end up like Everley.

In the waiting time they taught themselves rudimentary Chinese by scraping out the kanji and the words in the dirt. When they got cigarettes from the Red Cross, they used the packets to write what they called 'pointy' cards. English with the matching Chinese kanji. If they got out of the camp, they could use these 'pointy' cards to communicate with the Chinese. Once outside, they would have to meet Chinese rebels of all persuasions if they were to locate an American army base.

This was the hope.

Theo tried to gain what knowledge he could from the Americans who had any knowledge of China. It was hopeless to pretend they weren't intending to escape. Almost everyone knew, but no one else wanted to attempt it. Surprising though, what you could find even in somewhere as deprived as Woosung Camp. When Theo was on tea duty one day in the mess hall, he noticed a sharp-edged metal scoop used to get the tea out of the sack.

He bent deep over it and shoved the scoop into the top of his trousers. For the rest of 'tea duty' he scooped with his hands until he could get it away. Griff had made a hiding place under the officers' bunks which had bases made of solid wood. He'd prised a plank out of his to make a handy storage area beneath.

You couldn't keep food there because of the rats, but anything else useful, like paper and cardboard packaging found its way there, even if it did get gnawed.

Finally, the weather was perfect; damp ground and a persistent fog still wreathing the camp.

The woman in the shack had been a godsend. She knew now when they would send and receive. Their messages were getting through because Zofia replied every time.

Now at last they could send her the date of escape.

Zofia shuffled from foot to foot, impatient, waiting for Charlie to give her the day's deliveries. She was keen to get moving so she could call at the pharmacy on the way and see if there was another message from Theo. And she needed to send one, to tell him she'd moved.

Charlie finished his list and handed the envelopes over. Zofia put them in the waist bag she always wore, put on her coat and told Hilly to hurry. Hilly was fussing with a silk scarf, tying it this way and that to see what looked best.

But when they got downstairs, she found Zha Wei in the hallway standing right in front of the door.

'Excuse me,' she said, making to go past him. He stuck out an arm to prevent her, and she smelled the tang of his brilliantine. His hair was always well-oiled, and his face clean-shaven and reeking of aftershave.

'She's not to go out.' He pointed his stubby finger at Hilly.

'What do you mean?'

'Olga says she's a risk,' he said, 'so she's to stay indoors. We don't want our business compromised by some bitch who doesn't know what's going on.'

'I do know what's going on,' Hilly whispered, but she shrank away at his belligerent tone.

'No,' Zofia said. 'That's not how it works. If she's not going out, then neither am I. And then who'll deliver the messages?'

'You want to be awkward?'

'You've had no trouble from us before, so I don't see any reason why we shouldn't just carry on.' Her heart was thumping, but she tried to stay cool.

He moved a step nearer until his obsidian eyes were level with hers. 'You want to disappear? There are many like you who just disappear. No one knows where they go. You want to be one of them?'

A threat. Zofia's jaw tightened but she didn't drop her gaze.

'A little advice, that's all,' Zha Wei said. 'She stays here, understand?'

His breath was in her face. She was caught. She needed to get a message to Theo, but at the same time she didn't want to leave Hilly alone in the house with Zha Wei. She hesitated.

'Go without me, Zof,' Hilly said. 'I can help Olga and Charlie. I don't want any trouble.'

A slow smile spread across Zha Wei's face. 'You heard what the little lady said. She's more use in here than out there with you.'

Zofia looked from one to the other. At Hilly's pleading face, and at Zha Wei's implacable one.

'You want to stay at the Blue Lilac, you have to work. That's the rule around here.' Zha Wei opened the door and gestured at Zofia to go out.

Zofia turned to Hilly. 'You sure? I won't be long, I promise.' Then she turned to Zha Wei. 'If anything happens to her when I'm gone—'

She didn't finish because the door slammed behind her.

She stood for a moment in the shadow of the house. Tilting her head to look up at the window, she saw Charlie's face looking down at her.

You're no hero, she thought. *You're useless. You only think of yourself, of saving your own skin.*

She pulled up the coat collar and set off at a smart walk to try to deliver her packages. The correspondence was addressed to Zha Wei's contacts in the south of the city, to whom she had made deliveries before. After, she'd go the pharmacy, and hope for another message from Theo. But all the time she was berating herself, a feeling of dread in her belly. *Stupid. You shouldn't have left Hilly.*

She raced to leave the packages at the drop points as fast as she could, and hurried to the pharmacy with a sense of trepidation. She feared that Jun, the pharmacist, might laugh at her for turning up so often. On a previous occasion she'd even seen Biyu's husband and his distinctive cycle-rickshaw outside.

'No message.' Hai Jun had informed her gravely that Biyu was only there to pick up some cream for a dose of athlete's foot.

So now she almost dreaded these visits where she was so often disappointed. And the worry about leaving Hilly alone wouldn't go away. She waited behind the other people in the queue, preparing herself to receive the same response.

The person in front of her was an elderly man in a fur cap, wanting a treatment for his gall stones. Whilst his medicine was being prepared in the back room, she overheard him talking to his neighbour. Their voices were low, and they presumed she could not understand Shanghainese, but the mention of the name *Zha Wei* made her start and sharpen her concentration.

'It's got to be him,' came the old man's voice, 'Every time we arrange to take out a patrol, they change their route or change their times.'

'We've stopped giving him the maps of the roadblocks too because if we do, there are always twice as many Japs waiting for us. He's working for the Kuomintang.'

'We should never have trusted him, he's a double dealer – always was.'

'There's rumours he knows where that English sailor is. The Japs are desperate to catch him and the government have already offered Zha Wei a hundred dollars to tell them where he is. They want one over on the Brits, see.'

'Does Zha Wei know where he is?'

'He knows all right. But he's holding out for more cash.'

Their conversation was interrupted by Jun returning with their herbal pills wrapped in a paper bag.

Zofia fidgeted from foot to foot. She was torn. She must get back home – warn Charlie that Zha Wei was planning on handing him in. Not only that, but she could see what would happen. Zha Wei would tell everyone Theo had talked, and blame him for the betrayal, and this fired her with outrage.

'You again?' The pharmacist seemed amused.

Zofia was unsettled, forgetting why she'd come. 'Oh. Any message?' She was about to turn away, her mind on Charlie and Zha Wei's treachery. But then Jun grinned and placed something on the counter in front of her. A brown packet tied with string. 'For me?'

A conspiratorial smile and a nod.

She took it to one side and opened it, all the time aware Jun was bolting the door, locking her in.

She began to protest, but he held up a hand in peace. 'A friend of Ming Biyu's is a friend of ours. We do what we can against the Japanese.' Jun's English was almost perfect.

'You speak English!'

'Not in front of most people. But it is useful. I learned at the university when I did my pharmacy training. My wife is an English teacher. Was. She was killed in the uprising in Nanjing.'

'I'm sorry. How awful.'

'So I moved here, nearer my parents. I keep a low profile. I just wanted to say, if you need anything, you can rely on me.' He gave her a meaningful look.

She sat down and undid the small parcel. It contained a scrap of newspaper, with Theo's writing on the blank part at the edge of the page where there was no newsprint. Just the sight of his writing, that there should be this message at all, made her face hot. She told herself to concentrate as she turned it this way and that to read the short message.

> *Bring the clothes and shoes we asked for to the crossroads at the corner of Woosung Road. A couple of jerseys from my wardrobe and the bank books and cash from my briefcase. Any other money if you can get it. The others will need the things I asked for.*

She paused. Obviously Theo didn't know Charlie and Zha Wei had taken most of his clothes, or that she'd moved house.

> *We can't implicate our Chinese friends in our escape. They can be useful to so many more if we make it out. So you must wait at the crossroads just up the road from the camp. We'll find you there.*
>
> *Our friend will collect you from the place where you pick up this message, on Thursday between ten and midnight, to take you to the rendezvous point.*
>
> *I hope you have managed a boat. My fingers are crossed. Keep your head down and look like a peasant. I can't tell you how much this means to us to have someone on the outside. We would not get far without good shoes or cash, or a means to get away.*
>
> *So this is au revoir in advance – there will be no time for us to talk, I'm afraid – for I do hope I will see you again. When I do it will be when all this is over and we can celebrate in a civilized way and have that dinner at St Pete's.*
>
> *T*

'Good news?' Jun asked.

'I think so.' She didn't know what to tell him.

He waved a palm at her. 'Don't worry, I don't want to know.

Many secrets pass through here, and my mouth is always closed. Like you, I would like to survive to the end of this war.' He smiled.

'Then there is one small thing you can help me with. I need an antiseptic. Have you a herbal cream for that?'

He nodded and went to a small drawer at the back of the shop. He opened it and took something out.

When he placed it on the counter, she saw it was a small pink tin of the Western brand, Germolene.

He grinned at her. 'Whoever your friends are, they might recognize this.'

'Exactly what I need,' she said.

'There will be no charge. And take a stick of liquorice for the girl who waits outside. Where is she today?'

'At home. She has work to do.' She didn't want to reveal too much.

She thought of Hilly back at Zha Wei's and a panic rose in her throat. 'Thank you, but I have to go.'

And then she was outside and rushing down the road, her thoughts tumbling in turmoil, taken up with Theo's escape from Woosung Camp. Even if he escaped, he couldn't come back to Shanghai. But how was she to find him a boat? And even then, how would he get out of China?

The difficulty of doing what Theo tasked her to do, with Zha Wei watching their every move, was frightening. Thursday. Only two days away.

But then she slowed. There was the checkpoint, and she had to look as if she was calm and not draw attention as she passed through. She prayed it wouldn't be the same man who had asked her to dance.

Not him. Thank heaven.

She handed over her papers and the Japanese man looked into her eyes for a moment. It was like being cut with a knife. Could he see the panic inside her?

But he folded the card together and pushed it back in her hand.

It was at this precise moment that she realized that the Japanese for her had ceased to be saviours like Sugihara, and had become the enemy. It made tears spring to her eyes.

Once close to the house she took a deep breath. Not only was there the problem of Theo, but also the fact that Zha Wei was going to give Charlie up to the Japanese. He was just trying to squeeze more money out of them. Olga would be in trouble too for harbouring him. And what would become of her and Hilly then? She couldn't keep it to herself; she'd have to tell Charlie, and that was a conversation she wasn't looking forward to at all.

Chapter 29

Charlie was in the hallway when Zofia returned.

'I need a word,' she said, glancing over her shoulder to check nobody was within earshot.

Charlie was guarded. 'What is it?'

'I overheard men in the pharmacy. They were saying Zha Wei knows where the English sailor is and is negotiating with the Kuomintang to hand him over.'

'It's just rumour. Take no notice.'

'They were definite. And as soon as the Nationalists have you, they'll crow over it, and then that'll be the end for you. Public execution.'

She saw him take it in and then reject it. 'Zha Wei needs me. I'm the one who's in touch with Blighty and who's supplying his network with news from the BBC.'

A car drew up and one of Zha's men, Chow, a short man with a bristling crew cut, appeared at the door.

'Remember,' hissed Zofia, 'he needs you only as long as the price is higher to keep you alive than sell you. He's a thug and you know it.'

Chow gave them a look as he passed, but Zofia carried on

speaking. 'It's not safe here. You must talk to Olga and try to find an alternative.'

'Oh, shut the hell up. You've been against Zha Wei from the start even though—'

'Even though what? He threatened me and threw Theo out of his house?'

His angry face was inches from hers. 'The only thing I can do is to keep the communists sweet until I can persuade someone to get me out of here—'

He stopped mid-sentence as Zha Wei appeared. He'd obviously been summoned by his acolyte and didn't like them conspiring. He put a hand on Charlie's shoulder. 'Join us for a game, Charlie?'

He was steered away. Obviously he'd no choice.

Zofia watched him go with a sense of impotent rage before heading up the stairs.

A strange childish sing-song was coming out of the door.

'Hilly?' Zofia turned the handle and went in. She could smell sex before she'd even got two feet inside. Hilly was sitting on the bed stroking the smooth satin of the counterpane. Her face was tipped forward, her hair falling around her face. The singing stopped.

'What did he do?' Zofia asked.

The fact that Hilly didn't raise her head made her certain.

'I didn't mean to do it,' Hilly said. 'He made me lean against the wall and lift my skirt. Don't be angry.'

'I'm not angry with you. I'm angry with hm.' She grabbed a towel and threw it to her. 'Go and wash every trace of that man away. Now.'

Hilly jumped up, and in that moment Zofia saw the swelling around her eye, and the bruises at the top of her arms. She said nothing, but the tight feeling in her chest grew into a solid knot. When Hilly came back smelling of soap, Zofia had already packed their bags.

'We're leaving,' she said. 'Put your coat on and wait for me here.'

She stormed downstairs and demanded to see Charlie.

'He's busy,' said Chow.

She pushed by him.

'Hey! You can't—'

His words faded as she marched into the gaming hall, where the men were at roulette, surrounded by several prostitutes and croupiers leaning over the tables. The room was heady with smoke and cheap perfume. She ignored the other Chinese men at the gaming tables, but the bodyguards enabled her to pinpoint the squat figure of Zha Wei with the big, padded shoulders to his striped jacket. Charlie would be at his side, she knew.

Charlie heard her footsteps and turned, staring at her as if he'd seen an apparition.

Around the edges of the room Zha Wei's men watched her curiously, this woman in a coat who looked so out of place.

'You bastard,' she said. She swept the chips off the table before Zha Wei where they fell with a clatter on the floor.

Zha Wei turned slowly. 'You'll regret that.'

She turned to Charlie. 'He had sex with Hilly.'

'She asked for it,' Zha Wei said, giving Charlie a complicit smile.

Zofia turned her burning gaze on Charlie. 'Don't you dare support him, you lowlife. You know she can't consent. Her face is beaten black and blue!'

'She was happy enough.' Zha Wei shrugged. 'Enjoyed it.'

'She's not one of your whores, she's still a child. Charlie, tell him.'

Zha Wei rested a warning hand on Charlie's sleeve. Charlie stayed silent, his eyes glancing guiltily away.

They were now hemmed in by his men, hovering on the balls of their feet, like animals surrounding a kill. Zha Wei released Charlie, waved an impatient gesture, and immediately she was barricaded by a group of younger men. 'Escort her back to her room and lock her in with that other bitch. Any trouble, you know what to do. I'll deal with them later when I've finished my game.'

'Charlie!' she shouted, but he ignored her cries as they roughly muscled her back upstairs and propelled her through the door. She leapt for the handle as the key scraped in the lock.

She stayed looking at the door a moment. She'd thought Charlie was a friend. But he hadn't lifted a finger to help them and now he was colluding with Zha Wei. She understood why – he was trying to save his own skin, but his betrayal cut deep.

'Did they lock us in?' Hilly asked, her eyes wide and frightened.

Zofia's thoughts whirred. It was obvious they'd have to find a way to get out. 'Did you pack?'

Hilly shook her head. 'What will they do to us?'

'Nothing. Because we won't be here. As soon as Charlie or Olga come to the door, we're getting out.'

Chapter 30

Inside the camp, Theo and Griff were making intricate preparations. They couldn't go until the next night under the dark of the moon. Griff had calculated it, the message had gone to Zofia, and now every hour they had to wait made them more on edge. Today was damp and colder, the sky grey with a haze of drizzle. It didn't make the waiting any easier or fill them with confidence.

Griff had made maps of the terrain outside the camp by speaking to other prisoners.

'Griff says there are thousands of American military in China now,' Theo told Lennie. 'They want revenge on the Japs who caused Pearl Harbor.'

'Yeah. I heard that too,' Lennie said. 'One of the other Aussies has a crystal radio. Hush-hush though. The Chinese have welcomed the Yanks, they're calling them allies.'

'Griff thinks we can make it to one of their airstrips.'

'Dream on,' said Lennie. 'I also heard that any foreigners found by the Japanese outside Shanghai would be shot.'

'Oh great. Cheer me up, why don't you?'

After the mid-day break Lennie and Theo returned to the garden, but there was no sign of Griff.

'Where's the major?' Lennie hissed.

'Latrines? Stomach trouble?'

'He never mentioned it.'

He didn't return all afternoon.

Theo began to be uneasy. He turned to Lennie. 'What shall we do?' Theo asked. 'We can't go without him. He's the one with the maps and the plan and everything.'

It soon became apparent what had happened. The guards had found the long pole with the hook on the end of it when they searched his billet and fearing it to be some sort of weapon, had beaten him and tied him to a post to stand out in the rain. Fortunately, they hadn't grasped its true purpose, but it was still terrible news.

'Shit,' Theo said. 'The last thing we need. The message has gone out with the date on it and everything's all lined up.'

'I guess we just abandon it then,' Lennie said. 'We don't know how long they'll keep him there. The last one was left there for three days. Try for another date once he's back.'

'We can't. There's a woman outside risking her life for us. She'll have a boat and everything. We have to go. But without Griff, once we're out we won't know where we're going and where the villages or the American bases might be.'

'We've only two choices,' Lennie said. 'Go, or give it up. Which are you going for? And don't tell me you're going to be stupid.'

Theo sighed but kept his mouth shut. Could they still go under the wire without the major? It seemed impossible. But they'd got this far, weeks of planning, carefully building contact with Ming Biyu and Zofia. He was stubborn enough not to want to give up. And besides, there was Zofia; she'd be waiting. Hopefully with new shoes.

Griff was still standing outside tied to a post. Upright, back straight and with an indomitable expression. Everyone ignored him because that was the safest thing to do, but it made Theo unspeakably angry to see him there. By nightfall, Griff was hanging forward, his clothes drenched.

Theo didn't sleep that night thinking about him, the pain of having his arms tied like that, the inability to sleep. He prayed like he never had before.

In the morning, Griff's legs had crumpled more and only the post was holding him up. They went to the garden as usual, but halfway through the morning they saw two Japanese guards go over to the post and let Griff off. He crawled away then stood unsteadily to stumble towards his billet. Nobody dared to help him; they knew what they'd get if they did.

After Theo grabbed his lunchtime slop of congee and dishwater tea, he went to sit on the concrete path where Lennie was slurping his.

'Griff's free,' he said. 'We can go.'

'No we can't. You saw him. He'll not be fit.'

'Wanna bet? He's Mr Invincible, right?'

Lennie coughed, then rolled his eyes. 'You got some kind of a death wish?'

'Imagine the three of us on the other side of that wire. Free to go where we please. Free to find the Americans and get out of China and this hellhole for good.'

'You've watched too many movies.'

'Aw c'mon Lennie. Let's go see him. We won't push him. It's just we're so close to freedom I can taste it.'

Lennie looked up over his bowl. 'Tell me I'm not going to regret this.'

Chapter 31

The Blue Lilac

By nightfall, Zofia had everything packed and ready to go. The door was still locked and she was just waiting for any chance to leave. She'd hoped Charlie or Olga would come and she'd banked on being able to negotiate her way out, though she dreaded Zha Wei appearing at the door.

But though it grew late, nobody came. 'It makes me feel funny, being locked in.' Hilly's eyes were anxious. 'D'you think they'll let us out tomorrow?'

'I don't know.'

Tomorrow. A lurch of panic. Theo's escape was tomorrow and they still had to get to the pharmacy with the men's supplies.

Zofia couldn't sleep. She was fully dressed in a pair of loose trousers with a skirt over it, a cardigan, and a Chinese padded jacket she'd got from the market.

She couldn't settle because her mind was restless. She still hadn't found Theo a boat. She didn't know how she could, and she hated letting people down. And the fact Theo might get out of the camp but then be recaptured made her heart pound.

'What's the matter?' Hilly broke into her thoughts.

'Nothing. Try to sleep.'

Biyu's husband, Ming, was going to wait at the pharmacy, and then take Zofia by cycle-rickshaw to the crossroads near the camp, where she was supposed to hide until Theo came, hand over the stuff, and tell him where to meet the boat. Ming would leave immediately after the drop-off, so if anything went wrong nobody would knew he'd been part of it.

But now, stuck here, not only had she arranged no boat, but there was Hilly to consider too.

Zofia weighed up the dangers. If the Japanese caught them, they could be shot for helping someone escape, no doubt about it. But it was a risk she understood, if it was only herself. She'd no right to drag Hilly into it. But then again, there was no chance she'd leave her to the clutches of that mobster Zha Wei.

When sleep came it was disturbed; she kept waking with a sick feeling in the stomach.

'Will Charlie come for us? Will they let us out today?' Hilly's questions couldn't be answered.

The morning passed slowly. Surely someone would come?

But no. The afternoon dragged on. Every time she heard footfalls on the stairs, Hilly got up and backed herself against the wall. But still no one came with food or water, though there was a sink in the room so they could at least drink. Zofia banged on the door and shouted, but it fell on deaf ears.

Zofia wore a restless path on the floorboards, pacing, unable to be still. They'd have to break out somehow. Night-time was the best time to go – when Zha Wei was busy downstairs with his gambling friends and the liquor was flowing. Most nights he kept his makeshift roulette table open, and Chinese men and Japanese soldiers would come to try to gamble back what they'd lost before.

Once dusk fell, Zofia tied the men's things Chinese-style, in a long piece of material criss-crossed over her front and knotted at the back. 'We can't wait any longer,' she said.

Hilly's expression was wary. 'What are we going to do?'

'Here, put these on. We are going to get out of here,' she said. She passed Hilly a pair of trousers and a jacket intended for the men.

Hilly was wide eyed. The bruises on her face were turning yellow and purple. 'Do I have to wear these clothes?' she said.

'Better to blend in.'

'I'm scared. He won't like it if we run away.'

'I know. But that's why we're going. So he can't hurt you anymore.' She shook the trousers at Hilly, who reluctantly took them.

'How are we going to get out?' Hilly asked, as she struggled into the clothes.

'The window's our only chance.' A flat roof of what had once been the public bar was about six feet below them, extending onto lawns that were now unkempt and bedraggled.

Hilly winced as she peered out. 'It's a long way down.'

From below, Zofia could hear the low voices of Zha Wei's men in the hall. There was always someone by the front door keeping watch, ready to warn Zha Wei if the Kempeitai or anyone else came by. A gramophone was playing jazz music in the distance and every time a door opened it blared into the hall.

'Here, help me. But we have to do it quietly.' She gestured to the dressing table. 'Let's stick this in front of the door. To stop them getting in.'

Maybe it would hold them up if Zha Wei or his men came after them. She switched the light off in the room for the same reason.

Just as they were doing that, a wail of sirens blared. A flash of headlights.

What now? They peered out into the dark.

The Shanghai Police. Coming up the road that curved alongside the scrubby grounds.

Two cars drew up in a screech of rubber in the car park. A

slam of doors – two policemen from the first car. Four Japanese soldiers from the second. The police strode around the corner towards the front of the house, the soldiers following, rifles at the ready.

Hilly turned to Zofia. 'Have they come for Zha Wei?'

'I don't know. Ignore it. Help me with the window.' Just one more problem they could do without.

Zofia redoubled her efforts on the frame, trying to prise away the fly screen. It was stiff – the wood had swelled in the damp.

Hilly watched her wrestle. 'It's stuck,' she whispered.

'If I can just get my fingers underneath, I can do it,' Zofia said, pulling hard.

'No, let me!' Hilly grabbed it and yanked. Suddenly it gave and clattered to the ground.

They both froze, expecting someone to come. But the noise of music and men's voices carried on and nobody came. Until the blare of the jazz stopped, like someone had cut the wire.

Shouts and a woman's screams. Scuffling, banging doors. Running feet.

Hilly was staring out. 'It's Charlie and Olga,' she said.

Zofia put her arm around Hilly's waist as she went to see.

They'd got Charlie. Caught between two Japanese men who were dragging him away towards the car park. The defeated set of his shoulders said it all. Zofia realized in that moment that Charlie, who'd seemed such an enormous presence, was a puny man after all, just as short as the Japanese. It filled her with sorrow. Olga was frantic, clawing and shouting curses, and wriggling to get away. But there were too many men, and they bundled them into the police car.

In a squeal of tyres, the cars drove off.

As their tail-lights receded, Zha Wei strode out onto the drive to watch them go. His broad back and squat figure made Zofia want to throw a brick at him. The double-crossing bastard must have finally been offered the right reward.

'Where will they take them?' Hilly's voice was small.

Zofia didn't want to think about it. It would be the end for Charlie, after all this time and effort. What a waste.

Another insidious thought crept into her mind … with Charlie and Olga gone, they were even more at the mercy of Zha Wei and his thugs. Or maybe the police would come back for them too.

She waited for Zha to disappear again around the side of the house. 'We've got to get out.' Once he'd gone, she attacked the window with new urgency. She shoved the screen under the bed while she tried to grapple with the catch. It was clogged; the brass slider had been painted over with gloss paint. Desperate to free it, she resorted to using a nail file to scrape off the paint around the catch. It seemed to take an age, with Hilly impatiently breathing down her neck. With a heave and a tug, it came free and she could push up the sash.

'I'll go first and help you down,' Zofia said.

'I can do it.'

'Then don't wait, just come straight after. The hard part will be getting off the roof, and we might make a noise. It's close to the bar window, so we must get away across the garden. Run straight towards the hedge at the back. Okay?'

A nod, though Hilly was blinking as if she'd suddenly realized it wasn't a game. 'We can't go!' she suddenly said.

'We can. Come on. Just follow me.'

'Zha Wei will catch us.' Her voice wavered with terror.

'Not if we're quick.' Zofia made sure her bundle was tied tight around her chest, then crossed her fingers and slipped one leg out of the window, her blood pounding at her throat. She looked back and said, 'Ready?'

Hilly didn't answer, but was gripping the edge of the window, her eyes fixed on Zofia.

Zofia dropped softly onto the flat roof. It held her weight and she thought the noise had only been a gentle thud. She gestured frantically at Hilly to come after her.

But she needn't have worried; Hilly was already half in and out, baggy trousers hitched up around her thighs, and she threw herself out with an ungainly sprawl, landing with a great thump beside her.

Zofia flinched. That was loud.

Panicked, Zofia ran to the edge of the flat roof and peeped over.

Banging behind them. Someone trying to get in the bedroom. Then more crashes as the door bashed into the dressing table.

'Quick!'

The scrape of the dressing table legs on the floorboards. Chinese voices at the door.

Beneath them, on the floor below, a window opened and a man's head looked out, then disappeared inside.

'Now!' Zofia levered her way over the edge of the roof, clinging on with her fingers to the edge as she put her foot onto the only foothold – the horizontal drainpipe. She braced and let it take her weight whilst her fingers grappled the edge until she could finally let go.

Her feet hit the concrete path and her knees buckled and gave way. A pain shot up her legs, but she was already on her feet and gesturing urgently to Hilly.

Hilly's anxious face appeared looking over. 'I can't!'

'You have to. Just lower yourself down. I'll catch you.'

A whimper and a shake of the head. Behind her, the light flashed on in the room. Which meant the men were in.

'Quick! They're coming!'

The voice of Chow shouting; Zofia made out the word for 'window'. She signalled wildly at Hilly to jump.

It was enough. Hilly shuffled to the edge and then let herself scramble over the edge. She almost flattened Zofia as she fell, but they were away, clinging to each other, haring in a half crouch towards the dark shadows of the hedge.

They pushed their way through rough sticks and into the garden of the next house, then ran like rabbits to the one after that.

Behind them they heard Zha Wei's men yelling and then a flashlight whipped back and forth across the trees. In the garden of the next house there was a summerhouse, and they dived behind it. Its windows were broken and there were cigarette ends peppered around it as if people had used it as some sort of meeting place.

Zofia looked back at the lights of the house, and her heart seemed to stop for a beat.

'Come on!' she said dragging Hilly into motion again. 'We're going to Jun at the pharmacy.'

'Why?'

Zofia didn't answer. She didn't want Hilly to know anything. Any kind of knowledge was dangerous. She stumbled breathlessly through the dark gardens trying to find a way to the road. She was desperately unfit for running, she realized.

She was tugging Hilly behind her by the arm.

They were out, but she didn't know if they'd be in time to help Theo. In the next street she heard men shouting in Chinese. 'Run,' she said, desperate to get away from Zha Wei's men. The bundle of shoes bounced uncomfortably against her chest.

She stopped dead as they reached the main road. Two Japanese soldiers were walking up towards them. She yanked Hilly back into the shadows.

Chapter 32

The day of the escape arrived. Theo could see Lennie was tense and sidled over to him. 'Relax. We need to behave like it's any other day.'

'I am relaxed,' he snapped. But Theo could see the vein pulsing in Lennie's neck and the way his shoulders were set like concrete. His cough was worse too.

He didn't feel much better himself. His stomach cramped in a way that almost made him double over, and when he was using the trowel, his hands were slippery with sweat. All the tools they used in the garden were signed in and out by the guards and then locked away, except one small trowel, which Griff told them was broken and had managed to smuggle out for repair.

Griff hobbled to join them and Theo breathed a sigh of relief. He'd spoken to him the night before and despite the state he was in, Griff had insisted they should carry on. 'A plan's a plan,' he said.

They continued planting. It was beans they were sowing – long rows of them. About the only thing they could get. Ming Biyu's pak choi was actually sprouting. Every now and then Theo looked over the fence to her shack and saw the cycle-rickshaw sitting outside. The husband should be leaving any moment now to go into Shanghai to meet up with Zofia.

The thought of it made his belly contract.

The day seemed interminably long. He watched Griff wincing whenever he moved, and heard Lennie cough again. He vacillated between wanting to call it off, and the sweet pull of freedom.

By late afternoon, Theo just wanted to get it over with. To know if he was going to live or be a corpse on that electric wire. He wondered about Zofia and whether she too was as nervous as he was. She was taking a risk for them, and she could never know how much that was appreciated. Three men pretending to be interested in gardening, all the while staring death in the face. He glanced at Lennie, who was a wasted man in comparison with the big burly chap who had met him at the gates when he first arrived.

Night fell. Theo had counted the patrols and knew their exact routine. Griff was to make his way from the officers' section and knock softly on their barracks' door when the coast was clear.

Theo and Lennie were ready, though Lennie continued to cough. His cough was a worry Theo was loath to broach. Each time he coughed, Griff sucked in his breath in a disapproving manner, and Lennie would look sheepish and turn away.

Theo and Lennie tied sacks around their knees to cushion them as they crawled across the no man's land between the gravel path and the fence.

'You okay?' he asked Lennie, whispering in the dark.

'Better than ever. You're a pal. If we get out of here, I'll—'

'When. When we get out of here.'

'When … I'll buy you a beer. Deal?'

'Deal.' Tears pricked his eyes. He knew Lennie should really be in a hospital, not trying to crawl under a four-thousand volt fence, and he knew he was responsible for this foolhardy idea.

To busy himself, Theo wrapped his hands in sacking, and that stung like the devil because he still hadn't properly healed from the burns. The sores kept getting infected, and nothing he tried could cure it.

At last, the soft knock came. Theo glanced at Lennie, at the whites of his eyes in the dark. Lennie clapped him on the shoulder to show he'd understood the signal. Theo reached for him and felt his thin ribs as they hugged wordlessly for a long second.

Out of the back door of the hut, the one usually kept locked but which they'd unscrewed. The door creaked and they held their breath as Griff silently greeted them, his eyes glistening bright, his mouth taut under his bristling moustache. Griff softly closed the door behind them and waved his hand in a gesture that meant 'hurry'.

Theo dropped to his knees. The lights bounced off the fog and Theo began to crawl rapidly toward the fence. Lennie's breath was hoarse in the back of his throat as he followed him.

Don't cough, Theo prayed.

Griff was bringing up the rear, behind them.

The gravel path was flinty and Theo was glad of the padding on his knees. He had to stay low, under the swirling fog. In the distance he could hear the footsteps of guards marching.

His heart thumped in his chest. There'd been two other deaths apart from Bradford's where the men had been shot 'accidentally'. He'd no doubt that if the guards caught them, they'd shoot.

To his ears the sound of the crunch of gravel was unmistakeable. But no men came running. Behind him, he heard the too-loud scrape and rattle as the other two navigated the path. Once on the scrubby grass, he kept on moving forwards, panting with effort, anxious not to hold up the two behind him.

At the electric fence he could hear the tick of it, the electricity throbbing through the wires. He felt for a piece of soft ground and drew the tea scoop out from his trousers. He began to dig frantically. As he flung the earth back the others arrived to help. Lennie had a sharpened stick, and Griff was using the trowel.

The metallic sound of it as it hit the earth would bring the patrol, he was sure, but they'd passed now and their footsteps were receding.

After five minutes of frantic digging there was a shallow depression under the wire. Theo's mouth tasted of earth and their fog-damp clothes.

Another frantic bout of shovelling. 'Is it enough?' he whispered to Griff.

Griff peered into the gap. Then he crossed his fingers and gestured at Theo to go through. This was it. Theo lay on his back. They'd practised this. Shuffled on their backs on the floor of the billet. That way they could see how much clearance was under the wire. He had a sudden image of limbo dancing at one of the rowdy Shanghailander's parties one New Year's Eve.

Don't think. He began to push his way through by shunting with his heels. His nose was centimetres from the wire and its pulse.

He stopped a moment to breathe, aware he'd been holding his breath all this time. Slowly he inched underneath, eyes fixed on the deadly silvery strand above him, and then finally he pulled his legs through by dragging his body under with his elbows. As soon as he was clear, he ran in a crouch to the outer fence and began to dig in the shallow hollow where they'd left messages in the bamboo.

A split-second image of Zofia flashed into his mind. He hoped she would have clothes and shoes waiting, and a boat out of here.

Within what seemed like seconds, Griff was there next to him, jamming his trowel into the stony ground, throwing up earth and stones. Here the ground was harder and Theo's fingers were raw and numb with cold and damp. Lennie still hadn't appeared. 'What's up with Lennie?'

'Hole was too shallow for him and not wide enough for his shoulders,' whispered Griff. 'He has to dig it out more.'

Just then they heard steps on the gravel path. They'd been too noisy.

They both dived to the ground hoping the dark and fog would cover them.

But what about Lennie, stuck out there next to the fence?

They stayed still, until shouts made them brace, as if for impact. They'd seen him.

Theo and Griff flung earth up, digging like dogs after a bone.

'Time to go.' Griff wriggled his way under, a hair's breadth from the electric wire.

As soon as his feet were through, Theo was scrabbling after him.

A miracle he didn't touch the wire. But there was no time for thought. By now the flash of torches was slicing into the fog. Theo tasted dirt but he was through. He went a few more yards on his stomach, his face inches from the ground, before he dared to stand into a crouch and follow the disappearing figure of Griff as he dived into a field. From there he pitched into a run.

Theo hared along the road to the crossroads. Behind them the flare of torches through the fog. Theo cast about, running this way and that. There was nobody waiting for them.

The crossroads was deserted. No sign of a rickshaw, or of a person.

He searched manically, in case something had been left for them – a parcel, a note, anything.

Zofia hadn't come. It was like being hit with a baseball bat.

Thoughts zipped through his head. Had she been stopped? Arrested. Oh God, not that. Had she decided it was too risky?

Two shots rang out; sharp noises that made his heart skitter and leap. At first he thought they were firing at him, but then he realized with a sickening lurch, it would be Lennie.

But he couldn't stop, Griff was calling to him. He'd abandoned the road and was already leaping over the ditch and heading across the field.

Theo stood a moment as if glued to the ground. He'd been

so certain he'd see Zofia that her absence had sucked the power from his legs.

Torches swung and he was aware of a slice of light cutting into his arm almost like a physical blow. He burst into movement and ran, the pant of his breath loud in his ears. Which way?

To run was torture – his feet in his makeshift shoes stumbled and staggered on stones making his eyes smart, but he daren't stop. He spotted Griff as he zigzagged through the field, and caught up with him just as he flung himself into a ditch. Theo leapt in beside him.

'Where now?'

'The side of the field. See that smoke? The shack? They'll head for there, ask the Chinese what they saw. So left. We have to go left.'

'To the river? But what about Zofia?'

'Forget her. Too dangerous.'

'No. We need the shoes and the clothes,' Theo said. 'The camp clothes mark us out as escapees. And I can't travel in these sandals, they're disintegrating already. We should give her a few more minutes.'

'You want to die like him?' Griff gestured back to the wire.

Theo felt Griff's words detonate inside him. He had a sudden urge to run back, to drag Lennie away.

The staccato orders of the Japanese guards pierced through the fog, followed by the scuffle of footsteps around the wire.

'For God's sake, keep moving,' Griff said, yanking him forward.

Theo's eyes were wet but he stumbled along the edges of the fields, battling on painful feet through the white fog which came in patches. When it thinned, they scuttled along like beetles, fearful of being seen. When it thickened, they allowed themselves time to take a few snatched breaths.

Theo wanted to turn back, go to the rendezvous point, but the Japanese were on to them now, and Griff was right, they had to put distance between them.

At the river, they'd get a sampan. That had been the plan – Zofia would have found them Chinese clothes, and she would guide them to into the countryside, to a sampan to take them upstream.

The rosy idea in his head instantly died. Everything had gone wrong.

The outside world looked so different in this shifting light. They kept stumbling into holes, their feet unused to walking such distances. At least Griff had sandals, even if they were only made of old rope. They were both shaking with cold and fear.

The fog thickened so they could hardly see a yard before them, but they could hear the lap of water, the distant foghorn of a ship on the river.

Griff grabbed his arm. 'Slowly,' he whispered, 'we don't know who's out there.'

They crept forward until the sound of voices halted them in their tracks.

Japanese. They recognized the cadence of the speech.

Griff's hand tightened on his arm, fingers digging in.

There were several men, by the sound of it. A patrol.

Very slowly, they eased their way backwards, hardly daring to breathe.

One minute he was upright, the next tumbling backwards, dragging Griff with him. He hit his shoulder on something and then a freezing wash of water welled over his head. The river. It was behind him not in front. They'd got disorientated in the fog.

He struggled to breathe from the shock, arms flailing to find the bank. But then he realized the patrol was on the bank. He could already hear them.

Griff was in the water too. 'Swim,' Theo managed to choke out.

The water was full of debris but there was no choice but to follow the current.

From the bank, the staccato sound of gunshots.

The Japanese were firing at the water. Griff floundered beside him. He wasn't a strong swimmer, but desperation was forcing him into a splashing crawl.

Theo swam close to him. 'No splashing,' he said, through chattering teeth. 'They'll hear us. Slow and smooth. Look for a boat, any sort of craft.'

Thank God for the dark, and the fog which hung over the river. The river was vast and they were weak, so there was no way they could swim across the four hundred yards against the current, even if they could see where they were going. They needed a boat to get to the other side and safety.

Theo was aware of commotion on the bank, but he didn't dare stop. Bullets hit into the water behind him, but he didn't turn. He was already beginning to tire, and Griff was moving so slowly he was almost at a standstill.

Theo scanned the banks for some sort of hiding place.

Through the wreathing mist a jetty stuck out into the water. About a hundred yards ahead. He waited for Griff to drift towards him.

'I can't go on,' Griff gasped. 'I can't feel my legs or arms.'

'You can,' said Theo through gritted teeth. 'Grab my waistband.'

Slowly the current carried them downstream until they were within reach of the jetty.

A Chinese man, old and wrinkled as a prune, was tying up his boat and stared at them through the fog, but he didn't say anything, just watched them as they moved through the oily black water.

'Shit,' Theo thought. 'That's torn it.'

Theo and Griff each grabbed one of the stanchions and wrapped their arms around it.

Above, feet scuffling and thumping on the wooden planks, Japanese voices. He guessed they were asking if the man there had seen anyone. Theo knew enough Chinese to understand the old man was saying he hadn't.

Thank God.

He heard expletives and a slap and the noise of someone falling heavily on the planks above them, before the footsteps faded away.

By now Griff was almost unconscious, clinging to the post as if frozen there.

Theo hadn't the strength to climb out. The Chinese man must have been hit and be out cold. They waited another ten minutes before Theo thumped on the underside of the jetty.

Finally, a scraping noise from above, and the next thing a voice. 'Wait.'

Theo understood the Chinese.

After what seemed like hours, voices returned. The man had gathered some friends, and a boat was sculling alongside. They were hauled dripping into the sampan. By now both Theo and Griff were unable to speak. Theo bowed and made a trembling greeting with his hands to the man who was now sporting a cut and bruised cheek. Two of the other men threw a blanket around their shoulders, but they were so frozen they hardly cared. All Theo wanted to do was sleep, and he must have lost consciousness for the next thing they knew they were being dragged out of the boat and into a small house where there was a fire lit and two women staring at them as if they were ghosts.

They made Theo and Griff strip off their wet clothes and wrapped them both in cotton quilts.

They were exhausted, but Theo allowed himself a small thrill of elation that they'd escaped. They were safe. For how long, he didn't know.

Chapter 33

In Soochow, Haru watched the splash as his soldiers shot the two rebel women right there on the wharf of the canal, next to their illicit cargo of gunpowder. It had been concealed in tarpaulin inside the burlap sacks of grain they were supposedly ferrying. When his men had lifted those sacks, they'd weighed too light and a sharp bayonet had revealed the truth, as the black powder cascaded around their feet.

They'd blurted out their Red Army contacts readily enough when his men held up their baby sons by the ankles and threatened to gut them there and then. Then they killed them anyway, just as they had the women, who were floating face down after them as a warning to anyone else from the CCP.

Haru swayed slightly on his feet, a little nauseous, observing everything through the grainy filter hanging over his eyes. His men were scooping up the precious explosive and putting it into metal containers. He left them to it and went back to his lodgings, rubbing at his eyes, and hoping the desire to vomit would wear off.

At the beginning, he hadn't meant to use *Chandu* so often. The troops were given paregoric, a tincture of opium flavoured with anise and camphor; he'd tried it himself and found it underwhelming. When he told his new friend, Pau, the chief of police, about his persistent headaches, Pau smiled and suggested he try smoking the 'gentleman's saviour' – an opium pipe, something banned by the previous government and rare to find these days.

Haru was reluctant, but he was so desperate to relieve his pain, he eventually agreed. Pau brought round the opium pipe, and Haru felt obliged to give it a try or lose face. He eyed the pipe Pau prepared and handed him with scepticism. Despite opium's fearsome reputation, he'd be able to handle it, he was sure.

He inhaled the hot, bitter vapour. The rush of pleasure it gave him was astonishing. The first time he smoked it, he drowned in a kind of euphoric daze, the war drifting away from him like hazy wallpaper. He'd felt like a child again; the pain had gone entirely, and he was sinking in a luxurious feeling of being cocooned in ultimate safety.

The next day he thought a little more couldn't do any harm, so he ordered Pau to bring him a bigger supply. After that, Pau turned up most days, and despite his initial doubts, he was lonely and Pau always had a good supply of the black stuff, and a tale or two to tell whilst he prepared the paraphernalia of the pipe and lamp. The painstaking ritual of lighting the lamp, of rolling the pill of opium was an essential part of his smoking experience. There was something Zen about this careful arrangement of tools and attention to detail.

Haru glanced at his watch. Today Pau was taking him to meet another government contact of his, a dealer who was a connoisseur and would supply him with better equipment for the taking of it. Haru was impatient as the time ticked by, hovering at the back window to the street, fidgeting with his uniform belt buckle. He'd lost weight, he noticed with surprise.

He was a little agitated because Pau was late, and he hadn't had his smoke today. Of course he didn't actually need it, but it was the only thing to relieve his headaches. He began to understand why his men were so insistent on their ration of paregoric. He remembered the sheer terror of the initial fighting and how, no matter how many Chinese he dispatched, there always seemed to be more of the devils.

He could wait a few more hours, he told himself, because he wanted to have the best opium paraphernalia in Soochow. Now he'd tasted it for himself, he found the whole history of opium fascinating. Pau had told him that antique pipes were carved by master craftsmen, from rich materials like ivory, jade, tortoiseshell and shagreen, and he was keen to see such things. He missed the aestheticism of Japan, finding most Chinese objects gaudy and crass. Perhaps these would be different.

Aah! There he was now. He watched his portly friend struggle from the ferry. Haru had grown to welcome the appearance of Pau, always so deferential to him, sweating in his Western-style suit and greasy tie. Pau had arranged a rickshaw to take them across the many bridges to the south side of the city, and it was waiting on the street side of the house.

'Now you will see real craftsmanship, Kimura-san,' Pau said as Haru followed him out. He used the Japanese honorific and Haru smiled. A wary trust had grown up between them.

The rickshaw man weaved between the traffic; despite the chill he was bare from the waist up. They drew up outside a Chinese fan maker's shop. The fans in the window display dazzled Haru's eyes with their colourful silks and painted dragons and phoenixes. The gentleman in charge, an unsmiling individual in a silk cap with a tassel, his upper lip sporting a drooping moustache, took them through the rattle of a beaded curtain and upstairs into a warren of smaller rooms. One of these rooms had lacquered cabinets of deep red and black inlaid with tortoiseshell and brass.

Pau translated for him when the man brought out a few trays of smoker's accoutrements and arranged them on the table. The fan man introduced himself as Ping Kuan, but told Haru to call him by the American abbreviation PK. He sat down behind his collection and told Haru the opium trade routes had been blocked by war and the illegal flow of opium from India cut off. Fearful of losing their opium monopoly, the French had encouraged Hmong farmers to expand their opium production, and this was distributed privately within China through a network of Chinese middlemen, including PK.

Haru listened, but his eyes were already caressing the mysterious objects before him. A typical smoker's layout seemed to consist of a hardwood tray with mother-of-pearl inlay and miniature, spittoon-shaped pots on which to rest the pipe bowls. Small silver scissors and spoons, ivory picks rested in their own square dishes. Their intricacy enchanted him, the abundance of chased floral decoration.

He picked out the most lavish set, an enamelled tray which had a filigree lamp in the shape of a dragon, along with several inlaid ivory tools.

Pau negotiated the price.

'No no,' Haru said, feeling the tendons of his neck tense. 'Too high.'

'These are illegal objects,' Pau protested. 'PK risks arrest merely to keep them.'

'With a friend in the police like you?' Haru was having none of it. As soon as he saw the enamelled tray with its tiny tools, he knew he must have it. Here was civilization embodied in these desirable objects, which had obviously been manufactured for rich men. 'I will give you twenty yen.'

'Robbery.'

Though Haru didn't understand the words he understood the tone and shake of the head. 'You will agree to my offer, or your shop will be requisitioned.' His power as occupier couldn't be denied.

Pau looked uncomfortable and acrimonious words were exchanged between the two men. PK was obviously telling Pau he should never have brought Haru here.

Needless to say, the tray and its contents were carefully wrapped in paper.

'I'll take the other two trays too,' he instructed Pau.

More argument, and more haggling, until finally they were wrapped too. Haru found it impossible to leave them behind. It was as if he'd discovered another world beneath his own. One where dreams would insulate him from the real world. In the real world were questions he didn't want to answer, questions like why hadn't he written to Zofia, but only to his mother? Questions like, if they were to occupy China for any length of time, how would they subdue such a large population?

For though they had beaten them savagely, and tried to instil fear in them, he recognized that China, as an idea, was much bigger than all its inhabitants. And no matter how much terror they inflicted on them, somehow the fear had turned in on itself like a mantis and begun to eat him alive.

Chapter 34

At the pharmacy, the door opened at Zofia's first frantic knock. The Japanese patrol had held them up for a good twenty minutes and they had run the last half mile.

Seeing the expression on Zofia's face and Hilly's black eye, Jun gestured them inside and locked the door behind them. He swished back the red curtain with a rattle of its brass rings and took them into the adjoining room.

Zofia rested her hands on her knees to try to catch her breath.

'You're too late,' Jun said. 'Biyu's husband has already gone. He waited more than an hour.'

Zofia sat down heavily on the floor, suddenly pouring sweat from running. 'We couldn't get here any earlier, we were locked in our room.'

'I'm so sorry,' Jun said.

Zofia slumped, head in hands. 'What shall I do?' When no answer came, she raised her eyes and was surprised to see the room was lined with shelves of books and scrolls, and calligraphy paper and ink was laid out on a table where Jun had obviously been working when they interrupted him.

Hilly was staring at the calligraphy and then at Hai Jun's ink-stained fingers. 'Did you paint this?' she asked.

'I did.'

'It's like dragons. The writing's like coiling dragons, and clouds. I like it.'

He smiled. 'I'm glad you approve.'

'I was supposed to make a delivery to Woosung Camp,' Zofia said. 'I've let them down. They were relying on me, and I've let them down.'

'Why don't I make tea,' Hai Jun said, 'and then we'll decide what to do.' He went to lock the door.

'Don't let him lock us in!' Hilly said.

'It's okay,' Zofia reassured her, 'Jun's a friend.'

'I'm Hilly,' she said. 'The police came, flashing lights and everything. And I had to climb through a window to escape.'

'Is that so?' Jun seemed to accept their predicament. He put his own calligraphy away, got out fresh paper and showed Hilly how to hold a brush the correct way and dip it in the ink, then how to make swirling Chinese characters on the weighted-down rice paper. His willingness to show her in such a patient way made Zofia feel she could trust him even more. He seemed to understand by instinct that Hilly needed order, and he supplied it.

The tea was reviving, hot and bitter, and had something in it that calmed her.

'Do you think you can tell me what it's all about?' he asked. 'I'm a good listener.'

He barely moved as she explained, without using Theo's name, about the men trying to get out of Woosung, and that one of them had recently lost a son. She was supposed to be taking them clothing and shoes and a boat to get away. She bit her lip. She'd failed on all those counts. She unstrapped the bundle to show him. 'How will we know if they've got out?' she asked.

'Not much goes on that we don't know about – the pharmacy is a place where people talk. They talk while they wait, enjoy the gossip and the news. And many who come here are members of the Chinese Communist Party.'

'Are you in the CCP?'

'No. I'm not a member of anything. I just listen, that's all. My calligraphy teacher told me that listening is the way you find out the most. Try it. You'll see.'

She was quiet only a moment before she asked, 'I know it's an imposition, but can we stay here? Just for a night?'

'We can't go back.' Hilly looked up from where she was swirling the ink in the pot with a big brush. 'It was Zha Wei. He locked us in.'

'Zha Wei?' He raised his eyebrows.

Zofia sighed. She'd already told him so much; what was the harm in more? 'We were staying on the Bubbling Well Road with Zha Wei. At the Blue Lilac.' She lowered her eyes in embarrassment. 'He locked us in because I objected to the way he treated the women. He punched Hilly.'

'I've got a massive black eye,' Hilly said proudly. 'It's going all yellow.'

'So it is. I can make you something for that. Why didn't he want you to leave?'

'Because we were working for him and I found out he's double-dealing – pretending to be a committed member of the communist party, but at the same time selling information to the Kuomintang and the Nationalists.' She didn't mention Charlie although her story hardly made sense without it.

Jun just listened. Finally, she fell silent, the only sound the tinkling of the brush in water as Hilly washed it.

Jun brought out an ointment for Hilly's face, and a bedroll filled with some sort of soft grain filling. 'Here. Get some sleep. Tomorrow we will work out what to do. There's a sink in the kitchen where you can wash and a mirror to see where to rub in the ointment.'

He padded around the room in his cotton slippers, clearing away the calligraphy materials, stacking them carefully and pegging up Hilly's work to dry on the line by the window. He bowed them goodnight and they heard his footsteps creak up the stairs.

'I like him,' Hilly pronounced. 'Can we stay here forever?'

'Let's get some sleep,' Zofia said. She too was looking for a place to call home. She was tired with running, with trying to think everything through. And she was tired of looking after Hilly, though she would never ever tell her that. She was worried too, about after the war, what Haru might make of Hilly and the whole situation. That's if they even found each other again. It had been so long now, that she was beginning to doubt it. Hilly had nobody else but her. She couldn't trust anyone else to know Hilly the way she did.

The next morning, they awoke to the smell of something frying and soon they were seated at the calligraphy table with plates of scrambled eggs and fried noodles with onion and chilli. 'I have to open the shop,' Jun said.

'We'll wash the pots,' Zofia said.

'I'll close at midday and then we can talk, and see if we know any more about your friends.'

Hilly wanted to go outside to chat with her friend the chestnut seller, but Zofia told her it was better to stay indoors. Zofia watched out of the upstairs window, fearful Zha Wei might come looking for them.

Customers came and went. As Zofia kept vigil, below her the mutter and mumble of voices continued amid the clack of the abacus and clink of coins.

Halfway through the morning, she stiffened as three familiar men strolled toward the pharmacy from the direction of the city. There was no mistaking Chow's swagger. He was one of Zha Wei's toughest men, and he was accompanied by two others whose names she didn't know, also dressed in Western-style suits. They made an intimidating group, walking three abreast as though they owned the street, and she watched two Chinese women jump into the road to avoid them.

Zofia moved back away from the window, but stayed behind the shutter to watch the road beneath. The men stopped to talk to the chestnut seller at his stall, surrounding him in a threatening manner. Her stomach tightened as she heard them ask him if he'd seen two Western women, one dark, one blonde.

She couldn't hear his reply, but the men stayed there a few minutes looming over him. One of them picked up a bag of chestnuts and began eating them without paying. By the seller's body language, she could see his discomfort. His eyes flicked back and forth, searching the crowd for someone to come to his aid.

He shook his head vigorously and pointed up the road. Chow and his men walked off, and the man crunching on the chestnuts threw the empty packet down onto the street where it was immediately seized by one of the stray dogs from the next-door alley.

All this had made Zofia's mouth dry. Her hands trembled as she stepped back.

'What's the matter?' Hilly asked, sensing the change in atmosphere. 'What's going on?' She pushed past her to get to the window. Zofia tried to drag her back out of sight, but it was a struggle because Hilly was as tall as her now.

'Let go!' Hilly shouted, pulling free. 'I want to see.'

'Keep away from the window! It's Zha Wei's men. They mustn't see us.'

She saw the name register and Hilly jumped away as if she'd been scalded. 'Don't let him in,' she whispered.

'It's all right,' Zofia said, trying to calm her down. 'Here, give me a hug.'

They hugged and Zofia stroked Hilly's back, wondering how she'd ever got this job that seemed to be half mother, half friend.

'Will they come back?' Hilly said.

'Is everything all right?' Jun called from the shop at the bottom of the stairs.

Zofia let go of Hilly, who backed away at the sound of footsteps, but was relieved to see it was only Jun.

'I've locked up,' he said. 'We're closed. But I've found out something. Hilly, would you like to do some more calligraphy? I've left the brushes out for you in the room downstairs and some things for you to copy. If someone rings the bell, don't answer it, fetch one of us instead.'

Hilly glanced to Zofia, but seeing her stern look, huffed, 'I get it. You want me out of the way.' She slouched downstairs.

Jun sat down opposite Zofia and began to count a basin of pills into bottles of a hundred. After a moment, he leaned forward on his elbows. In a low voice he said, 'There was definitely a break-out at the Woosung Camp last night. One man dead, two got away.'

She had to ask, though she dreaded the answer. 'The name of the one who died?'

Jun shook his head and continued to count pills.

She waited while he screwed the top on the first bottle.

He put it aside and picked up another. 'No information. All we know is two men tunnelled under the wire. The third got caught and was executed. The Japanese have patrols and planes combing the surrounding area. None of my contacts has any information, but they're saying the Japanese are angry. They don't like to lose face and they're determined to track the runaways down. These are your friends, yes?'

Zofia nodded dumbly. *Please make it Theo who got away.*

She was quiet a moment taking in the bad news, then she picked up another of the bottles to help count. The counting became like a mantra, *let him be safe, let him be safe.* When it was full she looked up. 'Zha Wei's men came this morning. I saw them talking to your uncle outside.'

'Yes. They're looking for you. Third uncle came in the shop to tell me. Uncle acted old and stupid and told them he wasn't sure, but he'd seen one Western girl heading towards Cha Pei. They've gone off there, on a wild goose chase. Third uncle knows you are here, but he won't tell. He's absolutely trustworthy. But there's a problem. My mother-in-law's house has been targeted by the Japanese and she has been given two days to move out.' There was apology in his eyes.

'And you want the room. Yes, I see.' She pushed the full bottle towards him.

'I'm sorry but she is a not a woman who can keep her mouth closed. Already I am warning people not to leave messages here.' He held up his arms in a gesture of surrender. 'But I couldn't turn her away. Her daughter … my wife – we both lost so much. And though she's anti-Japanese, she's old school – she believes in the ruling Nationalists not the CCP.'

'So where can we go?'

'I've put a word out to try to get you out of Shanghai, to a CCP safe house somewhere in the country, where the Japanese army are not so active and where Zha Wei's men won't think to look.'

'Is there no way to get out of China?'

A sad laugh. 'Without transport? No. The distances are too great. Even if you could convince someone to let you cross a border. The borders are all fortified and manned by Japanese. And you stand out as Westerners. No. Your best chance is to go somewhere remote with friendly Chinese, somewhere you won't be noticed by the Japanese. Not an urban area. Somewhere rural, where there are peasant farmers who will hide you.'

Zofia had to be content with that. The noise of the rattle of pills in the bowl continued as they sorted. They both reached for the bowl at the same time and their hands brushed each other. She grasped his hand. 'Thank you. You've already done enough. I don't know what we would have done without your help.'

'It's nothing,' he said, extricating his hand. 'It's good to practise my English on people who speak it well. The Japanese frown on it now – we all have to try to speak their language.'

'You'll let me know if you hear any news about the men who got out of Woosung?'

'It means a lot to you, I can see that.'

She lowered her eyes. Guilt swamped her. She shouldn't feel this way but couldn't seem to help it.

'But your friend Hilly, she's young. She's a responsibility.' His expression was grave.

'When I first met her,' Zofia said, 'I didn't know her age. By the time I realized how young she was, we'd bonded. She was traumatized by the Nazis who took her parents. War is a cruel master and I suppose you take love where you can.'

'True. But in China we don't speak of our ills. No matter how much we suffer. China doesn't like people to see their weak ones. And everyone has to be seen to be working.'

'We can work. As long as we're together.'

Jun finished counting the pills into the last of his bottles and took them downstairs.

Zofia paused to listen, imagining Hilly's concentrated expression as she used the pen and ink. She heard the low hum of their voices, Hilly's laugh.

It'll be all right, she told herself.

When Jun came back he said, 'She's still drawing.' He smiled. 'She told me she won't go anywhere without you because you need looking after.'

Zofia's eyes filled with tears.

Chapter 35

When Theo awoke the next day their fisherman rescuer introduced himself as Xin, and a bowl of proper rice and vegetables was served to them by his wife. She had her hair dyed black, though she was obviously about seventy years old.

Griff too had revived, though he was coughing. 'Swallowed too much water,' he said. In his bedraggled state he looked a much smaller, less imposing man. 'Thanks,' he said to Theo. 'You saved my bacon.'

After a lot of gesticulating from Xin, Theo realized he was miming 'upstream', and 'sampan'. But they had to go at night. Xin mimed engine noise – planes circling overhead, and trucks full of soldiers.

Griff didn't take part in this conversation; he was quieter than Theo had ever known him. But he obviously understood the Japanese were searching for them. At the end of it, he said, 'I wish we still had our pointy cards.' But their carefully copied 'pointy' cards were lost to the river. Theo's pockets had been full of a mush of cardboard, and his 'shoes' had gone the same way.

Xin's wife seemed concerned about Theo's feet which were filthy and covered in small wounds from running on rough ground. Buzzing flies kept settling there, and Theo had to bat them away.

The woman tutted and persuaded him to soak his feet in a tin basin of warm salt water. It stung like crazy, but the dawn had arrived and with it, more light. The pain made him alert enough now to look around his surroundings and see they were in a concrete tin-roofed dwelling, and he was sitting on a bare earth floor. He guessed it to be about twelve feet by twelve and furnished with a brick firepit, and a few shelves for rice and provisions.

A faded photograph of Mao was the only decoration, and this portrait sat next to jars of pickles and an ancient oil lamp. A fishing kit of lines and weighted nets was hung near the door. Xin gestured at them to wait inside while he went out with his nets.

'Where did you say the nearest US airfield is?' Theo asked Griff.

'Nearest official one is in Laifeng in Henan province. One of the men in the camp was ex Chinese-American Intelligence Agency. Said he took his orders from Laifeng. Their headquarters are there. Maybe they can get us out. There's a small airfield.'

'American troops?'

'Doubt it. Not a proper unit. They use it for reconnaissance – aerial photography – getting pictures of where the Japs are and which infrastructure's been destroyed by the CCP. Broken railway lines, sabotaged substations, telegraph wires down. All that kind of thing.'

'How far is it?' Theo slapped away a mosquito.

'Too far. He reckoned about six hundred miles.'

'Geez.' They looked at each other, knowing even six miles to be too far in the state they were in – malnourished, weak, and Theo hardly able to hobble.

They dozed most of the afternoon and evening as Xin's wife ground rice flour to make dumplings which they ate ravenously. When she lit the soybean oil lamp that evening, they sat up expectantly. Theo's feet had been bandaged with clean cotton cloth, and though Griff still coughed, his face had regained a little colour. Both of them needed a shave, the few days bristle turning to beards.

The door opened into the black outside to reveal their fisherman friend Xin, holding a barely operating flashlight. 'It's time,' he gestured.

'Looks like this is it,' Theo said.

They stood up to follow him, and as they hobbled out of the door, they bowed their thanks to his wife. She fussed around them, then whipped down the portrait of Mao and pressed it into Theo's hand.

'No, no,' he protested at this gift.

'Best take it,' Griff said. 'It might give us some kind of passport to the Chinese rebels. Show 'em which side we're on.'

'Ah. Good thinking.' Theo stowed it carefully in his pocket. All his clothes were still a little damp and he hoped the picture would survive.

They had no choice but to follow the flickering flashlight because presumably it was avoiding Japanese checkpoints. Theo's trousers chafed against his soft skin. He was unused to walking, especially through marshland, muddy rice paddies and knee-deep dykes. Behind him, he could hear Griff's rasping cough, though he tried to keep it quiet.

They walked across country for perhaps five or six miles, skirting roads and bridges until they came to a small creek.

'*Lao baung yu!*' A greeting popped out of the dark.

Astonishingly there were three armed men waiting there to load them aboard their sampan.

Xin greeted them enthusiastically with slapping of the backs, then bowed and grinned, and gestured signs of good luck before they boarded, and it did feel like leaving relatives behind. They had been so kind, and the journey ahead was so uncertain. Even Griff gave Xin an army salute.

The boat slicked away into the dark of the reeds, the water

silently reflecting dim swathes of the passing cloud overhead. Theo prayed these armed men could be trusted. Eventually they punted into the big river where there were still the glints of a few boats night-fishing. Just before dawn, their rowers pulled into the side of the bank, saying they could go no further. The roofs of a village were silhouetted against the glimmer of the sky.

Griff struggled out and offered a hand to Theo as he followed. 'The village?' he asked, pointing.

Vigorous shaking of the head and an indication to go the other way. 'Japanese,' was all they would say.

The tallest of the young men reached into the bottom of the boat and handed Theo a machete. Theo couldn't imagine using this on any human being, but the Chinese youth was insistent, so he bowed his thanks and took it, determined to ditch it as soon as possible. Nothing spelled asking for trouble as much as a man armed to the teeth with a big metal knife.

Theo soon understood why they'd been given the weapon – ahead they might run into the puppet Chinese troops of the Japanese. They were to strike out across the fields to the next hamlet so must take care, and should look for a woman called Tang. They'd find her on the edge of the cluster of dwellings in a big house with a lamp burning outside.

'Even in the daytime?' Griff asked as light was already pinking the sky.

'Yes, yes!' Agreement from their guides. Griff thanked them and strode off purposefully into the gloom and Theo hurried after him, wincing every time a foot hit the ground. Thank God for a little light because the fields were more like bogs and Theo's feet were already protesting despite their bandaging.

'Did he say how far?' Theo asked.

Griff stopped. 'No. Can you carry on?'

'Not much further. I need shoes. My feet are in shreds.'

Griff bent down to untie his sandals. 'Here. We'll share until we can get another pair, okay?'

Theo was too grateful to protest. 'You're a pal.'

Griff smiled. It was the first time he'd seen much of a smile from Griff, and it was like gold. He immediately felt cheered, and the sandals certainly helped.

Theo waved the machete at him. 'Shall I keep it?'

'No. A liability. I think give it to this woman Tang. She might have a use for it.'

Theo had never used a weapon in his life. He'd never needed one in a boardroom. They moved slowly now, careful of Griff's bare feet.

The house with a light was more like a big hut, and it seemed Tang was expecting them. She was a big-bellied matriarch tottering on the stumps of bound feet – the barbaric practice of binding the feet to make them small had since lost favour amongst the communists. Theo, who was still limping, could imagine the pain all too easily.

'Welcome, welcome.' At first they couldn't make out what she was saying, but then Theo realised it was English, but with such a thick accent he hadn't recognized it. 'I expect you,' she said. 'My son, he bring you here. Now he go to town to see your friend Jun.'

When she received no response she said, 'Jun – American pharmacist.'

Theo glanced to Griff. Neither of them knew what she was talking about.

She saw their puzzlement and laughed a gleeful cackle. 'He take messages, send messages. Very useful man. He ask my son for news of you. Everyone laugh that you walk under the wire. Make Japanese mad.'

They warmed to her good humour immediately, and the fact she was clearly on their side. Theo held out the machete to her with a bow, and she exclaimed loudly but seemed pleased. She ran to fetch a bottle and offered them a glass of *Kaoliang*, the local corn liquor. Being so early, it went straight to Theo's head, but Griff seemed to relish the burning effect and said the bitter brew was good for his throat.

'Where are you going now?' she asked, her bright eyes full of curiosity.

'Laifeng,' Griff said, 'in Henan.'

Her eyes opened wide. 'Not back to Shanghai?'

'No. We want to get home. To America.'

This seemed to be such an outrageous idea that it silenced her. She tutted in deep disapproval and then left them sitting there whilst she went out.

'What's going on?' Theo asked.

Griff gave his expression of *not a clue*. 'I think we upset her.'

They sat uneasily, getting ready to run.

But they needn't have worried. She came back with a map. It was stained and soft with use. The cities and villages were printed only in Chinese, but she was able to point to the ones where there might be trouble. 'Not here,' she said, pursing her lips, 'or here. You go this way.' She traced a route with her finger.

Griff asked for a brush or something to write with. She returned with a Western-style fountain pen. 'Long time since, I work as *amah* for Americans in Shanghai,' Tang said in her thick accent. 'I stole this pen!' She seemed to think it a great joke. 'I keep. Now Americans have it back!'

Griff inked the villages to avoid with a circle and put a small tick next to the ones under control of the communists. 'But it change all the time,' she said. 'The Japanese, they keep disappear.' She winked. 'Nobody know where they go.' An uproarious laugh.

Theo and Griff pored over the map for a long time. Only now did the six hundred miles on the map seem real. 'How long do you think it will take us to walk there?' Theo asked.

'Realistically? Months,' Griff said. 'And that's if the terrain's passable and we manage to avoid Japanese troops all the way.

Do you think it's worth it, or shall we find somewhere to sit out the war?'

Theo couldn't countenance the thought. 'Haven't you anyone waiting for you at home?'

Griff shook his head. 'Before I worked for the Shanghai Bank I was in the army. There was a girl, but she's probably married with a bunch of kids by now. You?'

'A wife. Evelina. And two kids.' He still couldn't bring himself to say one child. Jimmy was still his boy.

'What about the woman who was supposed to be helping us, the one back in Shanghai?'

'It's complicated. There was something about her.' He shook his head. 'Don't ask about her.'

Griff gave him a long slow look before he coughed and reached for another dose of *Kaoliang*.

Chapter 36

At Jun's house Zofia and Hilly were cooking. The downstairs kitchen was stacked with medicinal herbs, different kinds of dried fungi in jars, and paper packets of salt and spices.

Shouts from outside. Zofia pressed her face towards the small, screened window to see a Japanese patrol passing by, with several prisoners manacled together. She saw them coming down the road, the men bruised and battered, the Japanese marching rigidly behind them. When these Chinese men stumbled and fell over, the Japanese soldiers beat them until they got up again. Savagery.

Zofia could not look away. These men doing the beating could be Haru. Her gentle husband was somewhere out there in this cold-hearted army. The Japanese at war were terrifying. A completely different nation to the Japanese in peacetime. Could these brutes be the same people who waxed lyrical about the spiritual qualities of cherry blossom, or the soulful qualities of the moon? It didn't seem possible.

But wasn't it the same the world over? That people could hold the evil and the good together in one person, like riding two horses? She looked over to where Hilly was slowly stirring the rice in the pot, her face rapt with concentration. Except Hilly, she thought. Despite being abused, she had a kind of purity that came from being able to let the past go.

Hurrying footsteps up the wooden stairs.

'Your friends,' Jun said, bursting in, all smiles. 'We know where they are. Two men, one English, one American, and they are right now with Li Tang – she's one of the friends of the CCP.'

'Did you say an American?'

'One Brit, one Yank.'

Zofia had to prop herself up on the wall. She was weak with relief. 'Where are they?' Zofia asked. 'Here in Shanghai?'

'No. It's quite remote – about twenty miles away.'

'Can we go there?'

He sighed. 'I knew you'd ask. But it's dangerous. The roads are full of Japanese roadblocks. And you are easy to remember. Two Westerners leaving Shanghai. And if you are caught or followed then it will put your friends in danger too. The Japanese army – well, their ways of asking questions are brutal.'

She'd just seen it. 'But your wife's mother is coming. We have to go somewhere. You said it yourself. Why not there?'

Zofia and Hilly waited by the road, dressed in their Chinese clothes, the bundle of men's clothes and shoes at her feet. The night was dark with gunfire and explosions in the distance. It didn't make them feel any more confident. A night soil truck was going to take them down the road towards the village where Theo and his friend were hiding. Jun said smuggling was often done by night soil truck because the smell of excrement put off the Japanese from stopping it as it passed.

When the truck arrived, it was driven by an old woman and her daughter. Zofia hadn't had any idea what to expect, and now the sight of it took her aback. The back of the truck was a stack of a double row of metal compartments. Each compartment was about three feet square and housed the barrel of night soil from an individual residence. The woman driving hopped neatly down and opened up one of the hatches to reveal an empty compartment.

The space was tiny. 'In here,' Jun said. 'You can hide.'

Jun had brought out a small stool to help them climb in, but Hilly wasn't having any of it.

'No,' she said firmly. 'Forget it.'

'We have to. Look I'll get in first and then you can climb in next to me.'

'I don't want to hide in there. It stinks. And it's too small.'

'It's only a short journey. Let's just try.'

She took hold of Hilly's arm to encourage her, but Hilly was becoming tearful. She pulled away and slapped at her. 'No. What if we get locked in?'

'Calm down. We won't get locked in. And I'll be in the compartment right next to you.'

Hilly's mouth crumpled as if she were about to cry. 'Please don't make me,' she pleaded.

Zofia tried again to lead her towards the truck.

'No! Leave me alone!' Hilly hit out with a fist catching Zofia in the eye, then wrestled herself away.

The two Chinese women were watching this with dubious expressions. She saw Jun explaining to them what Zofia had told him, about Hilly's fear of small spaces. They kept looking over to her, and then shaking their heads. An argument ensued and she couldn't understand what was going on, but they climbed back into the truck and started the engine. Seconds later, it drove away.

'What was all that about?' Zofia asked, her eye still watering.

He took her aside. 'They won't take you. They think Hilly is too much of a risk. They're worried she might make a fuss and then the Japanese might stop them and they'll get arrested. They don't mind taking guns and ammunition, but they're saying now, no people.'

Forty minutes later they were walking, each with a tied bundle of the precious men's clothes. Jun was between them. No doubt he was as keen to offload his troublesome guests as they were to leave, though he was too polite to say so. The women kept their heads down as Jun led them through the dark. Zofia could tell they were headed for the river by the tang of the saltwater from the incoming tide, the smell of engine oil and the slight whiff of fish. Dangerous – the Japanese patrolled the harbour and the landing stages.

But Jun led them for about four miles in the dark until he came to a collection of sampans by the river. The biggest one had a disintegrating thatched roof that had been replaced by sheets of canvas tarpaulin.

A hurried conversation ensued between Jun and the ragged family on the boat. The head of the family was a tiny man with no teeth and a face as polished as old shoes, who went by the name of Pan. After much negotiating and the handing over of a small package of medicinal herbs, a deal was struck and Pan nodded.

Jun brushed away their attempts to thank him. 'He'll take you to Li Tang's house. There are patrols at the next bridge. Keep your heads down and keep out of sight. After that there'll be patrols, but on the banks. I've told Pan to stay in the centre of the river and hope no patrol boat passes. Okay?'

'Okay,' Zofia said, but she saw Hilly was shivering with cold and trepidation.

'Be mindful of the risk they take for you.'

Zofia took hold of Jun and hugged him, though he didn't want to be hugged. 'And you took the same risk. I'll never forget.'

A woman on board who looked like perhaps she was Pan's daughter helped them get on board.

'We must be silent,' Zofia warned Hilly. 'Patrols are on the river.'

Hilly didn't reply. She was staring at the two children who were shifting themselves out of the way under the semi-circular awning, and moving a canvas-wrapped parcel to the side. By the smell of it, it was their day's catch – two big fish and a few other grey tiddlers, slippery in the damp canvas. The children scooped up one that escaped and with a grin, slid it back amongst the rest. They were two boys, she guessed six or seven years old and from the way she behaved, the woman was obviously their mother and Pan the grandfather.

The children pointed to a pile of burlap sacking and Hilly lay herself down on there and curled up like a nesting bird. It made the children giggle and stare. Zofia was always amazed at how Hilly could sleep – falling into deep slumber at the drop of a hat. Whereas she was always worrying about something and it often led to sleepless nights.

The Chinese grandfather poled his way through the silent waters. Fortunately, the tide was with them as they headed up towards the first bridge.

'You get down now,' mimed the daughter, gesturing for Zofia to flatten down. Ahead of them, white Japanese soldiers' uniforms stood out in the dark, where they were policing the river traffic. Their bayonets gleamed dully in the reflected light.

The grandfather kept to the middle channel, avoiding another sampan travelling downstream. As they approached the bridge, Zofia held her breath. Beside her, a sleeping Hilly was oblivious to the danger.

A splash next to them, and then another one. Suddenly a rock plummeted through the thin canvas roof and hit one of the children on the shoulder. The daughter scrambled to quieten the crying child.

'Ay, ay! It's what they always do,' the woman said in Chinese, gesticulating. 'Japs throw rocks at us for fun. Try to sink the boat.' Zofia could just about make out the gist of what she was saying.

Another splatter of stones on the roof, and then a bigger piece of rock. This time it hit Hilly on the leg and she sat up sharply with a cry.

'Hush,' Zofia said, placing a hand over her mouth. The dark passing shadow told her they were right under the bridge. The roof they were under held the boots of men who would want to interrogate them, or worse, if they were caught.

The boat nosed out again into the channel, whilst Zofia huddled close to Hilly, gripping her hand tight. Behind them the Japanese were shouting and taking aim at another boat. After a heart-stopping ten minutes they were clear and the river settled into quiet. But the fact they had been so close to being discovered made Zofia's stomach churn.

Their Chinese friends also relaxed, the children giggling together, and offloading the stones into the water. Zofia persuaded Hilly to lie back down and sleep, though she didn't dare doze herself. She was on constant alert, as if her body was on fire.

When dawn came, the grandfather pulled in to a small creek and immediately they were surrounded by armed Chinese with cloths wrapped over their noses and mouths.

'Stay low,' the woman said.

The men didn't seem very friendly. They demanded to see the catch, and the daughter dutifully brought it out. They took the two big fish and left the family with only the few tiny ones. Only then did they let them off the boat.

The gang of men stood silently as Zofia and Hilly got off.

Zofa caught the eye of one of the men who was staring intently at them.

With a wag of the head, he indicated she should follow. Her eyes were on a level with him, but she didn't blink. Just hauled Hilly after her. The daughter and the young boys followed her as they were led through thick undergrowth towards a clearing and a few huts.

'CCP,' said the daughter, as cowed as they were.

The other men stood guard as the leader of the CCP guerrillas knocked on the rough wooden door of the biggest hut. A thick-set older woman answered and greeted the family effusively. She obviously knew them, and the children scampered inside immediately.

This must be Li Tang. She glanced up at the two women and her lips pursed at the CCP man. 'No,' she said. 'No more.' She seemed to be protesting something, but he argued with her in a dialect Zofia couldn't understand, until finally she stood aside and the rest of them entered the cramped interior.

She saw two men, both Westerners, lurch to their feet. Both were skin and bone and wearing dark blue ragged clothes. It was a moment before she realized the one propping himself up on the wall was actually Theo.

Chapter 37

Theo heard the commotion at the door. Two young boys skipped in but then stopped short when they saw him and Griff, as if hauled back by a string. They backed away until an old man and someone who was obviously their mother came in.

He stood up awkwardly to greet the newcomers. Two more people were coming in and then he was almost knocked off his feet.

A figure flung herself towards him and wrapped her arms around him. 'Theo!'

He was so shocked he could hardly speak. 'Hilly?'

'We found you!' She was grinning, her blonde hair falling out of the scarf covering her head.

But already he was looking for someone else.

She was there in the doorway, looking at him as if she'd never seen him before. Of course – he must look so different. But their eyes locked on to one another, and she took a hesitant step into the room.

'Sorry we're so late,' she said. 'We brought you what you asked for.' Her face was pink and now she wouldn't meet his eyes. She had a cloth bundle slung over a shoulder and she squatted down to open it on the floor.

He dropped to his knees opposite her, unable to believe she was actually here. 'What the hell …?'

She was unwrapping the bundle and spreading out the things inside. 'Your shoes,' she said, 'and some Chinese clothing.'

'My shoes?' He could hardly believe it. The rest of the people had gathered around, their faces serious. Suddenly this pair of leather shoes looked impossibly glamorous – the shine of the leather, the tooled eyeholes for the laces, even the laces themselves.

Griff said, 'Well, I'll be damned.'

'Oh, Griff, this is Zofia—'

'And Hilly,' said Hilly. 'We're friends of Theo's.'

'But what are you doing here?' asked Theo. 'Why aren't you in Shanghai?'

'It's a long story and—'

But it was interrupted by Griff who was exclaiming over the contents of the parcels. 'Good Lord! There's another two pairs of shoes here. These ones are enormous … oh.' He stopped, realizing.

'They were for Lennie,' Theo said to Zofia. 'But he didn't make it out.'

Whilst this was going on, tea was being made by Tang who had produced a large pan and many small cups. There were still voices outside the hut, and Tang kept going in and out with cups of tea and small bowls of peanuts, so he guessed the band of men must still be loitering outside.

He saw Zofia's anxious look towards the door. 'It's all right. The men outside are guerrillas – fighting against the Japanese. They'll be asking Tang if you are spies for the Japanese and what you're doing here.'

'We can't go back. We got involved with Zha Wei and he threatened us. The Kempeitai took Charlie and Olga. Zha Wei was working for the Kuomintang. Of course he'd deny it if anyone from the CCP was to enquire. But I had to get Hilly away.'

'So how did you know where we were?'

'Jun the pharmacist. He was so kind. He put us in touch with his fishermen friends and they brought us here.'

'Sounds like a very useful man. So what will you do now?'

'Where are you going?'

The directness of the question and its implications floored him. He couldn't even get over the fact she was here because time had become elastic and it seemed years since he'd last seen her. 'We'll be trekking to Henan province. We're going to try to reach the American base and get a flight back to the States.'

'Then we'll travel with you.'

Theo was caught. He took in the fact she too was thinner with a haunted look about the eyes. He knew he wanted to see more of her, but he knew travelling with women would not only make their journey harder, but also make them more conspicuous.

His throat was tight with emotion. 'I'll have to talk it over with Griff,' he croaked.

She nodded, as if she'd expected as much. 'I was so sorry to hear about Jimmy,' she said.

Theo looked at the ground. Sympathy hurt more than just pretending it hadn't happened.

'We can't go back,' she said again, a desperation in her voice.

A clatter on the roof as the rain began. Hilly was drinking tea, her eyes flicking to where Griff was putting on Chinese clothes, and pushing his feet into the shoes they'd brought. 'Just a little big,' he said. He tore a strip from the ragged bottoms of his old trousers to wrap his feet.

Tang came back into the house and looked taken aback to see Griff in new Chinese clothes. 'You leave today,' she announced in her thick accent. 'You have map, okay? Not safe here. Take your girlfriends too. Too many strangers.' She looked pointedly at Zofia and Hilly.

Griff came over to whisper to him. 'We can't take them with us. You know we can't.'

'We can't leave them here either.'

'Then we'll have to leave them along the way.'

'What's all the whispering?' said Hilly.

Theo wondered how he could explain to Griff about Zofia and Hilly, and Charlie and Zha Wei, but then realized it would only make things worse. He'd find out about it all soon enough.

The leader of the local CCP had unwrapped his scarf from around his mouth and now he was waiting outside, rifle over his shoulder, to lead them out into the wild country beyond.

The rain was teeming down, and the women seemed surprised to be made to walk immediately. He dare not look at Zofia, or at Griff who came alongside him to complain.

'If it wasn't for those women, I think we could have stayed longer. They were never part of any plan.'

'Zofia brought the clothes you are wearing. Did you want to go the rest of the way with one pair of disintegrating rope sandals between us?'

Their guide, Tang's son, who moved like a panther, was already on his way, so Theo strode on through the splatter in his leather shoes, which now seemed to barely contain his painful, swelling feet. If he could catch up with him, he might be able to get more of an idea of where the next shelter might be. Theo hurried until he was alongside. When he thanked Yang's son for being their guide, he gave a gruff grunt and told Theo in English his name was Tang Yingsha. He was taciturn about their destination, just saying, 'Village ahead. I leave you close by. CCP will take you further.'

The women followed behind, rain soaking their shoulders as they struggled to keep pace through rice paddies and thickets of jungle. Theo turned once or twice to throw Zofia a sympathetic look of encouragement. After a few miles, they heard the buzz of engines and planes circling above. 'Get under the trees,' said Yingsha, gesturing urgently at the women.

The sound brought fear to Theo's throat. Under dripping foliage, he watched the Japanese plane loop over and over, all the time knowing it was them they were searching for. They hunkered under the trees until the engine hum died away.

'I can take you one mile more,' Yingsha said. 'Then, I return. My mother gave you a map?'

'That's right,' Theo said.

'Then let's look.' They unfolded it and spread it out, trying to keep it from being soaked by the dripping trees. 'You are here, and you go here and here. Not here.' Yingsha pointed to where one of the villages had a tick next to it.

'Your mother said here was okay,' Griff said, frowning.

'No. The Japs have burned it down. Could still be soldiers there. You go this way.'

Theo and Griff looked at each other. It seemed even the map was unreliable. The women looked uneasy, shivering in their wet clothes.

'How much further?' he heard Hilly ask.

Griff rolled his eyes. Theo quelled his frustration, knowing there would be many more miles as long as the daylight lasted and even then he didn't know where they would end up.

After another mile of a rough track through a thicket of bamboo, Yingsha stopped. 'Straight on, follow the track along the plain. Keep low but don't go near the river. Too many patrols. This village.' He tapped it on the map. 'There may be people there to shelter you.'

And with that, he disappeared again, back the way they came.

So now they were on their own. Somewhere in the vast hinterland of Shanghai. And Theo had no idea if they would ever be able to get out of China alive.

Don't think of it, Theo told himself. One step at a time.

Zofia was well aware that Theo and his friend Griff had not expected their company. It filled her with guilt. But they had nowhere else to go and the thought of getting out of China to freedom, no matter how impossible, was like a light at the end of some dark tunnel. Theo was a man she could trust, her instinct told her that. But what she hadn't been prepared for was the foul weather and the relentless pace of the guide.

Their shoes were unsuitable for trekking and they had no waterproof clothes. The Chinese cotton jackets they wore absorbed the water like blotting paper. When the planes circled them, she suddenly realized how impossible the whole idea was; they would be targets for the Japanese wherever they went. The thought made her shudder.

When the guide had gone they walked a few more hours. By now it had stopped raining and their clothes were steaming from the exertion of trying to keep up with the men. Zofia had no watch but guessed at how much time had passed. Though they had flasks of boiled tea supplied by Tang, these were nearly gone and they'd need food and water soon.

'Can I see the map?' Zofia asked Griff.

'No need.' His manner was prickly. 'I reckon about another ten miles before we make the village. Just try to keep up.'

Zofia felt his condescension like a slap, but said nothing. She had to grit her teeth. She'd got Hilly into this mess, and she'd see it through to the end.

Chapter 38

Haru emerged from his opium-soaked dreamland to find Endo hammering on his door, telegram in hand. A message from Commander Onozaka demanding he call him.

There was a field telephone on the landing of his house, but Haru had never used it. This small world he inhabited over the reflections of the canal had become smaller since he'd discovered the *Chandu*. Now he watched his men's brutality to the passing traders with a detached eye, knowing any discipline they once possessed had been eroded by war, the cheap ubiquity of Chinese lives, and the throwaway animal availability of sex whenever they wished it.

The fact he had to pick up the telephone now and be connected to the real world of the army made Haru nervous. He knew things had slipped, that he was viewing the world as if underwater.

The voice on the other end was like a whip. 'Kimura. Activity in your area has slowed. We have had no reports of smuggled weapons or insurgents for some time. What is going on in Soochow?'

'Nothing, sir. I mean, we are doing our best.'

'One of your men says you are rarely seen outdoors these days.'

'That's a lie.' Who was it? The sneaky little rat. 'I admit I'm not popular with the men. Some don't like to submit to the necessary discipline.' Sweat began to run down his neck. He passed the slippery receiver to his other hand.

'You know the penalty for lack of zeal and traitorous thoughts about our Emperor?'

He did, but he tried not to think about that. The question didn't seem to need an answer because Commander Onozaka was still snapping at him down the telephone. 'You are to intensify all your searches. Two of our enemies have escaped from Woosung Camp, an American and a British man. They've been on the run for a week, and so far they have evaded all our attempts at capture. The Chinese are using this escape as propaganda, saying we can't catch a monkey in a cage. They make a mockery of us.'

'What makes you think these men will come here?' Haru was already thinking how unlikely that would be, and whether he could get away with doing nothing at all.

'A peasant we brought in says he saw two tall white men pass by him in the company of other Chinese men, they were headed up into the hills near the village of Qianyan. We think they'll make for Soochow. Overhead planes haven't been able to locate them. You must organize all your units to step up roadblocks and checkpoints on the canals.'

'Shall I contact you directly if I find them? Or the local police?'

'Contact me first. We'll need to interrogate them about who helped them. They must have had outside help. Then we'll make an example of them as a deterrent to anyone else who is foolish enough to try it.'

'Yes, sir. I'll see to it.'

'I'm thinking of transferring you to a fighting unit,' Onozaka said. 'Unless of course, I get results.'

They could do that, he realized. Shunt them around like chess pieces, and there was nothing he could do.

When the call was ended he found he was shaky. That clipped voice had the power to put the fear of hell into him. And he knew he'd have to follow orders because there was an informant in his ranks, bleating back to Onozaka. Haru ran through the ranks in his mind, searching for the most obvious culprit, but came to realize with a hollow feeling that he knew none of the men well enough to say. He had no friends in the army. It could be any one of them.

He'd let things slide, and now his skin was on the table.

He'd sort it out tomorrow. He'd galvanize every man into action.

But tomorrow. Tonight he needed his little slice of peace.

Chapter 39

Zofia paused to catch her breath, as Theo's friend Griff, a man she found intimidating with his abrupt and abrasive manner, strode on ahead, splashing at a punishing pace through the muddy terrain. To her relief, Theo slowed and waited for her to catch up. She noticed he was limping. Indeed, he looked far from the urbane businessman she used to know.

'Does he know where he's going?' she asked, pointing ahead to Griff.

'He planned the route, so I suppose so,' said Theo. 'He doesn't like it though when things don't go to plan.'

'You mean, like us.'

He fell into step beside her and said in a low voice, 'Why do you want to do this? I worry about the danger. You'd be safer to stay in one of the villages. We could meet the Japanese at any time.'

'Because the war could go on for years.' And then quieter, 'And I'm sick of war. And there's Hilly. I feel responsible. It might be safer for her in the US.' *Please, don't leave us behind.*

'America's not what you think. No place is. We always think life will be better somewhere else. But it's what's inside us that's hell.'

'But you're trying to get out, aren't you?'

'Because we're wanted men. If the Japs catch us, though, they will kill us all. And it will go worse for the women.'

'Why are you whispering?' Hilly called from behind. 'I'm thirsty, I need a drink.'

'Hush,' Zofia said, 'We need to be quiet, remember? No loud voices.'

'But I'm thirsty.'

So much water and rain, so many paddy fields, but nothing to drink. 'We've run out of tea,' Zofia said.

'There should be a stream a little way ahead, past these rice fields,' Theo said. 'Griff looked at the map earlier. Maybe it will be clean. We can stop there and fill our water bottles.'

'Where will we sleep?' Hilly asked.

'In the next village. Only another eight miles I think. And it will be dark by then, anyway.'

'Eight miles!' Hilly was not impressed.

'After that we're headed to Soochow,' Theo said. 'It's a bigger place but there are more Japs in and around it. It has canals and links to other big towns.'

A sigh, and Hilly trudged ahead of them.

'She's coping well,' Theo said.

'Because she doesn't know the half of it. But I'm glad. When she gets stubborn, heaven and earth can't shift her.'

He smiled, and she was glad the talk of them staying behind had stopped.

After another hour of plodding they came to the stream which fed into a small pond. The stream edges were pulpy mud but the pond had a shale-like edge and a small man-made platform where they could fill their flasks. It seemed locals must use it for washing or feeding livestock. They'd seen oxen in a distant field not long ago. By now it was dusk and even though it was cooler, the mosquitos were biting over this standing water. Zofia slapped them away from her arms as they dipped their flasks into the viscous cold of the pond.

'Is it safe to drink?' she asked Theo.

Griff, who by this time had already filled his flask and was waiting for them impatiently, said, 'If the locals use it, I don't see why we shouldn't. Be quick, we need to make the village before dark.' He glared at them accusingly, as if they were responsible for holding him up. 'I'll go ahead in case there are Japanese troops.'

And he was off again, stomping into the shadows in his too-big shoes.

After a while they came to some criss-crossed paths that had obviously been used as footpaths by locals and as they climbed upwards they realized they must be getting nearer the village. There seemed to be no animals grazing and Griff came to a halt on the path.

A flock of carrion crows wheeled away from them, squawking into the mist and clouds.

They came up to see what he could see. But it wasn't what he could see, it was what he could smell. The unmistakeable stench of wet soot and decay, with some other darker stench beneath.

They walked forward more slowly now towards the blackened remains of houses, ruins on the charred hillside, all roofless, collapsed in on themselves. It was eerie, this patch of charred earth amongst all the green.

'Don't look to the right,' Griff said.

Of course they all did, and it was to see a pile of bodies, half burned, half decayed. The last few carrion crows flapped away, reluctant to leave their feast.

'The Japanese,' Griff said. 'They have this policy called the "Three Alls". Kill all, burn all, loot all.'

'Do you think all the villages are like this?' Hilly's trembling voice echoed what Zofia was thinking.

Griff shrugged. 'We'd better see if anywhere's been left intact. We need shelter. But I don't suppose there's anyone left here who can help us now.'

'I want to go home,' Hilly said.

Zofia suppressed a deep sigh. *Where was home? They were both rootless.* 'Come on now, we'll find somewhere to sleep.' She took Hilly's arm.

'I don't want to go there. It's a bad place.'

'You'll be safe with us,' Theo said, cajoling her.

Griff had stopped again and was staring back at them. He seemed to have only just realized that Hilly was not just 'another woman' but her own individual person. By his expression, he was not best pleased.

A flash of moving colour in one of the houses, and his attention was broken. 'Did you see something?'

'Someone's still there.' Zofia had seen it too. 'There's a wisp of smoke from that chimney. Or maybe the building's still burning.'

'Japs?' Theo asked.

'No. Why would they be hiding? More likely Chinese.'

'Shall we go on?' Griff asked.

'Let's risk it. We need somewhere to bed down, and maybe they'll be friendly.'

Griff kept going and they followed him warily up the dirt track leading to the village. Even the vegetation was burned. Blackened stumps of trees and burned-out iron-wheeled carts were strewn either side, along with the remnants of metal cooking pots and other detritus indicating people had been trying to move their possessions away.

Zofia scanned the buildings for any sign of movement, but there was none. The place was uncannily silent, although she had the distinct feeling they were being watched.

They were close to the village when without warning a man leapt out and shouted '*Zi bou!*' His hands were up telling them to stop. A small Chinese man in traditional peasant clothing.

Griff took another tentative step forward.

'No! No! *Jin zhi!*'

'What's he saying?' asked Hilly.

'Dunno,' Griff said. 'But he doesn't want us to come any further.'

Theo had paused and was squinting ahead. 'Is he armed?'

'Doesn't look like it,' Griff said, edging forward again.

The man crouched down, scrabbled to pick up a brick and then hurled it in their direction. Griff ignored it, arm outstretched in a gesture of peace.

The man kept shouting and gesticulating and throwing bricks until there was a deafening crack and the road exploded, shooting debris up in a plume of dust, spattering shrapnel into the air. Zofia and Hilly dived to the ground, unsure what was happening or what had caused such an explosion.

Griff pressed a hand to his cheek which was dribbling blood from a gash to the face. 'Get back,' he yelled. 'It's a mine. That's what he's trying to tell us. The track's been mined.'

In front of them a large crater pocked the road, right where they would have walked. Zofia felt her knees turn to feathers at the thought of it.

'Will there be more?' Hilly's face was white with shock.

Zofia helped her up. 'I don't know. Go slow. Look for any bumps where something might have been buried. Stick by my side, hear me?'

The Chinese man was gesturing with both arms, waving them off the track. They didn't need to be asked again. Stepping gingerly, ears buzzing, they moved off the main track and into the soft undergrowth on the side of the hill.

'Careful!' Theo said. 'They might have booby-trapped other places too.'

'Bastards,' Griff said. 'They've rigged it so people will be blown up if they return.'

As they got closer to the village they stepped around more craters where mines had been detonated, and had to avert they eyes from the ruined carts of villagers, their bodies laid out in sheets next to the track.

The Chinese man was waiting for them. Theo showed him the portrait of Mao.

He spoke no English but nodded at them, pleased, then pointed to the sky making imaginary circles.

So the planes were still searching for them. This was bad news.

He was filthy, now they saw him close up, his skin peppered with cuts. He pointed to one of the potholes and shook his head.

They understood it to mean he was one of the few survivors. He looked tiny and solitary against the blackened village and the hill behind. On his short bandy legs, he led them up the hill to where there was a house on stilts, still almost standing. It was empty and there were gaping holes in one side of the wooden floor where fire had charred and burnt it away. A bed roll of blankets and some sort of straw was pushed to one side, and a tiny fire was lit in the surviving hearth.

He got out a tin mug and filled it with water from a blackened pan before offering it around. It seemed he had little. With gestures and sign language they gathered the Japanese had been there five days before. He was the only one still alive as far as he knew because he'd been out cutting wood when they came. He showed them the wood pile. He'd hidden under a tree and watched the Japanese soldiers go past like marauding ants. There had been nothing he could do to save his family. All murdered. His eyes filled with tears that he brushed away as if the grief shouldn't be there.

Hilly seemed to feel his distress and put a hand on his arm while he wept. She was dirty too, and her skin full of mosquito bites. No one had anything to say. The scale of destruction and the loss of life was too huge to comprehend.

The Japanese army had moved on, he said, gesturing to the south. She imagined them, like locusts devastating everything before them. The thought of Haru sat guiltily at the back of her mind.

Wu Jianguo was the man's name. They simply called him Wu, grateful when he cooked up a handful of rice and they shared it, though their stomachs were too full of fear to be able to eat properly. They were all grey with grime and exhausted. Just to lie down under a roof and sleep was enough.

Zofia watched as the others sank into sleep, but she was too anxious to rest. She understood the odds of them meeting Theo's pursuers or Japanese patrols were high. She feared that by moving west they'd find more villages like this one, and she wasn't sure she could bear it.

They stayed in the ruined village for three days, enough time for Wu to look at their map and point to more suggestions about where to go. On the second day, Hilly began to get sick. First she began vomiting, then she had a fever. Wu showed Zofia where to fetch clean water from a well and a spring further up the hill.

'What is it?' Griff said, standing well apart from the Hilly's tossing figure where she lay on the floor. 'Is it infectious?'

'I don't know,' said Zofia, frustrated. 'I'm not a doctor. It could be something in the water. Or it could be malaria. She was badly bitten down at that last creek where we filled our flasks.'

'Can we get quinine or anything like it?'

'I don't know. I'll ask Wu.'

She mimed a mosquito biting and pointed to Hilly. Wu shook his head puzzled, but finally he seemed to understand and went off up the hill.

Meanwhile, Hilly seemed to get worse and the men grew restless, particularly Griff. Zofia heard them talking in low voices outside the house as if they were arguing, and it did nothing to ease her worry as she attempted to look after Hilly. The fever was worse, and Hilly was delirious with it, writhing with pain in her stomach and head, and rambling in German.

Zofia dabbed at Hilly's forehead and neck with a cloth soaked in water, but it didn't seem to help. Hilly seemed to think she was somewhere else, and she sat up, fighting something and with staring eyes tried to punch Zofia in the face. Her flailing arms made it dangerous to be too close to her. Zofia was forced to withdraw and watch her thrashing from afar.

When she moaned long incoherent sentences Zofia couldn't catch, her distress was obvious, and it made Zofia's eyes water to see her.

Reluctantly, Zofia went outside to the two men. 'She's not getting any better. Please, can't you do anything to help?'

'Like what? There's no doctor here,' Griff said. 'No one for miles. Only Japanese.'

'I don't know – we should search the houses, see if we can find anything. Aspirin, anything at all. She's in a bad way.'

'I'll go,' Theo said.

Griff put a hand on his arm. 'Better not. Better wait for Wu. The houses could be mined too. The Japs set booby traps everywhere.'

So they continued to wait uneasily, though Theo ignored Griff and stomped towards the ruined houses.

'He's a fool,' Griff said.

Minutes that felt like hours passed, with Zofia gripping her fists, expecting to hear an explosion any moment. But after about half an hour Theo was back.

'You don't want to see what I've just seen,' he said, his face white.

'Any luck?'

He shook his head. 'Nothing I could recognize.' He went out to talk to Griff.

Hilly had got no better and was now listless, refusing to drink, battling enemies they couldn't see. Outside, Theo and Griff's voices reached her – they were arguing again.

When Wu returned, he had with him a bag of roots and a bunch of dull blue-green herbs. '*Qinghao*,' he said. Some sort of healing herb, she guessed.

But he seemed agitated and after much miming, they

understood from his arm waving and pointing that a second wave of Japanese troops was close by.

Griff got out the well-thumbed map and Wu showed them where he'd seen the troops.

Too close. Less than an hour away.

The men went off to discuss what to do, whilst Wu boiled water to steep the sage-like leaves. The strong, bittersweet smell of the herb filled the air.

Zofia tried to get Hilly to drink it, but she refused to even take a sip, closing her mouth tight against the cup so the hot liquid poured down her chin.

Griff called for Wu to join them outside, but Zofia couldn't think of anything else but trying to get Hilly to drink her medicine. In the end she had to fetch Theo to help, to hold her down while Zofia forced the cup between her teeth.

'We can't make her,' Theo said, letting her go. 'It's not right. Even if it's good for her. And we don't even know that it is.'

'I trust Wu. He saved us from being blown up. He seems like a good man.' Zofia sat back as Hilly leaned over to retch again. Nothing was left in her stomach, and the effort made her collapse into stillness. A dread settled over Zofia like a cloak.

Theo drew her to one side. 'I know you don't want to hear it, but we have to leave. We can't risk being here if the Japanese come again.'

'We can't. Hilly can't walk, she's not going anywhere. You've seen the state of her.'

Right then, Griff arrived, stepping impatiently from foot to foot. 'Have you told her?'

Theo dropped his gaze.

Griff swore and made an impatient gesture. 'We're leaving. Right now. Wu's going to show us a route away from the Japs.'

'What about Hilly?' Zofia asked.

'Your choice,' Griff said. 'Come with us, or stay behind with her.'

'I'm not leaving her. We'll carry her.'

'We can't. She'll slow us down. And if she starts shouting again, she'll give us away. Army rules are clear, never compromise the many for the few.'

'We're not in the bloody army now,' Zofia raged. 'And we're not leaving without her. I'll keep her calm, I promise—'

A noise in the distance made her stop to listen. Gunfire.

They all heard it and adrenaline shot up Zofia's spine.

Wu was gesturing and gabbling something at them, tugging at Griff's arm. It was clear they should leave immediately.

Theo dropped down next to Hilly. Awkwardly he tried to drag her up from the ground, but she was a dead weight. Zofia rushed forward to help, but she was too late; Wu had seen what he was doing and had taken hold of Hilly's legs, as Hilly groaned and protested.

'Quiet now, quiet,' Zofia urged her, one hand on her forehead trying to soothe her.

Theo and Wu carried her out of the house and began heading up the hill towards the forest of vegetation surrounding the village.

'It's asking for trouble,' Griff complained.

'You make me sick,' Zofia said. 'Even Wu is prepared to help us, and he owes us nothing. At least he has a conscience, even if you don't.'

Griff's jaw tightened and he looked shocked, but he studiously ignored her comment.

In the distance the gunfire continued and then further over to the right a black pall of smoke unrolled in the sky.

Scrambling, stumbling, they climbed upward into the cover of trees and shrub. Out of necessity, Griff took over carrying Hilly's feet so Wu could show them the route, but Hilly began to jerk and thrash again so they finally had to lower her to the ground so she could vomit.

From their vantage point under a thicket of waxy evergreens, they saw the smoke rising more thickly over to the east too, and on a path to their left a column of men weaving ant-like across the landscape. Japanese soldiers.

Theo looked despairingly at Griff. 'We're caught between them. Like pincers.'

'Just press on,' Griff said.

Wu, meanwhile, had come back with two sturdy pieces of bamboo. He took off his jacket and threaded the poles through the arms. Theo grasped the idea immediately and followed his lead, taking off his coat too to make a stretcher for Hilly. Griff was resigned to taking one end and so they proceeded, a little more easily than before, and Zofia was able to exhale with relief. It looked like they were going to stick together after all.

The terrain was unforgiving, stony tracks amongst damp evergreen vegetation. They kept to the higher ground to avoid the plain where the Japanese soldiers were moving below them in long columns. Zofia feared there might also be snakes, let alone the Japanese. But it was reassuring to have Wu, indefatigable on his wiry legs, leading the way, his hemp bag over his shoulder. On several occasions he seemed to sniff the air, and then turn away from what he could sense.

They walked for three days with no habitation in sight, sleeping at night where they fell. Carrying Hilly was exhausting, but Zofia too took her turn.

The food was meagre, and they were all hungry. Wu had a few provisions in his bag, wild mushrooms, edible ferns and some root-like vegetables, but everything had to be eaten raw lest a fire draw attention to their position. Hilly had got no better and her fever kept returning. She alternated between sweating and uncontrollable shivering. She hadn't eaten and was slowly starving herself to death.

In the middle of the night, she sat up and grabbed Zofia by the arms. Zofia, who had been asleep, found herself looking into Hilly's intense stare.

'It's time,' she said in English.

'Time for what?'

'My mother and father are gone now. I can feel it. Like something that was tied to me has let me go. So now it's my time.'

Was she rambling? There was something coherent in what she was saying.

'You're going to get better,' she said. 'You must take the medicine Wu's making. It's something for malaria.'

'It's not malaria.' Hilly said. 'They've eaten my heart. Such a big space inside, when you have no one.'

'You have me,' Zofia said. 'And Theo.'

But Hilly had lapsed into silence.

Theo heard her and came to join in. 'Is she any better?'

'She was talking, but she's gone to sleep again. It seemed to tire her out. I wish I knew what it was.'

Zofia sat beside Hilly every time they paused to rest, but it was obvious she was failing. She'd developed a rash on her upper body like small pinpricks.

'What do you think it is?'

'Griff says it could be malaria, or dengue fever,' Theo said. 'He saw them both in Woosung.' Whatever the label, they both knew she was getting worse.

When night fell, Zofia tried to sleep but she could hear the rasp of Hilly's breath beside her. She put her arms around her to keep her warm, but halfway through the night she went limp and lapsed into a coma.

Zofia tried to wake her, but she wouldn't come round. Zofia stroked her hair away from her forehead. Distraught, she got up to alert Theo, but he was sleeping and it was Griff who was sitting up, chewing on a thumbnail and watching the horizon. He gestured her to leave the curled-up Theo alone. 'Let him sleep,' he said.

'I can't get Hilly to wake up,' Zofia said, her voice thick with tears. 'I don't know what to do. Please, we have to do something.'

Griff stood up, easing himself as if his bones were stiff. His face was haggard and deep creases lined his forehead. 'Do you think it might help her if we pray?' he said.

She shrugged. 'Maybe. But I only know Jewish prayers. And she said her parents were Jehovah's Witnesses.'

'That explains why she won't take the medicine. They don't believe in it.'

'Why?'

'They think God should decide, not men. They leave it in his hands.'

'Then if you know some prayers, let's try, see if He'll hear us.'

'I know a few Christian ones. Shall we try those? It can't do any harm, and our voices might comfort her.' He walked over to where Hilly was lying, her face white as stone, her breath barely a whisper.

Griff knelt as if it pained his knees, but he brought his palms together and began to pray. He started with the Lord's Prayer which Zofia recalled having heard once or twice before from Daisy at bedtime. She listened and the words eased the panic in her heart. This was a different Griff from the abrasive man she knew.

At the end he fell quiet and put a hand on Hilly's forehead. He raised his other hand and said a blessing.

'Are you a priest?' Zofia asked him, surprised.

'No fear.' He gave a hoarse laugh. 'But I had a friend who was.' He turned to look up at her. 'We fought in the first war. He died.' He swallowed. 'Blown up in front of me. I'm just doing what he did to the lads who came out of the trenches.'

'Did it help them survive?'

He sat back on his haunches and slowly shook his head. 'No. But it helped us. Helped us cope.' He paused. 'And I sure as hell need them now, the prayers. It's bringing it all back, the first war. I thought I could control everything, but it went wrong right from the beginning, didn't it? We were supposed to be three men. But we lost Lennie, and it still haunts me ... we should have waited for him; how it must have hurt to watch us go under the wire without him. They killed him. We heard the shots.' He stood up and his face creased into an expression of pain. 'And now you—'

'I know. You've got us two women as well.'

'You shouldn't be here. I don't think I've enough strength to protect you if the Japs come. And I know men, and war. And the awful things they do.'

'But Griff, we don't expect—'

'But I expect it of myself! And I knew I couldn't do anything to help Hilly, and I didn't want to watch another person die. So I wanted to leave her behind. How selfish is that? You're right, I'm a selfish, unfeeling bastard.'

'We're all under strain, I didn't mean—'

But he was still talking, like a river in spate. 'I couldn't do anything for my men before either. Couldn't save a single one, though I tried. Dragged myself through the mud and wire to fetch them back, but it was hopeless. A whole platoon lost. Bloody stupid war.' He turned away, staring down the hill. 'And the map is wrong,' he said, agitated. 'I should have known it would keep changing. But I'm the oldest and most experienced, aren't I? And responsible.'

She tried to interrupt again, but he strode over and grabbed her by the arms.

'No. It's my fault. None of you are used to army discipline and now we're stuck out here in this damn hellhole, army rules make no sense to me either.' He looked at her with a kind of desperation in his eyes. 'I'm hanging on to them because I don't know what else to do, see? I'm so bloody lonely.' With that he let her go and walked away.

'Griff?' She tried to call him back, but when she looked back to Hilly, she was ominously still.

Zofia froze. She knew before she even touched her what she'd find. There was some feeling in the air she couldn't name. A feeling of utter stillness.

Stupefied, she reached out a hand, but it was obvious Hilly was gone. What was lying there was no longer Hilly. 'No ...' she whispered.

A great chasm opened in her chest. She wanted to shout and scream, but she knew it would do no good. Nothing could fill the vast silence inside her heart. So she lay down next to Hilly and held her hand tight in hers as it gradually lost all its warmth to the chill of the night.

Chapter 40

They had no tools to dig, so Griff and Theo followed the instruction of Wu, who covered Hilly's body with large leaves and weighed them down with stones. Zofia went through Hilly's bundle and took out her passport, and she was surprised to find a worn photograph in there too. It showed three people sitting on a bench in front of a view of the sea. It was a small image, but she could make out that it was a younger Hilly, sitting between her parents – a woman with flyaway blonde hair, and a man squinting into the sun. Hilly had plaits and an ice cream cornet in her hand. The sight of it made Zofia swallow hard.

She tucked it into her own things. Someone had to remember this family, broken by the war. Griff was silent that morning and didn't get out the map. He deferred instead to Wu, who lit incense and made prayers over Hilly's body before they had to move on.

Leaving her behind was the hardest thing she'd ever had to do. Theo took hold of her hand as they walked. He didn't say anything because there was nothing to say, but the dry warmth of his palm made it somehow more bearable.

Two more days of walking and they were footsore and weary. Every village they came to was a shell, and they avoided them all, fearful of mines. Griff trailed behind; he'd stopped marching as though they were on an army training exercise, his feet dragged and his shoulders sagged.

Wu had taken charge and his bouncing stride was always a little too fast for Zofia. Still she struggled on.

One of the villages still had a few chickens rooting about close by. Wu caught and killed one, so they risked a fire and had their first chicken dinner to go with the foraged vegetables. She'd never tasted anything so good, and the effect of the food was immediate. Their energy returned along with better humour. The only bitter thing was that there was no Hilly to share it with.

On the fourth day after going down into a long marshy plain, they came across an unusual sight. The bodies of Japanese soldiers piled at the side of the path between rice fields.

Wu grinned. 'Yes, yes!' was all he could say.

'Do you think guerrillas did it – people from the CCP?' Theo asked Griff.

'Maybe,' Griff said, 'but I daren't take anything for granted.'

A few miles further on, a miracle. A house that was intact. Granted, it was just a shack, but it had a dirt road leading to it, and in the distance they saw more houses. A small hamlet, all with the roofs still on.

Wu was more confident now and wanted to hurry on, but Theo and Griff were not as hardy as Wu and were weary with walking the whole day. Ahead of them they saw Wu go into the house and a few moments later, a whole family came out to stare. Wu was talking, obviously explaining who they were – and pointing back over the hill they'd just descended.

Wu beckoned to them, leading them inside, grinning with excitement. The woman of the house produced hot food, and they dined on hot rice, vegetables and peanuts, with what appeared to be a few shreds of salt pork. Knowing food was scarce here, Zofia ate it, ignoring the Jewish custom and the echo of her parents' horrified voices in her head. Every moment Zofia looked for Hilly, surprised she wasn't there. Her presence was so strong, it was as if Zofia brought a phantom with her wherever she went.

When they'd eaten, the man of the household, a long-faced farmer, took them up the road to meet a priest he said could speak English and the Shanghai dialect. Wu came with them. He seemed to have become a permanent fixture, and no one had the heart to send him away, even if they hadn't relied on him. Wu asked for nothing, but seemed to need their company. Zofia respected the fact he was so self-contained; that despite losing his entire family and his whole village, he focused on the practical – food, shelter and safety. She suspected in his eyes these Westerners were like stupid lost sheep that had gone astray and needed herding.

The priest was an aged man straight out of a Taoist painting, balding, with drooping white moustache and a long blue robe. Duan Hongliang was treated with great respect by the two Chinese men; his English was old-fashioned and polite, and Griff seemed to melt before his mild hospitality. He sat them down at a low table for more tea, and listened as they explained where they were going. A story Zofia suspected would have to be told many times.

The map was consulted again, and Zofia took it in for the first time. Before, she'd paid it scant attention. Now the scale of the journey seemed impossible.

Theo saw her face, gripped her hand, and said, 'Repeat after me – "we're going to make it".'

Transport was swiftly arranged with a local communist farmer to take them on to Soochow, and it was restful to let themselves be organized. Duan told them he had a friend in the city who could smuggle them out by boat, and it would save weeks of walking. Zofia glanced at Griff to see his face had softened, and something in him had given way; a rigidity had collapsed.

In the morning, Zofia heard the crackle of voices, and realized Duan Hongliang had a radio. She got up and limped to where the men were crowded around the set, all talking over one another in some consternation. When the broadcast was finished, he turned it off and shook his head.

'Bad news. My friend in the CCP says there are road blocks on every road. To get to Soochow now, you'll have to go by canal.'

Theo frowned. 'These road blocks – are they looking for us?'

He laughed. 'You are famous. Everyone knows about you. I'd heard of you from the radio before you even got here, though I never expected to set eyes on you!'

Theo's gaze turned to Zofia and she gave him an answering glance. There was nothing they could do except press on. They couldn't go back.

Duan was still talking, fingering his long moustache. 'You must be careful who you trust. Every Japanese will want the reward for catching you, and every corrupt official will want to help them.'

'Can't we avoid going through Soochow?' Zofia asked.

'Not if you want to meet with my friend. His name is Pau. He's the police chief for Soochow.'

'Won't he want to hand us in?' Zofia said.

'He's anti-Japanese. His position gives him the chance to help many people, and to find us weapons. He has access to the Japanese army supplies. No one questions him, he has authority. If anyone can get you safe passage, it's Pau. But be mindful when you meet him; know he risks his own head for people like you.'

Theo held out a hand to help Zofia into the dusty yellow truck which was carrying baskets of coarse-leaved cabbage and winter radish bound for market. Wu and Griff were already leaning back against the cab as Zofia and Theo joined them. They'd been told to keep low, and all of them except Wu had smeared their faces and arms with soya sauce which made their skin look weathered. Chinese clothes and head coverings disguised them to look like workers from the fields. The relief of being off their feet made Theo and Griff grin to each other as they bounced in the back of the metal pick-up.

Few other vehicles were on the road and they travelled on in silence except for the rumble of the truck's engine. The weather was cold but dry and they left a plume of dust in their wake. This must have drawn attention because there was one frightening moment where a Japanese plane flew low over them, but the truck just kept on moving and the plane banked away, leaving Zofia weak with relief. When more farms came into view on both sides of the road, their driver turned off and they bumped up a stony track until it petered out into a rough turning circle.

A few moments consulting the map with their drivers before they were left to go on foot through tea plantations. Women tending the bushes in the distance looked up at the strangers and shouted, but Wu gestured to keep walking and ignore them, so with her heart pounding Zofia kept her head down and followed the others. The men stood out for being so tall, and Zofia was nervous about the fact they'd been spotted. But no one came after them and after a couple of hours they saw the canal stretching like a long silver line through the adjoining fields. As they walked, the number of sampans grew, and Wu gestured to Theo they should turn away from the water.

'Thank God we have Wu with us,' Griff said.

The next few days were just trudge and struggle all the way.

They had directions to Police Chief Pau's house and a hand-drawn map from the old gentleman Duan. They reached the outskirts of Soochow at dawn one morning, but knew that in daylight they would be too obvious, so they waited until dusk had fallen before venturing into the city.

'Let's go in pairs,' Theo said. 'We look too much like a crowd.'

'I'll go with Zofia then,' Griff said, 'and you go with Wu.' Theo began to object, but Griff interrupted him. 'It makes sense. I'm used to fighting and better able to protect her. You can have Wu.'

Zofia couldn't object, though she would much rather have gone with Theo. They split up and went two ways, both avoiding the gate at the city wall as they were sure that would be guarded by the Japanese. She turned to see the tall and short figures of Theo and Wu walking away, and it gave her a pang. Both such good men. What would she have done without them?

Griff walked with his head down carrying his small bundle of possessions. In the dark no one paid either of them any attention. They were dressed the Chinese way and kept their eyes lowered. Beggars hovered on the corner of every street, but they didn't ask for money or stretch out their hands, obviously thinking them two of their own.

It was easy to tell it was a town under occupation, thought Zofia. A tension spiked the air almost as if it was seeping out of the brickwork. There were barely any night-time traders on the streets, when once Soochow would have been bustling with street-food vendors. She passed walls pockmarked with bullets. Was the tension in her surroundings, or in her? She shivered, a feeling of foreboding draped over her like a cloak.

'You okay?' Griff turned. Maybe he'd sensed something too.

'Fine. Just scared,' she whispered. 'I know the Japanese are here, but I don't know where.'

'Pau's house should be around the next corner, and Wu's got his head screwed on. Let's hope they've got there before us.'

Griff stopped at the next intersection where the houses were stacked up over a narrow alley. White *hanfu*, left out overnight, hung from a balcony – shirts swaying in the breeze like ghosts.

Griff held up a warning hand to prevent her coming further, then shot backwards grabbing her by the arm. He dragged her into a shophouse doorway, just as two Japanese soldiers walked past the crossroads at the end of the alley. She watched their backs, the bristles of their shaven hair beneath their army caps, the knives and pistols in their belts.

Griff was pressed up close to her, and she felt his body stiffen, ready to fight.

Their footsteps faded away.

'Now!' hissed Griff and hauled her out.

They pelted around the corner and squinted through the dark, searching for the right house. The one with the lamp on the balcony, Duan had said.

There were two houses with lamps.

Zofia hesitated. Which one? They couldn't afford a mistake. But then she recognized the kanji for 'police' on the sign outside. She beckoned furiously to Griff who was about to knock at the door of the other house.

He saw her and hurried over just as she gave a soft knock. A man came out onto the balcony and looked down.

'Hongliang Duan sent us,' she said.

'What did he tell you to say?'

She repeated the Chinese words. 'The red leaf never falls.'

'Yes. He radioed me. Wait.' He disappeared from the balcony, and moments later the door opened to reveal a short square man dressed in a Western-style suit. After a quick look up and down the street, he held the door open and they entered the dark hallway.

'Our friends, are they here yet?' Zofia asked him in Chinese.

'There are more of you?' He spoke English. What a relief.

'Two more. An American and a Chinese man.'

'Ah. I heard about the escape on the radio and wondered if they might turn up here. Most fugitives do.' He shook his head as he led them up the stairs to the first floor.

'You've heard nothing of the American then, and his friend Wu?' she insisted.

'Not yet.'

'It was easier to travel in pairs,' she said.

'Don't worry. They'll be along soon,' Griff said. 'They have the directions.'

Pau was business-like but brisk. 'The local commander of the Japanese army has ordered searches of the boats coming in and out of the city. They are looking for you. Nobody told me there was a woman, or a Chinese national with you. It makes it difficult for me to arrange onward passage. I'll do what I can, but I can't risk my own position. Many more people depend on my help. And if you talk, then when they've finished with me, my corpse won't be worth burying.'

'But you can help us?' Zofia asked.

'You must leave tomorrow because I can't risk you being seen in my house. Also, my priority is the two men, the ones who escaped Woosung.' He turned to Griff. 'You are the ones they are searching for. If necessary, the lady here and Wu will have to stay behind.'

'It's Zofia,' she said. 'And they won't go without me.' She feigned confidence, but she wasn't sure it was true.

Griff picked up on the fraught nature of her reply. 'It's okay. They'll be here by then.'

Pau's servant brought them tea and a bowl of rice broth. Pau thanked him with elegant gestures of his hands.

Pau's house was busy. He had a telephone that kept ringing, and his radio was on at a low level with the Japanese news broadcasting in a continuous crackling murmur. He seemed to be fielding calls from insurgents all over China. With the rapid Chinese speech, she couldn't keep up with it all, but kept her ears open for any news about Theo and Wu.

The idea of them leaving without her struck deep in her heart. If they left without her, what then? Even though it was more dangerous to stay with them, she couldn't bear the thought of Theo leaving without her now.

Chapter 41

In his house in Soochow, Haru was reclining in his bedroom, which he'd made draught-proof so nothing could disturb the flames of his opium lamp. The embossed texture of the cool enamel pipe pleased his touch as it rested against his fingers. It bore pictures of persimmon, bamboo and chrysanthemum, symbols that reminded him powerfully of Japan and home. The drug made his fingers tingle, and his eyes thrilled to the glowing colours of the enamel. He'd become an expert in his own pleasure, in the rolling of the opium pill, in the art of picking up the hot pellet with the needle to place it precisely in the pipe bowl. Ah, the exquisite bliss of the stream of warm vapour in his lungs!

When his telephone rang he didn't get up and answer it, leaving it to his servant to field the call. Who the hell had the nerve to call him at this time of night? He took another long suck at his pipe.

A tentative knock on the door.

'What is it?' He couldn't keep the annoyance from his voice.

The door creaked open and Endo's head appeared. 'Sir, a patrol has brought in a Westerner, an American. With his Chinese servant. The officer wants to speak with you directly.'

American? Haru's heart stuttered. This could be the man

Commander Onozaka was after. He struggled to his feet, slightly woozy from standing too quickly. 'Tell him I'm coming.'

Endo disappeared and Haru threw a *yukata* over his loose shirt. 'Yes?' He pressed his ear to the receiver.

The city police officer informed him two men had been apprehended just inside the city walls. 'One of them's American,' the voice said. 'He won't talk but description matches Theodore Carter.'

'Who?'

The policeman repeated it and Haru managed to make out the mangled American name. A sensation like an electric current ran up his spine. 'And the other man, the Brit?'

'No. Not Brit. Chinese.'

Chinese? A servant? Haru's head swam as his mind tried to grasp the possibilities.

The man was still speaking. 'What shall I do with them?'

'Detain them in jail. No food. No water. I'll interview them tomorrow.'

When the call was over, he returned to his pipe, elated. Heaven had favoured him, and he was about to reap the reward for all that rushing about and putting patrols on the canals. Even more fortunate, it would mean Onozaka would get off his back. War was wearying enough without Onozaka. The only way he could go home would be if the Emperor decided to surrender. And the chance of that was zero.

At Pau's house, Zofia couldn't stay still. The tea was cold in the pot, and yet there was still no sign of Theo and Wu. Meanwhile, Pau was engaged in rustling through papers at his desk, quite unperturbed.

The tapping of Griff's foot, an unconscious tic that showed his matching agitation, made Zofia want to scream. Every passing moment stretched out the agony of waiting for news.

When the telephone shrilled, both Griff and Zofia shot to

their feet. Pau gestured impatiently at them to sit whilst he went to answer it.

Just police business. Looters and licences. No news.

Zofia had to curb her desire to do something, anything, to ease the waiting.

The next time it rang they followed Pau to the door of the hall and hovered as he spoke.

'I see.' There was something in his manner, the way he turned to see if they were listening, that raised the hairs on the back of Zofia's neck. She craned to make out the tinny voice on the other end.

She took in Pau's Chinese words. 'You called him at home?' A sigh, then a pause as more information was given. 'Yes, yes, of course it was the right thing to do ... What time?' Another pause. 'I'll be there ... no, I insist. I'll need to interview his Chinese servant.' Zofia shot Griff a look, unsure if he'd caught the gist of it. 'Yes,' Pau was saying, 'Probably. Likely a member of the CCP.' More conversation about patrols and drunken beggars before he could get off the phone.

When Pau put the receiver back in the cradle he stayed looking at the wall, with his back to them.

'They've got them, haven't they?' said Griff.

Pau swivelled to face them and held up his hands. 'They're in Soochow jail awaiting interrogation by the Japanese deputy commander. He speaks several languages including English so he's going to interrogate your American himself. There's not a chance Carter or Wu will get out of there, except to be taken for execution.'

Griff sank onto a chair, his face white. 'It's my fault. We should have stuck together.'

'No, or we'd all have been in there.' She turned to Pau asking him, 'Is there nothing we can do?'

'There's no time before he's interrogated. If he talks, we're finished. If he doesn't talk, a house-to-house search will begin soon after, because they'll be looking for his British companion too.'

'Shit,' Griff said. 'We can't just do nothing. We have to try to get them out.'

Zofia appealed to Pau. 'Is there no hope at all?'

'Only to run.' But then he paced and thought for a moment. 'The commander is an addict, an opium smoker. We try to get them addicted as soon as we can, so we can manipulate them through their habit. The last commander here was persuaded to go alone to an opium den when he needed a fix, and we made sure he never got there. Or back.'

'Can we do something like that again?' Zofia asked.

'I could try to delay him, I suppose.' Pau was pacing the floor. 'I can get in there, no problem. They think I'm a collaborator, on the Japs' side. I know the commander well, and because I supply him with his fix, he thinks of me as a friend. But I don't think he'll listen to me – he's been well trained, and he's in terror of his superior, a man called Onozaka.'

'If you and I went in, is there any way we could all overpower this commander and get Theo out?' Griff was determined not to give up.

'Not a chance. Kimura will have his bodyguard with him, the jail's well staffed with Japs, and besides, I have to keep up the pretence of collaboration, even if I were a fighting man.'

Zofia blinked. 'What did you call him? The commander?'

'Kimura. Why? Have you come across him before?'

It couldn't be a relation. Could it? 'No. His first name. Tell me his first name.'

'Haru. Haru Kimura.'

Zofia felt the world spin to a stop. Her mouth was dry as bone. 'Tell me about him. How old is he? What does he look like?'

Pau shook his head. 'I don't know, young – in his twenties. Too young for this, like they all are. Skinny. Looks like all the rest of those monkeys.'

She stepped towards him, as if she would shake him. 'Don't speak of people like that! Do you know where this man came from? Where his home is?'

Pau gave a small chuckle. 'A small village outside Tokyo. He's done well for himself through the blood of my people. He thinks himself an intellectual because he studied in America. At Harvard.'

Harvard. Oh no. It was making too much sense.

'Why all these questions?' Griff had got hold of her arm. He must have seen the blood drain from her face.

'My husband's name. But it can't be. Haru was sent to army training in Manchuria in the North of China. Not here. Not anywhere near here. It can't be him. It's a common name, surely.'

'You know this man?' Pau had understood their conversation.

'I did,' she said bitterly. 'If it's the same man. But no. It can't possibly be him. He would never let himself be so … so …' She was lost for words.

'How can we be certain?' Griff pressed. 'Have you a photograph? Have either of you a photograph?'

Zofia nodded. But she was now moving on automatic, as if she was in some silent film in which the frames were ratcheting in slow motion. She went to her bag and drew out her papers. Nestled in there was a photograph taken on their wedding day by Rabbi Rabinowitz. She drew it out. When she looked at the man in the photograph he seemed like a stranger.

Wordlessly she passed it to Pau. He stared at it a long time. 'This you?'

She nodded, embarrassed. 'I'm his wife.'

'He looks different now.' Pau said. 'But there's no doubt. That's him. Wait.' He hurried to the adjoining room and returned with a Japanese newspaper. On a front side column, was a mug shot of a Japanese man. 'Commander Kimura' read the caption.

Zofia looked at it and her heart made a double thump.

'It's him, isn't it?' Griff became instantly animated. 'Then you can talk to him, persuade him to let Theo go.'

'I don't know. I can't think. It's too much to take in—'

Griff wouldn't let up. 'If it's him he'll listen to you, won't he? And he's been to Harvard, hasn't he, so he'll be sympathetic to an American, surely?'

'Don't be so certain. They're at war.'

Pau looked from one to the other as they were talking.

Zofia struggled to a chair, sat and put her head in her hands. If she was honest, the thought of seeing Haru again filled her with mixed emotions. Disbelief. A flutter of desire. A shudder of revulsion. She'd come to think of the Japanese as the enemy, and there had been no letters between them, no calls since Japan declared war on the US. He would have no idea she was even in China, let alone here in Soochow. She'd seen what the Japanese did to people – the brutal nature of the killing. The rapes and the burning of whole villages. And the time with Haru seemed hazy compared to the time she'd spent trekking through Chinese mudflats with Theo. Time had twisted and turned and taken her under too many bridges.

'I lost too many men last time. We can't let them take Theo,' Griff said.

'I know,' Zofia said. And it was only that thought that made her turn to speak to Pau.

'Can I come with you to speak to him?' she asked him. 'Griff's right. I'm his wife, he'll listen to me. And there's Wu, too. He lost his family and his whole village to the Japanese slaughter.'

Pau's face creased into disbelief. 'No. You don't understand. I know Kimura and he won't listen. Not to you, not to anyone. Only three things he'll listen to – the Emperor, his boss, Onozaka, and his habit, the opium. Not to any woman. Not even his wife. It would be a death sentence to give yourself up or admit you helped these men escape.'

'I have to try.' She stuck out her chin. 'And I have to see my husband.'

'You risk us all,' Pau said angrily, and went to the window.

Griff tried to ask her what was happening, but she batted him away. 'Please,' she said going over to touch Pau on the shoulder. 'I have a right to see him.'

'Then I'll show you where he lives, nothing more. You don't know me, okay? Afterwards, it will be up to you. Before you see him, I will do my best for you. I will make sure he has a pill of opium to smooth his mind, make him feel invincible. Perhaps then he will be generous. But he can't know I helped you. I'll escort you there, but then you'll be alone.'

'I understand. Will we see you again?'

'No. It's too dangerous for me to stay in Soochow now your friends have been arrested. Mr Carter will be tortured until he gives my name and all his other contacts.'

'Haru Kimura will listen to me, of that I'm certain. And if he doesn't, then it's my risk and you know I would never give either of you away.'

'Don't promise anything,' said Pau. 'Except to do as much for our Chinese friend Wu as you do for Theodore Carter.'

Chapter 42

Haru was just about to have his morning smoke when he heard footsteps on the stairs. He assumed it was Private Endo. He went into the main living room and shut his bedroom door against the view of his opium paraphernalia.

'Pau!' He was surprised to see him. Pau was usually an afternoon caller.

'You've heard, I suppose,' Pau said.

'About the American, yes. News travels fast in Soochow. And we'll soon have the other man too, the Brit.'

'Good. Do you know anything about the man who was with him? The Chinese man?'

'Not a Red Army soldier,' Haru said dismissively. 'Just an illiterate peasant from what I can gather. Probably bribed to act as guide.'

'I wanted to check you'd been informed,' said Pau. 'And I thought if I came early there'd be time for a small celebration,' he added. 'I've got some new *Chandu*. Superior stuff. I thought you might like to try it. It's supposed to sharpen the mind, just what you need on a day like today. I expect the American won't be very cooperative.'

'Good timing, friend. I was about to take my morning smoke.'

Haru opened his bedroom door again. 'How much for this new stuff?'

'Call it a gift. You have bought enough of my *Chandu*, I can afford to be generous occasionally.'

'It won't make me sleepy?'

'No. This is pure. Best quality. No residue, no side effects.'

'You'll join me?' He suppressed his irritation as Pau leaned over his opium tray, picking up one item after another.

'Not today,' Pau said. 'I have some paperwork to attend to at the office.' He dipped in his pocket and handed Haru a tiny ball of toffee-like resin wrapped in a square of greaseproof paper.

Haru examined it, already longing for its vapour. 'I'll see you at the jail later?'

'Yes, I'm curious to see your American. Pictures of him and his British friend have been posted all over Shanghai. Shall I tell Private Endo to order you a sedan?'

'Yes. Give me an hour or so, would you?'

Pau turned to go, and Haru was glad to wave him away. He had that tingling feeling that meant it was time for another fix.

The door banged and the house was blissfully silent. The American could wait. After all, he was locked up and going nowhere.

He rolled himself a pill of Pau's gift.

Ah, it was good. A slight musky scent and the vapour so cool and smooth.

On the canal path, no one paid Zofia any attention for she was in Chinese clothes and a straw hat that shadowed her face. Haru's house. Past a flowering plum tree and up the outside steps. She knocked but no one answered.

A push on the door and it creaked open. The upstairs room was warm and the air foggy with a dry smell from some kind of smoke. Incense? She took in the state of the room. Scrolls and papers littered the desk, along with sticky-rimmed cups and a bottle of *sake* lying half empty on the floor. A bookshelf had a range of books but they were all gathering dust. An ashtray overflowed with cigarette ends and half-smoked cigars.

Was she in the right place? Surely Haru couldn't live here?

She took off her hat, smoothed her hair, and called for him, tentatively. The other doors off this living area were shut. The ceiling fan obviously hadn't been used in months, for it was grey with cobwebs.

At her second call she heard something creak. A bed, or a floorboard. She took a few steps towards where she thought she heard the noise and called again.

Even after the first pipe Haru could tell this was stronger and sweeter than his usual smoke: it made his nose tingle and his limbs feel as if they were made of elastic. He drifted, watching the light shift on his scarlet brocade curtains, seeing in them the shapes of dragons, twisted fungi and cascading waterfalls.

When someone called his name, he thought he was imagining it. A light, female voice. His mind immediately pictured a Japanese geisha swaying in an ornamental headdress.

'Haru?' The voice had something familiar about it. A discomfort. It pulled at something disturbing in his chest.

He sat up, groggy, the room swilling over him as if he was underwater.

He wrapped his bare chest with his *yukata* and went to the bedroom door. When he opened it, he saw a tall dark-haired woman, dressed in Chinese clothes, standing with her back to him, hat in hand. How had she got in? Where was Private Endo?

The first thing he noticed was that her legs were bruised and cut. He hadn't asked for a cleaner or servant, so what was she doing here?

She must have felt the draught as he came in because she swung around to face him.

He put a hand over his eyes. The woman wasn't Chinese. She

looked like Zofia, but it couldn't be her, it must be the *Chandu* playing tricks.

'Where's Endo? What do you want?' he said, aiming for an authoritative tone.

She was staring at him as if seeing a mirage. 'He's gone out,' she whispered in English.

Her voice made him stagger back a few steps. 'Zofia?'

Time concertinaed. Was he here now, in Soochow, or back in Kobe? Impossible.

Zofia couldn't take her eyes away from this apparition. This man wasn't Haru. This gaunt man with sunken bloodshot eyes, wearing an old robe and stained slippers. She was struck dumb until he spoke her name.

The word seemed to come from a long way away. Time was tumbling, a life falling around her ears.

'Zofia?'

But no one else had ever said her name that way. She wanted to run, but her feet stayed glued to the ground.

'What are you doing here?' English words. As he spoke, his eyes raked around the room as if the answer might be there.

'They sent all Jews to Shanghai. Months ago. I only just found out where you were.'

'To Shanghai?' He still seemed unable to look into her eyes.

'I had to come. As soon as I knew you were in Soochow, I couldn't wait to see you—'

'You shouldn't be here.' He was backing away.

She put the hat down on a chair near the door and went towards him, her arms outstretched. 'Haru, what happened to you?'

'Nothing.' The words were sharp, dismissive. 'I'm doing my duty, as I'm supposed to.' There was something defensive in his answer and in a heartbeat she understood with total certainty there was to be no happy reunion between them. Her arms dropped to her side.

The disappointment was so sharp she inhaled as if stung by a wasp.

The shock had brought them both to silence.

In that split second, she decided to do what she had come for. 'You are keeping a friend of mine in custody. An American. I've come to ask you to let him go.'

His mouth twitched but he didn't answer. She watched him as he walked back towards the bedroom.

'Haru?'

'I have to dress,' he said. 'We will talk after that. You shouldn't have come.' He went back into a bedroom where a lamp shed a red glow and shut the door.

She began to feel uneasy. She'd thought to find the husband who had kissed her so tenderly when he left for war, and had vowed to write. Yet she'd never had a single letter, and this man was no longer the same man. How had he got that long scar on his cheek? She had the hollow sense she was confronting a tragedy.

And yet she knew she too had changed. Haru had missed swathes of her life; had never heard of Hilly or Griff. Wouldn't understand Theo or Wu and what they'd lost. She traced a pattern in the dust on the floor with the toe of her shoe. She'd asked Haru about Theo, and she was all too conscious she hadn't had an answer. The fear Pau might have been right, and Haru could actually be dangerous, began to rise, and her hands started to tremble. She held them clasped together, tucked tight to her waist.

Should she wait? She heard noises from the bedroom, but he seemed to be taking a long time. She told herself to breathe.

When the door opened again Haru was in uniform, and it seemed to hold him together, like a parcel wrapped in string. He had a gun belt with pistol and truncheon sagging at his waist. He was so thin that the uniform hung on his chest. He cleared a space at the table and indicated she should sit down on the chair opposite. The uniform alienated him, reminding her of the other Japanese soldiers she had seen, beating Chinese people into the dirt. At the same time, sitting there felt like being at a particularly unpleasant interview.

'How do you know this American?' he asked. The disdain in the word 'American' made her face flare with heat.

'I was tutor to his children.'

He pursed his lips. 'He is an enemy of the Japanese state. He was put in a camp for enemy aliens. He should have stayed there.'

'But Haru, he lost his only son to ...' she struggled to find the right word, 'to whooping cough and pneumonia. He wanted to go to his son's funeral.' It wasn't strictly true, but she wanted to move him, to bring some emotion to his blank-paper face.

'In war, many people lose friends and family. It is no excuse.'

He was treating her like one of his men, and it wasn't getting them anywhere. She reached out a hand to touch his, where it lay on the table. 'Haru, what's happened to you? Why are you speaking to me like this, like I'm a stranger? It's me, Zofia, remember? I'm your wife.'

He pulled his hand away and stood up. He was unsteady on his feet and grabbed for the back of the chair. 'You can't be my wife now,' he blurted. 'Not now we're at war. What would my men think? The West are all degraded capitalists, I see that now.'

'That's not—'

'No!' He swatted at the air. 'My wife must be Japanese. She must understand. See this?' He tugged at a piece of white silk knotted around his waist. It was decorated with hundreds of tiny red knots of silk thread. It's a *senninbari* – a thousand stitch belt. The Japanese women stitch these knots on soldiers' belts to wish them good fortune in battle. They throw cherry blossom over us in every town we go to. All through my training in Japan, women did this. As a symbol that we must fall like blossom and die for our country.' He shook the end of the belt at her. 'Women I have never met stitched these for me. Yet there is not a single knot there from you.'

'I didn't know, or I would have tied one for you. You didn't write, I had no way—'

'Because you can never understand the military in Japan. Because it is not comprehensible to a Western mind.'

She stuck out her chin. 'Then make me understand.'

'We fight till the last man dies. We fight even though we cannot win this war. Even though the Japanese Imperial Army will be defeated.'

'But the Japanese have taken control—'

'Ha!' He spat out the word. 'The Chinese try to kill us at every turn.' He was pacing now, words tumbling from his mouth. 'They pretend to be our friends but all the time they are plotting, plotting how best to make us look stupid. They laugh that we tried to take over a place so vast with our puny little army. But they can't steal our spirit. We will all die heroes.'

'You talk as if there's no hope, as if—'

He rounded on her, cut her off. 'I will never be able to go home. A defeated soldier can never go home. It would mean disgrace and dishonour for my family. My mother will lose her house, lose everything.' He was seeing something in his head she couldn't see. His eyes were not looking at her but at some picture in his head. 'I will never see the shape of Mount Fuji again.'

She stepped forward to try to comfort him but he shouted, 'Get away from me. Don't touch me.' Tears were running from his eyes. 'You have to leave. If you don't, I will have to arrest you. Anyone helping the American or the British must die. Those are Onozaka's orders. No mercy. I cannot be an ally to an American. If I'm not at war with America, then whose side am I on, what's all the killing for?'

'To fight for peace. For love and being loved. For compassion and beauty and doing good. Forget sides. They are just an idea in someone's head. Be a proper human being. Let my friend go. He will leave China and go home to his family, and no one will know he was here.'

A laugh that sounded on the verge of hysteria. 'And what about my family? Have they then to live with my disgrace? Be shunned by their neighbours, spat upon for their unpatriotic son?' He stepped towards her, his hand raised, fury in his face and she cowered, expecting a blow.

Instead, he fell towards her, arms outstretched. 'My poor mother.'

His body shook with it, and she held him around his thin, shaking ribs until the storm had passed.

Abruptly, he stepped away. His eyes were red and his uniform crumpled. 'Get out of here,' he said in Japanese, his voice thick with emotion.

'I want to see Theo Carter,' she said, raising her eyes to his. 'We walked from Shanghai through your killing fields. Where you'd left not a single house standing. Where you shot children and threw them into pits. How dare you talk of family? The Chinese man you have in your damn jail lost every single member of his family to your troops. His mother, his father, his two young sons.'

She'd gone too far. His face turned rigid. 'Get out.' The sudden movement as he pulled out a pistol.

The shock of it took her breath. She'd seen enough killing to be in no doubt he'd use it.

'Haru!'

He raised the gun, but his hand was unsteady. She ran.

She heard a volley of shots as she bolted. Pau had heard it too and was waiting for her just around the corner. He stopped her with a hand on her arm. 'Quietly. Walk quietly.'

'Where is Endo?' She tried to sound calm.

'Waiting with the sedan bearer. I told him to fetch a sedan to take Commander Kimura to the prison. I just asked him to delay until I told him it was okay. You can wait in my car whilst I do that.'

He guided her with a firm arm away from the canal, and to

his car. He opened the door and she clambered in, putting her hands over her face.

She'd failed. She'd lost a husband and a lover in the space it took to take tea. The fact that she couldn't help either of them made her press both hands to her forehead.

When Pau returned a few minutes later, he asked, 'He wouldn't listen?'

She shook her head, but no words came.

'A whole nation has lost itself here. The Japanese soldiers don't understand what they are doing anymore because they are no longer allowed to think or to dream. They must just obey. The Japanese government is using the noble idea of *bushido* to tell them what they are doing is honourable. It isn't. It's just using men like scythes to cut other men down. In their own army too. Kimura won't let himself be human because he's too afraid.'

The car moved off, driving slowly past the people in the streets.

Zofia pressed her sleeve to her eyes, remembering the man who had turned on her like a dog with rabies. Tears leaked out, tears for their younger selves, the hopeful lovers who had been crushed by the weight of war. Those people were gone for good, and it hurt deep within in a way she couldn't explain. She mourned that even an embrace had not been enough to bring those young people back.

No use to think of it. She dried her tears and blew her nose. Survival. That was all that mattered now. She couldn't even think of Theo and Wu. She would have to travel with Griff. They were the only ones left now. And in this life, it seemed you couldn't choose your travelling companions.

Chapter 43

After Zofia had gone, Haru went back to his bedchamber to fix himself another smoke. He needed to calm down. The noise of the shots had shocked him. That he'd fired the gun. His eyes were stinging. Had he imagined it all? Had Zofia really been here in the room? It was hard to tell now, what was a dream and what was reality. But then he saw the straw hat Zofia had been carrying, still on the chair by the door.

The sight of it made him nauseous. It had actually happened. Panic in his chest. What if Onozaka found out his wife was connected to the American? His head would be on the block.

Haru went to his opium tray. He needed another pipe. It was then he saw there was nothing on his tray. No small packet of the precious poppy resin. He'd smoked the new *Chandu*, sure, but the old stuff was still there, wasn't it?

He searched, wondering if he'd mislaid it. Frantically he tossed aside his papers, the cushions, emptied out his robe pockets, searching. He turned the room upside down and still no sign. He called for Endo, who shrank away from his rage and swore blind he hadn't seen it and nor had he seen anyone but Pau enter the building. Pau had asked him to call him a rickshaw, that was all, and it was waiting outside to take him to the jail.

Haru wrestled with the conundrum. The only people who had been in here were Pau and Zofia. Why would Pau take the opium? He was selling him the stuff. But then it seemed unlikely Zofia could have stolen it; she never even entered his bedroom.

He tried to be calm. Inhaled deep breaths into his lungs. He could manage without it for a day or two, he was sure. He always had a fix before work, but he wasn't reliant on it, he'd always been able to leave it alone when he needed to. No need to panic. He'd go to Pau again this evening and see if he could supply him with some more of the good stuff.

Just the thought of that made him restless. He needed to move; his legs were twitching. He'd have to keep busy, keep his mind off the feeling, the sensation that his insides were becoming liquid in a most unpleasant way.

He hurried out to the waiting rickshaw and told the coolie to take him to the jail.

The night before, Theo had resigned himself to the fact there was no way he was going to get out of this predicament. The only regret he had was that he'd somehow got Wu into this mess too. He looked over to where Wu was sitting cross-legged on the hard tiled floor. At least this was a police cell, and not the hellhole that was Bridge House, though he suspected they'd be taken somewhere very similar soon enough.

The Japanese guards outside his door spoke no English and only a smattering of Chinese, not enough to try to say anything to them or ask for food or water. They had been brought nothing since they were arrested. Theo was aware though, that his stomach had shrunk, and he'd got used to the light-headed feeling that lack of food brought.

Wu was resourceful, pulling a button off Theo's shirt and showing him how to skim it across the floor to land on a particular tile. A primitive kind of bowls. They occupied themselves with this a while, taking turns until the hopelessness of their situation made playing a game seem too frivolous. In mutual unspoken recognition, they stopped and lapsed into silence.

Theo wanted to show Wu how glad he was of his company and how sorry he was they'd been caught. He went over and took hold of his hand, making a squeeze and then pumping it up and down. Wu seemed surprised and tears glistened in his eyes. He picked up Theo's button from the floor, kissed it, and put it carefully in his pocket.

Neither of them slept. Theo was preparing himself to resist torture, determined not to blurt out the whereabouts of Zofia and Griff, or give away their contacts – the priest Duan and the police chief Pau. Wu was very quiet, but intoning under his breath what could be prayers.

When the morning came, two guards took Wu away. He heard them open up the cell next door and then the clang as it shut. So they were to be separated.

Shortly after, a Japanese man arrived, in army uniform, with a private bodyguard at his side. The bodyguard entered first, and two prison guards waited outside. Theo made a quick assessment but saw they were all armed and the bodyguard had a pistol trained on his chest. A folding table and chairs were brought in and set up.

The Jap was emaciated-looking, and his uniform ill-fitting, although once he could have been handsome. Theo guessed from how the other man deferred to him that he was Commander Kimura, who they'd been told would interrogate them.

'Do sit down, Mr Carter,' Kimura said in English. Theo started. The accent betrayed a distinct American twang.

Theo sat. Who was this man? No doubt deliberately chosen, to get him to talk.

Kimura sat down opposite him. He was sallow and unhealthy-looking, with thin wrists poking from his uniform sleeves. His red-rimmed eyes, the pupils like pinpricks, seemed to roam over his face. 'You are Theodore Carter, I take it?'

Theo made no move at all.

'It is best to cooperate,' Kimura said in a polite conciliatory tone, though his forehead was peppered with beads of sweat. 'Things are always more civilized that way.'

I can't say I've witnessed many examples of civilized behaviour from your side so far.

'I believe you ran a shipping company in Shanghai. Carter & Co. That must have been an interesting venture. It is a shame you are no longer able to run it yourself.'

What did he think he was achieving by this small talk? Theo looked down at the stained table top where there were many marks of cup rings and cigarette burns. Involuntarily he twined his hands to feel the hard, round scars, the burns from Bridge House. He'd say nothing.

Kimura was shifting on his chair as if sitting on pins. 'I lived in America for a while whilst I studied. Such a pity our countries are at war. And we know all about you. Our researchers have been busy. We know you have a wife and two children.'

One child.

'They must be missing you and will be anxious to have you home. We admired your daring in escaping from Woosung, though it was unwise. It is bound to delay your repatriation, and I'm sure you don't want that.'

If you ever let me out of China, which I seriously doubt. Theo looked up and gave Kimura a venomous look.

Kimura's face hardened into sharp angles and planes. He seemed to be in pain, one hand clutching his stomach. 'You might find it amusing to refuse to talk, but I am finding it somewhat tedious. So, I will ask you this only once, understand me? Where is Major Griffiths? You were travelling together. We have had multiple reports of two Western men. You were seen in the rice fields by the Soochow canal, accompanied by a Chinese peasant, and a Western woman. Tell me about her.'

He would say nothing about Zofia. His silence was deafening to his own ears.

Kimura stood up and turned to one of the soldiers who was watching by the door. 'Yoshiko. Give him a taste of it,' he said gesturing him out. The American order was obviously for Theo's benefit.

Theo stiffened, waiting for what might come next, what torture they might bring. Instead he heard the clang of the door next to him, thuds and then Wu's shouts of pain. They were beating Wu. He could imagine only too vividly what was happening to his friend who had done nothing to deserve it.

Kimura was watching for his reaction, but seemed unable to be still; his hands twitched and his face was white as marble.

After a few minutes of listening to the grim sounds from next door, Theo could bear it no longer and he stood up.

'You bastard,' he said.

'Ready to talk, Mr Carter?'

'I'll talk. Just leave him alone,' Theo shouted. He wouldn't give anything away about Zofia. He just wanted to stop the noise of the other man's suffering.

'Yoshiko!' Kimura called him off, like calling off a dog.

Groans and cries from next door. Theo repressed the urge to vomit.

'Tell me about the woman.'

'There is nothing to tell. I know nothing about her, only that she wanted to get out of China.' The thought of Zofia was so intense it hurt.

'Her name is Zofia. She's a Polish refugee of Jewish extraction. How about we start with that?'

Theo knew his face must have showed his surprise, but he didn't understand why Kimura was asking if he already knew.

'I know nothing about her,' he said. 'She's just a hanger-on.'

'In that case why did she come to see me this morning and beg for your release?'

Theo didn't believe it. Why would she? Why would she subject herself to that risk? It was some kind of trick.

But now Kimura looked really unwell; he was panting and clutching his stomach. He shouted for Yoshiko and the guards, who came running.

Too late. Kimura vomited into the corner, the spray spattering the walls. 'Lock him up,' he said thickly, before staggering out.

The door clanked shut, the sound reverberating in his ears. This time he was alone.

He called to Wu through the wall. 'Wu, are you okay?' He didn't know if the other man could hear him or understand. There was no answering reply.

Theo sat on the floor, the cold eating into his emaciated sitting bones. Whatever the Japanese commander Kimura was suffering from, he hoped it wasn't catching. And how had he known about Zofia? Was it true she'd been to see him?

It didn't seem right, her trying to rescue him. It should be the other way around. He'd always thought of Zofia as brave, and because of it, he was a little in awe of her, scared of what she might think of him. Would she think him soft? She'd walked all that way as if she had some sort of iron will inside her, something that couldn't be broken. It was both inspiring and intimidating.

Haru squirmed, remembering the embarrassing incident where he'd vomited right in front of that American. Pau had arrived shortly afterwards to find him telling the guards not to let Carter out until he came back to finish the questioning.

'What about the Chinese man in the cell next door?' asked Pau.

'He's dead. Refused to cooperate.'

Pau's mouth tightened in disgust. Haru felt a momentary sliver of guilt, but he was still too much beside himself to heed it. He shouted at Pau to fetch him a fix so he could smoke it right there and then.

Pau looked at him with what seemed like contempt. 'No. Not here in the jail. You are unwell. You need to take some time at home. I will bring you a small amount this evening, when I'm off duty.'

He'd begged him to make it sooner, and the begging made him feel like an insect. He'd lost his power, he realized all at once.

'Go home, Kimura,' Pau said, leaving off the honorific for the first time. 'Change your clothes, and wait for me there.'

So Haru called a rickshaw and then staggered blearily down the edge of the canal to his house.

Every hour Pau did not come was more hell. Haru felt as if he was being devoured from the inside, as if snakes were writhing in his bowels. He was empty now, but the pain persisted until he thought he'd go stark staring mad. Haru spent a night in his house unable to go anywhere as withdrawal brought on more bouts of vomiting. He actually thought he might die. He became a madman, tearing at the bedclothes, hurling books and ornaments across the floor, hardly able to know what he did. He wanted to tear the world to pieces, the way the smoke was destroying him.

He cursed Pau, he cursed himself, he cursed the world.

The grunts and groans were visceral, like a child brought up by wolves. How had he let it get to this? It had crept up on him, underhand, this Chinese curse. But he couldn't think of that now. He needed to throw up again.

A knock on the door. 'Sir, are you ill?' Private Endo must have heard the noises from his rooms.

'Go away.' He retched again.

'Can I—'

'No!' Haru bellowed, his throat rasping. 'Go away! *Byouki!*' *Byouki. The kanji for mind and disease.*

The footsteps receded. He heard the telephone's shrill ring and Endo pick up, and his whispering that the commander was unwell. A stomach problem, and yes, he'd keep them informed.

He imagined Onozaka on the other end of the phone, his downturned mouth, his fleshy cheeks. This scene was mixed up with visions of curling smoke from smoking villages. The words Zofia said burned in his mind. The killing fields.

And the picture of Zofia, dressed like a Chinese peasant, was part of this nightmare. She had looked at him with pity and he could hardly bear it, because he was ashamed of himself, of what he'd become. He'd been afraid to look her in the eyes knowing how these hands that touched the bamboo pipe with such exquisite tenderness, had turned into instruments of terror. The room stank of vomit and excrement and his uncontrolled body filled him with disgust. He was in the land of fire and brimstone, and he knew it was because evil had consumed his soul.

For two days he stayed locked in his room, wrapped in blankets soaked with sweat, amid the detritus of his destroyed life. He saw himself clearly from above, a skinny man crawling on the floor, the trembling membrane of his skin pale over his ribs.

On the third day he woke with a silent clarity and a raging thirst. He staggered to the sink and drank water. Oh the sweetness of that water!

Then he cleaned. He shouted to Endo to leave him hot water and plenty of cleaning cloths outside the door. It took a whole day of cleaning to scrub away the stains. He opened the windows even though the weather was cold and cloudy, and he looked out of the window to inhale gulps of fresh air. Elation filled him that he had survived, that the birds outside the window still sang.

The tray of opium paraphernalia rested on the table by his bed. It looked tawdry in this daylight without the soft red glow of his candle lamp, and he immediately thought to get rid of it. But his hesitation brought on fresh agony because by the fact he resisted throwing it away, he was hard up against the sheer fact that the demon inside him was still clinging, refusing to let it go.

His devil mind protested, 'You don't really need it. It's there, just in case.'

Two parts of him were at war and he felt tears drip from his eyes. Was he going to let everything he'd gone through be for nothing?

In one rush of movement, he grabbed the tray and hurled the whole contraption from the window, where it clattered down onto the canal path. He gasped as he saw the pipe roll into the water, but quelled the urge to chase after it. He was done with it.

He was panting as if he'd climbed a mountain, before he dropped to his knees and wept.

It was sunset before a greater thought came. He was in control of himself at last. Though he knew that he would have to give his life for Japan, Onozaka was no longer the arbiter of his life. What was left of this existence, he would live by his own conscience. When night fell, he washed and dressed in his best Japanese clothes, his *hakama* and *montsuki*. Then he began to recite the old Shinto prayer of purification, the *norito* from his childhood, an honouring to the natural deities all around him. Wind, water, stars. A peace descended on him, and within it he pictured Zofia, the young girl he'd met on the train from Lithuania.

Japan would lose the war, and he would have to die to set an example to his men, but he felt the urge to give her something to remember him by. Something better than the vision of a man in torment.

Chapter 44

Zofia and Griff had been waiting three days for news of Theo, but no news had come. Zofia dreaded hearing he'd been executed and couldn't sleep for gnawing fear. Griff was restless too, cooped up indoors. Pau had decided there were too many patrols to risk getting the two of them out by boat, and he was awaiting some shift in circumstances that would make it possible.

Pau had talked to the warden at the jail, and tried to persuade him to let him interview the American prisoner, but the officer refused. Too scared. Commander Kimura was in charge; they were waiting for orders from him as to what to do.

Zofia was tight-lipped about what had happened on her visit to Haru. 'He threatened me, and it's safe to say we'll get no help from him.'

Now though, Haru Kimura had mysteriously disappeared. Pau had been to Haru's unit and discovered he hadn't been seen for days. One of his men had telephoned Haru's house, and his servant had answered it and told him he was ill.

'So he's still alive,' Pau said. 'I did wonder. I thought he might have been ambushed by someone from the CCP.'

The knock on the door startled them all. Pau put his hand

on the revolver in his belt and slowly went to answer it. When he came back, he said, 'Bad news. Japanese soldiers asking me to give you up. They asked for you both by name. They've got Carter with them. He must have talked. There are cars outside, and the house is surrounded by soldiers. I'm to take you down and you're to go with them.'

'What about you?'

His expression was stoic. 'Orders are, I'm to see Kimura tomorrow. But I'll see if I can find a way to disappear before then.'

Zofia relayed this news to Griff. 'I guess we've had it,' he said. 'But at least we'll go together.'

He turned to Pau and held out his hand. 'Thank you,' he said. Pau took it and then pulled him into a rough embrace.

'I tried, my friend,' he said.

'I know. None of this is your fault.'

Pau led them downstairs and around the front of the house, to the road where three matching black Buicks waited, engines idling, one behind the other. Two Japanese soldiers stood outside the house and a third was there to open the door of the middle car, his rifle ready. It was an intimidating sight.

Zofia turned to Griff. She saw all at once how old and faded he was. 'Good luck, Griff.' She let him climb into the back seat first, then followed.

The driver said in English, 'No talking. The car behind us has orders to shoot.'

The door slammed, the driver got in, and the car in front of theirs slid smoothly into motion. Their driver pulled away after it, and the engine noise warned her that behind them, the third car too had set off. A glance behind showed it was full of Japanese soldiers.

The figure in the front passenger seat turned around. It was Theo. There was only time for a glance, and Zofia didn't know whether to be happy or sad. She tried not to blame him for giving them away; she was just glad to see he was alive.

They drove for three hours. Zofia didn't dare ask to stop, though her bladder was bursting.

Eventually, the car pulled over. Zofia wondered if they were going to be executed there and then. Theo took hold of her hand as they headed towards the trees. The feel of it made her eyes blur.

The soldier indicated his flies, so perhaps this was just a comfort break. Theo walked behind the tree reluctant to turn his back.

The other car behind them had stopped and two of the men got out and had their rifles trained their way.

There was no place to run.

But the shots didn't come, and they were able to relieve themselves under the stares of the soldiers.

After this brief stop, they drove again until it was almost dusk. The first car seemed to contain a dignitary because it was always waved through with a salute. She wondered if they were being taken to a worse kind of prison, one where they would be tortured then killed. Some pheasants squawked and flashed out of their way back into the undergrowth. The road grew rutted and rough, and they were stopped twice at checkpoints but waved though.

Zofia peered through the dark but there was nothing to see except burned-out villages, and beggars that scuttled out of view. She was bone-tired but dared not even doze.

Without warning, the car ahead of them stopped.

The driver ordered them out. Griff, whose legs were stiff from sitting, almost stumbled. She glanced wildly around. Trees. Bushes. A dirt road. They were in the middle of nowhere. Ahead of them was a barbed wire fence and another checkpoint.

A camp. She felt tears come.

Theo was out of the car too.

'Go,' shouted one of the men. 'Now before we shoot!'

All was confusion. Theo grabbed her hand, uncertain where to run. From behind, a rifle shot hit the ground behind her. She stumbled forward. The cars were turning on the dirt track.

The car which had been in front drove slowly past. The window slid down.

Haru. She was too amazed to react. His eyes were wet. 'Good luck, Zofia. Remember me.'

'What?' she could not answer because his car was already grinding after the others, down the dirt track, leaving the three of them alone.

'Where the hell are we?' Theo said.

Griff was approaching the wire tentatively. 'Good God,' he said. 'They're flying the stars and stripes.'

'No.' Theo went to have a closer look.

They peered through the fence. A long low building made from corrugated iron and wood. He was right, the flag hung limply, but there was no doubt what it was.

They'd been brought to an American base.

Zofia turned to Theo and they screamed and jumped up and down in a mad kind of embrace. Over her shoulder she saw Griff, standing apart.

She grabbed him and drew him into their embrace. 'The three musketeers,' she said. 'All for one and one for all!'

'Guess we'd better find the gate,' Griff said, his face red. 'But boy, will we have some questions to answer.'

Haru didn't speak to his driver as the convoy drove away. He wasn't supposed to know the base was there, but Japanese intelligence was always better than the local population suspected. It would be taken out eventually, but it was doing little harm to the Japanese army being only a field hospital. Only that morning he'd had a memo from the Japanese Imperial Headquarters, saying the push was now to capture Sichuan province and he was to be redeployed there.

He was sure now that it was Pau who had not only supplied him with opium, but also deprived him of it, stealing it just when it mattered most. He had been his only friend in Soochow. His only friend in China. He would not give Pau away. His death would achieve nothing, after all, not when Haru would be far away in Sichuan.

Enemies and friends, how close they were together. Just two sides of the same coin.

Chapter 45

The US base was a hospital station for injured American pilots. There was no individual in charge, just three young doctors responsible for several Chinese men in training. The single other patient was a Chinese magistrate with multiple bayonet wounds, who'd been attacked by the Japanese and left for dead. A freckle-faced doctor called Bradley checked the new arrivals over, cleaned up the wounds on Theo's face and Griff's feet and then let them sleep.

Zofia was disorientated despite the fact they were safe in hospital, amid the purifying smell of ether and disinfectant. She still felt as if she was moving, and knew that whatever happened she would not be here long. She kept reseeing Haru's face as he looked out of the car window. The split second in which he'd appeared young again. His face had cleared and she could almost believe he was the man she used to know. What had happened to him? What he'd done was a kind of love. Maybe the greatest kind of love.

To let her go and find a life with another.

If only it were so easy. With Theo, she couldn't dare hope for anything. It was all still raw. They were too electrified by what they'd been through to be able to rest. Every noise made her jump and her heart pound. She imagined it was the same for Theo and Griff – like dogs that had been beaten and were ready to snap.

At last, she did sleep, the dreamless sleep of the exhausted. The next morning a Chinese student brought her tea. It smelled of gasoline, but it was hot and wet, and she thought she'd never tasted anything as good as that green tea as she sat between white army sheets.

Further along the ward Theo and Griff were already up, sitting on the metal and canvas chairs provided. The sound of laughter made her get out of bed to go and join them, though her body ached and her knees were stiff.

Theo was telling the American doctors how they got to the hospital. A little crowd had gathered around them, leaning in to hear all the details. 'Where are we?' she heard Theo ask. 'Not Laifeng, I presume.'

'We answer to them, but no, you're in Nanyang. And the Japanese actually brought you to our gate? Sheesh.'

'We knew someone in the Japanese army,' Zofia said, heat rising to her face.

'Can you get us home though?' Theo asked.

'I don't know,' Bradley said. 'We'll have to contact the government at Chungking, see what Madame Chiang says.'

'Who's Madame Chiang?' Griff asked.

'General Chiang Kai-shek's wife. He speaks no English, and our boss never learned to speak Chinese. So all discussions have to go through her. She's the one who really rules the roost.'

'Can planes really land here?' Zofia said.

'We've got room, sure, but we've only ever had one guy do it. Bringing in an emergency appendicitis case. But we'll get on to Madame Chiang, see what she says.'

In the end they had to wait three days for the flight to be okayed. It turned out the Brits were anxious to get Griff out, because he was some kind of war hero and they were willing to pay the Yanks for the privilege.

'You dark horse! You never told us anything about that,' Theo said.

'It was in the last war. No point bringing up the past.'

'They said you dragged four wounded men from no man's land.'

'They all died.'

'But you tried,' Theo said. 'That's the point.'

Negotiations went on, but Griff refused to be evacuated without Theo and Zofia. He dug in his heels and argued that Theo was an American citizen, and Zofia was a refugee.

Zofia was touched by this, and her thanks made Griff smile in a way she hadn't seen before. 'Where will they take us?' she asked.

'Kunming, I expect,' said Dr Bradley. 'It's not in Jap territory. From there, over the hump to Calcutta. And then – wherever you like.'

'Blighty, I suppose,' said Griff. 'What I'd give for an English pint.'

Zofia couldn't listen anymore. India. Another culture, another place to feel a stranger. The thought of travelling again made her want to weep. And she had nowhere to go from there. Griff would go to England, and Theo to America. But she had no place to call home. Poland was still occupied, as was Lithuania. She'd always wanted to go to America, had dreamed of it for so long. But now the possibility was there, she was afraid to take it. She knew nobody there. She was a refugee, one of thousands. No one would want her.

She went out of the hospital doors and into the compound, and started to walk away, the crunch of rough dirt and gravel underfoot.

Uneven footfalls, and she glanced behind to see Theo hobbling after her.

'Don't make me run,' he called after her. He slung an arm

around her shoulders. 'Come with me,' he said. 'I can't go anywhere without you now. And once we're in America, you can decide then.'

'I can't stay with you. What about your family? Evelina and Daisy?'

'I pray they're still alive. And of course I'll search for them, once I'm out of China and there's some sort of peace. The Philippines will be the same as here, though, impossible to find them there. Even if the war ended tomorrow, they will have been in a camp like Woosung for a year, and we're all so changed. But you're my family now, too. You and Griff. We're all different from how we were.'

Zofia remembered Daisy's heart-shaped face, and tying the ribbons on her braids, back there in Shanghai; it seemed like lifetimes ago. 'They'll be alive,' she said fiercely. 'You have to hang on to that hope.'

'And what about us?' he said, grasping her arm. 'I'm not going to let you leave me now, you know. I will always love my daughter, but I've learned along the way that the most important thing is trust – it's when someone's got your back. Evelina ... well, she never thought of me as anything but a convenient wallet. Without you, we wouldn't be standing here now. We've both made vows in the past. Mine were to the wrong person.'

'Mine too. But I feel so guilty.'

'Let's not waste time on guilt. If war has taught me anything, it's that life is short. Too short for guilt, too short for grieving.' He reached to draw her into his arms. 'Come with me,' he whispered. 'I can't imagine any life there without you in it.'

Zofia felt the thud of his heart through his shirt, and knew no matter what had happened, there was a kind of homecoming there.

Epilogue

Chicago, Illinois. Winter 1947

'Careful, the steps are slippery,' Zofia warned her friend Judy, as she opened the door.

'Bitter out there,' Judy said, taking off her gloves and putting her purse on the chair. 'Forecast is for more snow, too; you'd better get Theo to salt the path.' She turned and rummaged in her purse. 'I'm just bringing you those raffle tickets I told you about, for the Chicago Woman's Club. Five for a dime.'

Zofia went to the kitchen to get the money, and by the time she returned, Judy had taken off her coat and was peering into the perambulator in the hall.

Bonnie, the cocker spaniel, let out a low growl. She thought it her job to guard the pram and considered the hallway her personal domain.

'Take no notice of her,' Zofia said, scooping baby Teddy from his nest of woollen blankets.

Teddy put out his plump pink arms reaching to try to grab her hair. 'Oh no you don't, you little horror,' she said, hoisting him up and prising his fingers away. Instantly he began to cry.

'There, there,' she soothed him. 'Who's this? Say hi to Judy.' She held him out and the crying stopped as suddenly as it had begun.

'Doesn't he look like Theo?' Judy said. 'Same determined expression.'

'Stubborn, you mean.' Zofia laughed. 'He's teething. Teddy, I mean, not Theo! Coffee?'

'Yes, please. I'm frozen. That wind could cut glass.'

Zofia plopped a kiss on Teddy's forehead, 'Be a good boy for Mommy.'

She rested his soft, hot cheek against hers, before gently putting him back and handing him a teething ring. 'Theo should be back any minute, he finishes early on Fridays.' She glanced through the glass in the door to see the blur of a streetcar as it rumbled past.

Almost immediately there was a bark from Bonnie and the noise of skittering claws on the linoleum.

Zofia tried to grab Bonnie as she shot past but failed. 'I guess that'll be him now.'

'That dog's got second sight,' said Judy.

Zofia went to the window and watched Theo strolling easily up the street, his overcoat collar up and a newspaper tucked under his arm. She still felt a small thrill of pride whenever she saw him coming home. He was skirting the mounds of slush on the sidewalk as the streetcar squeaked away. Soon the streetcars would be gone, Theo had told her, replaced with modern buses. He was still in transportation, but now he worked for the newly formed Chicago Transit Authority, and his office was in the middle of the city.

Zofia fetched a tray with three cups, not two, and put the water on to boil.

Despite almost being old enough to be his mother, Judy greeted Theo with a coquettish, 'Look who's home!' as he bustled in and hung his Homburg and damp coat in the hall. From the kitchen,

Zofia heard him trying to persuade the excited dog to get down, so he could make a fuss of his son.

They made polite small talk as they drank coffee, though Judy did most of the talking, about her husband Vernon who worked for the Olsen Rug Company and travelled a lot, and about the people next door. Finally, after conversation stalled, Judy looked at her watch and made her apologies. Zofia stood up to help her into her coat and gloves.

'I thought she'd never go.' Theo let out his breath in a sigh.

'She's just lonely,' said Zofia, sitting back down, 'what with Vernon away and everything.' From the window she watched Judy totter down the steps, and across the tramlines to the other bungalow.

'Yes, we're lucky,' Theo said. 'Somehow I seem to have won the lottery – to have you and Teddy, and steady work back where I belong.'

'Me too. But I never thought America would be like this. I imagined a swanky New York apartment like in Hollywood films. Not cold and damp and trying to dry diapers in the yard.' She grinned. 'I wouldn't swap it though. Imagine being Rita Hayworth and having to watch your waistline every minute.'

'Wait long enough and Chicago will be just like New York anyway.' Theo said, abandoning the coffee cup to fetch a whisky and soda. 'Every day we're building new roads, more asphalt, more towers of glass and steel.'

'It's all moving so fast. Sometimes I can't imagine that places like Shanghai still exist. Places with coolies and rickshaws.'

'They're still fighting, you know. The Communists and the Nationalists. I read about it in the *Tribune*. It's hard to believe their war's still going on.'

'I'll never forget Shanghai. What we left behind.'

'Funny how it sticks, isn't it?' Theo paused a moment, thoughtful, glass in hand. 'But it's an old pain now, and we both have those. The people who won't come home.'

She sat down because their faces came back instantly. First Jacek, her brother, of whom she'd been able to find no trace. One of millions of souls lost like flotsam to the tide of war. Then Hilly in China. And now Haru. She'd gritted her teeth and written to Haru's mother, but received no words of condolence, just a copy of the citation of his death in combat, and even though it was expected, she couldn't help but be shocked at the flood of pain it brought with it. The sheer waste.

Theo's family too had perished. He'd pulled all the diplomatic strings he could to get some news of Evelina and Daisy, and when the reply came – the letter that said they'd both died – he'd pressed his lips together and put the flimsy slip back in the envelope without a word.

Later that night in bed, she'd held him as he wept in the dark. Only the next day did he tell her that Evelina and Daisy been liberated from Santo Tomas Internment Camp and put in a field hospital suffering from malnutrition. It had been shelled by the Americans. His own side. They had both died instantly. The irony and senselessness of war still made her want to rage.

So many losses, so much heartache.

Theo seemed to read her thoughts. 'We can't change it. The past's gone.' He put down his whisky and held out a hand to help her up. 'Time to get Teddy ready and take Bonnie out for her walk.' Bonnie jumped up again at her name and the word 'walk' and wagged her tail. 'Come on, Mrs Carter, look lively.'

'Okay, boss,' Zofia said, smiling. 'Mrs Carter' was their own private joke. When they arrived here, everyone just assumed she was Mrs Carter. Nobody ever questioned it or asked if they were married. She'd just gone on being Mrs Carter, and she supposed she would be Mrs Carter now until the end. They'd never tried to go anywhere since the war. This piece of solid ground in the suburbs of Chicago was enough for them.

Theo didn't let go of her hand and took her in a comforting embrace. She felt the slight roughness of the back of his hand, the scars from Shanghai, and squeezed it, before she leaned in against his shoulder, enjoying the warm solidity of him, the faint scent of Scotch. Together then, they turned to look out of the window at their tiny postage stamp of a garden.

'Your little plum tree is doing well,' he said. 'Mr McGregor would be proud.'

She laughed, remembering their first lesson together. 'Our little piece of Shanghai,' she said. 'Flowering in winter, just the way it should.'

A Letter from Deborah Swift

Thank you for choosing *The Enemy's Wife* and I hope you enjoyed the book, which was one I really loved researching and writing. I love to hear from readers, so do come and find me on my website www.deborahswift.com. If you would like to keep in touch you can also subscribe to my monthly newsletter which contains news of my books, interesting snippets of history, and bargain reads. If you join the community you will get a free WW2 short story delivered to your inbox.

Sign up here: https://dl.bookfunnel.com/e6izwznl1e

Last Train to Freedom

1940. As Soviet forces storm Lithuania, Zofia and her brother Jacek must flee to survive.

A lifeline appears when Japanese consul Sugihara offers them visas on one condition: they must deliver a parcel to Tokyo. Inside lies intelligence on Nazi atrocities, evidence so explosive that Nazi and Soviet agents will stop at nothing to possess it.

Pursued across Siberia on the Trans-Siberian Express, Zofia faces danger at every turn, racing to expose the truth as Japan edges closer to allying with the Nazis. With the fate of countless lives hanging in the balance, can she complete her mission before time runs out?

The Silk Code

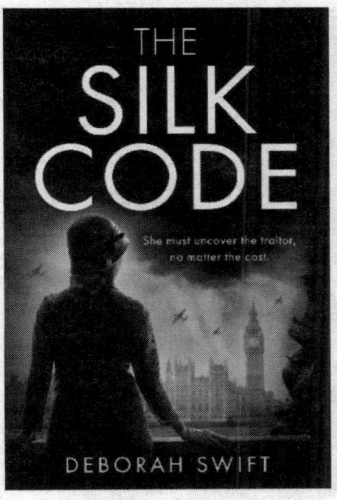

Based on the true story of 'Englandspiel', one woman must race against the clock to uncover a traitor, even if it means losing the man she loves.

England, 1943: Deciding to throw herself into war work, **Nancy Callaghan** joins the Special Operations Executive in Baker Street. There, she begins solving 'indecipherables' – scrambled messages from agents in the field.

Then Nancy meets **Tom Lockwood**, a quiet genius when it comes to coding. Together they come up with the idea of printing codes on silk, so agents can hide them in their clothing to avoid detection by the enemy. Nancy and Tom grow close, and soon she is hopelessly in love.

But there is a traitor in Baker Street, and suspicions turn towards Tom. When Nancy is asked to spy on Tom, she must make the ultimate sacrifice and complete a near impossible mission. Could the man she love be the enemy?

The Shadow Network

England, 1942: Having fled Germany after her father was captured by the Nazis, **Lilli Bergen** is desperate to do something proactive for the Allies. So when she's approached by the Political Warfare Executive, Lilli jumps at the chance. She's recruited as a singer for a radio station broadcasting propaganda to German soldiers – a shadow network.

But Lilli's world is flipped upside down when her ex-boyfriend, **Bren Murphy**, appears at her workplace; the very man she thinks betrayed her father to the Nazis. Lilli always thought Bren was a Nazi sympathiser – so what is he doing in England supposedly working against the Germans?

Lilli knows Bren is up to something, and must put aside a blossoming new relationship in order to discover the truth.
Can Lilli expose him, before it's too late?

HISTORICAL NOTES

If you have read the first in this series, you will know we left Zofia and Haru in Kobe, after they escaped Soviet Lithuania on the Trans-Siberian Express. Between August and November 1941 the Japanese moved all the Jewish refugees in Kobe to Shanghai in order to consolidate the Jews under their control. Shanghai was a haven for Jewish refugees, as most countries denied entry for Jews fleeing the violent persecution by Nazi Germany. Nearly twenty thousand Ashkenazi Jews from the rest of Europe had also fled to Shanghai. They were settled in what was known as the Shanghai Ghetto, the one-square-mile area of Hongkew (Hongkou). Meanwhile, in preparation for retaliation against the attack on Pearl Harbor, young men like Haru were conscripted into their National Service in the Japanese army.

The International Settlement in Shanghai in 1941

The International Settlement was a city within a city. An island of Western lifestyle dominated by the British and American concessions, which were ruled by an Anglo-American council.

South of the settlement was the French Concession, where many wealthy 'Shanghailanders' lived in luxury in palatial houses. Surrounding the settlement was the Chinese nation controlled by the Chinese central government in Nanking, but recently occupied by the Japanese. The Japanese occupied the Hongkew District of Shanghai in 1937 after they had invaded eastern China. So it was only a matter of time before they would over-run the 'Pearl of the Orient' – the international settlement of Shanghai, and the wealthy centre of trade in the Far East.

The British Government declared the International Settlement indefensible in 1940 and withdrew the army, and the Americans followed suit shortly after. However, thousands of defenceless British and American citizens such as Theo continued to live and work in Shanghai. There was also a large population of stateless White Russians like Olga who had fled the Russian Civil War, along with Jews like Zofia who had escaped the Nazi persecution of Europe. This was an era where whole populations were on the move.

Japanese-occupied China

The Japanese at this time were fearsome opponents. Japanese army training was brutal and uncompromising. An eyewitness from *The Guardian* newspaper records what it was like in Japanese-occupied China.

> *Trenches have been dug across the racecourse near Kiangwan. The railway station of Kiangwan has been completely destroyed and the college opposite is a burnt-out shell ... the trenches are full of Chinese dead, most of them surprisingly youthful ... No Japanese dead are to be seen anywhere. While*

> *foreigners are kept away from the battlefield, very many Japanese civilians are now to be seen, some of them accompanied by their wives and children. They are allowed to visit these scenes of horror and desolation. Japanese fathers show their sons the dead soldiers lying in the trenches. Some of the visitors seem to be inspired by the Samurai spirit, for they wander amongst the desolation with rusty swords in their hands collecting souvenirs.*
>
> (Unknown author, 'The Shanghai battlefield', *The Guardian* (March 1932))

However, China was so vast that despite Japanese aggression, pockets of resistance remained everywhere. The Chinese population itself was locked in an ongoing civil war between the Nationalists and the Communists. Britain officially signed the International Settlement over to Chiang Kai-shek's government, in the Sino-British friendship treaty, while Shanghai was still occupied by the Japanese. Yet the civil war in China continued, with Mao Tse-tung's People's Liberation Army engaged in a fierce battle against Chiang Kai-shek's Kuomintang. In 1949, Shanghai fell to the Communists, and the Nationalists fled to Taiwan.

Capture, Camps and Internment

The character of Charlie (Bob Dering) was based on the story of real-life hero James Cuming from Sheffield who, unlike Charlie, did actually manage to escape from occupied China after being aboard the *Peterel*. His story is told in the book *The Lonely Battle* by Desmond Wettern.

The experience of internment at Woosung Camp is well described in J. G. Ballard's novel *Empire of the Sun*. Surprisingly, people did escape. There were two failed escape attempts from Woosung. Five men including the Wake Island's Commander W. S. Cunningham dug under the electric boundary fence to escape, but they didn't make it far: they were captured by Chinese puppet forces and handed over to the Japanese.

Eyewitnesses claim two successful further break-outs, but Theo and Griff's story is based loosely on the real experiences of Commander C. D. Smith of the US Navy who was able to escape Shanghai into Chinese guerrilla territory and make his way to an American base. A brief article on him can be found online at History Net https://www.historynet.com/, and Smith is the hero of the book *Officially Dead* by Quentin Reynolds.

Selected Further Reading

Secret War in Shanghai – Bernard Wasserstein
City of Devils – Paul French
A Foreign Kid in WWII Shanghai – George A Kulstad
Kings of Shanghai – Jonathan Kaufman
Empire of the Sun – J. G. Ballard
Pearl Harbor – Randall Wallace
Birdless Summer – Han Suyin
Opium Fiend – Steven Martin
Tales by Japanese Soldiers – Kazuo Tamayama and John Nunneley
Horror in the East – Laurence Rees
Kamikaze Diaries – Emiko Ohnuki-Tierney
The Lonely Battle – Desmond Wettern
Officially Dead – Quentin Reynolds

Note on English spelling of Chinese place names.

In this novel I have used the modern phonetic spelling of places and locations, except if the word also occurs in conversation where I have used the 1940's version from witness testimony. Suzhou for example was spoken of then as Soochow, and Huangpu as Whangpoo.

Acknowledgements

Thanks must go to my agent Mark Gottlieb and to all at Harper Collins for bringing this book to publication. In particular I would like to thank my excellent editors Sophia Allistone and Cari Rosen for their skilful suggestions and support. But it is you, the readers, with your feedback and encouragement, who have kept me writing all these years, so many thanks to you for choosing this book from all the millions of stories on the shelves. With thanks too to the following work, Barbara Barnouin and Changgen Yu, *Zhou Enlai: A Political Life* (Hong Kong: Chinese University Press, 2006), for the paraphrased 'rather mistakenly kill a thousand innocent people, than allow a single Communist to escape' referenced in Chapter 25 of this book.